Alpha on the Hunt
MY LUNA STOLE MY SONS

JESSICA HALL

Copyright © 2023 by Jessica Hall

All rights reserved.

No part of this book may be reproduced in any form or by any electronic or mechanical means, including information storage and retrieval systems, without written permission from the author, except for the use of brief quotations in a book review.

CHAPTER ONE

Elena

Never before in my life have I derived such pleasure from watching someone squirm. Throughout the entire meeting, I could feel Axton's eyes on me. He must be wondering how I managed to obtain those photos. However, there are a few things I discovered while living with him. Axton meticulously documents and keeps everything. Unfortunately for him, he has a flaw. A flaw that I'm certain will change now. He uses the same password for everything, including his computer and Google Drive. The same password that he also used for his safe. I couldn't believe my luck when I accessed his email using that very password.

I was certain he would have made alterations or chosen an alternative, but once I obtained his email, logging in became effortless. Not only that, but I saved and forwarded all his files to my email address. Subsequently, I modified his password and included my phone number, ensuring he cannot change it without verifying through the code that will be sent to my phone.

Thank you, Khan, for telling me the password to that safe. And because I am feeling rather petty, I changed all his passwords on everything. Including the ones to his TV apps, and added him to some girlie subscriptions, so he should be expecting his first magazines any day now.

His new reading material includes Woman's Day, Women's Health, and A Woman's Revolution Magazine. I've replaced his newspapers, men's catalogs, and car subscriptions. I also updated his app preferences to chick flicks and added parental controls last night. He can't watch anything above PG without my permission. Fixing it will be an added headache for him, and I intend to be the biggest fucking migraine he's ever received.

Additionally, I enrolled him in online anger management classes, so he'll receive daily emails on controlling his man-baby tantrums.

However, sitting in this meeting, I notice a few things have changed. Titles have been altered, packs passed down, and a few fresh faces sit at the oval table of alpha douchebags. Among them is an overly flirtatious Alpha Cane, who I discovered is one of the smaller pack alphas, whose numbers have grown just enough to enter the council. Alpha Thomas and Alpha Soyer are also present; I am quite familiar with Alpha Soyer and Thomas, but not so much with Alpha Cane, although they are the only ones I recognize.

Which I find odd because this city comprises four major packs. The smaller ones are never worth mentioning and aren't classed as packs within the city; they are that small. But now, there are eight alphas, not including myself here. The tables have turned and Axton's rule has allowed new entrants into this rat race for the city throne.

Now we have two extra Alphas that seem to hold some power here, no doubt in Axton's pocket because they seem to agree with everything he has to say. And lastly, a new face I don't recognize who seems to want to challenge Axton at every turn.

"Which packs handle city borders?" I ask, trying to figure out how much power Alpha Cane and Alpha Osiris have in the city. Alpha Osiris, however, doesn't seem to get on well with Axton, almost as if they are competing against each other. I try to rack my brain where I have heard that name before.

"He is Elder Stiles' estranged son," Lexa reminds me. Oh, that is right, Elder Stiles, the old fossil has three sons, but none have lived here for as long as I remember, making me wonder why he is here now and also where his father is. Did he take over his father's pack?

"Nightfall, and Crident," Axton answers, pointing to Alpha Osiris, and I raise an eyebrow at him. He didn't seem to be happy with that, so I know the tension I feel between these two, is real. Yet, it is clear power-wise Axton holds all power in the city, or did until I walked through these doors.

Glancing at Alpha Osiris, he nods once. "My pack has just reached limits to be considered council-worthy. I can't risk any of my men at the moment, or I risk my seat," Alpha Cane tells me, and I nod. So that means he is paying the city for protection then.

"I want to pitch in, but-" Alpha Soyer looks over at Axton. "Tension in the city is high. We want everyone accounted for, and too many running the border patrols are difficult to track," Alpha Soyer adds.

More like Axton doesn't trust anyone. So Osiris seems to have something over Axton, or Axton just doesn't want to deal with him. Either way, clearly something has happened between them two.

"Well, let's end this meeting until next Friday. Undoubtably, I will have to deal with Derrick now," Axton tells everyone, dismissing them and cutting me off from asking about how my father's old pack fits into all this. Needing to get back home to bring the boys back to the city, I reluctantly start packing up the documents I brought with me when Alpha Cane clears his throat across the table from me.

"Out of curiosity." I glance at him. Alpha Thomas shakes his head at Alpha Cane and leaves talking to Soyer, while Osiris, I notice, lingers with Alpha Cane.

"Are you going to finish the sentence Alpha or am I to guess what it is you're curious about?" I reply. Alpha Osiris snickers and clamps a hand on Cane's shoulder.

"They're mates!" Alpha Osiris hisses at Cane.

"Well, obviously. But they don't seem very-" His words are cut off by a feral growl from Axton.

"Yes, we are mates," I answer the question that Alpha Cane couldn't seem to spit out.

"But are you together?" He seems genuinely curious. I suppose it isn't like it is a secret. We are both on opposing sides, and we have done nothing but argue throughout the entire meeting.

"Our relationship is none of your business, Cane. You've been dismissed. Now leave. I need to speak to my mate!" Axton snaps before I can answer.

"Sorry, I was just curious," he mutters, quickly gathering his papers. Alpha Osiris smirks and follows him out, and I notice Eli and Marco all but run from the room with them. I watch them leave while feeling the deadly aura threatening to suffocate me. It radiates off Axton like a brewing storm getting ready to unleash havoc. I jam the documents back in the folder when I see him rise from his chair out of the corner of my eye. Mentally cursing I didn't run the moment everyone was dismissed, I brace for the argument I know will happen.

CHAPTER
TWO

"Bastards ditched us!" Lexa snarls, knowing we should have been one of the first to leave. Axton slaps the envelope on the table in front of me.

"Where did you get this?" Axton demands.

"You really should change your passwords, also two-factor authentication is another way to secure your accounts." I chuckle, grabbing my documents. Turning to leave, Axton steps in front of me, his eyes flickering as he steps so close my ass presses against the table-top. Lexa growls at him, caging us in, while the stupid bond flares to life at his proximity.

"What do you think you're doing, Elena? You already had me sanctioned. And now this? What are you going to do, blackmail me?"

"Why? Don't you like having the tables turned against you?"

"This gets out. You'll fucking ruin me!" he snarls.

"Like you ruined me." I retorted. Axton growls, the sound threatening as his aura slips out menacingly.

"I swear, if you have shown anyone these–"

"You'll what? Get all growly, threaten me? Anything new, Axton? Because you've been that way since the day I met you. You have a sex tape of me. We've been there, finished that scandal already. The entire city saw it, so what are you going to do next? Hmm."

"You do not want to go to war with me!" he snarls.

"You're right, I don't, but you have left me no choice. The only difference is, you have nothing else on me, but I have enough to ruin you. You fucking the head of the supernatural council's wife isn't the worst of it. Is that how you got away with everything? Did you blackmail her too? Or maybe it's the fact your trucks have been running drugs across the borders for—" his hand clamps over my mouth and his head turns toward the door.

"Shut up, not here. Marco is out there!" He hisses at me and I almost burst out laughing. If only he knew the person behind his illegal operations was Marco! He may be by the book within the council, but his dealings outside his work are not as stellar as everyone believes. There is a reason Sondra and Floyd were never on anyone's radar.

"Marco is the least of your problems, Axton. Same as the photos of you screwing Mrs. Xander. But just so you know, I have the sex tape too. If you threaten my pack again, I may just send it off to every news station in the state."

"Don't you fucking dare!" Axton snarls.

"Threaten my pack and I will end yours!" I tell him before shoving past him. I walk toward the door when he grabs my arm just as the door opens. Axton lets go and Osiris enters. He stops at the door, clearly not realizing he stepped into the middle of our argument.

"Everything alright?" he asks, hurrying toward the table. He grabs his wallet that he left behind and stuffs it in his suit jacket pocket.

"Yes, I was just leaving." I tell him, quickly escaping Axton while I have the chance. Only the moment I step out, I walk into Alpha Cane, who is walking back into the conference room.

"Sorry," he mutters, stepping aside, and I slip out the door. I move toward the entrance and almost groan when I see Eli step into my path. Marco, I could see through the glass doors, was leaving, pulling out of his parking spot. Fuck.

"Axton?" I ask as Eli approaches, and he nods once.

"We need to get out of here!" Lexa hisses at me, while my eyes scan the exits about to bypass Eli, just as Osiris and Cane come back out chatting together.

Before Eli reaches me, Osiris stops next to me and Eli backs off. I have no idea what he is playing at, but it is clear he wants to get under Axton's skin. But right now, I am trying to escape the very same man, so I will willingly play along.

"Cane and I are about to head over to the casino for a drink. You should join us. Soyer and his mate are meeting us there." Osiris states just as Axton stomps out of the conference room toward us. Seeing him getting closer out of the corner of my eye. I panic.

"Sure, what time?" I reply. He seems a little shocked that I agreed, but he does not know the ball and chain Axton is trying to lock on my damn ankle.

"Ah, we are headed there now. Can you walk with us?" Cane answers, motioning for me to follow. I do, only to have Lexa growl in my head.

"What are you doing?" she snaps at me.

"What I need to do, Axton looks like he is about to club me over the head caveman style and drag me back to his damn lair!" I retort, and she huffs, knowing I am right.

"One drink, then we leave." I nod to her in agreement, but it works. Axton won't cause a scene, and Eli knows better than to challenge an alpha in an attempt to stop me.

Slipping out the doors, I can feel Axton's eyes boring into the back of me, and that feeling does not leave as he follows us across the road to the RSL Club.

"One drink, I gotta drive!" I tell Lexa, who seems antsy for some reason, as we enter the club and head for the bar. Alpha Cane, I noticed, is bubbly and not the typical alpha asshole I am used to.

Alpha Osiris is more of an observer, he doesn't speak much, but when he does, he is quite articulate and blunt.

"So is your mate/not mate, going to follow you everywhere?" He asks as the waiter hands me a glass of coke. I glance at Axton at the end of the bar, watching us, and he looks livid. Shit! Exactly how am I going to escape the city if he follows us like a damn shadow?

Unfortunately, I do not have time to answer his question when I see Axton sit up straighter just as my father shoves open the huge glass doors with a bang.

The door rattle draws everyone's attention to him. Sucking in a breath, I turn to face the man who is on a warpath and headed straight toward me.

"Here we go again!" Lexa growls, annoyed in my head. Alpha Osiris moves to block him, which surprises me the most.

"Derrick." Osiris growls threateningly.

"This Alpha best not be thinking I am some damsel in distress!" Lexa snaps, insulted at his actions.

"Step aside, Osiris, I have business to take up with my daughter!" my father orders.

"Not here you don't, and certainly not in my club." Osiris growls.

My father scoffs, looking between Alpha Osiris and me, and I go to tell them both I'm leaving anyway when my father speaks. "What? Are you fucking him too? Have you no shame, Elena! Just like your mother, a fucking whore!" My father yells in my face, and I feel Lexa press forward as my hands fist.

However, before I can even react to my father's words, a fist connects with his face, and he grunts, his head snaps backward, and blood spurts out of his nose. I blink, stunned for a second when I feel an arm wrap around my waist.

Alpha Osiris jumps and I see Security all watching as my father curses before stepping toward me when Axton suddenly shoves me behind him. "Call my mate a whore again and see what happens, Derrick. I will break more than your fucking nose!" Axton spits at my father.

CHAPTER
THREE

My father snarls and swings back at him. Axton moves quicker though, seeing it coming before hitting him again. His hands grab my father's shirt, ripping him toward him and head-butting him. The resounding crack of their heads clashing makes my teeth ache as my father goes down like a sack of potatoes. Cane erupts with laughter, making me look at him. He lifts his glass and nods.

"Well, I guess your mate doesn't hate you as much as I thought," he chuckles. Osiris groans and looks over at Axton, then shakes his head and lifts his hand, waving his guards over.

"Get him out," he orders, and they grab my father.

"Really, Axton, this better not be in the fucking papers tomorrow!" Osiris snaps.

"If it is, I'm sure your reputation will still stand, Osiris. You're good at putting the blame on others. Don't make out you didn't tell him where she was. Derrick knows better than to step into your establishments without permission." Axton snarls.

"No idea what you are talking about," Osiris says, yet the way his lips tug in the corners and his eyes flicker dangerously, I could see the snake he is beneath the facade. Some intuitive sense that I have just been set up filters through my thoughts.

"I was just being friendly." Osiris replies, his eyes moving to me.

"No, you were hoping to get back at me by fucking with my mate. Now, this will be your one and only warning. Elena is off limits. Pull this shit again, and I don't give a fuck how far up the supernatural council's ass you are. It won't stop me from killing you." Axton snarls, his tone ice-cold.

I have no idea what I have just gotten into the middle of, but something has clearly gone on between these two in the past. This plan to have a few drinks with me was far more sinister than just council members checking out the new Alpha and competition in the city.

Lexa, instead of urging me to escape Axton, is urging me to listen to what we are just witnessing. It makes me wonder if this is also why Axton followed me over here. Mostly I thought it was to drag me back and demand the boys, but seeing him now I wonder if it were to see what Osiris was up to as well. He could have easily dragged me out the moment I stepped in here.

"I'm sure Elena can speak for herself about the company she keeps?" Osiris smirks at Axton and his eyes move to mine.

Axton growls, taking a step toward him when I grab his hand, lacing my fingers through his. He stops, his body tensing only fleetingly, certainly not enough for Osiris to notice. He squeezes my fingers.

"And now you know her answer." Axton growls, lifting my hand slightly, and I step closer to him.

"Silly girl, you won't last in the council if you aren't playing on the right side of it. Being a woman, you're at even more of a disadvantage. I was willing to help you."

"This was a power play!" Lexa snarls angrily that we didn't pick up on it. My father's pack is the second largest and because I was so focused on Axton, I walked into a trap. One that could have seen me challenged for a title I am yet to claim within the city.

"Now that is where you are mistaken, Alpha. I am not disadvantaged. Once I take my title back, I step into power. I will hold the second-largest pack in this city. Therefore, you will be at a disadvantage. But you know that, that is why you invited me here." he shrugs, neither denying nor admitting what he did.

"And you think you're better off with him. That's the only reason he wants you now, to take your pack. I would have let you be, Luna. He'll just make you his bitch." Osiris laughs, walking off before I can answer. Lexa growls angrily in my head. Axton shakes his head, tugging on my hand while I glare after the man.

"Well, I guess he showed his true colors. I guess I'll come with you lot then! I thought he liked me. Now, I'm wondering if he liked me a little too much. I ain't nobody's bitch, and certainly not interested in the D!" Cane chuckles, hopping off his stool. He stumbles, making me wonder how much he has drunk in such a short time. I reach out and grab his arm when Axton growls at me.

He grabs Cane's arm to steady him. "This political shit is hard. I should have stuck with mechanics. But nooooo, Dad and Pete had to just die on me, making me Alpha!" Cane huffs.

"I tried to warn you, Cane."

"That you did, Alpha Axton." he slurs.

"Eli!" Axton calls out, and he instantly rushes over, grabbing Cane's other arm from me.

"Man, what is in those drinks? I think he was planning on making me his bitch. I think he slipped something into my drink. Thank the Goddess you're here, Axton. My ass isn't bitch material." Cane slurs.

"As if I would let my mate wander off with the likes of him, and you. Don't think I didn't catch you checking her out!"

"Guilty, but I'm harmless, you know that."

"Luckily for you, I do know that," Axton tells him before glancing around and waving his hand at Eli.

"Eli, make sure he gets home, and organize his patrols to be on the lookout."

"Lookout for what, you think he likes my ass that much?" Cane snickers.

"No, but Alpha Osiris is up to something, and Elder Stiles has been missing for a few weeks since he returned, we can't be too careful." Axton answers. Elder Stiles is missing? I have so many questions which the man of the hour, Axton, seems to have the answers to. I don't really feel like getting into another argument with him, so I know those answers will have to wait. But it makes me wonder if mom knows because she never mentioned he was missing.

Alpha Cane stumbles. "Maybe we should–" I begin to offer my father's warriors to patrol Cane's borders.

"No, Eli will handle it, and take care of him."

"Wait, you think Osiris did something to his drink?"

"No, Cane doesn't drink, his father was a bad alcoholic. Yet, he has stepped into a role he was hoping would be left to his older brother. Unfortunately, Osiris got to him before I could," Axton answers as we watch Eli haul him out.

"Then why would he drink?" I ask and Axton sighs, glancing around before he looks back at me. "Not here," he mutters, wrapping his arm around my waist and tugging me closer. Axton leads me out of the club and back toward the council chambers.

"Alpha Cane?" I ask.

"His father and brother were both killed a few weeks back in a car accident. Cane has never wanted the title. It was forced on him. I tried to warn him off Osiris, but Cane thought Osiris was just being friendly. Osiris doesn't do friendly, so you need to steer clear of him."

"Okay." I tell him, a little disappointed I didn't see through his facade, though Lexa was on edge, the moment we stepped into the club with them.

"Okay?" Axton stops in his tracks to look at me.

"Huh?" I ask, confused.

"You'll stay away from him?" after what he told me, I would be insane not to! Why would I question that? I don't trust any of them anyway, though Cane does seem harmless.

"I'm nobody's bitch." I tell him. Axton smirks.

"No, you're not. But I still thought you would disagree since I said it," he chuckles.

"So I shouldn't agree. Should I go back? Maybe I should. He did say I could be his Luna?" I mock and turn. Axton growls, and his arm tugs me back to him.

"You're only allowed to be my Luna, nobody else's," he snarls.

"Calm your farm. I am nobody's Luna. Not unless you want to be a Lupha." I chuckle.

"A what?" I shake my head, not willing to repeat what Michelle keeps calling him behind his back.

Axton's brows furrow, and I become very aware of the fact that he still has me in his grasp when I should be trying to get back to the boys. He is supposed to have them for the weekend. That thought suddenly saddens me, knowing I am handing them over, but I have enough battles on my hands and custody is not one I want to add to the list.

CHAPTER FOUR

I step out of his grasp, changing the subject back to Alpha Cane, wanting to know more about the new Alphas and what I'm up against. Axton tugs me back to him. "Promise me, you'll stay away from Osiris, forget everything else Elena. He is bad news. If you promise me anything, promise me this."

"I don't owe you any promises, Axton." He grits his teeth and looks away from me. "But I promise I will stay away from Osiris," I tell him, he lets out a breath and nods once.

"What did he do?" I ask. I can see his genuine concern regarding that Alpha, yet he has given no explanations.

"I think he killed his father. But there is more, I just have no way to prove it." His eyes flicker to Khan briefly with his mood shift. Lexa tugs at me, the mate bond enticing me to move closer to our mate the moment Khan breaches Axton's surface. Her brain doesn't seem to be as badly affected by his presence as it is for me, maybe because I am in this form and not hers. But either way, lately I have been at constant war with what the bond keeps demanding now he has marked me and what rationality knows.

"We need to go, Elena." She reminds me.

"So, Alpha Cane, how do you know so much about him?" Axton shrugs, letting me go, but grabbing my hand, he presses the button on the lights for the crossing, and we wait for the lights to change.

"I am capable of crossing a road by myself." I tell him, trying to jerk my hand from his grasp. His grip tightens, and he leans down a little.

"You're about to run from me again, it won't kill you to hold my hand. Besides, right now, I know Osiris will be watching on the cameras. It is best to look like a united front, despite the shit storm you created for me in the council chambers." he tells me. My eyes move to the club roof to see the little dome surveillance camera attached to the cladding.

I sigh and pull my hand away. Axton growls at me, but I ignore him, stepping closer to him and wrapping my arm around his waist.

Axton drapes his arm across my shoulders, tugging me closer and pressing his lips to my temple. He chuckles, "Wow, I would have settled with you holding my hand," he whispers next to my ear, then laughs.

"United front, remember? I can act the part." I tell him. He better not be lying, but something tells me Osiris really is watching.

"What if I don't want you to act the part?"

"No, you want to make me your bitch and steal my packs?"

"Joined packs are an added bonus, but that is not what I want from you, Elena."

I say nothing to his words, knowing often what he says and what he means are two separate things. His actions speak volumes. Axton may be semi-decent now, but I haven't forgotten his threat back at the council or when he found us.

The light changes and we cross the road. "You never answered about Alpha Cane?" I remind him, changing the subject away from his constant mixed signals, it makes me wonder which side of him I am dealing with now. The man's personality changes faster than I can shift.

"You'd think with his multiple personalities, we would have found one we actually like by now!" Lexa huffs.

"Let me know if you find one that is tolerable. His personality shifts are giving me whiplash." I tell her.

"Be like trying to find a rainbow pig with wings or a unicorn that farts confetti. Impossible!" she retorts.

"He's being okay-ish now."

"He is probably waiting for us to get close enough to his car, so he can stuff us in his trunk, and whisk us off to this basement that he is so fond of locking us in."

"That won't happen. I won't allow it."

"Yeah, because I will bite if he does!" she growls, wandering off when Axton speaks, finally answering the question I have repeated a couple of times now.

"Cane's father was an abusive alcoholic, we went to the same high school. His brother was a dick, just like his father. For a while, we were friends, still are. We just lost contact over the years, and he moved to live alongside humans not long after his father and brother moved to this city."

"So that's how you know him? Cane is from your old city?" Axton nods.

"Yes, but that's not how I know him, I know him from the pits. His father used to run underground fights through one of my father's clubs. If he lost, his father would beat the shit out of him. Lyle was one of my father's friends. Eli and I cleaned him up a few times before my grandfather reported the club's underground facilities, which in turn had my grandfather banished from the pack for a while. But he got it shut down, temporarily at least."

"Your grandfather reported his son's club?"

"Yep, Cane wasn't the only one that used to be forced into the pits. My father said I was too soft, that my mother pampered me too much."

"So, when did your grandfather come back?"

"After dad went bankrupt, he wanted my grandfather's money to bail him out, but he left it all to me and my mother. Mom demanded he be allowed to return." Axton tells me while leading me through the parking lot.

"And he listened to her?"

"He had no choice. Eventually, she signed everything in my name. Mom refused to give her half to my father, knowing he would have control. The moment she signed everything to me, he killed her for it." Axton tells me as we stop next to my car. Axton lets me go and takes a step away from me while I rummage through my bag for my keys.

"Hold this." I thrust the folders I have toward him, and he takes them while I dig for the damn keys. Axton, however, decides to flick through the pages.

"Are you really going to get your father to submit to you?"

"That's the plan."

"He won't like that. His pack is loyal to him."

"Yes, but he won't have a choice soon." I tell him.

"What do you mean?"

"He'll submit." Is all I tell him, not wanting to give away all my plans, especially to a rival Alpha. Axton certainly didn't need any more ammo to use against me.

He closes it and sighs. "You know I can help you, right?"

"And what would the price be for your help, Axton? I don't need it or want it."

"Well, you know where I am if you do want it!" I glance at him, finally finding my keys, and he hands me back my folders.

CHAPTER FIVE

"And why would you help? You hate me, remember? I'm the whore that ran off with your sons?"

"You're not a whore. I say shit out of anger. That doesn't mean I always mean what I say."

"No, but your actions say otherwise," I remind him. "You had no issues calling me a whore, thinking I ran off with Jake!" I spit at him bitterly.

"Because you ran off with another man!"

"A man who was a vampire, one who used his compulsion on me and killed my best friend! You act like I asked for that to happen."

"Don't act like you did nothing wrong. You chose to leave." Axton argues. He still doesn't get it.

"Wait, so I am a whore when you say it, but my father says it, you get offended on my behalf?" I scoff, shaking my head.

"You're still my mate and the mother of our children." I shake my head, personality number twenty-something slipping out. Should we call this one doubt, regret, or is this one simply a facade to gain pity or to make me feel guilty of what Jake did? "And I don't hate you.

You're just stubborn and had me sanctioned not to leave the damn city for two weeks."

"You threatened to take our sons and kill my pack! What did you expect?"

"Not for you to fucking sanction me and put me on damn house arrest!"

"And when those two weeks are up, Axton, then what?" he shrugs and doesn't answer, instead changing the subject.

"Next meeting is on Friday, can you bring the boys? Eli will watch them, or I can organize Tieriny to watch them while the meeting is on. I want to see my sons." Axton tells me.

"You don't want them for the weekend?" I ask him.

"Of course I do. But clearly you don't intend to give them to me because you didn't bring them with you."

"Yeah, because it is a meeting. I was bringing them to you this afternoon before you went on a warpath over the photos and threatened my pack again!" I snap at him. Axton's eyes flicker to Khan before he shoves him back and steps closer to me. His lips tug into a sneer and I take a step back from him, my ass hitting my car door as I fist my keys, ready to stab him with them if he tries anything.

"Don't bullshit me, Elena, not when it comes to them. I know you're just saying that, so I'll let you leave," he growls, and I roll my eyes at him.

"Either you want to see them or you don't, but either way, I have to get back to them."

He tilts his head to the side, watching me. "You know I want them."

"Then fine, but I need to get them and drive back." I tell him while unlocking my car with the key fob. When I go to open the door, his hand grabs it.

"You're not fucking with me?"

"I'll see you at 5PM." I tell him. Climbing in the car, I toss my stuff onto the back seat and reach out to close the door, but he still has a hold of it.

"You'll come back with them?" Axton asks. Man, do I need to send him to get his ears checked? Is he deaf? I just told him I would.

"Yes, I'll see you at five." Axton glances toward his car and I pull on my door, he presses his lips in a line, but he lets go, stepping back. I shut the door and start the car, Axton stands there for a minute before I wind the window down, the heat of the day making the car extra stuffy.

"Ah, I feel sick knowing we are just leaving them with him for the weekend!" Lexa mumbles and I am not looking forward to it either, but what choice do I have, either I let him see them or fight him in the courts which will be added stress. Not only that, I know he would demand to get fifty-fifty custody. I would rather give the boys to him every weekend than go a full week without them.

"I'll see you at 5, Axton. Do you have formula and diapers, or should I bring everything?" I ask him.

"I have a formula, but what is their diaper size? I will have to grab some," he tells me, still looking quite hesitant to let me leave.

"I'll grab an extra box on the way home. But you have everything else?" he nods and I sigh.

"I'll see you soon," I tell him, putting the car in reverse.

Lexa stirs, her mood instantly shifting as it sinks in fully that we would be without the boys for an entire weekend. However, as we leave the city, my phone rings through the Bluetooth speaker. Sondra's name pops up on the screen. Moving my finger over the button on the steering wheel, I hit the answer button.

"I'm on my way back." I tell her.

"Have you passed town yet?" she asks me.

"No, but about to reach the town limits. Why, what do you need?"

"Can you stop by the pharmacist for me and pick up my scripts?" she asks me. Lexa whines in my head, knowing that means she is in pain. Sondra refuses to tell anyone she is dying besides me and Marco. She doesn't want the women to worry, but holding this secret is growing heavier with each day. And every day I notice the subtle signs: she is nearing her end, her lack of appetite, her tiredness, weight loss, and the sometimes weird moods she gets in. Sondra is tough as nails, but every so often when we talk, it is like she is saying goodbye, as if she is worried it will be the last words to pass between us.

"I'll grab them. Do you need anything else?"

"Mmm, maybe one of those lemon meringue pies?" she says, and I chuckle. Sondra asks for the same thing every time I go into town, and it seems to be the only thing she can stomach a couple of bites of besides drinking her tea.

"Okay, see you soon." I tell her, hanging up and driving past the turnoff for the ranch. Crossing the town borders into the sleepy little town, I drive to the pharmacist, passing Taylor's general store that has its windows boarded up.

"I can't believe she is dead." Lexa mumbles, without her store here, everyone is forced to go to the city or neighboring towns for food supplies.

"Yeah, and now we must be extra vigilant." I tell her.

CHAPTER SIX

Elena

After picking up Sondra's pain medication, I race home to my sons. The women are out working the ranch, tending to the animals or picking fruit and vegetables from the fields. It's hard to wrap my head around the knowledge that we've created this peaceful little piece of tranquility out here. It was once a rundown ranch, the fields of vegetation dying out, the cattle not being tended to the way they needed. The main house has since received an uplift and everything is now flourishing out here.

Pulling up, Sondra is waiting on the porch in her rocking chair, my mother staring at her worriedly, which makes my brows furrow in confusion as I climb out of the car. Luke is up the side of the house, chucking wood into a wheelbarrow to take to the women and inside the packhouse.

"Hey, El," Luke calls out, and I give him a brief wave before climbing the few steps to my mother.

"What's wrong?" I ask my mother, nervously glancing at Sondra. She frowns. Worry is etched into her facial features, and I wander over to Sondra. Her eyes are closed, and her face is peacefully relaxed. Just as my hand reaches out to touch her to ensure she is breathing, she speaks, scaring the living daylights out of me.

"I know you weren't about to check if I was breathing. If I am dying, it will be dramatic and preferably with your father's head resting in my lap as I croak my last breath."

"Gees, Sondra, did you have to play dead right until I touched you?"

"You were the one going to poke the dead if I was. Serves you right to sneak up on an old woman like that!" She smiles, opening her eyes, yet I can see the pain pooling in their depths. Her eyes don't crinkle in the same way. They're also a little glassy, making me wonder if that is why she had them closed, not wanting my mother to see how watery they are.

"You old bat, I have been watching you for the past ten minutes and not one word, not even when I called out to you!" my mother scolds her.

"Aren't you werewolves supposed to have good hearing? Can't you hear my old ticker pumping the blood through my body? I may look as if I have one foot in the grave, but I can assure you, dear, I still have outstanding balance. I won't be tipping over that edge to the afterlife quite yet," Sondra retorts.

I smirk and shake my head, turning to look at my mother, who throws her hands up in frustration before stalking back into the house. "Kinda creepy, the way your mother watches me while I am resting, like she was waiting for a new wrinkle to appear," Sondra huffs, reaching for the paper bag in my hand, and I pull it away.

"You scared her."

"I scare many people, though no one here needs to fear me. I owe these women for my past failures. I'm the last person they need to fear," she states. My brows furrow, wondering what she means. Sondra owes us nothing. We all owe her. So I don't know why she would think she owes any of us.

"Care to tell me what you mean?" I ask her.

Sondra tilts her head to the side, looking at me. "We all make mistakes. Some are just bigger than others, some are redeemable, and some aren't. I just hope I have done enough when the day comes, and I finally meet my maker." She states, looking out at the women working, a sad smile pulls at her lips.

"What could you have possibly done that needs redeeming?" I ask her.

"Countless things, things I am not proud of. I should have spoken up, maybe then there wouldn't be all this mess. Fear makes people react differently. I was scared then. But I'm not now."

"Sondra, are you alright?" I ask her, beginning to worry. She rarely talks like this, yet when she does, she gets in these weird moods.

Sondra sighs, turning her attention back to me. "Promise me that when you take down your father. You make sure he hurts. I want him to hurt the same way he hurt all of you."

"My father? Sondra, what is going on?"

"Nothing you need to worry about now. But I know that monster, just like I know your mate. The apple doesn't fall far from the tree with that one, but I'm glad to see you aren't made from the same roots your father is."

Her words confuse me, and I want to ask more when she points to the pills in my hand.

"I have said enough for now. You have places to be and people to destroy. Don't feel guilty for ruining them. I can assure you, Elena, that those you destroy deserve it."

She takes her pills from my hand before I take them back from her when she fumbles to pop them from the foil covering. I hand her two, and she raises a very thin brow at me.

"You're only allowed two," I tell her, checking the packet.

"Those doctors are all quacks. Besides, they're weak as shit," she says, clicking her fingers at me.

I sigh and roll my eyes, popping another out and handing it to her. "No more, you'll be high as a kite," I tell her.

She narrows her eyes at me, but relents when she realizes I wasn't giving her anymore. "Spoil my fun then." She huffs, reaching for her tea. I watch as she chews her tablets before swallowing a mouthful of tea.

"Don't you have to take the boys back to your mate for his weekend visit? Why are you loitering? I can ward off the grim reaper myself, stop fussing and get ready." she waves me off dismissively. I turn to head inside.

"And tell your mother if I catch her holding a mirror below my nose again, I will whack her with it. I don't enjoy holding my breath. It's short these days." She huffs.

"And you wonder why she was watching you?" I retort. Sondra smiles wickedly. The crazy old lady I love returning.

"Well, she thought I was dead. Figured I would act the part." She chuckles, and I laugh, walking inside to check on the boys.

As I double-check their diaper bag, ensuring they have every little thing they could need, my anxiety reaches an entirely new magnitude. Lexa ripples beneath my skin nervously, not liking what we are about to do, but also understanding it is necessary.

"Why don't you stay in the city for the night? That way you're close, and it may help your anxiety?" my mother suggests.

"And stay where, at one of his hotels, or should I ask dad if I can sleep at home?" I snap at her without meaning to. My anxiety comes off in waves of anger and for the past hour, anyone who has crossed my path has copped a mouthful of my snappy mood.

"We can manage a few nights without you, besides you need to reclaim your old pack back. Why not work from the city? The council chambers are right there, which is where you need to be to get whatever it is you're looking for. We can manage; we did for years," Noleen tells me.

"Doesn't matter where I am. It's them being in his care that has me nervous."

"More reason to stay in the city!" Michelle adds, and I roll my eyes, scooping Bane out of his rocker while my mother grabs Kyan. She follows me out to the car, and I buckle them into their car seats and toss the diaper bag onto the passenger seat.

CHAPTER SEVEN

"We'll see you on Monday." my mother tells me.

"I'm not staying in the city." I remind her.

"Yes, you are, sweetie. You just refuse to admit it," she says, wondering off before I can answer. Glaring at her retreating figure, I start the car.

The drive to the city takes twice as long because I am trying to delay the inevitable. By the time I reach Axton's packhouse, he is standing out front, his arms folded across his bare chest. I roll my eyes, why does he have to be half-naked? I growl in annoyance when Lexa answers me.

"He came back from a run. He didn't think you were coming, and it set Khan off," she tells me.

"You can't know that!" I state.

"I can because the stupid bond gets stronger by the day now he has marked us. I have been catching glimmers of it through this one-sided bond," she snaps at me. This was the first time she has openly admitted to her struggle with the bond. I constantly suffer when within his proximity, but Lexa had clearly been hiding her struggle from me.

Axton stomps over, grabbing my door when I shove it open. "You said 5 PM." he snaps at me. I growl, not in the mood for his tantrum.

"I am forty minutes late, Axton. Calm down. This is hard enough." I tell him, opening the back door. He says nothing as I reach in and start unclipping Kyan first. Instead, he walks around to the other side to retrieve Bane. The moment he reaches in, a vicious growl tears out of me, one I didn't mean to make, some bizarre possessive growl leaving me.

Axton looks at me, and I shake the feeling off while reminding myself he is their father.

"Elena?" Axton questions, and I swallow, closing the door and grabbing the diaper bag from the front passenger seat just as Axton closes his door. He smiles down at Bane, quickly kissing his head before looking at me expectantly. I stare at him for a few seconds when Lexa snarls at me.

"He wants the bag and Kyan!" she reminds me as my brain decides to stop functioning, leaving me standing here staring like an idiot. My voice is robotic as I tell him the boy's formula dosage and rattle off useless information I am sure he won't need about their sleep schedule and explain every little thing in the baby bag, half of which he probably won't use. Axton takes the bag, chucking it over his shoulder.

"So are you going to give me Kyan?" he asks, staring at my son I am clutching, knowing once I hand him over, I have no reason to stay any longer. My mother was right. I am staying in this damn city. Driving away was going to be hard enough, let alone actually leaving here altogether.

"Elena, I am perfectly capable of watching them for the weekend," Axton states, holding out his free arm for him. Gritting my teeth, I hand him over, and Axton clutches them close just as the first drop of rain falls, hitting me.

"I should get them inside." Axton states, and I nod. My actions feel pre-programmed and automatic as he sidesteps me. Before I can make an even bigger fool of myself, I rush to get in my car before reversing out and turning onto the street, knowing if I don't leave. I will camp in his driveway.

Without looking back, I head for the city borders, determined to leave, except as soon as I see the border patrols manning the exit, I pull over because I suddenly can't breathe. My chest feels tight, and my hands are clammy as I clutch the steering wheel in a death grip.

"Pull yourself together, Elena." I scold myself. Yet no matter how much I want to prove everyone wrong, I end up turning the car around and heading back toward the packhouse.

I flick the lights off as I pull up and park in front of the hedges where the car is hidden from view. The rain is pouring down, obscuring my view completely, as I shut the car off and admit defeat.

My entire body prickles with goosebumps, and my senses are extremely heightened from the adrenaline pumping through my veins, thanks to my panic attack.

Lost in the confines of my mind as I conjure up any excuse possible to knock on his door, so I can check on them. I don't notice anyone approaching the car until Axton is tapping on the window. "You know I can feel when you're close, right?" he asks, and I blink at him. His shirt is drenched from the rain that is beating down fiercely as the storm continues to brew, darkening the skies as the thick clouds close in on the city.

I stare out at him, wondering how he noticed me lurking like some creep when he opens the door.

"Are you going to sleep in the car or come in? Can you decide quickly because it is freezing out here, and I am now drenched!" he asks.

"I can stay?" I ask him in shock.

"You're my mate, Elena. Of course, you can stay, although I am shocked you actually managed to leave the driveway. Your damn anxiety has been giving me anxiety," he chuckles.

"I need to head back," I answer, while also trying to remind myself.

"Get inside, Elena, you're not going anywhere, and I don't feel like spending all night worrying about you sleeping down the end of my driveway," Axton says.

"Now, Elena, or are the boys and me sleeping in the damn car with you?" I press my lips in a line, not liking to admit defeat when it comes to this man.

"Fuck!" I whisper under my breath.

"We can if you like," Axton chuckles. I glare at him, and he shakes his head with a laugh.

"You said it, not me. I was merely taking you up on the offer."

CHAPTER EIGHT

"That is not what I am offering!" I growl, pulling my keys from the ignition. I should go home. This wasn't my plan.

"Why are you still hesitating?" Axton questions.

"Because my pack is without an alpha if I stay," I tell him, the words leaving my lips taste bitter, knowing I should be home by now.

"I sent Eli and a few of my men to patrol your borders already, so please tell Sondra not to shoot them!"

"You did?"

"I won't leave your pack defenseless, Elena, so yes. I knew you wouldn't be able to stay away for long. You'd fret for them. They are still under one. All she-wolves fret for their young, especially when you are breastfeeding." I chew my lip when another thought occurs to me. If Eli isn't here, that means we would be in his house alone unless he has a nanny to help with the boys.

"Wait, if Eli is gone, who is inside with the boys?"

"They're asleep, and I'm just meters from the door. They are perfectly fine and safe tucked in their crib."

"How would you know that when you're out here?" I snap at

him, climbing out of the car, and he rolls his eyes at me before reaching into his back pocket. He holds up a baby monitor with a little screen. Showing the boys sleeping together in their crib.

"See, now you know your pack is safe; the boys are safe. Can we go inside?" I look at the huge house when Axton snatches my keys and slams my door shut. He hits the fob, locking it.

"Come in or sit in the rain," he says, heading towards the front door. I growl, marching after him.

I am as drenched as he is by the time I reach the door. The rain outside intensified, seemingly eager to wash me away. Yet, stepping inside the packhouse, it is toasty and warm. Axton heads for the stairs, and I close the door, staring at the lock before shaking my head and locking it. It's not like he can order me.

"I can, but I won't," Axton answers, reminding me once again just how much stronger the bond is for him. It won't be long before he can hear my thoughts, as if they're his own at this rate.

"Not quite hear them unless you mark me, more of a sense of them like they are mine." Axton shrugs. Wow, the invasion of privacy just climbed higher on the ladder of creepiness.

"Coffee?" Axton asks. And I nod, following him upstairs to the kitchen when he stops by the linen cupboard. He pulls a towel out, handing it to me before speaking again.

"It's only because I spent so much time around you today. Once you go back home, don't worry. It will be like starting over with the bond." His words offer me little comfort. Yet, I could see what he said bothered him.

"Are you seriously that uncomfortable being here by yourself with me?" he asks.

"Last time we were by ourselves, you had me locked in that prison apartment. The time before that, you knocked me up. So sorry if I don't exactly trust being on my own around you." I retort.

"I can keep my hands to myself. I'm not Jake. I'm not going to rape you, Elena." Axton growls, his eyes flicker, and that is the first time he acknowledged what happened with Jake wasn't by my choice. He walks into the kitchen, and I follow, drying myself the best I can with the towel.

"You're safe with me. Even if you don't want to believe it because you hate me, that doesn't mean I would do what he did?" he growls, reaching for the mugs off the shelf.

"Because locking me up was so much better. And nothing like what he did," I reply sarcastically.

"I would never force myself on you, despite what I've said in the past, Elena."

"Are you sure? Because you wanted to lock me in your basement earlier?" I retort.

"Doesn't mean I would rape you, kidnap you, yes. But I won't force myself on you. Besides, you'll come to me soon enough anyway when you go into heat." Axton laughs.

"Wow, how romantic? He'll kidnap us but not rape us. Oh, I'm glad he draws the line somewhere!" Lexa huffs.

"I have suppressants. My mother got them for me." I admit while ignoring Lexa, not wanting to think too hard about the fact I just locked myself in a house with him.

"You're not taking them." Axton shoots me a glare, and I scoff at him.

"I mean it, Elena, those things are dangerous. You deny your heat too long when you do finally go into heat. It can kill you!" he snaps at me.

"Wait, have you already gone into heat?" he asks, and I roll my eyes.

No, I haven't needed to take them yet. She only got them for me today while I was at the council. She and Michelle went with the boys." Axton lets out a breath.

"Good, don't take them. You don't need to."

"I am not having sex with you!"

"Why not? It's not worth risking your damn life, Elena. And it's not like we haven't fucked before."

"I'm not risking my life, Axton. They're perfectly safe, or they wouldn't sell them." I shake my head.

"Yeah, if you're mated to a common wolf. We are both alphas. Your heat will be intensified tenfold. The pills will be lethal if you reject the bond for too long. I get you don't want to complete the bond. I am not asking you to mark me; I'm just asking you not to risk your damn life when I'm right here!" he snaps, handing me my coffee.

"And if you reject me," he starts to threaten.

"Let me guess, your basement has my name on it?" I retort. He smirks.

"I rather you in my bed than in my basement, but if you reject me, I may just have to move my bed down there," he chuckles.

I say nothing, not wanting to argue over something that hasn't even happened yet, nor will I allow it to happen. I follow him upstairs to his room. He opens the door and wanders over to his bedside table, setting his mug down, before removing his drenched shirt and tossing it in the hamper. I watch him feeling awkward and out-of-place while also trying to keep my eyes off him; the bond urging me closer.

I can't help but admire the man, he has always been handsome, but now I can really look at him, my eyes roam over the hard muscles of his back when he turns drying his dark hair with a towel hanging from the hook by the bathroom door. My eyes trail down his body, taking in his tattoos that cover his left shoulder and part of his chest, down his abs, before dropping lower to a V-line that disappears into his jeans. Luckily, Lexa pulls and snaps me out of it.

"Are you trying to send us into heat? Stop gawking, pervert!" she snaps.

"I was only looking," I mumble.

"Look at the walls, the floor, the damn ceiling, just stop being a creep. It's bad enough we are in his room, his scent is driving me insane, and your wandering eyes are not helping!"

"Am I really being a creep though if he is technically ours?" she growls at me.

"Eyes to yourself!" she snaps when he looks up. His eyes take in my clothes and he nods toward the closet. "You can help yourself. Take what you want?" he says. My mind, when flooded with his scent, went instantly to the gutter, wanting to take something that involved removing my clothes, not putting any on while I devour his–I shake my head, coming to my senses.

"Elena! Don't make me come out there!" Lexa scolds. "Ceiling, floor!"

"There are extra towels in the bathroom. You remember where everything is?" I nod, watching him. Axton moves into his attached office, which has been turned into a nursery.

Seeing the boys, my anxiety instantly leaves and the mate bond fog fades into the background; both are snuggled up nice and cozy as Axton tucks the surrounding blanket around both, ensuring it is tight when he looks over at me.

"Thank you," he murmurs before looking back down at their sleeping faces. I swallow that strange feeling of guilt for keeping them away from him sweeps over me. After inspecting them, Axton exits the room, leaving the door slightly ajar.

"I will get you some clothes. You can do what you want. Why are you being awkward?" Axton questions while I watch him walk into the closet.

"Probably because she wants to have her damn way with you!" Lexa snarls at me.

"I do not." She scoffs, and we argue. She is being ridiculous.

"One step into his room, and you suddenly turn brain-dead," she yells at me. Axton clearing his throat makes me jump; I blink at him. He holds a shirt and sweatpants, smirking. He hands them to me. "Thanks," I mutter, taking them. He chuckles, and I raise an eyebrow at him, watching as he grabs his own clothes.

Gosh, he has a nice ass.

"Thank you. I like yours, too," Axton snickers. My face heats, and I instantly turn away, marching into the bathroom and shutting the door before I make a bigger fool of myself.

CHAPTER NINE

Spending the night with Axton is awkward. We have barely spoken since I stepped out of the shower. And I have kept my distance since. The bond is yearning for him and being locked in a room filled with his scent is making the bond nearly impossible to ignore. Yet Axton looks perfectly comfortable when he walks back into the room holding two plates.

The smell of steak reaches my nose, and my stomach growls loudly. Adding another embarrassing thing I can't control. "Hungry?" Axton chuckles.

"Yes, I'm still breastfeeding. Well, mix feeding, I'm always hungry." I tell him, and he nods, setting the plate on my lap.

"Just because I'm technically taking them for the weekend doesn't mean you can't breastfeed them," Axton says, while sitting down with his own dinner.

"Will you stay the whole weekend?" I chew the inside of my lip. Lexa has been constantly at me about what a terrible idea staying here is. Yet she can't bear the thought of being away from the boys. The anguish is not worth it. A few uncomfortable nights aren't so bad, right?

"I would offer to stay at your place, but I'm still on house arrest, and I don't think Sondra likes me. I worry she'll shoot me in my sleep." Axton chuckles.

Sondra's words about the apple and the tree linger in my mind. The way she spoke was as if she knew Axton's father and mine. What is her connection to our families and why does she feel guilty?

"Elena?" I look at Axton, lost in my thoughts.

"Pardon?"

"I asked if you were staying the entire weekend, or if you are going home tomorrow?"

I could go home and pump, but I would worry for them and produce too much milk to freeze, anyway.

"I can organize Eli to stay the entire weekend. My men will watch over your pack," I nod, grateful because my boobs were killing me, and the shower turned into a milk fountain the moment the hot water touched me. Just the thought of leaving them here makes my anxiety peak. Not that he can't look after them. He has already proved he is quite capable. Which brings me to more questions. Why is he so good with kids yet his people skills suck?

Cutting a piece of my steak, I pop it into my mouth, pondering my thoughts, and almost moan at the taste.

"I didn't know you could cook," I tell him and he stops chewing. He swallows before clearing his throat.

"I'm not completely useless."

"I never said you were," I retort. He shrugs.

"I used to cook for my grandfather after my mother died."

Tilting my head, I watch him for a second, wondering if I should ask if he knows Sondra or ever heard of her before.

"Your father killed her, didn't he?" Axton nods, but says nothing on the matter.

"How old were you?"

"Seventeen."

"So you were seventeen when you killed your father?" I blurt out.

"No, he would have killed me. I was nearly eighteen."

"I thought you would have had at least a wolf. How else could you challenge your father?"

"I did have my wolf. Khan saved me that night."

"But you just said you were seventeen?" Axton sighs, leaning back in his chair and folding his arms across his chest, watching me.

"Why do you want to know?" he demands and I shrug,

"Curiosity.... And something Sondra said." I admit.

"Sondra? The old lady you live with?" I nod my head, wondering if I said too much.

"What did she say?" I shake my head, not wanting to answer and anger him or refuse to let the boys back there.

"Well, I am not answering your questions unless you answer mine. Besides, you have enough shit against me; I am not going to give you more." Axton tells me.

"I wouldn't use your dead parents against you, Axton. I am not cruel."

Axton clenches his jaw, but I could see he won't answer unless I do, and now my curiosity has peaked tenfold.

"Fine. Sondra mentioned she knew your father, but she wouldn't tell me how. She said that is why she helped us because she felt guilty she couldn't save them, and that she knew my father, too."

"Your father?" Axton says, leaning forward and almost putting his elbows on his food. He growls, setting his plate down on the coffee table.

"How does she know your father?"

"I don't know. She wouldn't tell me anymore." Axton sighs and his brows furrow.

"But that is why I asked. I wasn't looking for anything to use against you. I just wanted to know what her link is to you and my dad."

"I don't know her, so I am not sure. I know Marco and he said he is related to her, though?" Axton seems thoughtful for a second while I nod my head.

Axton frowns, a strange look crossing his face. "But she is human?" he questions, confused.

"Yeah, he is her brother-in-law, not a blood relative."

"Her brother-in-law, but Marco only has one brother?" he questions. I nod, yet the look he has on his face is like he knows something.

"Why are you pulling that face?" I ask.

"Because I know Marco through my father and mother, Marco's brother... ah.. What's his name...Gee, I haven't seen him since I was a kid. He and my mother had a huge fight."

"Floyd?" I offer, and his eyes widen, and he quickly nods.

"Yeah, Floyd, he was friends with my father. He is how my father met my mother, but I do not know how that links to your father."

"So what is Floyd's link to your father?"

"Does it matter?" Axton shrugs. Well, yes, because I want to know why Sondra feels guilty, but I can tell Axton would not answer. But I also want to know how he killed his father without a wolf.

CHAPTER
TEN

I cut off another piece of steak, chewing slowly, wondering if he will answer about Khan saving him.

"Is it really bothering you that much?" Axton asks, and I look at him.

"About how I killed my father?"

"I never asked that?"

"Yet I can feel your curiosity over it," he says, grabbing his plate.

"You said you were seventeen. But we don't get our wolves until 18."

"Once my grandfather was back, my mother agreed to sign everything over to him. We were eating dinner, Eli was staying the night and I remember dad was in a great mood because he was drunk. I just assumed it was because we bought this place and were moving soon." Axton pauses, staring down at his plate, his hand fisting around the knife.

"This packhouse?" I ask him. Axton nods.

"Yeah, mom was excited; she said this place would be a fresh start. Mom purchased it two weeks before we were moving the pack here."

"And that's why you lived in the apartment, not here because it was your mother's?" Axton nods sadly.

"So what happened?" I ask curiously.

"Dad was living away. He was living here for a bit to sort out things here. Mom and dad were constantly fighting, so it was a good break for her. Anyway, he came home. He handed her the paperwork. Mom asked if she could sign after we finished eating dinner. When we finished eating, he slid the paperwork over to her. Mom signed it and gave it back to him. My grandfather was talking to me. I had another fight in the pits, and my hand was broken, so we were discussing my opponent." I open my mouth to ask how he broke it, but he shakes his head.

"Anyway, mom made this strange noise, which made me look at her to see my dad had stabbed her in the throat with a steak knife. I was in shock and just stared at her. It happened so quickly and abruptly, and dad was in a good mood, so I didn't think he would do something like that." Axton stares at the knife in his hand, his eyes flickering for a second.

"He just kept stabbing her. My grandfather shifted and Eli ran for help. My grandfather tried to protect her. She was still alive, bleeding everywhere, but her wolf was a quick healer. She had to be living with my father as her mate," he tells me, looking lost in some haunting memory.

"I tried to stop her bleeding and dad almost killed my grandfather when he shifted. That's when I got Khan. His voice suddenly appeared in my head and screamed at me to drop the barrier between us. I didn't know how; I tried. My father's wolf ripped her to pieces in front of me. He broke both my legs and my arm when I tried to stop him. I was bleeding out, my grandfather was also hurt badly. He went to finish my grandfather and Khan smashed through the barrier and I shifted."

"So you killed him?" Axton shakes his head.

"No, I tried, but my father's wolf was a monster, and Khan was brought on by my fear. Khan attacked him and ripped into him, but we were still no match for him. If it wasn't for Eli, I would be dead."

"What did Eli do?'

"Got my father's gun and shot him. It didn't kill him, but distracted him long enough for my grandfather to shift once my father turned on Eli. My grandfather knocked him out. Forced him to shift back."

"So, when did you kill him?"

"A few weeks later, he tried to cover up my mother's death. People were asking questions. So, I contacted Marco. But Marco's hands were tied. Pack business is handled within the pack. Still is. Dad tried to get my grandfather to take my name off everything, but he refused."

"So you challenged him?" Axton shakes his head.

"How I killed him is not something I will tell you."

"Why?"

"Because Alpha titles are handed down or challenged for, or given to the oldest child when a parent dies."

"I don't understand. The title would have been yours unless you killed him in cold blood?" Axton says nothing.

"You did, didn't you? That is why there is so much media speculation about how you became alpha?"

"Marco helped cover it up. He told the council he witnessed the challenge in the pits."

"Why would he do that?"

"Because my mother was Marco's niece." I nearly choke on my food at his words. I shake my head, knowing Sondra had no children.

"Sondra had no kids."

"Yes, but Floyd had a daughter. That I am certain of," Axton states.

"Floyd died. He was human? I met him."

"Floyd wasn't human. He was a werewolf like Marco before he was changed."

"Wait, when was Marco changed?" I ask.

"I don't know. I know he is a lot older than Floyd, decades older."

"But wouldn't that make Marco your uncle?"

"Yes, but also no. My mother was estranged from her father. She hated him, and Marco tried to convince her many times to leave my father, but she was his mate and she eventually had me. So by blood we are no relation technically."

"What do you mean?"

"Marco and Floyd weren't blood brothers, but they were both raised by the same people. Both were orphaned in rogue attacks. When the foster carers were killed, Floyd was only a child. Marco used to work for my father. Until he died, luckily he had vampire blood in his system, so he came back a vampire. Not long after, Marco and Floyd's foster parents died. Marco raised his foster brother and became a council member, wanting to look for those responsible for killing them."

"No, we have to be talking about someone else." I tell him, this seems so far-fetched, I am struggling to keep up. Axton only shrugs.

"Marco from the council?" he asks. I nod my head.

"Well, that is the only Marco I know, unless you know another? Yet, I never knew Sondra, so maybe Marco has another brother?" Axton offers.

"Another brother called Floyd?"

Axton laughs. "I'm just telling you what I know. Your guess is as good as mine."

"We'll question Sondra when we get home," Lexa tells me. Yes, we would definitely sit down to have a chat about this.

CHAPTER ELEVEN

We spend the rest of dinner in silence while I pondered on the sleeping arrangement. I can't sleep in here. I don't trust myself, not with the bond acting all haywire.

"I'll take the couch. It's fine Elena. Stop stressing." Axton growls angrily when one of the boys wakes. Axton sets his plate down, forgetting his dinner and wandering into the nursery. Picking up his empty plate and mine, I go to the kitchen to make a bottle and return to find Axton already has one. I groan, waving the bottle at him.

"There is a kitchenette in my office," Axton says.

"You didn't think to tell me that?"

"You were gone when I came out, and I have no mindlink with you. I wasn't going to yell out to you and wake Bane." He says, while Kyan fusses, not wanting the bottle. He is fussier than his brother, preferring the breast and sometimes difficult to settle. Bane could be just as bad, but Kyan lately has refused the bottle, which was one stressor of them coming here.

Axton rocks him, trying to settle him, yet he continues to cry when Axton looks over at me, his eyes moving to the shirt that I'm wearing. "He won't take it, and I already changed him, too."

Moving toward him, Axton has a silly smile on his lips, and I take a second to realize why when I feel milk filling my bra and running down my stomach.

"Crap!"

"It's fine. I have more shirts, but try to feed him. He won't take the bottle while I get you another shirt. Axton passes me over Kyan when Bane suddenly starts crying, and I whip my boob out. Kyan chomps down on it, making me hiss when he doesn't latch properly and I have to adjust him.

Seconds later, Axton comes out with Bane and I watch as he changes him, then gives him the bottle. Holding him in one arm, he moves to the closet and returns with a fresh shirt, and places it on the bed where I'm sitting. Bane, however, has no issue accepting his brother's bottle, and Axton moves to sit beside me.

Shuffling over, I lean against the headboard, turning my gaze to the TV and trying to ignore his presence beside me. For the most part, it works, until I feel tingles rush across my arms, making my eyes fly open, not realizing I had dozed off.

My heart races for that split second when I notice my arms are empty, and I think I've dropped him. "He's fine, I've got him," Axton murmurs, his hand tugging my shirt down.

"Though you might want to change your shirt again." Looking down, it's soaked, and I groan. Without thinking, I tug it off, only remembering Axton is standing right there, and I just flashed him. Ripping the shirt down, he has his gaze on Kyan in his arms, and I let out a sigh of relief.

"Was he slipping?" I ask, and Axton looks over at me.

"No, but you looked uncomfortable with your neck craned back." he shrugs, moving to set Kyan back in his crib. Some part of me wanted him to remain, so I wouldn't have to be alone with his father. Yawning, I nod before moving to the couch and laying down, glad it is finally bedtime because I can ignore him.

"I'll sleep on the couch. It's hard as a rock," Axton tells me, but I would not kick him out of his bed.

"Elena!"

"I'm fine sleeping here," I tell him and Axton mutters under his breath and shakes his head, then grabs the TV remote.

Axton puts on a movie. "This one alright?" I wave him off, not caring what he chooses, knowing I will fall asleep in five minutes, anyway. Grabbing the fleece blanket laying on the arm of the couch, I tug it over myself, settling under the blankets to face the TV.

Axton, however, moves to his desk that was removed from where our son's nursery now is and has been placed under the window. Sleep comes easily, or did until I felt sparks rush over the backs of my thighs and under my back. I jolt awake, my hands flailing in the air, and I grab Axton's shoulders. Still half stuck in a dream state, I felt like I was falling.

"What are you doing?" I growl, trying to settle my now-racing heart from the heart attack he almost gave me.

"Shh, go back to sleep," he whispers.

"Put me down." I all but snarl at him, and he growls back at me.

"You're sleeping in the bed. Twice you've nearly rolled off that couch and I can't sleep knowing you're in the room yet out of my reach." I blink, trying to clear my hazy vision when he places me in his bed. Yet, his bed is a million times better than the hard leather couch I was sleeping on, and this one has a pillow!

I snatch his pillow, tucking it between my legs and using the other for my head. Axton huffs and shakes his head, walking off and returning with another. He narrows his eyes at me, while I yawn, eyeing the new pillow half tempted to build a barrier between us. However, that seems like far too much effort.

Axton climbs into bed and sighs loudly, and I roll over, giving him my back when Lexa stirs nervously, coming forward.

"I don't like this. We shouldn't be this close. It's not a good idea." Lexa worries.

"We're just sleeping."

"It's not the sleeping part I'm worried about."

"Sleep. If he tries anything, you can rip him a new asshole." Lexa growls in disagreement as I bury my face in his pillow, soaking up his soothing scent, when Axton chuckles behind me.

"I can see what you're doing." My eyes open, and I peer over my shoulder at him. He arches an eyebrow at me, a coy smile on his lips.

"I'm not doing anything?"

"You're scenting my pillow, Elena," I peer down at it.

"I was not!" I tell him, outraged at the accusation.

"Really, so you just sounded like a pig sniffing out truffles because you weren't scenting my pillow?" my face heats. Surely, I was not that loud. I sniffed it subtly.

CHAPTER
TWELVE

"It's fine. I am playing around. But if you want my scent, I am right here." he smiles at me, showing all his pearly white teeth, and I roll my eyes.

"If you're here, you might as well take advantage of the bond, Lena. I definitely won't complain if you want to scent me," he teases before chuckling. He pats his chest, and I look at him, my eyes tracing over the tattoos that are on his left pec and shoulder.

"Don't you dare!" Lexa growls at me, but what would it hurt, besides I know I would sleep better, and I hardly sleep with the boys? One night couldn't hurt, right?

"Are you trying to send us into heat?" Lexa growls angrily.

"I'm breastfeeding!" I tell her, annoyed at her dramatics. Besides, he is our mate.

"We are too close. You are asking for trouble," she warns, yet I purse my lips, fighting temptation, the bond yearning for its mate.

"Lena?" Axton laughs softly. "Come on, you know you want to." he smiles, his eyes flickering to Khan, and I feel the bond tug at Lexa, who sighs, giving in and as soon as she lets go of the restraint, I didn't realize she is holding in a death grip, I all but throw myself at him. It was like someone pulled back a slingshot, and the moment she let go, I was launched at him, embarrassingly so.

The bond flares at the offer, and I didn't realize how much Lexa was suppressing the bond until she let her control go of the control I didn't know she had. Axton makes an oomph sound as I crush him and my face flames, making me wish the bed would open up and swallow me.

Instantly, I go to move off him, but his arm snakes around my waist, pulling me back and tucking me closer. "Stop, I know it's the bond. You're not the only one fighting it, Lena." Axton murmurs before pulling my arm across his waist. I settle against him, tossing my leg over him, only for him to grip my thigh and drag my leg higher.

"But let's not test my self-control too much," Axton growls when I feel his lips press against my forehead. I yawn, his scent enveloping me and the bond finally settles, while exhaustion sweeps over me like a tsunami.

"I don't like this. We shouldn't be this close." Lexa murmurs, yet I can feel she is relishing in his scent and the feel of his overly warm skin.

My eyes close, and I feel my face fall slack as my entire body turns to putty as sleep takes me.

"This is how it should have been from the start," Axton whispers just before I pass out.

The sun beaming through the slight gap in the heavy drapes wakes me. I groan, the light making my eyes flutter to find I am still laying on Axton. I sluggishly try to find the reason I have awoken, yet the boys I can see on the tiny monitor on the bedside table next to Axton are fast asleep.

"I warned you, I warned you, but you never listen to reason." Lexa huffs. I sit up, wondering what she is talking about.

"Why did you wake me?" I growl at her, lifting my head off Axton's chest. I admire his resting face, like this I could almost forget why I am fighting the bond. He looks peaceful, and my eyes roam over his face, taking in every part, from his long lashes, lashes I wish I had. Down his straight nose to his full lips. He is handsome.

"Yeah, until he opens his mouth, and his attitude ruins everything." Lexa mumbles.

"He was fine last night, and I had the best sleep." I yawn, looking at his tattoos on his chest.

I peer down, finding I drooled all over him, and I gasp. I wipe my mouth, mortified, while my stomach cramps viciously. Trying not to wake him, my hands hover over his chest, wanting to wipe it off before he notices I caused a puddle on his chest. I swipe my hand over it, only smearing it more, and he moans at the touch while I grit my teeth, knowing if I keep touching him, the bond will wake him.

"Crap, I need some tissues." I hiss at Lexa. My eyes scan the room to see a tissue box sitting on his desk. I carefully remove my leg from across his waist and drag the blanket back. Axton stirs and I climb out of bed, wondering why I feel wet.

Sneaking out of bed, I creep toward the desk and pluck some tissues out when I feel something warm trickle down my leg, making me stop dead in my tracks. "Please be pee, please be pee." I squeeze my eyes shut. Glancing down, Axton's boxer shorts are drenched in blood and I swear the blood drains from my face.

Looking at the bed, I see Axton's clothes are ruined and so is his bed. It looks like a massacre took place in the bed.

"A massacre of your uterus lining!"

"Lexa... What should I do?" I panic.

"Well, for one, I think you'll need more than tissues. You might as well give him your uterus. You shredded most of it on him anyway," Lexa growls at me while I stare in horror.

"But I'm breastfeeding," is all my mind conjures up.

"I told you not to get too close, and now in a few days you'll set your damn heat in motion!" Lexa snarls when he stirs, he pats the bed, where I was laying, rolling over and straight into the ruined mess I made of his bed.

I gasp, wanting to erase last night, or go back and choose the couch. Anything as he sits up. Shame washes through me and tears prick my eyes. What have I done? Axton grumbles, lurching upright, and my eyes widen impossibly more when I see him lift his hand, which is drenched in blood.

"Elena?" Axton murmurs, half asleep, and staring at his hand in confusion.

"What the fuck! Elena?" Axton jumps up in a panic. Unable to face him, I race for his bathroom, slamming the door shut and locking the door.

CHAPTER THIRTEEN

Axton

A I feel a cold draft where Elena was sleeping with me. Rolling over in bed, I feel for her trying to tug her closer when my hand hits the air and something wet. My eyes flutter dazedly when the scent of blood hits my nose.

Wiping the spot with my hand, my brow furrows, and I open my eyes to see my hand is red. Confusion wraps around me as Khan stirs, nervously picking up her scent and blood. Blinking, I stare at my hand and then glance down at the bed to find it looks like a ritualistic sacrifice has taken place while I slept.

Panic slivers through me, making me wonder if something set Khan off. "Elena?" I mumble.

Khan shoves forward in a panic, and a gasp escapes me. "What the fuck! Elena?" I choke out, sitting up to find I am soaked in blood. Looking around in a panic, Elena darts across the room and locks herself in my bathroom while I toss the blankets back that cover my legs.

Placing my feet on the ground, I lift my legs, finding a puddle of blood on the floor.

"She's bleeding. Why is she bleeding? What did you do to her?" Khan snarls at me.

"What did I do? You mean, what did you do!?" I snarl back at him.

"I would never hurt her!" Khan growls at me.

Shaking my head, I call out to her. "Elena?" I get no answer when I feel her embarrassment smash through me. Standing, I walk over to the bathroom and knock on the door.

"Elena! What's wrong? Did I do something?" I question, looking down at my ruined boxers and my stomach, which is drenched in drying blood. She doesn't answer, and her embarrassment makes my face heat when one of the boys starts crying from the nursery.

Fuck! What should I do? I can't grab them like this!

Rushing into the nursery, I turn the mobile on above the crib, hoping the music calms them down, before searching for the binky for Bane. He fusses and I rock his bundled form with my hand, hoping he doesn't wake Kyan.

Finding the binky jammed down the side of the crib, I pop it in his mouth, and he gums it viciously, so I know he is hungry. Looking around, I reach over to the change table, snatching the baby wipes. Yet, I only manage to smear the blood more.

"Khan, help me!" I snap at him.

"With what? We need to check Elena! She is hurt!" Khan snarls when I curse, only to notice Bane has dozed off, though he has managed to roll into his brother, and gone was his binky, and he is now slobbering on his brother's hand that escaped the wrap.

I try to pry Kyan's fingers from Bane's munching lips. One eye flutters open as I pull the fingers out. His lip quivers and I know he is about to let out a blood-curdling scream when Khan snarls in my head,

"Quick plug it, he'll wake the other pet sperm!"

Holding Kyan's little wrist, I shove his fingers back into his brother's mouth in a panic. "That can't be hygienic!" I mutter, watching Bane munch on his brother's fingers.

"Leave him be, not like he can gum them off. Besides, good that they assert dominance now, the strongest will win the gum fight!" Khan tells me.

"If we come back and his fingers are gone, we know who the next Alpha is!"

"What?" I question his logic.

"He's fine, check Elena. They're twins, they have the same germs!" Khan snaps at me when I go to pry Kyan's fingers from Bane's mouth, now worried Bane will find a way to gnaw them off.

Sighing, I listen, sneaking out of the nursery and making my way back to my bathroom. I tap on the door, cringing as I do, not wanting to wake the boys again.

"Lena, open the door!" Shame washes through the bond, scaring me and Khan shoves forward and breaks the door down.

"Khan!" I growl, rubbing my now aching shoulder just as Elena yelps and jumps into the shower, ripping the shower curtain closed.

My eyes go to the tiled floor where I can see she has tried to clean it with towels and Elena makes a strange noise. Ripping the shower curtain back, she stares at me. Her eyes go wide and mine trail down her body to see her covered in blood. My hands reach for her and I tug at her shirt, only for her to slap my hands.

"You're hurt. Let me heal you." I growl at her.

"I'm not hurt!" She growls, making my eyes dart to hers when it dawns on me. Her face reddens, taking on the color of a beetroot. Her hands move to cover her face.

"Wait, that's..." I look down at the tiles. Why is there so much blood that can't be normal?

"Real smooth jackass, you can see she is embarrassed!" Khan retorts.

"Are you sure you're not hurt?" I blurt because this seems excessive. Maybe she has internal bleeding, or....

"Or what, fool! Her guts fell out! She sacrificed her uterus to the period gods!" Khan snarls.

"Perhaps?" Khan shakes his head at me, and my eyes move back to Elena.

"I ruined your bed," she whispers, peeking between the gaps of her fingers.

"I didn't like that bed anyway," I tell her stupidly. "I mean, I can clean it, it's fine." I internally facepalm myself at my word vomit. I was making this so awkward!

"Let's just get cleaned up, and then I can run down and grab your purse to find some plugs, or... what are those things called?" Elena blinks at me.

"Plugs?"

"Yeah, the... you know...the blood plugs, the cotton things with a tail." I make a plugging motion with my fingers.

Elena blinks at me. "You mean tampons!"

"Those things, good for nose bleeds, though maybe you might need to jam in a few." I tell her, reaching past her and turning the shower on when her embarrassment gets even worse.

CHAPTER
FOURTEEN

"It's fine, Elena, it's no big deal."

"I don't use tampons, I also don't have anything with me." She whispers and I look at her.

"Don't girls carry those things, or are supposed to?"

"I'm breastfeeding!" I blink at her, wondering why her breastfeeding matters in such a situation. Are tampons toxic?

Reaching for her shirt, I force it off her. "What's that got to do with anything you can still breastfeed?"

"No, I haven't had my periods because I'm breastfeeding, so I haven't needed to carry that sort of stuff."

"Then I'll go find some. Surely, we have something here!" I mutter, reaching for her pants. She shrieks, slapping my hands away, and I raise an eyebrow at her.

"Seriously, Elena, you left the contents of your uterus on me, and you're worried about me seeing you naked when I'm wearing your insides!" Her eyes widen and her face reddens impossibly more.

"Why would you say that?" She cringes and I shake my head, ripping her pants down and tossing them aside. I shove her back under the stream of water only for her to shriek and her back arches as I step in with her, her breasts smack against my chest.

"Freaking cold!" she squeals, and I chuckle, feeling the water to find I turned the wrong dial. I quickly adjust the temperature when she pushes me away.

"I'm not showering with you."

"Well, I'm not going to the store looking like I sacrificed my mate to the period goddess, so you'll get over it!" I tell her, reaching for the soap behind her in the niche. She sighs, and I go to wash myself when she snatches the soap off me.

"Don't touch it!"

"Touch what? It's touching me! I can't keep it. Whatever it is, I am apparently keeping that you don't want me to touch!"

"Just... it's gross."

"Elena, I love you, but I draw the line at wearing your insides on me like a body mask!"

"Don't be disgusting!"

"You're the one wanting me to leave it on. I'm all for you marking your territory, but I think I rather you pee on me!" her face turns purple, and she presses her lips in a line.

"I'll wash you!" she snarls, trying to clean it off. This woman is insane, her embarrassment making her act irrationally. She washes my side and abs, and her touch sends sparks everywhere, my cock twitching when she shrieks and jumps back.

"On second thought, you can wash it off," she says, staring at the ceiling, unable to meet my gaze. I glance down, knowing I have an erection from her touch, before smirking.

"Are you sure? I wouldn't want to touch it, don't want to get blood on my hands." I chuckle and she glares at me. Taking the soap from her, I wash myself.

"Now you're playing with it!" she scolds after a few seconds and I look up to find her watching my hand. Her face heats, knowing I caught her looking at my cock.

I step closer to her, pushing her against the shower wall, and she sucks in a breath. "Axton!" she snaps. "What, you caused it? I think it's only fair if you fix it." I purr at her.

"I'm bleeding!" she says, outraged.

"I hadn't noticed... But that wasn't a no!" I point out and her mouth opens and closes like a fish as I press my body against hers. "Blood doesn't bother me," I whisper.

Her hands go to my chest, but I grip her hip, my fingers digging into her skin, and I kiss her. Her lips are soft and she gasps. Taking advantage of her parted lips, I force my tongue into her mouth, deepening the kiss, and groan when I feel her kiss me back.

Grabbing her hand from my chest, I move it to my crotch, and she jerks, coming to her senses. "Axton!" I shrug and hold her hand in place.

"We're mates, Elena."

"That doesn't mean I want to fuck you!" she growls when I feel her fingers wrap around my cock, I fight back a groan and I know it's the bond, but I am having far too much fun watching the way she reacts to it without knowing.

"Are you sure?" I ask her and her eyes narrow.

"Positive."

"Then why are you stroking my cock?" I whisper and she shrieks, letting me go. I chuckle and peck at her lips, deciding to leave her alone.

"Asshole!" she growls, snatching the soap off me to wash herself.

"That I am, but I'm your asshole!" I laugh before stepping out of the shower and reaching for a towel just as one of the boys starts crying.

Elena whimpers and I glance back at her, her face looking rather pained when she covers her breasts. Only the moment she touches them, milk spurts from them like a fire hose from the added pressure, and I shriek at the force my eyeball is assaulted with.

I clutch my eye and the motion catching me off guard; I trip over the lip in the shower and stumble backward. Elena shrieks, grabbing my arm, but momentum is not on either of our sides as I slip on the wet tiles and she lands on top of me with a thud.

"Ouch!" I mumble, rubbing the back of my head.

Groaning, my back hurts and Elena sits up. The boys scream their lungs out and I grip her hips just as she shakes her head in a daze. Sitting up, I go to ask her if she is alright when I am given a milk shower, milk spraying in my face, and some gets in my mouth. My hands grab her breasts and I gasp as grabbing them makes it spray out faster. I hold my hands in front of my face, trying to block their hazardous spray.

"Oh, my gosh, could this get any more embarrassing," she squeals, covering her breasts.

"Well, if it makes you feel any better, breast milk doesn't taste that bad," I tell her, wiping my face. Opening my eyes, her face is flaming once again, and I wonder if she will permanently turn red.

I laugh and she quickly climbs off me and I groan, finding I am once again covered in blood. Stepping into the shower, I wash it off.

"The boys..."

"Let 'em cry for a second, won't hurt them, they have to sort out which is the more dominant twin," I tell her, rinsing the blood and milk off.

"Pardon?"

"They're fighting over who eats whose fingers!" I huff as I quickly step out of the shower, shut the curtain, and grab a towel.

CHAPTER FIFTEEN

Stepping out of the bathroom, I wrap the towel around my waist and quickly strip the bed. The boys are quiet, and I can hear them babbling happily. Dumping the sheets into the hamper, I look at the mattress. It still looks like a small animal has been sacrificed.

"New mattress it is, then!" I breathe out.

"Just flip it over for now so she doesn't notice!" Khan tells me and I sigh, doing as he says before quickly ducking into the hall to grab fresh sheets. I make the bed, worried if she comes out, she will go back and hide in the bathroom. Once I am finished, I hear the shower cut off and move to the nursery.

Plucking the boys from their crib, I carry them back to the room and set them on the bed, and quickly make bottles. Upon returning to the room from the nursery; I see Kyan is using his knees to push up, and his head bulldozing as he squirms his way over to the edge. A very embarrassing feminine shriek escapes me.

My heart races when I see his tiny body go careening over the edge, legs kicking while he cackles. Khan shoves forward with reflexes quicker than mine and snatches his ankle. Kyan cackles as Khan lifts him by one foot, dangling the sperm spawn by one leg.

"And where were you going?" he questions, placing him next to his brother.

"Now stay!" Khan orders him while Bane squirms, trying to roll and push off with his knees, too. Khan grabs his feet, dragging his tiny body back into place. I flip him onto his back, earning a big, gummy smile from him.

"Are you trying to get me in trouble? I don't think your mother will approve of brain damage. Now, stay! And try to keep the injuries to a minimum." I scold him. He babbles happily, blowing raspberries and spraying spit all over his brother.

Shaking my head, I build a pillow barrier around them and rush into the closet to retrieve some clothes, grabbing the first thing my hands touch while keeping my head out the door and on the mini escape artists.

Coming back out, Kyan is eating Bane's face, while Bane has his mouth open like a bird looking for a worm. Shaking my head, I grab their bottles and check the temperature when I notice Elena still hasn't come out. Feeding the boys with one hand, the bottles gripped awkwardly; I try to dry myself before using the pillows to prop the bottles up.

I get dressed, keeping one eye on the boys while doing the buttons on my shirt. Turning to check the boys one last time, I find them holding their own bottles.

"You mean I was holding them when you can hold them yourself? Lazy babies." I tell them. Kyan answers with a very wet-sounding fart.

"And that's for your mother, so hold that thought." Moving toward the door, I push it open. Elena is sitting on the toilet, a puddle of blood on the ground, and I sigh.

"Good thinking. You stay there, and I will take the boys to buy tampons."

"Pads!" I nod, shutting the door and looking at the boys, their bottles now empty.

"Okay," I mutter, trying to figure out how to do this. I wish Eli was here to help. I need an extra set of arms.

"Looks like we are on our own," I tell them, scooping them up when I remember I need to change them. Sniffing Kyan, I nearly chuck the kid in the trash. He reeks.

"I thought I said save it for your mother?" I tell him, holding him at arm's length.

"Don't forget the other one!"

"Right!" I tell Khan, scooping Bane up, who thankfully doesn't smell like a smoldering turd.

Groaning, I stomp back into the nursery, setting Bane on the change table. I change and dress him, setting him in the crib before retrieving Kyan and his nuclear ass. The moment I undo his diaper, I am sprayed in the face. I gasp, choking on piss, while Khan howls with laughter in my head.

Grabbing the diaper I set aside, I chuck it on him and his water fountain when the kid rolls. I watch the stream curve as he rolls, his pee stream following, and I see him rolling off. Grabbing him, I roll him when he gives one last quick spray, which hits my chin.

I wipe my face. "All done?" I quickly change him, finding my fingertips covered in mustard-colored shit. A shudder runs through me, and I quickly wipe my hands with a baby wipe.

I grab another baby wipe and quickly clean my face to find him smiling at me, covered in pee, too. Growling, I pluck more baby wipes from the container and wipe him over.

"Just because your mother marked her territory on me doesn't mean you have to!" I tell him. He babbles happily, eating his hands while I quickly dress him. Once done, I grab my wallet and the boys before singing out to Elena.

"I'll be back soon. You wait there!" I tell her.

"Real funny, jerk!" she calls back, making me snicker.

It took me a good twenty minutes to work out how to undo the stroller; I even threw it in frustration, but it seemed to work as it unfolded. Sometimes brute force is required. Walking into the store, I find the aisle designated for hygiene products. Stopping in front of it, I see an entire wall of them.

Picking one up, I stare at it. Why are there so many options? Scratching my head, I pull my phone from my pocket and dial Elena's number. It rings out, and she doesn't answer.

"She might have left it in the car last night. Try Eli!" Khan tells me.

"What would he know about feminine products?"

"Well, you got a better idea?" I growl, knowing he is right, and the checkout boy looks pretty clueless, so no point asking him. He looks like he barely has two brain cells to rub together.

Dialing Eli's number, he answers after a few rings. "Alpha," he answers when I hear the phone beep in my ear, making me look at the screen. He opened a video call. Sighing, I answer it with his face popping up on the screen.

CHAPTER SIXTEEN

"What's up?"

"Do you know anything about pads?" I ask him.

"Pads?"

"You know pads, period pads?" Eli blinks at me.

"Are you having an identity crisis? Like I'm full support, but shouldn't pads wait until after the sex change?" What the fuck is he talking about? He keeps rambling.

"I'm pretty sure you still won't get your periods even with one," he looks at the screen thoughtfully and I raise an eyebrow at him.

"But this explains so much, your mood swings, your growing hunger. Alpha side effect? Or the hormone replacements?"

"Not for me, you idiot! For Elena!"

"Isn't she breastfeeding?" Eli asks. Huh, what is it with breastfeeding and periods? I growl and he jumps.

"Fine, fine, turn the camera around. What are the options?" I turn the camera around, showing him, and he whistles.

"Wow! Okay, all this for a bleeding snatch, okay I can work with this! What size is she?" Eli asks. Huh? Size, what does he mean? There are sizes?

"What do you mean?"

"You know, is she a loosey-goosey, a tighty—" I snarl at him.

"You did not just ask me that!"

"I'm only trying to help!"

"Hang on, I will ask one of the guys!" he says.

"Slater! Come here!" Eli calls out. I glance around to find the cashier boy watching me, curiously.

"What's up!" I hear called back in the background, and I pinch the bridge of my nose.

"We got a bleeder! Just get over here!" Eli calls out and I growl. Does he have to alert the entire world to the fact Elena has her period?

"You know anything about pads?" Eli asks him.

"You're bleeding? Where?" Slater asks.

"Na, Luna got a bleeding snatch and our Alpha is trying to figure out which snatch pluggers to buy." I'm going to kill him.

"What size is she?" Slater asks and I growl.

"I swear to god another person asks me about her pussy once more. I will banish both of you fools."

"Geez, Alpha, only trying to help. What are the options?" I turn the camera.

"Do they do a one size fits all?" Slater asks. I growl when Khan gives me an idea.

"Wait, ask her mother!" I tell him. Eli groans, looking back at the screen.

"No, that old witch shot me in the ass with a pellet last night!"

"Louise did?" I ask a little shocked.

"No, Sondra!" I blink down at him, and he rolls his eyes at me.

"Fine, but if I get shot, you're pulling the pellet from my ass," he growls. I stand in the aisle like an idiot waiting for him to walk to the house.

"What do you want?" I hear Sondra snarl at him, making me pay attention to the phone again.

"I'm looking for Louise."

"Not here. Now get off my porch." Eli growls and I see him go to leave.

"Wait, she is a female, ask her!"

"You ask her!" Eli says.

"Ask me what? Spit it out pup, I ain't getting any younger!" I hear her snarl, making me remember mine and Elena's conversation about the old woman last night.

"I'm not asking, you ask her. Here, my Alpha wants to speak to you." I hear the phone exchange hands as the screen goes black.

Then I see her face as she squints at the phone, holding it away. "Ah... why the fuck is your head on the screen? Your voice is bad enough." she snaps at me and I shake my head. I hear Eli explain it is a video call.

"What do you want? Louise isn't here!"

"I need to ask you about feminine problems. You're a woman." I tell her.

"Good observation, son. You're not a complete dimwit after all. Did you just figure that out?" she asks, glaring at the screen. Sighing, I glare back at her.

"Listen here, you old dragon; I just need to ask a question. No need to be a--" she raises an eyebrow and purses her lips.

"Fix it yourself. Call me a dragon you little mutt, I have taken shits bigger than you!" she snarls, handing the phone back. "It's for Elena!" I blurt. She pulls the phone back.

"What about Elena?"

"Do you know what pad size Elena uses?"

"What?"

"You know pad size! For periods?"

"Periods! I haven't had a period in twenty years. My old meat flaps dried and shriveled up years ago, along with my ovaries. What would I know about pads? Roll up some rags." she snaps.

"Surely you would know what women use!"

"That depends. Am I a woman or a dragon?" she snaps.

I press my lips in a line. "Just apologize to the old bat!" Khan snaps at me, wanting to get off the phone with her.

"I'm sorry I called you an old dragon. Can you answer the question?"

"And how did that taste rolling off your tongue?"

"Bitter, so can you help?" She seems to think for a second.

"Fine, show me." she huffs. "I can't see your screen is blurry. Oi, Michelle!" I hear her yell out before hearing a faint answer.

"What does Elena use for.."

"No, what size!" I tell her.

"What size pads does Elena use?" I can't hear her answer but it's clear she does answer.

"Apparently, she uses period briefs, better for the environment and cheaper," Sondra explains. I nod, looking for these period briefs before seeing a giant packet on the top shelf. I grab it down and read the front.

Extra absorbent and discreet. "These ones?" I ask. Sondra squints at the screen.

"They look like briefs to me!"

"Thanks," I tell her, hanging up and moving to the front of the store to where the checkout boy is waiting.

I pass him the huge bag and he raises an eyebrow at me. I shake my head and he quickly bags them and I pay. Leaving the store, I put the boys back in their car seats and clip them in before moving to the trunk with the stroller.

"No, lift and squeeze." Khan orders, as I try to make the stroller collapse. I try it but it doesn't collapse. After about twenty minutes, I am still struggling with the stroller, so I give up and try to jam it in the trunk. I slam the lid down, only for it to pop back open. Growling, Khan shoves forward and hits the trunk, a wheel pops off, and the lid creases.

"Khan!'

"It worked, didn't it?" I growl, muttering under my breath, and climb in the car and head home to Elena.

CHAPTER
SEVENTEEN

Elena

I stare at the wall, Lexa scolding me and blaming me for our shared embarrassment.

"Man, what is he doing? Why is it taking so long?" Lexa growls when I hear the downstairs door open. I sit up straighter, listening to doors open and shut, then hearing someone on the stairs. A few minutes pass when I hear the bedroom door open.

"Honey, I'm home!" I hear Axton sing out and I roll my eyes. "I come bringing gifts for the bleeding minge!"

"Can I bite him? I think I need to bite him!" Lexa snarls. I hear him rummaging around and talking to the boys when suddenly the door opens.

"Aha, I found you. I was wondering where you went." I glare at him, and he snickers, his hand behind his back.

"Just give me the pads!" I growl at him. My ass is going numb from sitting on the toilet. My nipples are so hard from the cold, I feel like they are going to leap off my chest and run for my bra that is in the room.

"I'll forgive you for your lack of thanks because I know you're hormonal and it is not your fault." Axton declares, and I consider letting Lexa bite him. He pulls his arm out from behind his back and tosses me a package. I catch it, wondering why it is so big. Staring down at it, my mouth opens while Lexa howls with laughter in my head.

"I did good, didn't I?" Axton says smugly, and I grit my teeth, turning to look at him. He has a smug smile on his face, and I narrow my eyes at him.

"Is this a joke? Where are the pads?" I ask, and his smile falls.

"Sondra said you wear period briefs, that's what they are!" he says, motioning toward the package. I hold it up, squeezing the wrapping.

"These are not period briefs, and when did you talk to Sondra?"

"Well, first I rang Eli, but he didn't know what to buy. Neither did Slater, and your mother wasn't home, so Sondra said those were it!" he walks over, snatching the package. He points to the front of it, showing me the diapers.

"See briefs!" I growl, snatching them from him and pointing to the writing.

"Absorbent and discrete adult diapers!" I screech at him. He gives me a funny look, making me question his intellect.

"No, they are briefs!" he slaps the picture.

"For old people!"

"It says nothing about old people on it!" He snatches the package and flips it over to see an old man standing in an adult diaper.

"No wonder the checkout boy gave me a weird look!" he mutters. "Sondra said these were it! And why would these be in with feminine products?"

I shake my head and growl. Axton wipes a hand down his face and sighs.

"Just put it on and I'll take you to the store so you can buy your own," he tells me.

"I can't wear this!"

"Well, I am not going back there by myself!"

I growl at him and he shrugs, folding his arms across his broad chest when one of the boys starts fussing in the room.

He glances over his shoulder, looking at the door. "Go, I'll figure it out!" I snap at him as I wave him away before staring down at the package. Axton leaves, shutting the door behind him while I tear it open. Lexa is still laughing uncontrollably in my head as I open the packaging and hold up a pair.

"They say extra absorbent?" She laughs and I huff.

"Don't be a baby. Put them on!" she cackles.

"Your commentary is not helping!" I snarl at her while pulling them on. Standing up, they cover past my belly button. I groan, this day just keeps getting better! I catch a glimpse of them in the mirror.

"Nope, definitely not!" I tell her about to take them off when Axton opens the door.

"Kyan is refusing.... Oh, la la, what have we here?" He purrs, wiggling his eyebrows. "I wonder if they do matching bras?" Axton snickers.

"Bridget Jones got nothing on you, baby," he sends me a wink. I growl at him and grit my teeth before stomping past him.

"Don't be like that, Lena, I didn't mean it!" he says, following me to his closet. I snatch a pair of his sweatpants off the shelf and grab a shirt off the hanger.

"Shh, shhh. Mommy is just upset you wear them better than her!" he coos, rocking Kyan. I shoot him a glare and he snickers, leaning against the door frame while I tug the shirt over my head.

"Don't get any ideas. I ain't changing your ass after seeing what came out of Kyan's this morning. I will take you out back and hose you down!" he warns.

"You are so lucky you're holding our son right now or I would—"

"Would what? Throw a tantrum and demand a bot-bot?" Axton snickers. I growl, and he holds up Kyan like a shield.

"Settle, you can beat me off later!" he winks at me. I'll beat him alright, but not the way he wants me to!

"Our sons are present. Contain yourself. If you are a good girl, I will give you my lollipop." I growl at him, and he snickers, darting out of the walk-in closet before I can grab him and strangle the life out of him.

CHAPTER
EIGHTEEN

I finish getting changed, stealing his clothes before walking out to the mirror and making sure my giant diaper can't be seen. I feel like I'm walking like a cowboy who just rode bareback for three days up a rocky mountain.

"See, you can't even tell. You got upset over nothing." Axton says and I glance at him to see Kyan was finally accepting the bottle. Bane is resting across his legs, already having finished his while Kyan is in his arms.

"Just let me finish feeding him and I'll take you to the store," Axton tells me, smelling Kyan's little head. Moving toward him, I grab Bane from his lap and snuggle with him, inhaling his scent.

"Oh, and you need a new stroller. I may have broken it."

"Excuse me?"

"It wouldn't fold down and I didn't have time to put the one in the shed together, so I stole yours. I'll get you a new one," he tells me and I roll my eyes.

When Kyan has finished his bottle, we all pile into Axton's car and we drive to the store across town. However, I notice the street is still super quiet.

"Curfew?"

"No, just not many people out lately. Most are too scared to go out alone and those that do go out in groups." I nod in understanding.

I try to get comfy looking out the window to see most stores haven't even bothered to open. Yet the longer we drive, the more uncomfortable I get. These diapers are not comfy!

"Will you stop squirming?" Axton hisses at me.

"It itches!" I tell him, scratching my ass cheek.

"I will get you diaper rash cream," he tells me and I growl, smacking his chest. He laughs harder and I fold my arms across my chest when he reaches over, gripping my knee.

"I'm playing. Stop getting so upset. No one will know."

"Except Eli, Slater, and Sondra!" he cringes.

"I tried to ring you, but you left your phone in the car, and why don't they have a one-size-fits-all?" I shake my head at him as he pulls up in front of the general store on the main street.

Climbing out, we grab the boys and enter the store when Axton walks off and grabs a cart.

"We don't need a cart," I tell him and he shrugs, buckling Kyan in and I sigh, before handing him Bane when he holds his arms out for him. Walking through the aisles, Axton grabs milk and a few other things while I'm too busy scratching my ass.

"Will you stop that? People will see!" Axton hisses at me.

"I have a wedgie!" I hiss back. Axton leans back and stares at my butt.

"Don't look!" I growl at him and he laughs. We stop in the feminine section and I see they don't carry period briefs or the brand of pads I like. Picking up a few, I read them before selecting a Libra brand.

"Those ones?" Axton asks, pointing at the package in my hand, and I nod.

"And what size are they?" he asks, looking completely serious.

"Size?" I question.

"Yeah, so I know for next time." he shrugs, reaching for them, but I chuck them in the cart.

"There aren't sizes, it's not a shoe! And regular, then you have super, mini and panty liners. It goes off the flow, not the size of your vagina!"

"Then you need the super. I've seen how you bleed!" My face burns at the memory and I turn to walk off when I hear him rustling on the shelf. Turning back around, I see him swipe the entire shelf into the cart.

"What are you doing?" I shriek at him, looking up the aisle.

"Stocking up!"

"I'm here for one more night! I can't use all those." I hiss at him.

"Years supply then." He shrugs and I growl, trying to put some back, but he slaps my hand.

"You won't get your lollipop!" he scolds, and I grit my teeth when I notice we have drawn the attention of other shoppers. He snickers. I growl at him, stomping to the front of the store, not wanting to make a bigger scene, when I hear Axton groan behind me. "Man, I was hoping he clocked off already," he whines.

"Who?" I ask, glancing at him, wondering what he is talking about.

"The check-out boy." he waves ahead and I look at the boy, who was not a boy but a young man, a little younger than me and I move toward check out, wanting to slap Axton.

I place the milk on the conveyor belt and the few groceries Axton grabbed and my one package when Axton reaches in and dumps an armful on the conveyor belt. My face flames when the man raises an eyebrow, looking at me, and my embarrassment grows stronger when Axton opens his mouth to comment.

"She has a heavy flow! Oh, and those diapers weren't for me but for her, just so we are clear on that," he tells the checkout clerk.

"Breathe, Elena, it is not worth life in prison," I whisper to myself. The man scans the first package of pads, then scans them again while Axton grabs his wallet out.

He grabs another package, and the register makes the same noise before he sighs, reaching for his microphone.

"Can I get a price check on?—" I snatch his microphone and growl at him.

"I have had enough embarrassment for one day!" I snarl at him and he jumps back away from me. Turning, I snatch Axton's wallet, grabbing the wad of 50s from his wallet and dumping it on the register.

Swiping the contents into the cart, I turn to look at the clerk. "That should cover it!" I tell him, "And keep the change." I stomp out of the store, fuming, and head for the car.

"You better be little spoon tonight, you just emptied my wallet, that was two grand you gave him! Your bleeding fanny flaps best give me something." I whirl around and he puts his hands up, laughing.

"Okay, I will still give you my lollipop even though you've been naughty and had a tantrum. Okay, BABY girl."

"Want me to bite him?" Lexa growls just as embarrassed.

"I'm considering it," I tell her.

"Go for it, I have a designated spot with your name on it." he points to his neck. Idiot, yet I can't help but smile at his playfulness. It's a nice change from his usual alphahole self.

CHAPTER
NINETEEN

On the way home, Axton stops at McDonald's and we order some burgers for lunch, yet while waiting in the drive-thru, sirens sound in the distance before police cars race past the restaurant heading towards Axton's territory. I peek at Axton.

"Wonder what's going on?"

"No idea, but they'll mind link if it is anything important," he assures me and I nod my head. The window opens, and the girl smiles at Axton, holding out a paper bag to him.

Grabbing the food, Axton hands me the paper bag and pulls out of the drive-thru and onto the road to head home. Yet as he drives, I notice the car slowing down, and he then pulls over.

"Ah, why are we stopping?" I ask, stuffing a fry in my mouth. Axton growls, making me jump, and one of the boys makes a noise. Leaning across the seat, I put Bane's binky back in his mouth and turn to face the front.

Glancing at Axton, I see his eyes are glazed over and he is stuck in a mind link. His hands grip the steering wheel tightly and his knuckles press beneath his skin, making the skin look on the verge of splitting. I wait for the mind link to drop. He clenches his jaw and his eyes return to normal, and I hear him curse.

"Is everything alright?" Axton says nothing.

"Axton?"

"Everything is fine. I just need to go somewhere once I drop you and the boys home," he tells me.

"So something is wrong?" he glances at me but doesn't add any more on the subject when his phone starts ringing through the Bluetooth. He declines the call only for the number to ring again, flashing across the dash.

Officer Ben Carlton. Axton growls, hitting decline. Yet when it pops up again, I answer it. "Just take it!" I tell him, knowing it has to be important if he keeps calling, but pulls back onto the road and continues driving.

"Hello, Alpha?"

"Yes, Ben. I have heard already. I am dropping my mate off at home first. Tell them to wait!"

The officer clears his throat. "I have already sent them in."

"Did Eli not ring you?"

"He did, but I had already sent them in. We've had so many reports come in and we linked them here."

"And did you find them?"

"Yes, Alpha. You need to come in. Alpha Osiris is on his way with Alpha Thomas."

"Excuse me? Tell them to wait; they are not to enter before Marco gets there. They trampled evidence last time!"

"Derrick is also headed in."

"How does he know about it?"

"Thomas told him, Alpha, he was at the station when the call came in."

"It's fine, Axton, just go do whatever it is," I tell him.

"How bad is it?" Axton asks.

"You need to come in." Axton curses and shakes his head.

As we come toward the turnoff onto his territory, he turns the opposite way and mutters under his breath.

"I'll be there in a minute!" he hangs up the call and I look at him for answers.

Coming around the next bend, I see the police cars all lined up out the front of one of Tieriny's restaurants. Leaning forward in my seat, Axton's entire demeanor has changed. Gone is the playfulness, and the Alpha has returned.

"I just need to go take a look at something,"

"Is it a robbery?"

"I'm not entirely sure, but wait in the car. Whatever it is, isn't good!" Axton tells me, pulling over between two cop cars. He climbs out, and I glance at the boys in the back of the car, wondering if Tieriny is ok. However, watching from the car, I grow increasingly nervous when I see one of the older officers talking to Axton, who keeps glancing at the doors to the restaurant.

He glances back at me in the car before quickly averting his gaze back to the officer when another comes staggering out the doors. Axton looks at him, but he rushes to the curb, throwing up in the gutter. Axton looks at him again and drops his head before disappearing inside the restaurant.

Waiting in the car, the boys start to grow antsy, and Axton has been inside for ten minutes when I see Alpha Osiris pull up. One of the officers tries to stop him from entering. He barges past, walking into the building followed by Alpha Thomas. Curiosity is killing me, and I notice ambulances pull up, but none enter and no one comes out.

"Axton said to wait here, Elena." Lexa worries and I look at the boys.

"I just want to know what is going on, or if it will take too long, I will tell him I'll head home," I tell Lexa, opening the car door. However, the moment I do, one of the officers spots me and waves his hands at me.

"Back in the car, Luna!"

"What's going on?" I ask, ignoring his Luna comment. The officer looks back at the doors to the restaurant and sighs.

"Just wait for Alpha to return," he says, and I shake my head, suddenly feeling sick, and I close the door.

"Luna! Wait in the car."

"Alpha, now wait with my boys!" I growl, and the officer looks at one of the senior officers, who nods to him. He walks over to me and I open the door.

"Sit with them for a second," I tell him, and he nods.

"Yes, Luna." Once again, I ignore his comment and head for the doors to search for Axton. Pushing the doors open, I step inside and am instantly smashed by the scent of blood and decaying flesh.

I gag, covering my mouth and nose, and look around the foyer before spotting officers through the glass double doors to my left. Walking over to them, I yank one open when Axton is suddenly in front of me, pushing me back out of them.

CHAPTER
TWENTY

"I said wait in the car!" he growls, grabbing me and spinning around. I growl, turning back when he grabs the back of my head, pulling me to him and blocking my view.

"Please go wait in the car," Axton whispers, and I can feel his heart racing beneath my hands, smell his fear of whatever is going on emanating from his pores. His fingers tangle in my hair.

"What's going on, Axton? Is Tieriny alright?" He makes a weird noise in his chest.

"Please, Lena, you can't unsee what's in there. Just go back to the car, I'll be there in five minutes."

I push off his chest, trying to see around him, only for him to step in my path again. "Axton! What about Tieriny?" he doesn't answer, but his jaw clenches.

"Go back to–" I shove past him, needing to know if my friend is okay, and shove open the doors and nearly throw up from the stench. It is amplified in here worse than in the foyer, and I retch, gagging and clutching my knees when the foul smell steals my breath.

"Elena, do as he said!" Lexa snarls at me, and I shake my head, pinching my nose.

Axton growls behind me as I gag again when I see a small red shoe with blue laces not far from me. Lifting my head a little, I notice the dead body of a child.

He is wearing navy-blue sweatpants with some cartoon character on them, and a white shirt, only the shirt is covered in blood, his skin is black from decay, his throat is ripped out and I gasp. My eyes move higher to look at his face when I spot another crumpled, disfigured body next to him as I stand upright.

A second later, a hand covers my eyes and sparks rush across my neck where Axton's lips press gently, his other arm wrapping around my waist as he pulls me back against him.

"That was a boy," I murmur in shock. Who would do that to a child?

"Please, wait in the car," Axton whispers.

"But—"

"Tieriny is dead, Elena," Axton murmurs, and my stomach drops. My blood runs cold in my veins and my heart feels like it is about to leap out of my throat.

Axton moves, pulling me with him, keeping his hands over my eyes, and I hear the doors close behind us. "How many?" I ask him, my eyes burning with tears.

"Twenty-nine, eleven are children," Axton whispers. So many.

"How could that many people go missing without you noticing?" I ask incredulously.

"All restaurants have been shut down, only essentials trades are open, Elena."

"Elena?" I nod, walking toward the foyer doors, wishing I listened to Lexa, and backed out of the room. Axton is right. I can't unsee the little boy. Needing to get out of here, I shove open the doors. The moment the fresh air hits me, I rush to the gutter, now understanding why the officer threw up because I am forced into the same predicament as I lose my stomach.

I retch, bile coming up and the lunch we bought when tingles brush my face as Axton grabs my hair, pulling it back.

"Come, I'll take you home." I shake my head, not wanting to be left in the packhouse alone with the boys after seeing that.

"I'm fine. I'll wait in the car."

"I'm done here. Marco just showed up." He tells me, and I lift my head, seeing his black car pull up beside Axton's, and then so does my father's.

Marco moves toward Axton, who quickly moves to the car. He reaches in and grabs his drink because I drank mine already. He hands it to me and I sip it, to wash the taste away, just as my father comes over.

"They found them?" my father asks. Axton nods his head and Marco curses, rushing inside.

"All of them?"

"Looks like we found one lair." Axton answers.

"Tieriny?" I shake my head.

"We think she stumbled upon them. Her body was fresh. She was found by the alarms which signaled the station." Axton tells him. My father curses and rushes inside.

I watch him, knowing I should be the one going in there since I technically own his pack.

"Let your father identify your pack members. You don't need to go back in there." Axton says, sensing my thoughts. I chew my lip, yet even Lexa is urging me away and I can't get the image of the boy from my head.

"Vampires?" I ask him and he sighs.

"We are starting to wonder if it's something more. Half the bodies were torn apart."

"Werewolf?" I ask. Vampires mostly drain their victims, not rip them to pieces, yet how do you explain the blood loss?

Axton says nothing, instead opening the passenger side door and motioning for me to climb in.

"He knows something," Lexa states, and I agree, watching as he slides into the driver's seat.

"You know something."

"We aren't sure. Not even Marco has come across something like this. It will cause hysteria if it gets out."

"So the council has just been sitting on information?"

"No, Marco and I have been, though I don't think we can hide it now."

"Hide what, Axton, tell me."

"We think it's a form of strigoi."

"Strigoi don't exist anymore," I tell him.

"We know, they haven't for centuries, but it's the only thing that makes sense, why we can't catch them also explains why sometimes we find fur at the murder sites."

"Fur?"

"Yes, vampires only need to feed once or twice a week. This thing is draining victims daily." I gasp in horror. I've heard stories, but these creatures were hunted to extinction. They are the very reason humans feared vampires in the first place.

"Strigoi can shape shift," I murmur, praying I remembered that wrong.

"Exactly."

"You think one is in the city?"

"I think it's not just hunting in the city; I think it's within one of the packs."

CHAPTER
TWENTY-ONE

Axton is quiet for the rest of the drive back to the packhouse. I didn't know what to say or even think about what he told me because it only gives me more things to worry about. Especially knowing it could be literally anyone. Yet, I could tell Axton was serious, he wasn't joking, and I can tell it scared him too.

"I don't want you and the boys out on that ranch, it isn't safe. You need to move back to the city."

Sighing, I glance at him and shake my head. "I can't uproot my pack or abandon them out there, besides we have had no attacks out there and if anywhere is unsafe, it's the city! That's its hunting ground."

"You are exposed out there. Omega women are no match for a strigoi, Elena! Not even I'm a match for a strigoi, no werewolf is!"

"Exactly! This has been going on for months, and it is clear whoever is doing this is targeting the packs within the city!" Lexa also agrees, most of the attacks have happened in the city, very few outside its borders, so why would I want to bring my pack to its hunting grounds? Axton growls and grits his teeth, his hands tightening on the steering wheel as he pulls on to his street.

Finally he exhales, his shoulders slump. "Fine, you're probably right but you need to agree to let my men remain on your borders."

"They can go where they please; just tell them to keep their distance from the women. Some are a little jumpy when it comes to men, but they can have full access." I give in knowing it will cause issues, but their safety and our sons is what matters. Besides, saying no to extra patrols would be foolish and only cause more arguments. I am sick of arguing with Axton at every turn, especially when things are kind of pleasant at the moment.

"I'll organize it before you leave tomorrow, don't forget the council meeting is on Friday; I may try to move it to Wednesday."

"I'll bring the boys and mom. She can watch the boys for us at the packhouse?" Axton nods his head, a silly smile on his lips as he pulls into the garage.

"What's so funny?" I ask him.

"Nothing, it's nice not fighting with you." I chuckle and shake my head, it is a nice change that for once we can agree with each other.

"If you have your men watching my borders, will you have enough to watch the city?" Axton nods his head.

"Yes, I will get the other packs to help. Clearly we need it now. We thought with so many missing, they fled the city. We had a few that did at the start when the attacks first happened." Axton explains as he climbs out of the car.

We grab the boys out of the car and take them inside. The packhouse is quiet as usual and I follow Axton to the kitchen with Bane on my shoulder and a bag in one hand. I set it on the counter while Axton digs through them.

"Crap, we are missing the bag with the milk and bread." Axton groans about going back out and grabbing it.

"Here, take Bane, I will go. I left the year's supply of pads in the car too." I chuckle. Axton takes Bane in his other arm, following me and turning into the living room while I go back outside. I am about to close the door behind me when I hear him sing out.

Stepping back inside, I pop my head into the living room. "Yep?" Axton smiles deviously as he sets the boys down on the play mat.

"Can you grab the tarp off the shelf along the back wall?" I nod and I am about to turn and leave again, wondering why he wants a tarp. "Oh, and in the glove compartment, I am pretty sure I have a yellow poncho. Grab that, too." A poncho?

He laughs and I look at him questionably. "Can't be too careful when the rivers run red." He chuckles. I grit my teeth and flip him off.

"I was serious about the poncho!" He sings out while I ignore him. Shutting the door, I race to the garage and open the trunk, finding the missing bag and see pads scattered through the trunk. I stuff a few packages in the bag, but give up on the rest. Shutting the trunk, I turn to head back to the house when I see a car sitting at the end of the driveway with its windows up, the dark tint making it impossible to see who is inside.

I start walking down the driveway when it slowly pulls away from the curb. Shaking my head, I head back inside the house yet something about that car nags at me, I've seen it before, I just can't remember where.

"Did you grab the poncho?" Axton asks, and I grab a package of pads out of the bag and toss it at him. "No!" it hits him in the head and he snickers.

"A car was sitting at the bottom of your driveway." I tell him.

"What kind of car?"

"A white one with tinted windows." I tell him.

"Probably someone lost; I get heaps that turn into the driveway to turn around since it's a deadend." He shrugs and I nod, taking the milk to the fridge when I feel arms wrap around my waist.

"You're probably being paranoid."

"And you're being clingy." I tell him, pushing him away, and he laughs.

"It's the bond!" He defends himself and I raise an eyebrow at him.

"What it is! You may want to ignore it. That doesn't mean I want to." Axton tells me.

Sighing, I ignore him. I am not forgiving him just because he is struggling with the bond.

"You had no issue giving into the bond last night!" Lexa growls, still angry with me.

"So, you're just going to keep ignoring the bond?" Axton asks.

"I'm not ignoring it; I am just choosing to think above it."

"Think above it?"

"I can't let the bond control reason, Axton."

"I said you can keep your pack, Elena."

"On paper!"

"Isn't that enough?" He demands and I shake my head. Axton growls, folding his arms across his chest. "And that doesn't make up for what you did!" I remind him.

"I can't take that back! I would if I could! You're living in the past, and need to get over it!"

"Get over it? That shit fucking haunts me! Who are you to tell me to just get over it, the shit you did to me I would never do to you." I shake my head at him.

"You left." Axton yells at me.

CHAPTER
TWENTY-TWO

"Because you gave me no choice, you're why I left, maybe I shouldn't have run the first time, I own that, I admit that was a mistake. Fuck do I know that was a mistake, I lost everything, lost my best friend, lost myself and when you found us, I would have begged to be by your side, and instead you rejected me. Even then, in my fucked up head I thought we would work it out, but... you know what, I'm not doing this. You fucked up, I fucked up, but at least I own my mistakes."

"You aren't the only one that lost everything! I lost my sons!"

"Did you, though? I still sent pictures, I let you know they were okay, I didn't have to do that. I could have disappeared for good, but I didn't... You're just angry because once I came back you realized I wasn't going to be your bitch anymore, that I won't be walked over, you realized I didn't need you, or a pack, anyone. You didn't lose anything. I'm here now and so are your sons, I didn't have to bring them this weekend, I chose to! So before you start making fucking demands, Axton, maybe start meeting some of mine!"

Axton scoffs. "I haven't demanded anything of you..."

"Really, you demanded to mark me, then demanded I not reject you again, demanded to see your sons. I kept my promises, but you, every time I ask for something in return it's no! Or you threaten my pack, or threaten to take the boys, when have I threatened your life?" He goes to open his mouth, but I hold up a hand, knowing exactly what he's going to say.

"Your reputation isn't your life, that's ego. You destroyed my reputation when you leaked that video, a video that almost cost me my life and our sons. Those photos wouldn't have physically hurt you, not that I would have leaked them anyway, not when that would hurt our sons in the end anyway. So tell me, Axton, when have I done the things you've done to me to you?"

"I've never threatened your life, not intentionally."

"Yes, you have. Those boys in there are my life. The reason I get up each morning, it's exactly why I agreed to let you have them because I forgot they're yours too." Axton presses his lips in a line and looks away. "I don't want to fight with you, Axton. But I won't let you walk all over me, either."

"So that's it? You've just decided the bond doesn't exist, doesn't matter?"

"That's up to you, I've seen how toxic bonds can be, the women on that ranch are proof of that, my mother is proof of that, I won't be our son's proof." Axton nods his head and then storms off angrily, and I shake my head. "He'll never get it until he sees fault in himself instead of everyone else." Lexa sighs.

"What about Khan?"

"He owns Axton's mistake, I swear the goddess got that shit wrong and Axton was supposed to be the wolf and Khan the humanity!" I chuckle because usually the wolf was the angry dominant one, not the human counterpart.

I put the rest of the groceries away before going back to the boys. Axton is lying beside them on the floor. When his phone rings, he rolls, pulling it from his back pocket.

"I need to take this. Are you alright to sit with them?" he asks, refusing to look at me.

"Yes," I find his question silly, but don't tell him that, instead just move to take his spot on the floor while he leaves the room. Flicking the TV on, I turn it to the news station.

As expected, the new channels are parked out the front of the police station waiting for statements and saying what they suspect happened. Yet when I flick to another station, an emergency city broadcast cuts the channel out. The news anchor goes on to speak about the restaurant and what they found; they list pictures of the missing people that were found, and I sit up when the boy I saw comes up on the screen, and I swallow when they identify him as being from Axton's pack.

Yet as the names are called out, I start to notice all of them are from Axton's pack, and my father's. Yet nothing prepares me for the next three faces that pop up on the screen. Alisha's parents and lastly, Tieriny. I have no idea how I will tell my mother all this. It seems unfathomable that one person is responsible for so many lives taken. Suddenly, the TV turns off and a feral growl sounds behind me as Axton drops the remote back in my lap.

"You didn't tell me Alisha's parents were a few of the missing people." I tell him, looking up at him.

"I was hoping we would find them alive," he mutters.

"I need to tell my mother." I shake my head, about to get to my feet, already dreading giving her that news.

"She already knows, she was the one who reported them missing. She didn't want you to worry, they've been missing since the first attack happened, just before you left last time." Axton tells me. She knew all this time and said nothing, even when I asked about them, she would say they were fine.

"I need to leave for an hour, are you alright by yourself or do you want to come with me?"

"Where are you going?"

"I have a pack meeting in the hall, my pack members are growing anxious, most of those killed were my people." I nod my head and glance at the boys.

"Just let me chuck some warm clothes on the boys."

"You want to come?" I nod, I didn't want to stay here in this huge house by myself.

"Elena, you know they'll call..."

"Luna? Yeah, a few of your officers called me Luna." I shrug, scooping the boys up off the floor, and Axton instantly takes one.

"And that doesn't bother you?" He asks.

"Nah, it's fine, Lupha," I snicker, climbing the stairs.

"Pardon?" I giggle to myself.

"Luna is fine. If that's what they want to call me."

"Why do I feel like I'm missing some inside joke?" Axton mumbles behind me.

CHAPTER
TWENTY-THREE

It is late by the time we return to the packhouse, just like Axton predicted. News of a possible strigoi has caused citywide panic. Families requesting to leave the city, and others wanting to hunt it down. But exactly how do you catch a ghost when it could be anyone, people accusing their neighbors, their friends, their rivals? It was utter chaos, and I could tell Axton didn't know how to cope with this added stress.

"I need to shower," Axton mumbles. After helping me get the boys tucked into their crib, I watch him move toward the bathroom, locking himself in, and I sigh.

It makes me wonder how my father is coping with the chaos in our pack. While Axton is showering, I check in with my mother, video-calling her to ensure everything is okay back home.

She took the news of Alisha's parents and Tieriny pretty hard, as expected. "When are you coming home?"

"Tomorrow afternoon, unless you need me back there now?" I tell her, and she shakes her head. "No, it won't change anything. I really thought they left when the others did. And Tieriny..."

"I'm sorry, mom," I tell her, chewing my lip, and I hear Luke call out to her. She looks away from the screen for a second.

"I need to go. I will see you tomorrow night. Give the boys a kiss for me."

"Love you." I hang up the phone just as Axton comes out with his towel around his waist. Tension rolls off him in waves as he wanders into the walk-in closet and returns a few minutes later with some boxer shorts on.

"Couch or bed?" Axton asks me, and my brows furrow.

"The bed, but I forgot your poncho," I tell him, and he half smiles.

"Damn it, we can build a pillow barrier then," he chuckles, climbing into bed. I yawn before quickly ducking into the bathroom to change, having showered quickly before we left. Coming out, Axton is watching the news, a deep frown on his face.

"One of Osiris's journalists accused me of being the strigoi," he laughs, shaking his head, and I look at the news anchor who is reporting knowing exactly whose pack she is a part of. I move toward the bed and tug the blankets back. Climbing into the bed beside him, I take the remote and shut the TV off.

"I expect to wake up with my blood still in my veins," I tell him, and he chuckles.

"No promises," he laughs before he tenses when I move, putting my head on his chest and arm across his waist.

"Ah.... Elena? You're voluntarily touching me?" he asks.

"Shut up. It's the bond!"

"Sure it is." He rolls, flipping me on my side and snuggling into my back as he slides his arm beneath my head.

"I was comfortable."

"Yeah, I don't want a repeat of last night. These are my favorite boxers!" He laughs, and I elbow him. Axton grunts, tugging me closer, his warm breath sweeping my neck as he presses closer.

"Stop fighting the bond." He purrs behind me.

"Stop being an asshole, and I'll think about it." I chuckle.

"Deal. But I need to ask a favor first?" Axton says, making me look at him over my shoulder, and he sits up, rolling me onto my back. A line creases between his eyes, and a frown settles on his face before he sighs.

"You don't want to merge packs or lose your packs," he says, then glances away.

"You already know that. What do you want?" I ask him, slightly confused about where he is taking this conversation, and he looks back down at me.

"You heard my pack tonight. We are outmatched severely right now. Osiris wanted your father's pack because it's the second largest. You have an army behind you if you'd use it. That is why Osiris went after you. He knows the power you hold once you take over. At the restaurant, he was talking about challenging you for your title, saying if we had control of your pack, we could better prepare the city."

"But my father has been allowing access?" I ask. Axton shakes his head.

"Kind of. He will only let his men patrol his borders, but he has 300 warriors more than any of the packs in this city, more than me."

"But your pack is the strongest."

"Yes, because all my pack members are trained, not just my men. But we are running double and sometimes triple patrols. My pack is tired, and your father won't help out. Osiris has his own agenda, and the other packs won't fall in line while Osiris and I are at each other's throats. They won't step in until there is a display of sides officially."

"So you want to challenge my father, challenge me?" Axton shakes his head.

"No, and I don't want you to, but—"

"You want me to take my title..."

"I can run your pack until it merges, but they won't listen to me wholly. They're loyal to your father."

"But a change of power won't make them either, Axton."

"They will if you claim me."

"That would make you their Alpha, giving you control over not only your pack but mine," I growl. Axton sighs.

"They'd still be yours."

"Yeah, but only on paper." I shake my head.

"Then you aren't going to leave much choice but to challenge your father and take your pack, Elena. I don't want to do that, but right now, we need help. If the human governments get involved, they will tear this city apart and dismantle the packs." I sigh because it has been happening everywhere. As soon as a city turns into a problem, the government steps in.

"I'm not marking you," Axton growls at me.

"You'll have to eventually, anyway. What happens when you go into heat?" I shake my head.

"Not yet. Let me think about how to deal with that when it happens, but I.."

"Elena, we aren't ready to challenge him yet. We've barely trained," Lexa worries. My plan was originally to force him to submit, but I haven't got enough evidence against him yet to make him do that.

"We have no choice," I tell her, and her mind instantly goes back to the night he nearly killed us, then the night we went to help mom and Luke.

"I challenge him and temporarily hand the pack over to you," I tell him, yet my mind is plagued with what if I lose?

"You won't." Axton suddenly says, picking up on my thoughts.

"But if I do, I lose everything all over again," I whisper.

"You won't," he says positively, yet I felt sick just at the thought.

"Besides, even if you did somehow lose, he won't beat the six-foot monster coming up behind you." Axton growls, his eyes flickering as Khan presses forward.

"Challenge him; worst-case scenario, I take your pack back for you. But I won't have to. You'll kick his dusty old ass." Khan assures me, making me chuckle before he gives Axton back control.

"Set the challenge for your title; I'll be right behind you. I know you don't trust me, but you can trust I will be there to back you up if you need it."

I chew my lip when another thought occurs to me. "If I take my pack back, what is stopping Osiris from challenging me once it's official?"

Axton smiles, leaning down and brushing his lips against mine gently. "He won't. He challenges my mate, he challenges me. It would be suicide, and he knows it. Your father he'll challenge, your father is old. Osiris knows he can beat him, but you?" Axton chuckles. "He would want to have his funeral arrangements prepaid and his eulogy ready if he comes after my mate," Axton growls before kissing me.

His lips move hesitantly against mine at first, gently like he fears I'll shove him away, but when I kiss him back he growls, delving his tongue between my lips. Sparks rush everywhere, and my stomach clenches as heat invades me when I pull away, feeling him move, pressing his body between my legs.

"What's wrong?" he groans.

"Are you forgetting something?" He looks at me questionably.

"Poncho!" I hiss at him. He looks at me funny, then his eyes widen slightly, and he laughs.

"No, I haven't forgotten, but your mind went to the gutter quickly. I was only kissing you." He snickers, and my face heats.

Axton presses his forehead against mine. "Although blood never fazed me." He chuckles, rocking his hips against me. His erection presses against me, and I growl at him, shoving him off.

"Fine, but come here and let me hug your butt!" He purrs, tugging me back against him.

CHAPTER
TWENTY-FOUR

Elena

"Here's the last bag," Axton says, holding it out to me. I take it from him, placing it in the trunk while he says goodbye to the boys. Shutting the trunk I walk around to the driver's side. We spent all day going over the evidence and unfortunately, it appears Marco and Axton are right, and it is a strigoi or some form of hybrid. But its ability to come and go without being seen or caught is quite distressing. We are still no closer to figuring out who it is.

Axton quickly kisses the boys' little heads, who are munching happily on their bottles. He shuts the door and sighs.

"I wish you would stay here."

"I'll see if Marco will lift the ban. I will appeal to the council for you tonight so you can leave the city."

Axton nods once, and I go to hop in the car when he grabs the door, a devious smile on his lips. I raise an eyebrow at him, eager to get home and check on the women when I hear a car engine. Turning my head, I see the same car from yesterday.

"That's the same car I saw yesterday," I mutter and Axton looks over at it, but it pulls into his driveway and then turns around.

"As I said, they always turn around here, go you should get home before it gets dark. I glance down the driveway one last time, shaking the odd feeling that I got away, turning back to hop in the car. Axton is still standing in my way.

"What are you–" His lips cut my words off as he grabs me, pushing me against the door of the car; the bond flares to life instantly and I kiss him back despite Lexa telling me we have to get home. When he eventually pulls away, I am breathless. "It's the bond!" He shrugs with a silly smile on his face.

"Sure it is," I tell him, shaking my head. Axton steps aside and I climb into the car.

"Make sure you message me when you get home."

Nodding my head, I shut the door and start the car, Axton walks inside and I can't help the silly smile splitting onto my face. Reversing out, I pull onto the road, suddenly feeling sick at the idea of leaving him making me stop.

"We have to get home," Lexa reminds me, but the bond was screaming for me to stay.

"Elena!" Lexa growls at me. Ignoring the feeling, I start driving, yet when I am coming out of Axton's territory, the feeling gets ten times worse.

"We need to get home so we can take those damn pills; I don't like this, Elena!" Lexa scolds me and I shove her back, yet as we head toward the borders leading out of the city, I see that car again. I watch it stop at the lights two cars ahead of me and a shiver runs up my spine.

"All this strigoi stuff has got you spooked. It's a common car!" Lexa reminds me.

Crossing over to the border station, I sigh when I see it turn off down a side street. I stop at the barricades, and grab my ID, handing it to the man before he lifts the boom gate and lets me leave. Halfway home, the boys fall asleep and I turn the music playing down and turn the AC up. However, while fiddling with it, my eye catches the rearview mirror and my heart nearly stops in my chest when I see that car behind me.

"Lexa!" I hiss and she comes forward, peering out my eyes; I keep my eyes on the road and the cars in front start to brake, slowing down for the intersection after my turnoff. "It's a common car, Elena." She tells me, yet I'm sure it is the same one.

We continue driving and I can see our turnoff coming. I slow down when the strange car suddenly overtakes heading toward the town.

"See?" Lexa says and I nod, feeling foolish as I turn onto the dirt road. Once home, I finally relax as I pull up at the driveway until I spot Eli leaning against the fence post. His clothes all wrinkled and his chin is resting on his chest. I stop and roll my window down.

"Is he asleep?" Lexa asks.

"Eli!" I call out and he jumps before clutching his heart when he notices it is me.

"Geez Luna, are you trying to give me a heart attack?" he chuckles.

"Why are you still here?" I question, Axton was supposed to swap the patrols over to give them a break.

"Double shift, while we wait for Axton to find more warriors." I shake my head.

"You need sleep!"

"I'm fine, though some of the others are feeling it. Slater hasn't slept in three days running purely off adrenaline and caffeine." he shrugs then yawns.

I grit my teeth and shake my head. "I'll handle it. Go home, Eli."

"No can do until Axton gives the order," he tells me. Shaking my head, I wind the window up and continue up the driveway, parking out the front of the house. The moment I pull up, I leave the car running for AC and grab my phone from my handbag. Axton answers after only two rings.

"You're home?" he asks immediately.

"Yes, but your men are falling asleep. Order them home until you find others to take over. Eli was asleep leaning against the front gate!"

"I can't for a few more hours; I just pulled a heap from the borders that were dropping."

"Order them home. We can run patrols for a few hours, Axton. They're no good to us asleep!" I tell him and he falls quiet.

"Axton!"

"Fine, fine. I will order them to go home. The next rotation starts at 9 PM. Can you wait till then?"

"Yes, we'll be fine. Order them home." I tell him before hanging up annoyed. We were perfectly capable of doing patrols.

Climbing out of the car, I see Michelle and Noleen rush over from the barn to help get everything out of the car. Grabbing the boys, they both wake and I juggle them in my arms when the front door opens and I see my mother in her robe and slippers, her hair a mess and she looks exhausted..

She looks like she spent all night crying but rushes to help me by taking Kyan. Climbing the last few steps, I find Sondra sitting in her rocking chair, staring out at the fields.

"She needs to tell us the truth." Lexa tells me and I nod my head in agreement.

When I stop, she turns her head to look at me and sighs. "Spit it out," she says and my mother stops.

"I know about Floyd," I tell her, gauging her reaction, and she purses her lips and nods her head once, her features turning stern like she knew this was coming and was just waiting for me to figure it out.

"Sondra!" I call out to her and she stares at the women working the fields and tending to the vegetables patches. "You and I need to talk."

"You figured it out." she states and reaches for her tea.

"No but I know you're hiding something, I know what Floyd was."

Sondra watches me over the rim of her mug, takes a sip before lifting her head and turning her head back to watch the women. "Settle the boys first." she says.

"So Axton is right?" I question, and I could see my mother staring at me, confused.

"Settle the boys, then I'll tell you about Floyd." She says then takes another sip of her tea, she sets the cup back down on the small table and looks at me leaning back in her chair.

"And I'll tell you why I killed him." she turns her gaze away and I look at my mother who holds the same shock on her face that I feel.

Of all the answers I was waiting for, that was not one I was expecting. My mother gasps, and I swallow but quickly nod my head.

CHAPTER
TWENTY-FIVE

I was gone for the weekend. Yet getting home, the place was in chaos and anyone would think I had been gone for months. Women had complaints, and orders for supplies, the accountant had left messages about the bakery and Marco had dropped off the appeal my father placed against the title. He was trying to say it was done while he was intoxicated.

Which is laughable because if you know my father, he isn't much of a drinker and when he drinks, it's never enough that he actually gets drunk. The man has control issues, and that extends to not being in control of his own body.

"Do that first! Get settled, then we'll chat." Sondra says, making yet another cup of tea. She watches me for a few seconds while she waits for the kettle to boil.

"Are you going over the documents Marco dropped off last night?" She asks me and I hold them up.

"Marco said he already rejected it, but he still had to drop them off."

"You and Marco are close?" I ask her and she shrugs.

"Yes, we are. We always will be. I met Marco first." She shrugs, pouring the hot water into the mug and jiggling the tea bag.

"How?"

"So curious." She laughs.

"I thought he was human. He lived in the apartment next to me. We may have dated for a while." She shrugs.

"Wow! I bet that didn't go over well when you met Floyd." I chuckle.

"Definitely not. I had no idea he had a brother, so it was quite a shock when Floyd came looking for him. He was caught up in some legal drama and needed his help, they hadn't spoken for a few months, and Marco wanted out of that lifestyle. When he came barging into his brother's apartment and found us in bed together, I would say that was definitely an experience I could have gone without." She laughs.

I blink at her. "And Marco just let you go?" I ask her.

"He believed it was the right thing to do. I was his brother's mate."

"And that didn't upset you?" I ask her.

"Of course I was upset. I thought I was going to be a journalist and marry Marco, and run off into the sunset. Instead, I got Floyd and was locked into a marriage and a life of crime and running from his enemies."

"But they got over it?"

"Marco accepted it, but Floyd? No, he never got over it. But he needed Marco and loved him still. He just always made sure to keep Marco busy and away from me, paranoid I would run off with him."

"Why didn't you run off with him?"

"Floyd would have killed me. After a while, I started to feel the mate bond. That was the most confusing part. Humans aren't mated by the moon goddess to werewolves. Sure, they can produce kids together, but destined mates?" Sondra shakes her head.

"It was unheard of. But we got the answers we needed, eventually."

"What do you mean?"

"Floyd had Marco look into my background. Turns out I was adopted, born to a beta and human woman. Only instead of getting the werewolf genes, I came out human. I have some genes, just not the right ones to make me a werewolf. So they got rid of me." She says with a sigh.

"Do you know which pack?" She nods her head.

"Yeah. Just not a good one," she says, taking her cup and walking outside when I hear the boys cry from their rocker in the living room.

Once I have the boys settled and tucked in their beds for their nap, I quickly change into my fluffy, soft pink butterfly pants and a white cami, excited to put on my own clothes, having left my dress at Axton's. Once dressed, I head downstairs, I am about to go outside to speak with Sondra when I walk past her, rummaging in the kitchen. Stopping, I see her trying to get the rum off the shelf above her head.

"Sondra, what are you doing? You can't drink on your medication." I scold her when she uses her walking stick to swipe it closer to the edge. She looks at me, stands on her tippy toes, and snatches the bottle off the shelf.

"I need it. All this talk of the past is stealing my sass. If I am taking a walk down memory lane. I will need this!" she tells me, tucking the bottle under her arm. "Grab my smokes! Let's get this over with!" She snaps at me, and I shake my head.

"I'm already dying. What will hurt? My life?" She laughs, and I sigh and grab her smokes off the fridge. We put them up trying to cut her back, but I also needed answers. After what she told me, I could use a drink already too, and we haven't even gotten to my questions yet.

When I walk out, I find her tipping her tea out over the railing. Her hands shake terribly as she tries to pour rum into the mug. "Fuck it!" She mutters, tipping the bottle to her lips and gulping it down like it is water.

I take a seat across from her when she pulls the bottle away, nursing it in her arm. She wipes her mouth on the back of her hand, looks at me, clicks her fingers, and I sigh, handing her smokes over to her.

She lights one and inhales deeply, and sits back. "What do you want to know?" She asks, leaving the smoke between her lips as she rocks back and forth. Pausing, I think for a second, where would be the best place to start before deciding on Axton's mother?

"I want to know about Floyd's daughter...." I tell her, and she swallows. She nods her head slowly. "You want to know about Phaedra." she muses, and her eyes turn glassy.

CHAPTER
TWENTY-SIX

I wait for her to say something, but I now had Axton's mother's name. I'll give Marco one thing: he is good at covering up for people. There are hardly any articles remaining about Axton's family or his life before he moved to the city like they just vanished, and now everything is secondhand info or rumor.

It makes me wonder how much he covered up for Floyd, his foster brother. Axton barely told me anything about his mother that I didn't already know about her, and he was very reluctant to talk about her.

"Phaedra, I didn't know about her until Floyd agreed and allowed that asshole to buy her. What a shock that was to know he had a family I never knew about, especially given that he stole the opportunity from me to have kids, made me have a hysterectomy not long after we met, and said his way of life was too dangerous to raise children in.

"So I didn't expect him to have any, and it almost broke me to find out he did. Though now I see it as a blessing, especially after what became of Phaedra. That was also around the time I met Mary and Petra," Sondra says, shaking her head and taking another mouthful of her rum.

"Who bought her?"

"Axton's father. Insufferable prick he was. I hated him from the moment I met him. You could tell he was a cruel bastard, and I thought Floyd had a sinister edge, but that man had no limits, no humanity. He claimed Phaedra was his mate."

"He was a terrible man, and Floyd knew that, making what he did worse. She didn't want to go with him, but he forced her, despite her not being able to recognize him as her mate. She was only fifteen, still a child. A year later, Phaedra had Axton when she was only sixteen." Bile rises in my throat that he would just sell her to a man because he claimed her as his mate, his own daughter.

"Floyd told her she was to settle her mother's debt to Ivan, Axton's father. Apparently, she ran a debt, and he was going to kill her and cut all business dealings with Floyd until he met Phaedra. I didn't know who she was until her mother tried to stop him."

"He never told you he had a daughter. He never mentioned her once?" I question. Sondra shakes her head.

"No, turns out he had an entire life before he met me; I was Floyd's mate. Human mates are unheard of, and I wasn't familiar with your world. This was just before I found out about my real parents, so when he said I was his, I never questioned it. I just knew I couldn't seem to stay away from him, despite knowing I should, despite loving Marco still. So I was shocked to learn about her and her mother, Mary. He left her when he found me, just abandoned her," she tells me.

"Wait, Mary was her mother? As in Petra's mother?"

"Yes, Petra was Phaedra's twin sister." She tells me, and the wheels start spinning in my head. This was so much to take in, and I was struggling to work out how all this information links to my father. Or is that another story?

"My husband was not a good man. That was the day I truly, truly realized that. I knew he was into something shady, knew about the drugs, the fight clubs he ran with Ivan, but trafficking, I didn't think he was capable of that." She says sadly.

"So, how does that link to the women here? I thought Petra escaped her abusive father and took the women with her?" I ask, looking out at them setting up for dinner.

"She escaped her abusive father, but it was never her father she was running from. It was the man she, too, was sold off to, her mate. Floyd didn't care for those girls. He saw an opportunity and if they wanted their mates, they would pay the price he wanted. He didn't care that they were his daughters, he cared what he could get for them." Sondra sucks in a sharp breath before shaking her head.

"I've done a lot of things I am ashamed of. One of them was not helping them sooner." She says with a faraway expression on her face.

"Sondra?" I call out to her, and she tilts her head, looking at me.

"For years, I watched Mary grieve for the daughters she lost. All this time, she lived only a town away; I asked Marco for her information. We became friends; I bought her that cafe. I stole the money from Floyd's safe, hoping to give her something to distract her from the loss of her girls. He was so mad, beat me up pretty good for it, but after a while, he gave up trying to keep us apart, knowing I would take the beating just to sneak off to see her." She tells me.

My stomach drops hearing that. It was like karma was out to get her, punished and punished again, and I now understood why she has such a hard exterior. But no matter the cold, unfriendly attitude, she still had a heart of gold beneath it all.

"It wasn't until I heard about Phaedra's death that I asked Marco to help me get Petra back," she tells me.

"Marco helped you?" I ask in shock. Axton said Floyd and Marco were close, but I'm surprised he went against his brother considering he gave up his girlfriend for him. Sondra nods her head and smiles sadly.

"Axton said Marco raised Floyd?"

"He did, but that didn't mean he agreed with the things his

brother did. Marco was furious when he found out about the girls, yet he loved his brother. He was always trying to fix him and get him to see reason. He thought by letting me go, I would somehow fix him since I was his mate, but some people are just bad and always will be. Floyd was one of those people."

CHAPTER
TWENTY-SEVEN

"So, after I learned Phaedra had died, I had him locate Petra and the pack she was in." Sondra looks out at the women setting up the yard and cleaning up after the kids, her eyes turning glassy, and a tear slips down her cheek. She quickly wipes it and clears her throat.

"We knew if Floyd found out, he would have stopped us, so we kept it from him. These women were slaves to their mates, purely kept for their sick amusement. Unfortunately, Marco couldn't do anything. Packs were handled by the alpha, and unless one woman came forward and complained, his hands were tied. Mary and I knew they never would. They were petrified and knew they would be caught. But not Petra. Petra wanted out, and so did a few others. We used to meet Petra in the woods and plan their escape. Despite that, she said the women were too scared."

"So, how did they get out?" I ask her, and she holds up her bottle of rum and shakes it. She takes a sip and sets it back in the crook of her arm.

"I had Marco get me concentrated wolfsbane. I gave it to Petra when I visited her and told her to poison their liquor at the next pack meeting; if you could call it that, it was basically an orgy, the women shared between the pack."

"So she poisoned them?" Sondra nods her head and purses her lips.

"Yep, they thought the burn was from the liquor until they started dropping like flies. They were supposed to run and meet us on the bus. I had been waiting with Mary by the river. Yet when Petra turned up, she was covered in blood and by herself." Sondra closes her eyes and rubs her temples before continuing.

"She was wailing, and we couldn't understand her. She was frantic, so I called Marco, and he sent me home. Marco then went out there with Mary. They found the entire pack dead, the women had killed them. Mary hid them out at the commune, and that's where they stayed. When I went home that night, Floyd accused me of trying to run from him. He stopped me from seeing Mary. He had his men wait with me at the bakery. They never let me out of their sight unless I was with him."

"So you never spoke to Mary again?" I ask her, but she shakes her head.

"No, I saw Mary, but I never saw Petra again after that until Mary went missing. One of his guards would sometimes sneak me out back to meet Mary. But once I aged, and he didn't, he knew I could never outrun him. So he left me be. I was just more careful. I would see Mary first thing in the morning when I opened the bakery, and she would tell me about the girls."

"It wasn't until she went missing a few years ago that I started snooping and then Jake told me she left, but each time his story made a little less sense. Petra told me the same thing when I questioned her when I spotted her in town. I knew she would never abandon Petra. And I honestly thought Floyd was behind it. I thought he killed her and sold her shop without me knowing, but when Floyd discovered Petra was here, I knew nothing good would come of it," she says, reaching for another smoke.

She lights it and sits back. "So I started poisoning him, bit by bit, until he was too weak to stop me. He started aging quickly, then slowly dying, until I eventually couldn't make up excuses anymore. Marco kept asking questions. For a while, it worked because I knew most of Floyd's contacts, and his men. But eventually, Marco insisted on talking to him. He came out here to check on me. I thought he would kill me when he found Floyd."

"But he didn't, obviously," she chuckles.

"He said if only I did it sooner. Yet he was still my mate and I loved the bastard, but I wanted him to suffer for his crimes, so he did for years!"

"But once my crop died, I finished him and shot him while he slept. Marco helped me cover it up, and he is—" she points to the hill where a lone tombstone sits.

"Right there. Marco helped me bury him. Now you know what I feel guilty about. It was that I didn't realize what a monster my husband was, what a monster Jake was until it was too late. I believed Jake blindly, thinking that it was Floyd."

"Yeah, Jake even had me fooled, so you're not alone there," I tell her, chewing my lip.

"How does this link to my father?" I ask her, and she shakes her head. Just as my mother comes out to help the women with the cooking. Sondra looks at her, then drops her gaze to her hands.

"That's a story for another day." She says, and I look at my mother, who is carrying out some baked buns.

"Are you hungry, Sondra?" My mother asks.

"No, dear. I think I might take a nap," Sondra tells her, and my brows furrow. Whatever she knew, she didn't want to say it in front of my mother.

Sondra then gets up. She sways on her feet, and I stand to help her when she brushes me off.

"Go help the women," she tells me, and I sigh.

"Do they know?" I ask Sondra, and she stops to look at me. I nod toward the women setting up for dinner.

"No, only Petra knew who I was and what I was to her father." I nod my head, and she glances at them.

"This pack wasn't just their fresh start, Elena. It was mine, too. My way of making it up to Petra, Mary, and Phaedra. They don't need to know. It was also my way of making it up to you." She tells me. I go to ask her what she means when I hear someone coming up behind me.

CHAPTER TWENTY-EIGHT

"Know what?" Noleen asks, coming up the steps and stopping behind me.

"That you and Michelle are on patrol after dinner at the front gate," I chuckle, and she groans.

"Really? Can't I go with Lacy? Michelle never shuts up! The girl could talk the legs off a donkey!" Noleen whines and I chuckle, getting up to help with dinner.

Everyone set out on patrol after dinner while I helped my mother and a few of the women clean up. Throughout dinner, I am distracted by what Sondra told me and the bond tugging frantically, craving our Axton. Even Lexa seems to be in a depressed mood.

My brief excitement at finally being home on my territory has dimmed quickly, but it also has me worried. Sondra is still hiding something, and we still have the issue of who the strigoi is or are. We aren't even sure if it is one or a lair of them. Taking the trash to the bin, I toss the huge black bag in while my mother stacks the chairs back in the shed.

A few women stand around the bonfire, their children are roasting marshmallows while they stand around and chat. Walking back to my mother, I hear my phone ring and stop. Pulling it from my pocket, I glance at it. I see Axton's name pop up on the screen in a video call and I can't help the stupid grin that splits onto my face.

My mother glances at me, and I hold up the phone. "Take it. I will finish cleaning up." She waves me away, and I turn to head for the house.

Answering it, I walk back inside, knowing he probably wants to see the boys. "Is everything alright out there?' He asks as I climb the steps, heading for my room.

"Yep, the girls are running patrols, and the boys are asleep," I tell him.

"Did you have a chance to speak to Sondra?" He asks, and I hold a finger to my lips. He nods once, and I head to my room, slipping inside, trying not to let the door creak and wake the boys and close the door.

I quickly wander over to the boys' crib and turn the camera around so he can see them. Facing it back the other way, he is smiling. "I already miss them, and you hogging my damn bed." He laughs.

"You'll see them Friday. I will make the appeal to the council once I get off the phone with you. If it goes through, maybe you can come out here beforehand." I tell him, sitting on the end of my bed, and he nods his head.

"Or maybe you come over tomorrow?" He asks, and I roll my eyes.

"I just got home! Besides, I don't want people getting the wrong idea, thinking we are suddenly together."

"We are! You're just too stubborn to admit it. Don't make out that you don't miss me. You forget I can feel you!" He says cockily.

"It's the bond!"

"Sure it is?" He winks at me.

"You're a fool, and tomorrow I will be busy. I have to dig up some dirt on my father. He already appealed to the council to have the title changed. Marco dropped the paperwork off last night." I tell him.

"Did he handle it, or do you want me to ring Marco?"

"No, he took care of it, but it just means I now have no choice but to challenge him or find a way for him to stand down. I really don't want to have to make him submit." I sigh. Lexa also worries, old fears tainting the idea and instilling fear.

"Do it from here, then. You'll have access to the council files off my computer, and I can help."

"It's not that simple. I have looked into my father's past before. There is nothing dating from before I was born."

"I can ask Marco or you could get his help?" Axton offers.

"No, I'm pretty sure Sondra has already, so whatever was covered up, I think it was before everything went digital."

"So you already checked the basements at the council?"

"No, that is why I want to come in, see if there are any old articles. Something about him at all. I checked the council data when I was at your place." I tell him.

"That's what you were doing before you left?" He asks, and I chew my lip. That wasn't what I was originally doing; I was looking into how Axton killed his father, but found nothing.

"Yeah," I murmur.

"Why do I feel like you're lying to me?" He asks.

"I can check your search history. You know that, right?"

"Might as well tell him, Elena." Lexa sighs. Either way, he would find out.

"I was trying to find out about your father's death at first," I admit. Axton presses his lip in a line.

"I'm sorry," I tell him and he nods.

"Not like I haven't looked into your files. It's fine. So do I need to worry about being blackmailed again?" He laughs.

"Oh, I have plenty of blackmail material. I don't need the council data for that." I snicker.

"I knew some men kept little black books but didn't think you were one and on your phone, of all places." I laugh.

"That doesn't bother you?" He questions.

"No, they predate me, and I noticed you haven't slipped an entry into it since you met me," I tell him.

"Yeah, I won't lie. I did try, but Khan is a stubborn asshole. Even when you were gone, he made sure I stayed away from women." My chest pinches, but at least he admitted it and he thought I ran off with Jake, so I can't really blame him for trying.

"I don't think I would have gone through with it, anyway. Women repulse me now I've met you, so thanks for that. Though I take better care of my hands now, the calluses were getting ridiculous." He snickers.

CHAPTER TWENTY-NINE

"If you're getting calluses, maybe you are doing it wrong. Pretty sure, you're supposed to stroke it, not rub the skin off it." I chuckle.

"Well, since you're such an expert, perhaps you should give me a demonstration. I might learn a few things." My face heats at his words while his eyes flicker, turning black.

"That's not what I meant."

"Are you sure? You're the one giving me a lesson on it. Do you offer tutoring? I could use a few hands-on lessons. My cock would be most appreciative of having an experienced teacher for Mrs. Palmer and her five daughters. Maybe you could offer oral tutoring?"

Lexa snickers in my head while my cheeks warm. "I don't mind paying, could do a clean swap, your hand for my fingers, tongue for your lips?" He laughs.

"I am about to hang up now!"

"Fine, fine, I will stop, but the offer still stands." I shake my head at him and go to hang up on him.

"Don't hang up! I will behave... promise. As much as I love

hearing about you wanting to get your hands on me, you need to tell me what you're doing about your father," he chuckles.

"I need to find evidence of his dealings with Thomas, for one. I know they used to work together. When I reported Thomas, he deleted files he told me were business dealings he had with Thomas, but he didn't want to get dragged into the mess."

"What was in the files?"

"I don't know, but I know they are linked to the garbage removal service my father used to own. I never questioned him about it, but now I'm wondering if I should have. Dad sold the business a year later."

"To Thomas?" Axton asks.

"No one of the smaller packs. I can't remember which one, but I know my dad freaked out when I started looking into Thomas. But after Marco dropped that paperwork off, I don't think I will have time to dig it up." I tell him.

"So when are you going to challenge him then? Have you told your mother?"

"Not yet; I will soon." I chew my bottom lip. Just the thought of challenging him makes me nervous because I know what a lethal beast he can be.

"You'll be fine. I'll be there, and if I think he is getting the upper hand, I will jump in.... Or you could let me do it."

"But then it will be your pack!" I remind him. Axton shrugs.

"Ours, I have no intention of taking it from you, but I also don't like the idea of him hurting you," Axton tells me.

"We are mates, Elena. I want you as my mate, by my side, not on opposite sides. What are you scared of? Just me taking your pack. I have told you I won't." I shake my head. There is more to it than that he just refuses to understand.

"It's the same argument repeatedly with you. I get that you have your reasons, but it doesn't change the fact that I am your mate! You have to give in, eventually."

"I won't lose my mother's pack, not once I finally get it back. We just need to wait for Luke—"

"I am not waiting for Luke to turn 18 for you to mark me, Lena!"

"Then what do you suggest? I don't trust you not to take my pack!"

"How can I build your trust when you trust me with nothing? I can't earn it back when you never give me a damn chance to!" I sigh, knowing it is going to turn into an argument. Axton curses and shakes his head before he presses his lips into a thin line.

"I don't know how else to fix this!"

"You can't. We'll just deal with it as it comes, but for now we—"

"I've already offered to sign the pack over to you. I don't know what else I can offer."

"I want nothing from you, Axton."

"And I just want you, not your damn pack!" He snaps before he exhales and mutters something I don't hear.

"I don't want to argue. Just think about it." He sighs, moving around, and I see him walking through the house.

"So what did Sondra say?" He asks, and I chew my lip, wondering if he knows his mother had a twin sister.

"Elena?" He asks, walking into some room when he sits down.

"I don't want to upset you," I admit. Axton sighs, and I notice he is in bed when he leans against the headboard.

"So she told you about your father and how she knows mine?"

"Not about my father, but she mentioned your mother," I tell him, and his face changes on the screen, and all I see are his tattooed shoulders and face showing he sat up.

"My mother? What did she say?"

"That your mother was sold to your father to settle a debt, and that your father claimed she was his mate?" Axton sighs.

"Yeah, my mother never spoke of her father. I knew her father sold her to mine when she was a teenager, and they are mates; he was just a shitty one. She didn't realize until she was of age that what he claimed was true." He shrugs.

"Did you know she was a twin?" Axton's brows furrow.

"She was an only child. Her mother died giving birth to her. Well, that's what my father told me." I shake my head, relaying everything. Axton seems shocked and confused. He lets me speak, barely adding anything until I'm done when he asks the one question I hoped he wouldn't.

"I still don't understand how Sondra knows all this. I know she knows Marco, but she is human. And why didn't Marco ever say anything to me?" He growls.

"Probably because he was protecting his brother," I told him reluctantly.

"Floyd?" I nod my head, pausing.

"So it is the same person. Floyd was her father."

"You were right. Floyd was her father and Sondra's husband, your grandfather. She admitted he was a werewolf. It's why Sondra helped us, because she couldn't save Petra, Mary, or your mother, Phaedra."

Axton grits his teeth.

CHAPTER
THIRTY

"I thought he was her father, but the rest I didn't know; I only met him once when I was really young and caught glimpses of him a few other times. But my mother was always careful, and we were never home when my father dealt with him, or she kept me away from him the few times he came to the house. She never openly admitted he was her father. But I overheard Marco refers to my mother as his niece once and reference Floyd. Mom got all weird, so I never asked. I can't believe they're the same person. Although it makes sense why my mother hated Floyd."

"But she said nothing else?" Axton asks, and I shake my head when I feel Noleen open up the mind link, only it cuts out a second later. I try to open it again. "Elena!" She says quickly, only for it to cut out.

"Everything ok?" Axton asks.

"Hang on. One of my Pack members tried to open the link."

"Tried?"

"Yeah, she cut out. Wait, a second. I'll find out what she wants." I stand up, glancing toward the window, when pain suddenly ripples through my chest, dropping me to my knees.

"Elena?" Axton worries when I drop the phone. My chest burns when the pain worsens, stealing my breath before it vanishes completely. Gasping for air, I reach for the window ledge, pulling myself up, but I instantly know what the feeling is. I just lost a pack member, Noleen. I instantly try to reach Michelle. The link is there, but it won't open.

Opening the window, I stick my head out and sniff the air, noticing the scent of his pack in the air. "Mom?" I call out to her as she peers out at the fields when she drops the box of deserts at her feet. The cupcakes roll across the grass, and her eyes go to Luke, who is at the trash cans, throwing the last couple of bags away.

"Luke, get inside!" She screams, running over to him. She grabs him, shoving him toward the house, and I see the other women turn to look at her when they all drop what they're doing and start rushing the kids toward their homes.

"Elena!" Axton panics as I peer out into the darkness, trying to catch my breath. I grip the windowsill and lean out. Only when I do, do I see eyes glowing back at me in the distance.

"Axton?" I panic and my eyes go to the crib where our boys are sleeping. My heart palpitates in my chest.

"Elena? What's going on?" I stumble for an answer because I'm not completely sure. But why is he here? And how did he find us? Turning my gaze away, I look to the driveway; I can just make out a car racing toward us with its headlights off.

The women downstairs look out into the fields, and the others try to hide the children, screaming, tossing themselves in front of the kids, and backing up toward my mother when she looks up at me. Wolves step out from between the barn and the mobile homes, and I gasp, realizing we are under attack.

Snatching the phone off the ground, I rush out of my room when Sondra comes out of hers.

"Elena?" she calls, and I grab her arms. "Lock yourself in the room with my boys. I will send Luke to you. Go!"

"Elena, what's going on?" Axton demands at the same time Sondra does.

"My father's pack is here," I tell him, and Sondra gasps rushing into her room. "Go, I'll get the boys!" She yells as I race for the stairs, still breathless from Noleen's tether breaking.

I run for the stairs, skipping a few in my haste when pain ripples through the pack link, and I stagger on the stairs clutching the banister. "Lacy," I curse, feeling her tether snap as I open the pack link, telling the women on patrol at the back end we are under attack and to head home.

"I'm on my way!" Axton says, but I can't answer him when my head is filled with my pack's voices.

Dropping the phone, I feel Lexa lurch forward, waiting for me to finish with the pack-link, when I hear my mother scream. My feet thud on the stairs as I race down them, hearing all the women screaming and the sounds of fighting. My mother is screaming for Luke, and he is for her when I burst out the door to find the car is the same one that followed me, and my father is trying to rip Luke into the backseat.

My mother grabs my father's arm when he grabs her hair, also trying to drag her to the backseat while my mother pleads for him to let Luke go.

It is utter chaos. Within seconds, my father's pack has us entirely surrounded, and the women are backed into a corner, trying to shield their kids.

"Let them go!" I snarl at my father, and I feel Lexa press forward, my claws lengthening, and my father looks up. He sneers at me, and I walk down the steps, tossing the phone onto a chair nearby. I can hear Axton demanding to know what is going on, but I can't speak to him and deal with the problem at hand.

"You dare sabotage my name, think you can kidnap my son and mate! Then have the audacity to claim my pack!" My father roars as his pack warriors close in around me.

"My pack, now let him go!"

"She moves; kill her!" My father orders his pack. I glance at my father's warriors, who seem unsure as they glance between us.

"Derrick, please, I will come back. Just leave Luke here. You're scaring him." My mother pleads while gripping his forearm.

He looks at her, and he cups her cheek with his hand. My mother leans into his touch, but I know better; I know she is playing along, for Luke's sake. Luke peers out at me, tears rolling down his face, which is blotchy when my father's hand on my mother's face turns from affection to cruelty as he grips her hair and her ear, jerking her closer.

"You rejected me, love. Now you'll learn what betrayal earns you." He sneers, and my mother's features harden like a rock as her canines slip out.

"You were always a fucking coward!" She snarls before shifting and attacking him.

CHAPTER
THIRTY-ONE

Gasps break out from my father's pack surrounding me, and I move to help her, only for them to close in, pressing closer.

"Elena, please." Ben, one of my father's warriors, pleads with me to not interfere.

"Stand down!" I snarl at them. But they just move closer, yet cast nervous glances at my mother and father when I hear her whimper. Casting my eyes back to them, my father has her white wolf by the scruff of her neck, holding her head to the ground.

My mother thrashes, yet she is weaker, no match for him. Luke is frantically kicking the door when I hear the glass shatter, and he tries to climb out the window.

"Submit!" my father screams at her, and I shake my head at Luke, telling him not to interfere.

"Derrick?" My father's gamma looks at him, unsure. "You're hurting your Luna." The man stammers, taking a step toward her. My father snarls in return when my mother twists her head, her eyes locking with mine.

"You know what she did! Know your place, or I'll banish you!" He growls, his aura smashing his gamma, forcing him to bare his neck and submit to him.

"Axton?" my mother asks through the mind link, and my stomach drops. My tiny pack is no match for my father's, and I'm no match to take them on, even being an alpha. We are vastly outnumbered, and with so many children present, it could quickly become a tragedy.

"He'll get here," I reply, glancing around at the women and opening the link.

"We need these children gone!" Lexa tells me.

"The moment I move, get the children out of here. They'll come for me. Get them out."

"But he's ordered them to--" the woman argues.

"I know — get them clear. Axton will come! We just need to hold him off." I tell them. Glancing around, I see a few of the women nod their heads, sizing up the wolves surrounding them, yet their eyes are on me like my father ordered. However, their eyes go to my brother when he suddenly screams.

"Let her go!" Luke screams, jumping from the car and thumping his back with his fist when my father backhands him. His little body goes flying toward the car, causing a dent in the door as he hits the ground, and my father's pack gasps in horror at what he did.

My breathing becomes shorter, witnessing his tiny body be flung away like trash. Luke crawls to his hands and knees, blood dripping from his head where he hit it on the side mirror. My father's gamma tries to go to him but is still on his knees; Ben whimpers, and the others try to fight against my father's command to go to him, but it proves futile.

However, that split second of distraction is my opening, and Lexa takes it as she shifts and lunges at him. Lexa tackles him, slamming him into the side of the car and tearing into him. He's forced to let go of my mother, and chaos ensues as the women run their kids to safety.

Claws rake down my back, and teeth rip into my side as my

father punches Lexa in the ribs, trying to get her off, while she tears into his shoulder on the opposite side.

Luke's scream is blood-curdling, and so are my packs when my father's command to kill me if I move has taken over his pack, and they start ripping us apart.

Lexa's teeth tear into his shoulder, and she refuses to let go despite his men ripping into her when my pack members jump into the fray, trying to pull them off her as she mauls him.

Lexa is flung backward by two wolves, and we are tossed back and off my father. His arm is barely attached to his body, and his wolf is quick to heal him when he rises to his feet. Blood drips off his fingers, and he staggers briefly when we watch him heal.

Lexa shakes her head, then rips into the wolf on top of her. Standing up, she shakes out her fur, spraying blood everywhere, when I see teeth coming straight at us, followed by a loud boom.

The wolf falls on its side just before it tears into us, and Lexa turns her head to see Sondra is the one to shoot it. She points the gun at my father.

My father's pack backs up, shielding him from her as she walks down the steps, yet my father barges through them toward her.

"Sondra?" He growls, and she cocks the gun, aiming it at his face.

"Get off my property!" She sneers. He raises his hands and smirks.

"I thought when I saw Noleen, it was a coincidence; I should have known you were fucking behind it! Though I'm surprised you are still alive!" My father snaps at her.

"Call your pack off. And submit to your daughter, now!" She glares at him, poking him in the chest with the barrel. My mother staggers to her feet, looking confused.

"You know each other?" My mother blurts. Her skin is drenched in blood, but besides being slightly banged up, she is alright. Luke tugs on her hand as she steps closer, while my pack and his look on in confusion.

"Call them off!" Sondra screams at him, and he smiles, backing up.

"Stand down! No one touches Elena." He orders his pack, yet his eyes remain on Sondra, whose hands are visibly shaking when one woman steps forward.

"You!" she snarls, and I see it is one of the older women in my pack, she is around Noleen's age. She points an accusing finger at him. "I recognize you..." she says, her finger shaking as she looks at me when I see Michelle and a few others finally reach us from their patrol areas. Relief hits me seeing Michelle; she must have swapped places with Lacey because she should have been at the front gate with Noleen.

"As you should. Derrick's responsible for trafficking a few of you here! It's why his father banished him from his pack when the women started going missing!" Sondra snarls, and whispers break out between my pack and his.

"It was you, wasn't it? You were the one who tipped him off! Just like you helped Bane shut down the fight clubs!"

"Of course, it was me, and you knew it, but you feared Floyd too much to even bother trying to do anything about it," she screams at him.

"And where is your bastard husband?" he snarls, looking at the house.

CHAPTER
THIRTY-TWO

"Dead, I killed him!" she snarls at him.

"You shoot me. How will you explain that to the authorities, especially with all these witnesses?" My father laughs.

"I'm the only reason you're even alive! He would have killed you had I told him you were still speaking to Mary and were involved with hiding Petra!" He sneers at her.

"Go on, tell them... tell these women who you truly are! Let's see who the bigger monster is!" He snarls at her before glancing at me.

"Elena knows who I am. She knows who Floyd was!" My father scoffs and looks at me.

The women all look at Sondra, clearly wanting answers. My mind is trying to fathom what I have just learned about my father. And my mother looks at him like he is a complete stranger to her.

"Derrick?" my mother gasps.

"Shut up! Stay out of this. Just get in the fucking car before I drag you into it!" he yells at her.

"She's not going anywhere!" Sondra says, drawing his attention back to her.

"Yes, she is, or my pack will wipe out everyone here." My father warns her.

"Elena's pack! She owns the titles!" My mother snaps at him, and my father growls, going to turn to her when Sondra jams the barrel of the gun under his chin. My father laughs and swats the gun away, then grabs her throat. Lexa snarls, and I force her to shift back.

"Dad!" I growl in warning.

"Of all the people you had to get involved with, it had to be her. Don't look at me so appalled, Elena. She isn't so fucking innocent, either! How do you think that sex tape got leaked? Marco leaked it! She owns the two stations it broadcasted on! Did she tell you that?" My father snarls as he tosses her aside. I look at Sondra, who lands on the ground. Her gun is tossed a few feet away, and she sits up.

"I didn't know what was on them. Marco only said it would get you off the council and make you look bad! I wasn't out to destroy her, but you!"

"And you got your fucking wish! But then you had to take it a step further and brainwash my daughter and my fucking mate!" He snarls at her.

He then turns to my mother and points at the car when his pack suddenly steps in his way, blocking him from her. My father scoffs, and I see Sondra get up out of the corner of my eye. I stare at her in shock; I knew she had shares in the stations, but I didn't think she owned them.

"Stand down!" He orders his pack, and his aura erupts, forcing them to their knees.

"I'll deal with you all when we get back! You dare go against your Alpha."

"Is what he said true?" My mother asks Sondra, and I look at her.

"Had I known what was on that tape, I wouldn't have aired it. I thought it was something to do with his dealings with Alpha Thomas," she says.

"I swear, Elena, when Axton rang Marco wanting access to the station, he said it would take down Derrick. I didn't know it involved you. Marco said Axton could be trusted. I didn't think someone would do that to their mate, or I would never have agreed." Sondra pleads to me.

"Get in the car, Louise!" My father snarls when she shrieks. Turning my head, I see he has her by his arm.

"Let her go, dad." I snap at him, moving toward Luke, who instantly runs to me.

"You would still go against me knowing what you know. Sondra betrayed you!" he bellows.

"Because of you! Not intentionally! Now let her go," he growls, ignoring me when she fights. He snarls at her and flings her aside.

"Fine, stay! But Luke is coming with me!" He growls at her as she hits the ground. I growl when he turns to face me. "Luke, now!" Luke hides behind me.

"1....2," my father counts, and Luke peers up at me.

"Go inside, Luke," I tell him. My father laughs and stalks toward me, and my mother rushes to help Sondra off the ground.

"He's my son!"

"But she's my Alpha!" Luke growls behind me, and I shove him back behind me.

My father glances at me and raises an eyebrow at me.

"Do I need to remind you who the real Alpha is, Luke?"

"Last chance, dad," I tell him. Feeling Lexa merge with me. My father scoffs, his eyes flickering as his aura ripples menacingly.

"I taught you, made you what you are, and you think you can just take my place! You were my student." He laughs, looking at his pack like he thinks it's funny that I would even think of challenging him for his title. Yet his pack looks at him disgusted after what they've learned about their Alpha.

"And now I teach you." I retort, and his laughing stops. He turns back to me and glares.

"You can try, sweetie, but you're no Alpha. I'm giving you a chance to come back to the pack. I'll even let you bring yours." He looks at the women behind me.

"But this ends now. We have actual issues back at home that need dealing with," he motions for Luke.

"Go inside, Luke!" I order, and he rushes off with my mother.

"You're making a mistake." My father growls, his claws slip out, fur grows along his arms, and he cracks his neck.

Lexa urges for control, and I let her have it. My claws slip from my fingertips, and my canines elongate as she takes control of my body. My skin ripples with her urge to shift.

"No, you did the moment you stepped into my territory! And now you learn the consequences of that!" I snarl, handing the reins to Lexa, and she immediately shifts, and so does he. His black and brown wolf charges at us, and Lexa doesn't hesitate as she runs full pelt at him when they clash in a violent display of claws and teeth.

CHAPTER
THIRTY-THREE

Axton

My heart thumps erratically when I hang up the phone, the bond screaming at me to get to her and our sons. The panic in her voice sends fear slivering through my veins, turning it ice-cold. A fear I've never known so strong sweeps through me, and I run for my bedroom door. My fear for them has adrenaline shooting through me, and I don't even bother to dress; my sole focus is on getting to them.

As I took the stairs two at a time, I nearly smashed my way through the front door, grabbing my keys from the hook next to it as I went. Stepping outside, the night breeze is warm, but I can smell the brewing storm that is fast approaching the city.

I race to my car, jumping in and reversing out; as I do, I hit the garbage bin, knocking it over and sending trash everywhere. "Shit!" I curse, spinning the car around and hitting the accelerator. My car bottoms out on the end of the driveway, and the tires screech as I race to get to them.

I try to ring the border patrol to ask them to have the gates open. Osiris's men should have just changed over from mine, yet I get no answer, so I try again. Not getting any answer from them, I toss the phone onto the passenger seat.

As I reach the borders of the city, I notice blue and red lights flashing ahead and slow down, wondering what is going on. When I approach, I find it blocked off by police cars, Alpha Osiris' pack members, and Alpha Thomas. Alpha Osiris stands in the middle of the road with his arms folded across his chest, with a smug smile on his lips like he is expecting me.

My car's tires screech as I slam on the brakes to stop from plowing into the side of the vehicles blocking the exit and Alpha Osiris. Cursing, I open my pack link. "Get to the fucking borders now!" I yell at my men.

"What's going on?" Eli mumbles, half asleep but becoming alert to my order. Chatter fills the link as my men wait for an explanation.

"Osiris' men aren't letting me out of the city! Elena is in trouble." I tell him.

"On our way!" I get from my men.

"I knew his men were acting weird when they swapped patrols as we returned to the city! I saw our men arguing over the scheduled times." Eli tells me.

"Just get here now!" I snap at them, cutting the link.

Switching the engine off, I toss the door open and climb out of the car, snarling. Thunder rumbles loudly, and lightning cracks and whips across the sky, briefly filling it with light, followed by another deafening boom that hurts my ears.

"What the fuck is going on? Move your cars now!" I yell at them, and Alpha Osiris casually strides over, a smirk on his lips. His eyes flashed at my command.

"A little birdy told me you were about to breach your court ordered council restrictions?" Alpha Osiris asks with a smile on his face.

"We were just making sure you were following your probation. What kind of friend would I be if I allowed you to breach probation?" He taunts, "I'm just looking out for you, Alpha." I turn my attention to Alpha Thomas, who is leaning against one barricade they have built.

My eyes are drawn to him when he pulls his phone out, messaging someone. He then quickly pockets it, and I grit my teeth, turning my attention back to Osiris.

"My mate's pack is under attack, Osiris. I will rip through your fucking men if you don't move. Your choice!"

"An attack? No, it's just a family reunion. Alpha Derrick was so excited to hear his Luna and son were coming back home. He is even considering letting Elena and the boys return home. Isn't this great news?" Osiris laughs.

My eyes flicker to Khan's as he presses forward hearing that. My stomach drops just at the mention of my sons and not knowing what is going on. Yet I can feel Elena is okay, furious, but okay for now. But I know this is a setup by Derrick.

Where Derrick is involved, his intentions are anything but family-orientated; the bastard has been trying to get his pack back any way he can, and now that's not working, he will try to force her hand by wiping out her pack. And Elena's pack is far too small to stand against that many without backup.

The fact they have this place blocked off and council members here to witness this was organized for some time.

Shaking my head, I turn back to my car, determined to drive straight through the barricades, even if it means running over him and his men. Only when I do I notice two of the supernatural council members surrounded by armed men standing near my car.

"You're making a mistake!" I tell them, seeing around ten council officers standing behind them. They lift and point their guns at me. And I snarl in response, pulling my phone from my pocket.

"You're not the only one with friends in high places, Axton. Not even Marco will get you out of this one when you have two council members here to witness your breach!" Osiris says behind me. I message Marco, demanding to know what is going on, and a second later, my phone rings in my hand.

"Where are you?" I demand when I answer the call placing the phone to my ear. Khan presses against my skin nervously, his patience running thin the longer we are stuck standing here.

"In the city, at the council, I've just heard; I am working on it! Someone sent through a message saying there would be an altercation. They have the city tech hacking your cameras for the street live feed. I'm headed there now."

CHAPTER THIRTY-FOUR

"So they're watching?" I ask.

"Nope, my hacker just locked them out. Do what you need to do while I work out who Osiris' puppet is."

"Well, you want to work on the two council court officials standing in front of me? They're refusing to let me leave! Elena needs me. Get them to stand down."

"I'm working on it. Elena sent in the appeal earlier tonight, but someone else rejected it before I could get my hands on it. It appears to have come from higher up; I am looking into it."

"Who?"

"That's what I'm trying to find out. Someone is pulling on strings within the council. I've been temporarily locked out of the database. Once I know who, I will sort it out. Until then, I am working with what I got to cover your damn ass," Marco tells me, and I grit my teeth, glaring at Osiris over my shoulder.

"And if I breach?"

"They'll shoot you, but we both know that's not enough to stop Khan. Let them; get to your mate, and I will handle the consequences." Marco tells me. I turn my gaze to the officers' dart guns and growl.

"Are your men on their way to help? Order your pack to get to her if you can't get through." Marco says, and I can hear him running through security checks at the council, the buzzers going off, and him yelling orders at the guards to let him through as he identifies himself with his council ID numbers.

"They can try to stop me, but they won't stop Khan," I tell him.

"Are you really foolish enough to risk the fines, the immobilization of your pack over a family gathering?" Osiris asks.

"I will handle the damage control and find out who's in Osiris's pocket! I can get you off on compassionate grounds. This is a family matter! Do what you gotta do!" Marco tells me, hanging up.

"You and I both know Derrick has not gone to her pack for a fucking friendly chat, Osiris. Call them off, or you can deal with the consequences," I snarl at him.

"And what consequences would that be?" he asks, sauntering over, and Khan presses forward. "Me!" Khan snarls at him, and Osiris stops.

"Are you challenging me, Alpha?" Osiris laughs.

"No, because you aren't a fucking challenge. That would imply you actually have the ability to stand against me!" I tell him.

"You think you can take me on?" He looks over his shoulder at his men, and I smirk when I see them back up quickly as my warriors come from all directions, their wolves filling the street.

I glance back at the two council members behind me who are playing witness for Osiris.

"Are you sure you don't have somewhere else to be?" I ask them, and they glance at each other nervously.

"Marco can't wait to find out who sent you here!" I tell them.

"Osiris said there will be a breach. We are merely observers!" one of them tells me. I cock my head to the side.

"No, you are in my way, stopping me from getting to my mate and sons!" I snarl at them. They glance at each other.

"We are observers," he repeats.

"Then observe this!" I snarl, handing the reins to Khan, who instantly shifts and turns back to Osiris. He growls, his suit tearing as he shifts, the fabric falling to the ground in tatters.

Khan snaps his jaws and charges at him at the same time my men charge at him, and the street quickly becomes a bloodbath as Khan tears through his men. The streets are coated in blood; Alpha Thomas flees the moment the fight breaks out, and so do his men, leaving Osiris to deal with the backlash like the coward he is.

Khan is covered in wolfsbane darts, and he turns his head, grabbing the one in his rump with his teeth, ripping it out as the poison burns through his system, making him stagger. He's been pelted with darts, but adrenaline has him still standing for now. Just as the last of Osiris's officers are taken out by Eli. The gun smacked the ground.

Osiris, realizing his pack stands no chance, growls. Seven of his men are now dead. One of mine has been lost; blood covers the roads and spills down the drains. Khan is drenched in blood, fur, and chunks of flesh torn off him, and Osiris is barely standing when I feel Elena's pain ripple through us.

Khan tenses and growls furiously. Stalking toward the Alpha, who shakes out his fur, spraying blood everywhere, Osiris' wolf snaps its jaws and whimpers as its jaw clicks, and one ear is torn up badly. Yet his wolf is weakening, and he is no match against Khan. Osiris shifts back, his form crouched on the ground before Khan. He growls, eyes narrowing as he bares his teeth at us.

He glances at his fallen men before he grits his teeth. "Stand down!" he orders his men.

Khan shifts back, and I start pulling darts from my flesh. "Little advice Osiris. Thomas always runs at the first sign of trouble." I laugh, and he gets to his feet; the moment he does, a dart flies past my shoulder, the feather grazing it.

Osiris grunts, and I look over my shoulder to see Eli with one of the court enforcers' guns in his hands. The dart hits Osiris in the center of the chest, and he gasps, ripping it out, but not before the blue liquid in the vial is expelled. He growls and staggers. Eli picks up another gun and pulls the dart from it, tossing it to me. I catch it and wander over to Osiris, who is as pale as a ghost.

He sways, and I grab him. "You need to build a tolerance, Osiris, as I have. Next time, do your research. Had you done this, you would know better than to come after me with pathetic wolfsbane darts. Wolfsbane has little effect on me. Maybe next time you'll remember that before picking a fight, you can't win!" I snarl, jamming the dart into his side.

CHAPTER THIRTY-FIVE

Osiris grunts and falls against me heavily, and I look over his shoulder at his men, who stand around warily, waiting to see if I will kill their Alpha.

"Get your Alpha to the hospital!" I order them, and two rush over. I hand their Alpha over to them, feeling Khan's anxiousness to get to our mate.

Looking over my shoulder, Eli is already taking over and nods to me, so I give control back to Khan. Too impatient to wait for the cars to move, he takes off, jumping over the barricades, tearing out of the city, and heading to our mate.

Elena's burning anger pushed us faster, and what should have taken us half an hour, we managed in twenty minutes. The ranch came into view, when we stopped at the front gates smelling blood.

We find Noleen first. Her throat is ripped out, and she is covered in cuts and grazes, blood drenching her hands, and I could tell she put up a fight. Her vacant eyes peered up at the night sky, her skin pale and cold.

Khan growls, sniffing the air and picking up another scent. He races up the driveway before spotting a younger she-wolf. This one lies in the middle of the road, and tire tracks are etched into her skin like she was run over first, and a knife is embedded in the side of her neck. Her skin is covered in blood, and her blond hair is drenched, obscuring most of her face.

Khan sniffs her and shakes his head, growling when he turns his attention to the ranch; I can smell Derrick's pack and see them circling around the packhouse. Fighting reaches our ears, and Elena is in a bad way but still fighting when Khan groans, pain slivering up his hind leg from her, and he takes off up the driveway, flicking up gravel as he pushes faster.

As we approach the front of the packhouse, I notice Louise trying to hold back Luke on the porch, who is thrashing, trying to escape his mother's grip; Sondra's head is bleeding as she sits on the step. Elena's pack is visibly shaken. Khan growls, and Derrick's pack and Elena's pack turn to look at him, and they quickly part, allowing him through.

Derrick's wolf is tearing into Lexa, her white fur covered in blood, but he is in worse condition than her, some part of his skin hanging off his side in a giant flap, and she wastes no time ripping on it every chance she gets.

Derrick's malted brown and black wolf bites into the side of her face. Lexa yelps, shaking her head to get him to let go, and Khan snarls and moves closer, about to jump in.

Lexa freezes. She turns, growling back at him and stalking toward Khan, a clear warning to back off. Yet the moment she turns her back, Derrick's wolf pounces on her back and starts ripping into the back of her neck. Lexa rears back on two legs and twists, her skin pulling from his mouth and spraying us in her blood when she attacks him with new vigor.

"She's worried we'll take over and strip her title," Khan tells me. Yet that fear has adrenaline shooting through her, and Derrick is barely holding on. Lexa is a savage, and Elena is clearly an alpha's daughter, her wolf lethal like any other alpha I've met. You can tell she trained all her life for the position. Lexa is savage but slightly smaller, she is quick and lithe on her feet. She maneuvers effortlessly and seems to know Derrick's next move before he takes it.

Her eyes zone in on the flap of skin hanging off his wolf's side that goes from his shoulder down his ribs, exposed muscle and tendons on display, blood pouring from the wound as his wolf tries to heal it but isn't quick enough before she gets a hold of it again.

Derrick's wolf whimpers as Lexa mauls him, his legs go making him fall on his side, but before he can get up, Lexa has his neck between her jaws, her front paws digging into the gaping wound, making his wolf whimper.

He thrashes beneath her, trying to get out from under her. Still, she digs her claws in harder, ripping on his neck and shaking her head viciously, his legs kicking and claws tearing apart her stomach, but she growls, ripping harder. Khan watches her blood spill onto the ground, coating the grass anxiously, not liking how much she is bleeding; she's losing too much blood.

"Wait, Khan, she's almost got him," I warn him, knowing if we stepped in before she backed off, she wouldn't forgive us. Khan snarls when she whimpers, but she doesn't let go but moves to get a better grip on his wolf. He nearly bucks out from under her, but Lexa expecting it is quick to retake the advantage, sinking teeth and claws into him when he whimpers loudly.

"She has three seconds, Axton. She's gonna drop if he doesn't submit!" Khan warns me, and he's right. Lexa is growing tired now. Her blood loss becoming too much. However, she is too stubborn to let him win, just as he is too stubborn to submit to her.

Derrick's pack, I notice, is cheering for Elena, urging her not to give in along with her own pack. So I know something major has gone down because his pack has always been loyal, he's done something to anger them. Turning our gaze back to Lexa, Derrick's wolf yelps, going slack and panting while Lexa holds his neck when

Derrick shifts beneath her. She loosens her grip, allowing the wounds to heal when Derrick taps the ground.

"Enough, you win!" he growls, giving in, and Lexa lets go of him, swaying on her feet when Derricks growls. Clamping his hands over the gaping wound, pushing the flap of skin back in place before baring his neck to her.

CHAPTER
THIRTY-SIX

L exa waits a few seconds to ensure he is indeed submitting to her before she shifts back. The moment she does, I fight the urge to race over and cover Elena's nudity, but the blood coating her does most of that when she gets to her feet. She is littered with injuries, her skin more black and blue than its usual sun-kissed tan skin.

The moment she rises to her feet, Derrick's pack drops to their knees. Her eyes scan over them, and they bare their necks to her. Michelle moves toward her as Khan shifts back, giving me control, and Michelle backs off when I grab her, helping her stay upright. She flinches when my arm wraps around her waist.

"Restrain him," she orders her new pack. Her breath wheezes, and her chest rises and falls heavily.

"Yes, Alpha!" they speak in unison, moving to do as she asked.

"Marco's on his way!" Sondra sings out from the porch, holding up a phone and shaking it. Elena turns, glancing over her shoulder, and Luke escapes his mother, rushing over and slamming against her. She grunts as his arms wrap around her.

"I'm fine," she tells him. However, she is anything but fine, her wounds taking forever to close, and I'm taking most of her weight.

"Get the door for me, Luke," I order him.

"Don't you dare!" Elena snaps at me, and I press my lips in a line. She doesn't want her pack to see how badly she is struggling to remain standing. My grip tightens on her, but I help her climb the stairs.

Cars in the distance, growing closer, have her look over my shoulder. "It's my pack," I tell her, and she nods.

"I don't have cells here to hold him," she mumbles to me.

"I'll have Eli take care of him; I'll make sure they grab Noleen and the other woman," I assure her, and she nods, stepping inside the door Luke is holding open when I hear our sons cry out.

"I'll watch the boys." Michelle races ahead of us and up the stairs to retrieve them. Approaching the stairs, Elena sucks in a breath, and I grit my teeth at her stubbornness. I scoop her legs out from under her, picking her up, and she growls, but I growl back at her.

"It's not a show of weakness. I'm your damn mate, and no one expects you to remain standing after winning a challenge." I snarl at her.

Her eyes dart over my shoulder to the front door, where I can hear my men's cars pulling up.

Opening the mind link, I tug Eli's. "We found two at the gates." Eli immediately tells me. "Slater is picking up the bodies," he assures me.

"Lock Derrick up back in the cells at the police station until Marco can arrive and take him in for questioning."

"Yeah, I'm already on it," Eli tells me, and I cut the link to find Elena watching me.

"Everything is being taken care of." I peck her lips before climbing the stairs, and she finally relaxes against me.

I take her to her bedroom, and Michelle fusses over the boys. Stepping past her, I move to the attached ensuite bathroom and kick the door shut before setting her on the edge of the bathtub.

"You're injured," she murmurs, her fingers grazing my ribs as I reach over and turn the taps on. I drop the plug into the hole and grip her hand.

"I'm fine. I'm healing; you're not!" I tell her. Standing, I move toward the sink, rummaging under it and finding some antibacterial soap. I pop the cap and sniff it, pulling a face at the stench. I quickly pour some into the tub; it will burn, but she doesn't stop me.

Moving toward the shower, I turn it on before turning back to her. Blood is caked on her skin, drying and congealing.

"Let me rinse you off before you get in," I tell her, grabbing her and helping her into the shower. I grab the shower head off the hook, and she hisses as I rinse the blood off, prodding some of her wounds to see how deep they are.

"Sorry," I mutter when she grabs my shoulder as I examine the one on the inside of her thigh. I grit my teeth, knowing if she let me, I could try to heal her with my blood or saliva when Khan reminds me we have wolfsbane still lingering in our system. It may not affect us, but it might affect her.

Standing up, her hand shakes as the adrenaline that runs through her abates. Now leaving her with the pain of it wearing off.

Helping her out of the shower, she moves toward the tub that is filling, and she sits on the edge.

"Everything hurts," she groans, gripping the side of the tub. I check the water before shutting the taps off and climbing into the tub. Sitting down, I open my legs and then sneak my arm around her waist, pulling her in with me to sit between my legs.

She hisses, the soap stinging her, and she grabs my thighs briefly before letting go and leaning against me.

"You could have taken over my pack if you stepped in," she mutters.

"We wanted to step in. You are hurt, but I knew you would be angry. Besides, I could tell you had him." I shrug, grabbing the loofah off the side and wetting it. Gripping her jaw, I turn her face up to mine.

"I've told you already, Elena, I want my mate, not your pack," I whisper, brushing my lips against hers softly.

"I just want my family back," I tell her, and she relaxes against me, exhaling. I kiss her temple before running the loofah over her.

CHAPTER THIRTY-SEVEN

Elena

Every muscle aches as Axton helps me get dressed in my pajamas. Since Axton has no clothes here, I have given him a pair of my fluffy purple fleece unicorn pajama pants. He looks ridiculous, yet somehow manages to still look sexy. Or maybe it's his muscular body and abs that I want to trace with my tongue that allows me to look past the fact he is wearing unicorns.

"It's the body; those pants look ridiculous." Lexa purrs, pressing forward as she watches him dry his hair with the towel. He hangs it up on the towel rack and then turns back to face me. He arches a brow at me and my very obvious gawking.

"Are you done perving; I would appreciate it if you didn't give me a damn hard-on, considering one of your pack members is on the other side of this door." Axton laughs.

"I'm not doing anything!" I retort.

"Can still feel you, Elena, and your arousal kinda gives it away?" He says, tapping his nose, and my face flames. He laughs, grabbing my hands and pulling me to my feet.

My entire body hurts as I climb into bed; Axton sits down next to me, watching Michelle trying to wrap a thrashing Bane. He isn't having it, wanting to remain free to kick and squirm; he did not want to be wrapped up like a baby burrito.

"I'll take him," Axton tells Michelle, and she glances over her shoulder at him and nods. Axton holds his arms out for Bane, moving closer to the edge.

Michelle's eyes dart to the purple unicorn pajamas I've lent him when she brings Bane over.

"Love the pajama bottoms; they suit you." She laughs.

"They are surprisingly comfy!" Axton chuckles while I try to find a comfortable position to lie in.

"Your mother came up. She sent most of your father's pack home, but a few remain wanting to help," Michelle tells me, I sigh. Everything that could go wrong tonight has. The night turned into a disaster, yet somehow we turned it in our favor, which is great but has created more work for us.

Eli has taken my father back to the city and will lock him in the city cells until Marco can send some enforcers to collect him. Although Sondra will have to face up for her crimes in the past, she doesn't seem worried, apparently. No doubt trusting Marco to take care of it.

Michelle hands Bane over to Axton, who quickly cradles our son. Only for Bane to stretch, turning stiff like a plank in his arms.

"He just had his bottle, and I've changed him," Michelle tells him, passing him his binky.

"Thank you," Axton tells her, sitting on the edge of the bed.

"Anytime, Lupha," she says, and he looks at her, but her gaze is on me.

"The girls were asking if we can organize new patrol rosters with your newly acquired pack?" Michelle asks, and I can see how bloodshot her eyes are from crying. Michelle and Noleen have always been close, I knew Michelle was hurting and looking for anything to distract herself.

"My men are patrolling, and I will help Elena set up a new roster tomorrow. Get some sleep Michelle; everyone will be safe now. My men aren't going anywhere." Axton assures her, and her eyes dart to him. She chews her lip nervously and nods once.

"Thanks, Lupha," she says before leaving.

Axton lays down with Bane lying on his chest. "I never realized she had a speech impediment," Axton shakes his head, rubbing Bane's back. I try not to laugh. If only he knew it is the nickname Michelle has come up for him and a title he doesn't realize was given to him now by my pack.

"Where did they take Noleen and Lacy?"

"Slater has taken them to the city morgue until you work out funeral arrangements," Axton tells me, and I sigh, rolling on my side. Axton moves on his side, setting Bane between us. He is wide awake, babbling and cooing, trying to talk.

"I really wish you would come back to the city with me; I know the city isn't safe either, but I had hell trying to get here tonight. I believe Osiris helped orchestrate this entire thing with your father. He was at the borders with council members and a heap of officials waiting for me to breach."

"Just let me talk to the women first and Sondra," I tell him. His brows raise, and I glance down at Bane, who is trying to eat his father's knuckles.

"You'll consider coming back to the city?"

"Well, I don't really have much choice. Eventually I will have to now that I have gained my father's pack. It will be too hard to run two packs in two locations."

"Yet you don't want to move back to the city." Axton sighs.

"No, it's not that. I just don't want to move back to my father's pack. Back to the packhouse." I tell him. Moving back there would be moving backward, not forwards, or that is what it feels like to me. I've just regained my freedom from him, only to end back up where it all started again. Axton sits up on one elbow.

"Da, Da..bl," Bane blows raspberries, spraying spit across my face. I chuckle, nuzzling his cheek and blowing a raspberry on it, making him cackle before putting his binky in his mouth, hoping he goes back to sleep and doesn't wake his brother.

Axton watches me for a few seconds. "Then open your borders to my side. Both packs share the border, open the borders and come move in with me at the packhouse," Axton says, and my eyes move to his.

"Then I can help with the boys and your pack." He offers, shrugging, and Bane spits his binky out and grabs Axton's hand, preferring to gnaw on his knuckles than his binky.

"But what about the women?"

"Move them into my pack's apartment building. The bottom three levels are vacant; they're used to my pack, anyway. At least you can monitor them until they get used to your father's old pack. They can stay there as long as they want until they adjust."

CHAPTER
THIRTY-EIGHT

I sigh when my thoughts go to Sondra. "And Sondra can stay with your mother in the penthouse. Sorry, but the old bat will cut me in my sleep." Axton says before I can even ask the question.

I chuckle. "I think you're growing on her." I chuckle.

He holds his fingers up, pinching them close together. "Maybe this much, but not enough for me to sleep without one eye open." He laughs.

"I'll have the packhouse to myself soon, anyway. Eli is moving in with Slater. Apparently, I'm insufferable to live with."

"And speaking like that is not helping you convince me it is a good idea." I laugh.

"Will you at least think about it? I want you and the boys close." Lexa presses forward. Yet after seeing Axton back down to her and not try to take over, she doesn't seem as reluctant.

"Maybe we should. We'll go into heat soon, anyway. At least until we figure out what to do next?" She tells me. Not only that, it would stop all this struggle with the bond.

"Da, Da..Dadda.." Bane says, making me blink down at his

squirming little body between us, thinking I misheard when Axton looks down at him too.

"Did he speak?" Axton questions, looking at me. My brow furrows, and I shrug, unsure if I misheard when Lexa speaks.

"No, that little crotch goblin best not have said dada first! Free-loading pint-sized traitor!" Lexa huffs angrily in my head.

"Say it again." Axton coos, squishing his cheeks, giving him fishy lips, and making him cackle.

"Come on, you can say it." Axton urges as we both wait expectantly.

Bane babbles and coos but doesn't repeat the mysterious word. Lexa purrs. "That right, my boy is not a traitor!" She huffs when Bane speaks.

"Dadda, Dadda!" He babbles, pulling on Axton's hand, trying to gnaw on his knuckles again. Axton sits up straighter, and I frown, feeling betrayed.

"He said Dadda!" Axton exclaims excitedly, picking him up and hugging him. Bane giggles as his father's stubble tickles his neck and face.

"He is confused and got our names mixed up!" I tell him while trying not to pout and sound bitter. It doesn't work because Axton raises an eyebrow at me.

"No, he definitely said Dadda, not Momma!" he tells me triumphantly. I shake my head, refusing to believe it and sticking with my hearing needs checked! When Bane repeats it, a little clearer, making sure there is no debate on whether he indeed said it.

"See!" Axton says, smugly holding him up like Bane is a trophy he just won. "Definitely, Dadda!" I glare at him, and he tucks Bane closer.

"Don't look at me like that. It's not my fault I'm his favorite!" Axton teases, and I scoff.

"I have been trying for weeks to get them to say mom, and you waltz on in, and he spits that garbage out first!" I growl at him.

Axton gives me a look like I just insulted him. "Garbage?" He growls at me.

"Yes, garbage." I huff.

"Someone is jealous and throwing a tantrum!" Axton tells Bane with a laugh before looking back at me.

"Why are you getting so upset? He'll say mom, soon enough, you'll see." He shrugs, and I growl at him.

"Of course I'm upset; I carried and birthed them, only for them to come out looking like you! And now my little womb renter spits out dadda first." I tell him, and Axton chuckles.

He looks down at Bane. "You better spit out, Momma, real soon, you've just put Dadda back in the doghouse, and I had barely got out of it!" He tells Bane, who just blows spit bubbles back at him. Axton lies back down and rubs his belly.

"So, about moving to the city?" He questions.

"I'll speak to the women and try to convince them."

"You could just order them." Axton retorts, and I shake my head, not wanting to force anyone's hand. I am about to tell him as much when a knock sounds on the door. Axton looks over his shoulder when the door pushes open, and Marco steps inside my room. Axton sits up, and his shoulders drop.

"You're making me go back to the city." Marco smiles sadly.

"I haven't had approval for restrictions to be lifted, although your breach is being removed on compassionate grounds until Elena can appeal to the council again. I've spoken to my superior, and he said no action will be taken, but until officially it is lifted, you need to return back to the city, so Osiris doesn't file a complaint."

"And Derrick?"

"Being transferred to the council as we speak. But unfortunately, I do need to return back to the city." Axton looks at me and sighs.

"How long will it take before the restrictions are lifted?"

"If Elena does it first thing in the morning, I can have it done by tomorrow afternoon." Axton nods his head, turning to look down at me.

"I'll do it first thing in the morning when I wake up," I assure him.

He kisses Bane's little head, and Marco walks out, shutting the door behind him.

"Argh, I don't want to go," he growls, frustrated.

"I don't want you to either, but it will be sorted tomorrow," I tell him, tucking the blanket back around Bane. Looking up, Axton smiles, leaning down and kissing me.

His tongue traces the seam of my lips and mine part, allowing him to deepen it. His tongue brushes mine, and his hand grips the back of my neck, tugging me closer as he tangles his fingers in my hair.

I kiss him, the bond thrumming at his closeness and reveling in his touch, only for him to pull away. He presses his lips to my forehead, and he sighs.

"I will see you tomorrow?" I nod, and he gets up, moving to the crib where Kyan is sleeping.

"Want him with you or leave him in his crib?"

"No, bring him over. Hopefully, Bane will go back to sleep." I tell him, and Axton leans in, retrieving him. He brings him over, laying him next to his brother. Bane instantly rolls into him, trying to eat his face before stealing Kyan's binky. Axton chuckles, taking Bane's and popping it in Kyan's mouth before he wakes over his stolen pacifier.

CHAPTER THIRTY-NINE

Axton

As I leave the packhouse, I immediately notice Eli. He is waiting on the front porch, his hands hidden in his pockets. As soon as he hears me step out of the building, his eyes snap to me, and an odd look crosses his face.

"Woo-woo, Alpha," he pulls his hands out of his pockets, raises them, and takes a step back. There's a mischievous glint in his eyes, which I'm sure is proof of what's coming out of his mouth next. "I love purple. It really makes your eyes pop. And those cheekbones, man, you sure you're not a model?" Eli snickers, staring at Elena's unicorn pajamas I'm wearing. Yeah, I should've seen this coming.

I sigh and pinch the bridge of my nose. My jaw is so tight that if I don't relax soon, I'll sport the worst headache known in history.

I don't want to leave. My entire being is screaming at me to turn around and go back inside the packhouse. All I really want to do is close that massive door behind me and hide away, if only for a bit longer with Elena and the boys. But alas, Marco is already covering for me, and I don't think he would appreciate me demanding more of him when his job is hard enough.

Eli nudges my side, so I look up at him. I expect another snide remark or a shit-eating grin, but I meet a serious facial expression. "They'll be fine. I will be here, and Marco is coming back. Derrick is in the cells. No one is getting near them," he assures me.

A loud breath leaves my lips as I glance at Marco. At that very moment, he nods toward his car. "I'll be heading back here once I drop you off," he assures me, and I press my lips in a line, looking back at the door.

The storm outside is already raging, but I'm sure it's not nearly close to the full power of destruction it holds above our heads. My eyes scan the area, and soon, I notice that most of my men are stationed under the porches of the woman's houses. They're standing just inside the open barn doors, out of the rain.

The rain is pouring so violently that it looks like the skies have opened up to release a monsoon. My mind is overtaken by nothing and everything at the same time until I'm snapped back to reality by Marco, who hits the button on his key fob, making the lights blink on his maroon Mustang.

"Ready?" Marco asks me, and I give him a stern nod.

We both duck out into the rain to run to the car. However, the speed and attempts to avoid the rain don't help much in our case. In weather like this, no one could be fast enough to get untouched from one location to the other.

Both of us are drenched the moment we step out from under the porch roof.

Reluctantly, I follow Marco back to his car and hop in. Marco instantly reaches over into the backseat and retrieves a tank top. He tosses it at me, then removes his jacket and throws it onto the back seat.

"Put that on so I can at least try to take you seriously with those damn pants on," Marco grumbles.

I laugh at his statement and put on the navy blue tank while Marco starts the car.

As Marco drives down the long driveway toward the highway,

my stomach twists, and my heart sinks at the thought of leaving Elena and the boys behind. The wind howls outside the car, and the rain pelts the window as Marco tries to navigate the windy road back to the city, although visibility is a bitch.

"Are you cold?" Marco asks me, reaching for the air conditioning button. I raise an eyebrow at him. "Sorry, forgot you're not human." He chuckles, leaving it off.

We still feel the cold, just not nearly as much as a human would. However, Marco has no sense of what is hot or cold. He can't tell the difference between temperatures, as everything feels neutral to vampires.

Although, this very fact makes me wonder who he has had in this car before me. Who was important enough to sit in this seat and, most importantly, to make Marco question if they were cold?

"So, which human have you been driving around with?" I ask, pointing to the AC.

Marco shrugs as if he sees no importance in the question or the answer. "Just Sondra." He shrugs.

I raise an eyebrow at him, remembering what Elena told me about Sondra and Marco being together before Floyd found her.

"I took her to her appointments last Friday after Elena left to go to your place. Sondra didn't want to ask her, knowing she would stress about leaving the boys, and now Floyd is gone. I no longer have to keep my distance, so I spent most of last weekend there."

"You stayed at the packhouse with Sondra?" I ask, a little shocked.

"Yes," he says, staring out the window, and my brows pinch.

I've never known Marco just to hang out with anyone. He is a serious workaholic and never takes a day off. Yet, he takes it upon himself to take a weekend off for Sondra. That explains why he could get to the city so quickly after the last attack.

"You're still in love with her," I tell him, and he glances at me.

"She was mine before she was Floyd's. I never needed the mate bond to love her, and I never stopped loving her. I was going to tell her what I was and ask her to marry me." He shrugs, "But then Floyd ruined that, and I knew nothing would impede the mate bond. Sometimes I think I should have killed him back before.." he trails off, not finishing the rest of what he wants to say.

CHAPTER FORTY

I know he blames himself for not preventing what happened to my mother and Petra. It also sucks because he would soon lose Sondra again.

She is an old woman, and despite that, he still loves her even though he could pass as her grandson. It is quite heartbreaking to think about loving someone, then losing them to your brother, only to get them back and having to prepare to lose them all over again.

I push those thoughts aside, knowing Marco does not want my pity. It makes me realize what I could have lost from my own actions.

"So, is there any news on who is working with Osiris?" I ask him, and he exhales loudly.

Marco glances at me, then returns his eyes to the road, looking grateful for the conversation moving away from his dying love life. He slows down as we approach the intersection leading onto the highway. Marco turns the blinker on and stops, waiting for the traffic to pass before he shakes his head.

"No clue, but I will find out. However, if the council questions you, I allow you to leave the city on compassionate grounds after learning your family was attacked by another pack. And the fight at the border between you and Osiris was because he was trying to stop you when you had permission to leave," he tells me, and I nod my head, then return my gaze to the window in contemplation.

There is hardly anything visible from the car up ahead, only the brake lights of the cars as they slow and try to follow the lines on the road. We are halfway to the city when Marco's Bluetooth rings loudly through the speakers, and a name comes across the screen in the dash: Officer Flint.

"Great. What does he want?" Marco growls, glaring at the name as if he's ready to rip out someone's throat.

"Not friends?" I laugh.

He curses under his breath. "Nah, I can't stand his whiny ass. He's a brown noser and can barely follow instructions." Marco tells me.

Taking the call, Marco mutters something under his breath and presses a button on the steering wheel to answer it.

As soon as Marco hits the brakes once again, he hisses. "What is it?" His voice is low and irritated while the cars in front of him jam on theirs. He curses, shaking his head at the traffic and blasting the horn. "Stupid humans and their crappy eyesight!" He snarls in a hushed voice.

All I can do is snicker at his irritation and behavior. Even I, with way better senses than any human, can barely see anything ahead of us. That fact alone says a lot about how bad the rain from the storm is.

"Flint, are you there?" Marco snaps at the Officer, but all we get in response is silence.

For a minute or so, all we can hear coming from the speaker is static, and some voice crackles, but we can't understand what he is saying. No matter how enhanced one's senses are, nobody would be able to take apart what the Officer is trying to say. It sounds like he is talking underwater in a foreign language.

After another agonizing minute of nothing but hearing the sounds of static, the phone cuts out. Marco grows visibly more annoyed and curses when the phone rings through the Bluetooth again.

"Can you hear me now?" Officer Flint asks in a muffled voice. He's still hard to hear, his voice barely audible, but at least we can understand him this time.

"Yes, what's up?" Marco asks, tossing his arms in the air when the traffic comes to a complete stop. It looks like there are more than a few cars in front of us, but weather be damned, I can't tell how many, it looks like a considerable line. I'm startled by another growl from Marco and the vicious blaring of the horn as he holds it on. "This is ridiculous!" He grits out through clenched teeth.

"Darn storm... are you there?" Officer Flint asks, and I sigh.

"Yes, I can hear you. What is wrong?" Marco snaps louder. It looks like no matter what the Officer says or does, even if it's not in his control, Marco grows more furious and forces his frustration on the unsuspecting fool.

"Ah, I can hear you now," The Officer says finally, and I roll my eyes. At this point, I get Marco's frustration because I'm growing just as annoyed as he clearly is.

"We have lost contact with the transport officers that picked up Alpha Derrick." Officer Flint says quickly in one breath.

My head instantly whips to the side to look at Marco.

"Probably the storm," Marco replies, and he has a point. Reception is shit out here, and the storm only worsens it.

"No, the last communication was an hour ago. We checked the car's tracker, and they parked it in a town nearby. It hasn't moved for an hour either. I sent officers out to check if they've broken down, but we can't reach them on the radio or on their phones." The Officer stresses. He isn't as quiet as he was moments ago. In fact, I have a slight feeling this guy might have a panic attack.

"How far out are–" Marco stops mid-sentence when a phone rings in the background.

"Hang on, that is them," Officer Flint says. We hold our breaths as we listen to the Officer talk quickly on the other phone. A moment later, he yells, probably because they, too, are having issues with reception. We hear something get slammed down while we wait.

"One second, Marco, while I try them on the other phone." Officer Flint mutters, and we listen to some shuffling around.

Silence follows for a few minutes, and traffic moves again.

"Fucking finally," Marco states, and I glance at him.

"You're in a terrible mood this evening." I laugh.

"Yeah, Sondra didn't get good news last Friday." He shrugs before we hear cursing and Officer Flint yelling at his co-workers.

My blood runs cold when the Officer finally picks up the phone again and speaks up again.

"They're dead, and Derrick is gone. They found the car on its roof just on the town border in a ditch," Officer Flint states.

CHAPTER
FORTY-ONE

Marco grips the steering wheel tightly and growls. "Find him. Put every available resource we have into looking for him!" Marco snaps.

"Yes, Sir. I'm already on it. We'll find him." Officer Flint tries to reassure us, but one thing about Derrick is that he is resourceful. He isn't someone easy to find or capture, especially if the dickhead is on a mission. And so it appears that he's on one right now, and I know anything he is up to will only cause a headache for Elena and me.

"Marco, that is not all, though. The officers have their throats ripped out, and their bodies appear to be drained of blood." My brows furrow, and I look at Marco.

"They are drained of blood?" Marco questions.

"Yes, Sir. It appears we now know who the strigoi is." Officer Flint states, but that makes absolutely no sense because if he were the strigoi, Elena would not have stood a chance against him during the challenge. Marco seems to think the same thing because he asks the very question I am thinking.

"Who knew Derrick was being moved?" The question leaves his

lips in a tone so calm that it sounds ice-cold. I have a feeling he's boiling inside, ready to jump out of the car and go after Derrick himself, but something's clearly holding him back. No doubt his need to do his job and return me to the city before he can go hunting for Derrick.

Officer Flint remains silent for a moment and hums. "Only those in the office and a few trusted border patrols from Alpha Axton's pack."

"No one else?" Marco questions.

Officer Flint falls quiet for a second, and we hear the shuffling of paperwork and movement. "Get me the log book, Trent!" Officer Flint snaps at another officer.

"Forget it. Just have that logbook ready, and I want the surveillance camera footage. I am about to cross the border. We'll meet you at the station." Marco says, hanging up the phone before Officer Flint can reply.

We stop at the barricades. Osiris' men are still on patrol with a few of mine and Alpha Thomas' warriors. Marco rolls down his window when one of Osiris' men taps on it, wanting his ID.

"Are you fucking blind? Can't you see the Council Emblem!" Marco snaps, and the man jumps and backs away from the car.

Marco curses and winds the window up. The boom gates lift, letting us pass, and I smirk at the man's frightened face, only to realize why he freaked out. The fear isn't there because of who Marco is but because his fangs are protruding past his lips, and he looks furious. In fact, right now, Marco looks like he's about to hunt someone down and rip their throats out just because he can.

"Are you alright?" I ask him, and he looks at me.

"Yeah, just sick of everyone being so damn slow. I want to get back to Sondra, but it looks like that won't be happening tonight! Why?"

I point to my mouth. His tongue darts out, running across his fangs, and he groans.

"Fuck! I haven't fed in a few days, which explains my short

temper. Sondra even clipped me about it before we left," he chuckles and shakes his head.

"Should you maybe sort that before we head to the station? They might think you're a strigoi." I tell him, and Marco laughs.

"Well, unless you're offering a vein, it can wait. They can think what they want," he states, uncaring. But I know seeing him like this will freak a few people out, given what has been happening recently. We don't need people putting unnecessary attention in the wrong direction.

"Head to the hospital," I tell him, and he shakes his head.

"I'm not drinking cold blood," I growl at him before looking around his car and finding a styrofoam coffee cup.

As I peel the lid off the cup, Marco shakes his head, looking all sorts of exasperated. I ignore the stubborn vampire as I allow my canines to extend and then bring my hand to my lips to bite the side of it. I fist my hand to allow my blood to drain into the cup. As soon as the cup is finally full, I let my hand heal and place the lid back on it. If not for the fact that it's filled with my blood, someone might mistake it for a fresh cup of coffee. Well, except for the smell.

As I hand the cup to Marco, he raises an eyebrow at me, but eventually accepts it and takes a sip. "What? It's fresh blood. Now drink it before you eat, Officer Flint," I warn him, and Marco laughs at me. He brings the cup to his nose and sniffs it. He can't be fucking serious.

"You aren't seriously being picky right now, are you?"

"God knows where you've been. Just making sure." He chuckles and takes another sip of my blood.

Not long after, Marco's pupils dilate, and he drinks more from the cup. He licks his lips and winks at me. "Fuck, I forgot how much better you guys taste compared to humans!" He groans.

I frown at him. "Hey, calm down, Romeo. Don't be getting any fucking ideas. I am not becoming your personal juice box." I tell him.

Marco just smirks. "Yeah, I haven't got time for a blood addiction, but thanks," he says, holding up the cup. I nod and return my gaze back to the road.

Soon, we pull up at the station, and Marco parks the car in the underground parking lot. Climbing out of the car, I groan, realizing I am still wearing Elena's pants. Shaking my head, I follow Marco inside, and he walks through the place like he owns it. He might as well since no one is stopping him, even when he sets the buzzers off.

"Where's Flint?" He asks the officer that is perched at his desk on the phone.

The officer raises his eyes and freezes for a second. Then regains his senses and enough common sense to slowly point a finger to the back.

CHAPTER
FORTY-TWO

Marco looks over to the interrogation room, shakes his head, and then walks over toward it.

"What part of having the log books ready didn't you fucking understand?" Marco shouts as soon as he steps inside the room.

Officer Flint attempts to stammer for an answer, but since none comes, he rushes out of the room. "Trent! The logbook!" Officer Flint snaps in the distance. I peer out the door to watch the man on the phone at his desk lift his head.

The man furrows his brows and blows out a heavy breath. "On your desk!" He retorts, sounding just as annoyed as the Officer looks.

"I just came out of there!" Officer Flint snaps.

"It's on your desk!" The man shakes his head, returning to his phone call.

"Why are you even here?" Marco says, shoving past Officer Flint and walking toward his office door.

I follow on his heels as Marco stops in front of a door and tries to open it. However, it's locked, so Officer Flint rushes over with his keys jingling in his hands. He fumbles with the stack of keys, and Marco snarls, grabbing the handle and ripping it off.

The door opens, and Marco hands the broken door handle to Officer Flint, who looks at it in disbelief. His mouth is open, gaping like a fish. A little more, and we'll see that jaw hit the darn floor.

"Useless mutts!" Marco snaps, walking in and looking down at the desk covered in crap, cups, food wrappers, and documents. Marco snarls and starts rummaging through it before finding the black folder.

He is about to open it on the desk, but then he glares at the Officer beside him. "How do you work in this filth?" Marco snaps at him.

The Officer leaves my side, clearly set on cleaning up the mess Marco so openly disapproves of. However, he doesn't get to reach the desk when Marco growls at him and uses his hand to swipe all the crap onto the floor with his arm and hand.

The Officer shrieks in surprise and jumps back. Marco ignores him and then sits behind the desk. His eyes focus on the folder as he slowly opens it. I move to the seat across from him and sit down.

Officer Flint stands there awkwardly as Marco's eyes scan the pages, flicking through them before he opens up the laptop. "Log in!" Marco snaps at him again.

My eyes follow every movement in the office as the Officer quickly does as he is told to and logs into his laptop. As soon as he does, Marco slaps his hands away. He turns the laptop, so I can see as well when he scans files on the surveillance system and opens them.

"What are you looking for?" I ask him, leaning forward a little to ensure I overlook nothing.

"Osiris was here a few minutes after Alpha Derrick was brought in. I want to see where he went." Marco slides the folder over to me, and I glance at the page to see Osiris' name scrawled on the line next to his signature when Khan presses forward. I stare at the signature and the handwriting, something nagging at me when Khan picks it up.

"That's not Osiris' handwriting," Khan says, voicing my suspicions.

I remain silent as I stare at the writing. My gaze focuses on the signature on the page, and I frown. It's vastly different. Perhaps someone who hasn't seen his signature wouldn't notice the difference, but I see it clearly.

Once I am certain and Khan also confirms my thoughts, I turn the folder around on the desk to show my discovery to Marco. His eyes set on me, so I point to the signature and name. Marco looks at it and then gives me a questioning look. "That's not Osiris' handwriting," I tell him, and Marco's eyes snap back to me again.

"Are you sure?" He asks.

I nod my head, then grab my phone and unlock it. Quickly, I scan through the files to pull up the one Osiris signed and filled out last week at the council meeting. I double-tap on the screen to enlarge it and show it to Marco. His eyes focus on the screen when he finally notices what I'm showing, and his brows pinch together.

"No, it's definitely Osiris. I remember him coming in not long after you hung up on me. I saw him myself and watched him sign in," Officer Flint says, crossing his arms in front of his chest as if it's me he has to prove something to.

Marco looks at the Officer and tilts his head as he asks, "What time was that?"

"About ten minutes after they brought in Alpha Derrick." Officer Flint shrugs.

Marco focuses back on the timestamp on the logbook. "He walks into the bathrooms but never comes out. Instead, I see another officer does," Marco mutters, dragging the words as if he already knows something.

"That is Officer Tuck," Flint points out.

We focus back on the screen and wait for Osiris to come out of the bathroom, but he doesn't. At this point, it looks like he has drowned in the sink or fallen in the fucking toilet. However, about twenty minutes later, we see more activity.

Officer Tuck returns to the bathroom, and soon after, Osiris emerges, straightening out his suit.

We watch how he logs out, writes and signs the logbook, and talks to Officer Flint for a few minutes. Both of them laugh about something, and soon after, Osiris leaves.

"Must have been taking a dump?" Officer Flint says, shrugging his shoulders.

Is he serious? Is this man really trying to come up with an excuse for all that we just witnessed? Both Marco and I look at him as if he has lost his goddamn mind.

"Get out!" Marco snarls at the unsuspecting man.

Officer Flint looks at him in pure shock. "What?" he stammers.

CHAPTER FORTY-THREE

"You fucking idiot, that is not Osiris! Or Officer Tuck! That is the fucking strigoi, and you let him slip right past you!" Marco shouts right as his fist collides with the desk.

The Officer looks at the screen. His face pales, and his eyes widen as he shakes his head in what even he knows is denial. "No, that is Osiris! I saw him with my own two eyes." Flint says, and I almost facepalm myself.

Marco turns in his chair to look at the Officer. "Are you really that stupid? Do you honestly think Osiris came all the way to the police station to take a shit just to leave right afterward? Have you not remembered anything about strigoi? We only just went over this last week after the last attack! Or are you truly that much of an imbecile?" Marco snarls at him. If he were human, I'm sure his face would burn bright red in the display of rage.

Marco rewinds the footage, only this time, we follow Officer Tuck, who goes down and speaks to Alpha Derrick about being transferred to the council chambers in the city. He then talks to the two officers guarding him and finds out the route and time the council enforcers are arriving. There would be no need for anyone working here to need to know the route or the time they were leaving.

"How is that possible?" Flint asks, staring at the screen in shock.

"Because strigoi can shapeshift, you fucking idiot! You couldn't even recognize the change in your own damn Alpha! How did you even get this job if you can't tell the difference by his aura alone, moron?" The tension in the office rises, and Marco's clearly at the end of his rope. I can't blame him, and I don't think I would attempt to save the fool if Marco decided to eat him.

"How was I supposed to know? I have never met a damn strigoi before!" Flint argues.

"You just did; in fact, you had a good ole fucking laugh with one! You know your damn Alpha. You should have realized by his mannerisms, even his damn signature!" Marco points at the writing in the logbook.

Flint shakes his head and tries to come up with an excuse, but it is clear that it isn't Alpha Osiris; they don't even walk the same, but it leaves the question of who else it could be. We scan the rest of the surveillance footage, but he just disappears once outside the doors.

"You couldn't tell by his scent?" Marco demands. I've been told up close that they have a very cloying scent of decaying flesh. This makes sense since, to become strigoi, a vampire has to feed off the dead. It is why feeding off the dead is illegal for vampires. They feed off the dead too much, it sends them crazed, rabid. It's also how they inherit these extra abilities.

A vampire feeding off the dead eventually kills them, and they come back as something more sinister. Back when I was younger, my grandfather told me stories of when vampires and werewolves were at war with each other, that some vampires purposefully became strigoi to gain an extra advantage, which ended up being a later problem in and of itself.

Those additional abilities make it so much harder to identify a strigoi and kill them. They are faster than a typical vampire and stronger. They can even compel/glamor other vampires and even werewolves. Marco only has the ability to compel me while I am in human form, but it's said that strigoi can compel the wolf's side too, which makes them harder to kill.

Unfortunately, population numbers grew out of control, and the human governments had to work with the supernatural council to eradicate them; it's also when the alliance started with humans and the supernatural.

"No, he was wearing a heap of aftershave, and it smelled cheap, too. Which I thought was a little odd, but he looked exactly like Osiris. How the heck was I to know?" his brows pinch, and he mutters something too soft for me to hear.

"Although, he was in an excellent mood, which is odd, especially after everything that happened earlier at the borders between you two," Flint says, pinching his lip between his thumb and forefinger.

Marco growls in frustration. "Get out!" Marco snaps.

Officer Flint jumps, glances at me, then he rushes from the room, shutting the door behind him.

"Fools, the lot of them!" Marco snarls. He rubs his temples and sighs.

"So what now?" I ask him, and Marco leans back in his chair. He tosses his arms up in the air.

"I have no clue. We are still no closer to figuring out who it is; for all we know, it may be the idiot we were just talking to!" Marco exhales.

"Nah, he smells alive," I tell him with a laugh.

"Well, with any luck, he killed Alpha Derrick; that would be one less headache to deal with!" Marco states, and I chew my lip, trying to think.

"What are you thinking?" Marco asks, and I look at him to find him watching me.

"Nothing much, trying to figure out why they would go after Derrick."

"No idea. Maybe Derrick is in on it." Marco clicks his tongue before leaning forward and typing on the laptop.

"What if it was to frame him? Throw us off their scent. Maybe we are closer than we think, and Derrick would be the perfect scapegoat?" I tell him, and Marco seems to think for a second.

"But why? It makes no sense," I shrug. We don't have enough information to come to that conclusion yet.

"Go back to Elena, knowing that strigoi is out there, and so is Derrick. I rather you out there than here. An emergency alpha meeting will take place in the morning, and I'll send out the message. For now, I'll deal with this; you go back to Sondra and watch over my mate and my sons." I tell him, getting up from my seat.

"Are you sure?" Marco asks, and I shrug. It's not like we could do much. Everyone is already out looking for Derrick, and now we are just sitting here guessing who it could be.

"I'll drop you home and then leave. Call me if you need me." Marco says, pulling his keys from his pocket.

CHAPTER
FORTY-FOUR

Elena

The boys fell asleep quickly once Axton left. However, I barely slept at all. All night, I was tossing and turning. The storm outside was horrendous, and every sound had me jumping, thinking we were under attack again.

It wasn't until early morning, when the light fills the room, ruining my stare off with the ceiling, that I roll. Only to nearly roll off the bed, my hands grab the corner of the mattress, and I cling to the edge of the bed, having forgotten I moved to the edge. So the boys don't wriggle their way to the edge and fall off.

Trying to pull myself up, I lose my grip. A shriek leaves my lips, my hands flail, catching air, and I am again staring at the ceiling. Only this time, I'm on the hardwood floor. I groan, sitting up, and Lexa groggily comes forward.

"Some of us need sleep, you know!" Lexa scolds while I rub the elbow that I landed on. The next second, I hear running footsteps, and my bedroom door bursts open. Marco stumbles into the room, looking disheveled and half asleep, in just his black boxer shorts and a white tank top. He exhales loudly, clutching the door.

"Jesus, Elena!" he sighs, walking over and offering me his hand. I take it, letting him pull me to my feet.

"When did you get back?" I ask him, remembering he left with Axton last night; I hadn't heard him return.

"A few hours ago," he scratches the back of his neck awkwardly, then yawns.

"Are you good?" He asks, and I glance at the boys, who are still fast asleep despite the loud thud I made when I hit the floor. I nod my head and lean over the bed. My body is still aching from challenging my father last night, but at least the pain is tolerable now and more of a dull ache.

"I'm going to go shower and get ready to head into the city. Are you going anywhere this morning?" Marco asks me, and I glance at him over my shoulder as I scoop up the twins from the bed. I quickly shake my head, cradling the boys who stretch in my arms before snuggling against each other and going back to sleep.

"Good; I need to talk to you when I get out. Put the kettle on," he tells me, turning for the door.

"Talk to me about what?" I ask him.

"Your father."

"My father? What did he do now?" I ask as I set the boys in their crib so I can make coffee.

"He escaped. We'll talk about it when I get out of the shower, but for now, coffee, and you need to send in the appeal to have Axton's restrictions lifted so I can approve it."

"Wait, have you told my mother yet?" I ask him while quickly shutting the door and following him down the hall.

"No, everyone was asleep when I got back." Marco shrugs, and I sigh. Great, this is the last thing we needed, but at least he has no pack to back him now. Marco disappears into Sondra's room, and I stare at him.

"Did he just go into Sondra's room?" Lexa asks, just as perplexed as me.

"Ew, gross, she is like a hundred years old." Lexa shudders, and I roll my eyes at my wolf.

"You don't think they... you know?--"

"Damn it, Lexa, why would you say that? That is not an image I want in my head!" I snap at her. I shake my head, shoving Lexa away with her vile thoughts about Marco and Sondra. It was far too early for that imagery to be in my head; she could have at least waited until after my morning coffee before putting those thoughts in my head!

Walking down the steps, I make my way into the kitchen. Sondra is sitting at the dining table in her floral gown and her fluffy slippers, her hair in rollers still while sipping her tea.

"Morning," I murmur, and she holds up her tea.

"Morning dear, did you get any rest?" She asks, and I shake my head.

"Barely any," I tell her while filling up the kettle. I flick it on, wondering what the commotion outside is that has everyone looking at the far paddock behind the massive garages and the house. I peer out the window, seeing the women coming out of their homes bundled up in their gowns and slippers as they move to the side of the house.

I try to see where they're going but only manage to headbutt the window, forgetting it's closed. Sondra laughs as I rub my head.

"You definitely need coffee." She chuckles when we hear beeping and machinery. My brows furrow, and Sondra looks over her shoulder at the double door leading outside.

"What's that noise?" She asks, and I peer out the window, now seeing women running up the side of the house toward the garages, when I notice Eli frantically dialing a number or texting on his phone while sending nervous glances up the side of the house where the women just ran to.

"What is going on?" I mutter, turning and heading for the front door, when I hear metal on metal. I stop, staring at the door, and Sondra gets up, also looking at the door.

Rushing to the door, I toss it open and step outside into the frosty morning air. The sun is far too bright for my bleary eyes. I hold my hand up to shield them from the morning sun and turn, heading up the side when Eli waves his arms frantically.

"Elena, wait! I'm taking care of it!" Eli rushes out, racing over to me when I stop dead in my tracks, and my mouth falls open in shock to see a huge digger knocking down the garages. Michelle is yelling at the crew of men to stop what they're doing, her hands waving frantically in the air while the other women talk in hushed murmurs.

CHAPTER
FORTY-FIVE

"What the fuck!" I yell, stomping over to the fence line, only to see the digger smash straight through it to pull down the other side. I jump back, and the women are also forced to move away as he starts demolishing it when I spot the foreman standing on the other side of the now broken fence line, looking over plans on the hood of his truck with another man.

Stepping over the broken wire fence, I march over to him, furious. "What the fuck do you think you're doing? This is private property!" I yell at the two men, only to notice more machinery filling the paddocks surrounding the property. The foreman turns around, clutching his hard hat before it falls off; he had spun around that quickly.

"What is all this?" I motion toward the construction site being cleared as the trucks moving in with demountable buildings on the back of the flatbeds mow tracks into the paddock.

"New subdivision, ma'am." The man says, and I growl, turning to glare at him.

"A new what?"

"The land was purchased a few months back. We are the

company assigned!" He says, and I look back at the house and our ruined garage.

"Then what the fuck are you doing pulling down my sheds!" I snarl at him, and he snatches the plans off the hood of his truck.

"That fence line does not belong to you. That shed is part of this land right until the back clothesline," He says, pointing out the boundary. I snatch the plans from him, glancing at them but not really understanding what I'm looking at.

"See, now, if you'll excuse me, I have work to do!" He snaps at me, and I scoff.

"Not past that fence line, you don't. Get that digger out of my yard!"

I start arguing with the man over where the boundary line is, and even my mother comes rushing out to help, yet the man is adamant that he has permission to rip it down and that multiple letters were sent out warning about the construction going on when a loud boom echo's around us. The foreman shrieks and ducks while I jump, the sound scaring the living daylights out of me.

Spinning around, Sondra shoots at the tires of the diggers before turning the gun toward us. Mom and I rush out of her way when she shoots out the windows of the truck.

The man clutches his hair and growls, rushing over to his car when Marco comes running out with just a black towel wrapped around his waist. His eyes widen when Sondra reloads her gun while she stomps toward the foreman and shoots at the truck again. She hits the side of the car and the man is forced to jump back. He turns on us, and Marco races over, snatching the gun from her hands.

"You fucking crazy bitch!" The foreman screeches at Sondra, only to cop the butt of the gun in his face. His head whips backward, and he clutches his nose, only for Marco to hit him again.

"Mind your fucking tongue, mutt!" Marco snarls at him, baring his fangs. His eyes flick to me, and I raise an eyebrow at his use of the word mutt.

"Not you, this buffoon!" He says, trying to shield the man from

Sondra. He grabs her around the waist, but not before she takes off her slipper and belts him in the head a few times while she screams at him about ruining her garage. The man shields his head from her blows, his nose bleeding, and the digger driver has stopped to witness his boss receive a beat down.

"Enough, Sondra. I will find out what is going on!" Marco says, looking back at the destruction they have caused.

"Who approved this job?" Marco demands, and I glance at the foreman, watching as he cracks his broken nose back into place.

"Nightfall city council." Marco tilts his head to the side.

"Who? Give me the paperwork!" Marco demands that the other man rushes toward the car and retrieve it before running back to us. Marco snatches it from his hand and looks it over, and curses.

"Pack up. This site no longer has the go-ahead!" Marco tells him.

"No, we have council permission and have already been paid—"

"I am the fucking council, and I have just removed the land title! Pack it up, or you deal with them!" Marco snarls, pointing to the slight incline heading back to the house. I look back at the house to see the women with pitchforks and shovels, anything they could brandish as a weapon.

The men look up at the hill, and the foreman gulps when I notice Eli cursing and dialing on his phone frantically.

My brows pinch together, and I turn back to the foreman. "Whose job is this?"

"Alpha Axton's." The man says, and I press my lips in a line.

"Yeah, you fucked up big time, girl. Now you'll have to answer to him!" The man retorts smugly, and Marco laughs, and I scoff.

"No, now he'll have to answer to me!" I snarl back at him, and the foreman laughs.

"You? You are damn nuts if you think he will even entertain this little land dispute! Who do you think you are?" The man laughs, and I growl.

"His fucking mate!" I snarl at him, feeling Lexa come forward just as furious that he would do this. Was this his way of ensuring I would have no choice but to return to the city? Turning on my heel and stomping back toward the house when I see Eli rush toward me.

"I'm trying to get a hold of him; he's been in meetings all morning and keeps blocking me out."

"You and your men get the fuck off my territory now!" I yell at him, and he stops, putting out his hands in some placating gesture that serves to anger me more when his phone suddenly starts ringing.

"Finally!" Eli says, looking at the screen.

"Is that Axton?" I ask him, and he nods. I snatch the phone from his grip and answer it.

CHAPTER FORTY-SIX

Axton

Logging into the council server while in the meeting with half the council, I check to see if my ban has been lifted. I growl when I find nothing showing she has even put in the appeal yet.

Tuning back into the conversation about the strigoi, I am antsy, eager to see Elena and the boys, when my phone rings on the table. Glancing at it, I see it's Eli. I reject the call.

He has been pestering me for the past ten minutes via mind link and I keep having to shove him out. His timing is impeccable. Grabbing my phone, I shoot Marco a text asking if Elena has done the appeal yet when I hear my name mentioned.

Looking up from my phone, I spot Osiris with a smug look on his face.

"Pardon?" I question.

"I've been speaking with the other alphas, and we are all in agreement," he states. My eyes flick to the seven alphas sitting at the table, not one of them able to meet my gaze.

"Agree on what?" I ask through gritted teeth.

"About you standing down. We want to run an election. Let the people decide who should hold the highest seat within the council. I had the paperwork sent off last night to the supernatural council of elders requesting permission for a status change."

"You did what?" I snarl.

"We just don't think it is a good idea to have someone with such disregard for the supernatural council law to be in a seat of power." Osiris smiles wickedly and my anger rises. My phone rings in my hand and I reject it, seeing that it is Eli again.

"You want to run against me?" I scoff, leaning back in my chair and folding my arms across my chest.

"We all agree. I am the next best candidate for the head of the council, and you've proven how you lack the capabilities to take on the job with so many deaths. The city is frightened and you've done nothing to extinguish that fear. If something isn't done soon, the human governments will get involved, which is not in anyone's best interest, certainly not the city's!"

"This city is thriving with me in this seat. You've barely been Alpha for five minutes Osiris and you think you can run an entire city?" I laugh.

"My name isn't painted with the deaths of those living in this city, Axton, so who do you think the city's population will side with?" Osiris questions and I want to wipe the smug look off his face!

"I own the largest pack in the city, and Elena is behind me, you can't win," I tell him.

"Exactly, which is why I had everyone involved in the upcoming election packs removed from voting, to make it fair, of course! Not only will your pack be removed from voting, but since Elena is your mate, her pack is out too, along with mine. Leaving the decision up to the other five packs and the human population that has been growing by the day." Osiris says and I glance at the other Alphas, all of them look at the table while Cane looks between me and Osiris.

"And you all agree with this?" I ask them.

"He has a point. You and Osiris can't get on long enough to work together, and nothing is changing, maybe a different—" I growl and Thomas' words cut off while I turn my glare on the rest of them.

"This is my city and I will fucking challenge all of you and strip you of your fucking packs if you go against me!" I snarl.

"That is exactly my point. You let ego and your mate bond with Elena get in the way of making decisions for this city." Osiris snaps, leaning across the table. Khan presses furiously against my skin, wanting to tear them all apart for going against me when Alpha Cane speaks.

"I just want to clarify that this has nothing to do with me. Consider me Switzerland," he states, and Osiris and I both look at him.

"Your time as head of the council is over, Axton. Stand down before you embarrass yourself." Osiris sneers.

"No. You will get everyone here killed. You can't run a city, you barely run your pack. Don't think I don't know about you filing for bankruptcy. Does your pack know how much debt you have got them in and who bailed your father out of it?"

Osiris growls and I hear the other alphas whispering amongst themselves. "Is that why you killed him, because he cut you off?" I snarl.

"I didn't kill my father!"

"Then where is he, Osiris? It's amazing how you return to the city and one of our elders goes missing the same fucking day." I growl at him.

"I know you did it. I know exactly what you were involved in. If I were you, I would stand down unless you want me to bring every single one of your skeletons out of the closet come election day."

Osiris laughs, standing up. "We all have skeletons, at least mine aren't in cold blood." Osiris chuckles, saying the one thing, not one of these Alphas would be game enough to say to my face.

"Marco did well to cover it up, but not well enough. I have all the evidence I need to ruin you. But I won't stop there. When I am done, I will not only take your pack and the city, but just to really kick you where it hurts, I will take your mate, too." He laughs.

"Elena would never be with you." I scoff.

"Are you sure about that? Because last I checked, she refuses to let you mark her and why is that?" He questions. Yet he was digging his own grave here, threatening my mate, and that hole was growing deeper by the looks on the other Alphas' faces.

"She is mine. I don't need her mark to prove that when she carries mine!"

"For now she does, but when you're rotting away in prison and she is trying to keep her pack and yours afloat, don't worry. I will take good care of her until you return." He retorts.

"Osiris! You are taking it too far!" Thomas snarls and Osiris smirks.

"I will take it further. Just make sure you pick the right side, Thomas, and remember who was there when you needed help!" Osiris snarls, turning his gaze to Thomas. Thomas purses his lips and averts his gaze to the far wall.

The Alphas murmur amongst each other. Osiris may have numbers on his side, but his comment about Elena I can tell does not sit right with any of them. Mates are sacred, and stating you would take one from another proves how low one would sink for his own gain.

"So that's what you'll do Osiris, threaten our mates if we don't agree?" Alpha Soyer speaks up.

"What? No," Osiris sputters, shooting me a glare.

"Now whose ego is getting in the way of rational thought?" I retort with a smile. Alpha Soyer nods and so do a few other Alphas, but each looks undecided still. Osiris glares at me.

"With that mindset Osiris, I can see you'll take this city far! What will you do next? Do you want to take a step back into the 30s? Are you going to tell your pack before they can take a mate you get to try her out first?" I ask him and he growls, his eyes shooting daggers.

"Because that is what you're suggesting, that once in a seat of power, you're allowed to breach our most sacred laws, taint them and twist them to use at your disposal? Are you okay with that Alpha Soyer? Can he try out your mate?" I ask him and Soyer snarls, his fist crashing down on the table with a thunderous boom.

"I'll kill him before he could ever try!" Soyer threatens before stalking out of the room.

CHAPTER
FORTY-SEVEN

"It appears you hit a nerve, Osiris. We don't take too kindly to threats to our mates in this city, even those of us that aren't mated, correct Thomas?"

"I may not see eye to eye with Axton or Elena, but there are some lines you don't cross!" Thomas retorts and Osiris' eyes move around the table.

"Switzerland!" Alpha Cane raises his hand, and I fight the urge to roll my eyes. We know he wants no part in any of this. He didn't even want to be Alpha.

Osiris laughs. "It was just a little healthy competition. I have no intentions of going after Axton's mate." Osiris quickly states, recognizing his mistake.

"Had you been in this city long enough, Osiris, you'd know the very law you threatened to break. We put it in place! Mates are off limits, and anyone that breaks that earns death. What happens between mates stays between mates only." I inform him.

"And I hear Elena has fought and protested hard to have that changed. Aren't all her pack members from abused mate bonds? You abused your own, from what I hear?" Osiris says, his eyes flashing, daring me to disagree so I don't.

"Correct. There need to be conditions added to that law, special circumstances with the ability to still protect what the moon goddess desired." I tell him.

"But that law depends mostly on the city in which you live?" Osiris questions.

"Correct, but nearly every city has adopted it, same as pack punishment remains within the pack," I state.

"Another law we have spoken of in the past and are thinking of changing?" Alpha Thomas states, coming to my defense for the first time since I sat at the head table. Usually, we are at each other's throats. Maybe he feels even more threatened, given his mate left him for another. Come to think of it, he fought hard to have the law introduced into our city and now I think I know why.

The supernatural council creates the laws, but overall it is at the discretion of the city councils whether they adopt them and make them their own.

"Am I correct in thinking this law was brought forth for debate since Elena was banished?"

"Correct. Elena, being my mate, should have protected her. It didn't, and I nearly lost her and my sons when her father beat her from an inch of her life." I tell him, my stomach sinking at the memory.

"The law was added a month later. Meaning, had it been in place, Derrick would have been forced to hand her over and she would have been placed under my protection."

"And yet his Luna broke the law when she rejected him," Osiris states boldly. Clearly, he hasn't even looked at the laws to know so little about the ones we protect in this city.

"As we said, conditions need to be made, but no, she never broke the law and neither did Elena when she rejected me and I her. The law states mate issues are sacred and handled between the mates.

Louise rejected Derrick. That was her choice, same as it was mine and his, to whether we accept it."

"And did you?" he asks and I growl.

"No, but it's handled between mates, and in my eyes, she did nothing wrong, therefore she's broken no laws!"

"But didn't she intervene last night when it came to Derrick?" my eyes flicker, he was getting on my nerves.

"No, she was protecting her pack! Which she is entitled to do. Her mother is part of her pack, and pack issues and relations are left to the Alpha to decide in discretion!"

"Ah, yes. I know that already, that law is universal. Not as many have adopted the mate's one yet. But from my understanding, Elena doesn't fall under the city laws."

"Protecting your pack from attack is a given. She doesn't need to be under city law for that one. It is an international law unless a werewolf city has it removed or clarified conditions for it." I repeat, like a damn parrot.

"Exactly my point, Alpha Axton," Osiris states.

"What point are you trying to make, exactly?" I ask him.

"Elena isn't part of the city, because she doesn't live in it yet. She doesn't fall under the city laws!"

"Pack business is not a city law, Osiris, it is an international one!"

"Correct, but the sacred mate's law is, therefore if I went after Elena, I would not be breaking any laws at all. Because she is not protected by the city. Therefore, she is fair game!" A feral growl tears out of me, and Thomas also snarls along with another Alpha. Osiris raises his hand in mock surrender.

"Not that I would, of course. I have limits. To give you something to think about, Alpha Axton. I would hate for a lesser man to know that information. It could cause you a lot of heartache!" yet I hear his words loud and clear and the threat behind each one.

I just made a fool out of him by meeting his challenge and now I have done something foolish myself. I have just put Elena and my sons at risk unless I can get her to agree to move to the city ASAP.

"I call to adjourn this meeting until the usual time on Friday?" Osiris says, and we all nod. My phone rings on the table and my mood has turned even more sour. The Alphas leave and I pick up my phone.

"Yes, Eli!" I answer it.

"Is this your fucking idea of getting along, and fixing things, Axton!" Elena's angry voice screeches at me and I sit up straighter.

"What?" I ask, trying to figure out what is going on.

"You took it too far this time. I agreed, I fucking agreed to be with you, agreed to accept the bond, but because I am not moving quick enough for you, you pull this shit!" she screams at me, her booming voice making me yank the phone away from my ear.

"Pull what? I have done nothing, Elena!"

"Nothing, they are ripping up my land! I thought we were past all this!" she snaps.

"Past what? I don't understand why you're yelling at me! Where is Eli?"

"Right here, and while you're on the phone with him, tell your men to get the fuck off my territory!" she screams at me. My heart races in my chest, feeling her rage like a blazing fire burning through me. I hear the phone being passed to someone.

"Talk to your fucking Alpha and get the fuck off my land!" I hear her snap at him before I hear his voice.

"Why haven't you been answering your damn phone or the mind link?" Eli snaps at me.

"I've been dealing with fucking Osiris, that is why! What the fuck is going on?" I snarl at him.

"Oh, she is pissed. You fucked up big time Alpha, she wants us gone."

"Will you tell me what the fuck I did?" I yell at him.

"You ordered the fucking subdivision being built out here. They came out this morning and started tearing the sheds down!"

"No, I canceled–" my blood runs cold when I realize I completely forgot about canceling it.

"You wanna do something because she's pissed!"

"No shit!" I tell him.

"Not her. Fucking Sondra, and she's armed. Call them off Axton before she shoots one of us!" I growl at him.

"I forgot! Why would I ruin everything when me and her were just getting along? I just got my boys back, for fuck's sake!"

"I know that, but Elena doesn't! She thinks you are trying to force her back to the city!"

"Yeah, well, she needs to come back like now. Osiris threatened her this morning, and she is not under city protection." Eli curses.

"So, what do you want me to do?"

"For now, move off her territory, remain on the borders, while I try to fix it. Just let me make some phone calls." I tell him, hanging up on him and instantly looking for the project manager's number.

CHAPTER
FORTY-EIGHT

Elena

Impatiently, I watch the project manager receive a call, and Eli informs me that Axton is on the phone with the manager. The project manager throws some nervous glances in my direction and waves for his men to stop what they're doing. Fury burns through me as I look at the damage they have caused. The garage is reduced to rubble, and sheets of tin, brick, and tiles cover the entire paddock where it stood; trash is scattered everywhere.

"Elena?" Eli murmurs behind me, but I don't glance back at him, instead watching and ensuring the workers leave.

"Get off my property," is all I tell him. After everything we have gone through recently, this comes as a massive slap in the face. I didn't want to hear his excuses. Who goes out of their way to destroy someone's property like this? There is no excuse worthy of this kind of behavior.

"He didn't realize—" my growl cuts his words off, and I turn to face Eli. He backs up and scratches the back of his neck awkwardly. I have no issues with Eli, but I won't stand for him defending Axton.

Not right now. Not while I am watching the devastation on Sondra's face.

"Don't... Don't feed me some bullshit that he didn't know! Even if he somehow forgot to call them off, he still originally planned for them to destroy the place. Destroy our home!" I snarl at him, and Eli bites down on his lip, glancing away, then shakes his head. "Look, I get you're--"

"You need to leave. Get your men and go!" I tell him, cutting him off. Furious, I stalk past him and back toward the house. Marco is trying to calm down Sondra, and he glances at me when I near the stairs.

"Please tell me you have spoken to Axton and have it sorted?" Marco asks, and I nod my head.

"See, they're leaving," Marco tells Sondra. Marco sighs, and Sondra exhales loudly, shooting a glare at him and nudging Sondra toward her rocking chair.

"I will make you some tea," I tell her as she sits down.

"And grab my smokes." She adds, and Marco gives her a disapproving look but says nothing about her smoking, so I nod. Walking inside, I turn the kettle on, grab a mug, and retrieve the tea bags.

Hours later.

After our early wake-up call this morning, we spent all morning and into the afternoon tidying up the destruction and sifting through what remained, trying to salvage anything we could. Most of everything is broken, and luckily Sondra had gotten rid of most of the cars that were stored there. However, the tools and farming equipment would cost a fair bit to replace or fix.

We dumped it into the huge skip bins, which I had the local garbage company drop off.

Yet as the day's heat slowly dies, I notice Lexa has become awfully quiet. Throwing the last sheet of tin into the scrap metal pile, I glance over to see both skips overflowing, and we still had two piles of scrap metal, a pile of salvage items that we now have to figure out what to do with, and another skip-worthy pile of debris left.

"How about we call it a day?" Michelle yells out to me while tossing some trash into the overflowing skip bin. I nod, wiping my forehead on the back of my hand and peeling the gloves off.

She is right. We've been at this for hours, we have made some progress, but it is stifling hot out here still. Walking over to her, she sighs; Michelle is also covered in dirt.

"My back is killing!" she groans, placing her hands behind her and pushing on her lower back as she leans backward.

"Yeah," I tell her breathlessly. This heat is really getting to me, and I feel on the verge of passing out.

"You're a little red?" Michelle comments and I touch my face before fanning myself with my hands.

"Aren't you cold?" she asks me while her eyes roam over me, and I glance down at my shorts and crop top.

"Ah no, we've been working our asses off." I chuckle, turning to look at the packhouse, and Michelle moves to follow me back to the house.

"The girl that just came back from patrol said she saw Axton's patrols lingering at our borders, she told them to leave, but they refused, stating they aren't on our land, so we can't make them," Michelle tells me, and I roll my eyes. I am not dealing with Axton right now. I want to strangle him, and if he was right in front of me, I might actually try it.

"I'll deal with it tomorrow. For now, I'm going to shower and feed the boys their afternoon snack." Michelle nods, and we both head toward the house when I hear Marco call out, making me stop. Turning back around, I see him toss a broken car motor into the skip bin as if it was merely a piece of trash he had picked up off the ground. The pile in the skip bin drops lower under its heavy weight.

"Are you heading inside?" He calls out, and I nod. He gives me a thumbs up.

"I will finish this last section and head in myself then!" he tells us, and Michelle and I head back inside the house. The moment I step inside, I am blasted by the air conditioning, and I sigh.

"Are you alright, dear," my mother asks from the kitchen, and I move toward her. She quickly fills a glass with ice-cold water and hands it to me. Within two large mouthfuls, I drained the glass and set it back in the sink.

"The boys went down for a nap ten minutes ago," she tells me, and I nod, yet she sniffs the air subtly, and I smell myself wondering if I stink. I can't smell anything, yet she watches me for a few seconds. Worry is etched into her features when she cups my cheek with her hand.

"Gosh, you feel like you're burning up?" she murmurs, her brows furrowing.

"Yeah, it's stifling hot outside." I groan.

"I just need to stand in front of the air conditioning for a bit," I tell her.

"Air conditioning? Elena, I have the heater on. It is not hot. That breeze is damn near icy!" she tells me, and I blink at her. Only then do I notice what she is wearing. She has a long sleeve top on and track pants, her fluffy white robe over the top, and she has stolen a pair of my slippers. It makes me remember Michelle and her comments outside.

My gaze moves to the air conditioning, and I see the temperature is on heat, my brows furrowed in confusion. I could have sworn it felt cold when I came in. Surely, I am not so hot that the heat feels cold.

"Maybe you should lie down and drink some more water." My mother worries, her eyes assessing me, and I roll mine at her. "I'm fine," I tell her, heading for the stairs so I can go shower. However, as I start to climb them, my legs go funny, almost like they are on the verge of giving out from under me. My vision darkens and warps as vertigo washes over me. I grab the banister, waiting for the dizziness to settle, but it gets worse.

"Elena?" my mother calls out, and I turn to where she stands at the bottom of the stairs just as Marco walks inside.

"All done, I will organize for some—" Marco stops dead in his tracks, a peculiar expression sweeping over his face. I blink as he blurs, my vision tunneling, and I can no longer feel my fingertips holding the banister or my arms. Marco sniffs the air, and a feral growl tears out of him just as I feel my eyes roll into the back of my head. The next thing I see is black.

I don't feel the ground when I hit it, I feel nothing, but I can hear Marco's voice.

"Call Axton. She's in heat!" Marco snaps at my mother, his voice sounding close.

"I thought... I just wasn't sure.... I knew something was wrong... but she-wolves can't smell heat!" my mother panics.

"Louise ring—" Panic courses through me at his words and with the last of my energy.

"No!" I order, the words sounding hollow to my ears when I lose all sense of everything, falling deaf and numb to everyone and everything around me, blinded by the blistering heat surging through me.

My skin hurts and burns when I groggily wake up. I nearly scream when I find myself in a bathtub naked, Marco holding my head above the water while speaking to someone over his shoulder.

My hands grip the tub's sides, and I try to sit up. The room spins, and my vision blurs at the motion as I reach for a towel, only for him to shove me back under. "You need Axton!" he snaps at me.

"You need to get out!" I tell him, horrified that I am naked in front of him, yet his eyes don't leave mine, even when he reaches over to switch the cold water tap on and my mother rips the plug out of the bathtub.

She lets the water drain while cold water pours in. My mother chews her lip, staring at Marco. "Now she is awake; I can give her the pills?" my mother tells him, and he presses his lips in a line.

"She needs her damn mate. She can't live on those pills. They will only hold it off, not stop her heat. She's an Alpha. They'll have barely any effect on her!" Marco snaps angrily.

"Listen to him, Louise. He's right." Comes Sondra's voice. Yet the more they speak, the more distant their voices become and the harder it is to breathe.

"I can't. She ordered me not to!" my mother argues, and I exhale, relieved to know they haven't told him.

"It's been three days, Marco can't hold her in the water much longer, and we have nearly drained the tanks!" Sondra says.

"He knows something is wrong; he messaged me asking why she won't reply to his text messages. Or let him video call the boys."

"I won't let you keep injecting her with that damn poison to numb their bond. It's been too long. Any longer, Axton will start getting sick himself." Marco growls.

"She's my daughter--" Marco cuts her off.

"And he's my friend! I won't risk her life any more than I would risk his, and leaving her like this, they're both at risk!" Marco snarls, the points of his fangs jut out from beneath his top lip.

"I am doing what she wants; I can't call Axton even if I wanted to!" my mother argues.

"Please, mom?" I hear Luke whimper distantly. Jeez, what is this! Is the entire damn pack in here!?

My mind races as I try to take in what they're saying.

Three days? I must have misheard. There is no way I have been unconscious for three days.

"No, just leave me!" I murmur, feeling the sickly feeling sweep back over me.

"Pass me that ice bucket! Sondra, and call Axton!" Marco snaps when I pass out once again before I can argue.

CHAPTER FORTY-NINE

Axton

Wiping the sweat from the back of my neck with my handkerchief, I put it in my pocket. I've been feeling under the weather for the last few days; some bug must be going around.

"Are you okay, Axton?" Alpha Soyer asks me, and I glance up at him.

"Yeah, just going to message Elena and see where she is." I tell him. Khan paces in my head as I send yet another text to Elena. She still hasn't forgiven me or appealed to the council's court, which is driving me insane. All I get are short answers or photos of the boys, she rejects all my calls, but I know something is wrong because I messaged and emailed her yesterday to tell her the council meeting has been moved a day early. Elena knows she can't miss these meetings.

Looking at the time, she is twenty minutes late already, and even Marco has been ignoring my messages. Not one reply from him in days. I know he is close with Sondra, but ignoring his obligations is out of the ordinary.

"Mindlink Eli." Khan snarls at me. Sending the message, I open up the mind link feeling for Eli's pack link.

"What's up?" he asks.

"Has Elena left yet?" I ask him.

"No, I haven't seen her in days, and the women won't let us near the packhouse," he tells me. "Why? Is everything okay?"

"I moved the council meeting a day early. She is late, and we are all waiting on her."

"I can ask Michelle. She is on border patrol this morning." Eli suggests.

"Yes, leave the mind link open, so I can hear what she has to say. Khan is convinced something is wrong," I tell him, and he groans. It is considered rude to eavesdrop because it is not only using the mind link but also Eli having to let me entirely in his head, meaning I can hear his thoughts which is a major invasion of privacy. Eli groans loudly.

"No, I'd rather walk up there and risk being shot by Sondra!" he whines.

"Just do it; I already know what sick thoughts run through your head; I have seen your magazine stash!" I snap at him. Nothing was more disturbing than finding out my Beta has some bizarre kinks.

"Fine," he huffs, opening the link further and letting me in his head. I can hear everything around him, hear his breathing when he hums loudly. La la la.

"What are you doing? Stop that!" I tell him, but he continues humming and chanting. Eli ignores me and continues.

"Michelle!" he suddenly calls out, making me jump. A few council members look over at me, but I wave them off, returning my attention to the mind link.

"Ah, what do you want? And stay on your side of the fence unless you want my damn claws in your ass and my teeth in your throat!" Michelle snarls at him.

'I wouldn't mind sinking my teeth into your neck!' I blink at what I heard of his thoughts.

"Axton wants to know if Elena is going to the council meeting today. They are waiting for her?"

"Ah... Elena is... she is..." Michelle pauses for a second, and Khan comes forward, also invading Eli's thoughts. "Get out, Khan. It's bad enough having Axton in my head!" Eli snarls through the pack link.

"Shut up; I don't care if you have the hots for Michelle. Where is my Luna!" Khan snarls at him.

"I don't have the hots for her!" Eli argues back with him, and I am about to lose my damn mind as they start arguing when Michelle speaks, shutting both of them up.

"Elena is sick...?" Michelle offers.

"What, she has been sick for days?" I question, and Eli asks her.

"Um...yes, she has a bad case of....." Michelle pauses.

"Runny bum!... Yeah, she got the shits real bad, been stuck on the toilet for days!" she tells Eli.

'Well, that was far too much information!' Eli thinks.

"Yeah, so tell your Lupha she is fine. We're all fine!" she tells him.

'Yes, you are,' Eli thinks, and I suddenly get images of Michelle sitting on his face.

"Eli, focus, head out of the gutter! Tell her to tell Elena to call me!" Eli's embarrassment hits me loud and clear. He does what I ask, and Michelle leaves to tell Elena.

"Well, that was fun!" Eli says, feeling embarrassed that I know he likes Michelle.

"Why are you embarrassed she is single? So are you!"

"She has a mate."

"Had! She killed him, remember? Marco said they were all from that dead pack. Therefore she is single, so feel free to date crazy pants, and teach her how to say alpha. For god's sake, if I were Elena, that would drive me insane."

"Huh?"

"Lupha, it's not even close to alpha," I tell him, and he laughs.

"But that's what you are; all the women call you that," Eli tells me, and my brows furrow.

"Pardon?" I ask.

"They made it up; I asked Michelle the other night because I thought I was hearing things. It turns out you are their Lupha since they already have an Alpha, and you're Elena's mate."

"What?"

"You can't be their Alpha. They have one already, so you are Elena's Luna, Lupha, Luna/Alpha Lupha!" Eli explains. I don't know what to think of his words, but it explains why Michelle keeps referring to me by it.

"Okay then, I have to get back to the meeting. Hopefully, she calls me; I can't get a hold of Marco either," I tell him.

"Really? He hasn't left. He's still here." Eli tells me. "I can get Michelle to tell him to call you?"

"He's still there?" I ask Eli.

"Yeah, he hasn't left," Eli tells me.

"Yes, please do," I tell him before cutting the link.

"Something is going on. None of this makes sense," Khan tells me. I have to agree, but until the ban is lifted, I can't do anything, at least I know she is safe if Marco is there.

Returning to the meeting, I can't seem to think straight. We go over more details of the strigoi attacks, and we are about to go on a short break when my phone starts ringing, and Elena's name pops up on my screen. Finally! I think to myself, and I hold up a finger, and Osiris throws up his hands when he is expected to wait.

"Finally, why aren't you taking my calls?" I ask her when I answer it.

"Is that any way to greet someone?" Comes Sondra's voice.

"Sondra?"

"Yes, now you need to get that ass out here. Elena needs you. And I am done watching her suffer."

"Excuse me?"

"Elena has been in heat for days now, with no end in sight, she ordered her pack not to tell you, but Marco has been holding her in the bath for days. I've just run out of water, and the injections are wearing off faster each time. Her heat is not breaking!"

My blood runs cold at her words, and it explains the sickly feeling I've had for days.

"Are you there?"

"Yes, yes, I'm here. I'm on my way." I tell her, hanging up.

CHAPTER
FIFTY

I snatch my keys off the table and shut my laptop before stalking toward the door, only for Osiris to step in my path.

"You wouldn't be thinking about breaching your conditions again, would you?" Osiris sneers. He laughs, looking at the other council members.

"You just heard my phone call, Osiris. Don't pretend you didn't." I snap at him and step to the side when he steps in my path again. He blocks me, but I haven't got time to waste, especially if Elena has been in heat for days, so I let Khan come forward.

"You can't leave the meeting, Ax—"

Khan punches him, cutting his words off, and Osiris clutches his bleeding face and goes to speak again, only for Khan to kick him in the stomach. He smashes through the door, and I blink in shock, my foot fucking killing with the force he used. Khan then steps out the door and over Osiris' body.

"You were saying?" Khan snarls at him, and Osiris puts up his hands. Khan shakes my head, giving me back control, and I turn to leave.

"Axton!" Osiris snarls when he grunts; I turn back to look at him to see Soyer standing over him. He dips his head to me, and I smirk, seeing Osiris knocked out on the ground when Cane steps out the door. "Well, he got fucked up!" I snicker and race for my car while trying not to limp.

"I think you broke my foot!" I tell him.

"Get over it. You'll heal." Khan snaps at me as I climb into the car. We race toward the borders, and I growl seeing Osiris' men on the borders, so instead of slowing down, knowing they will just delay me, I speed up, driving straight through the boom gates, wood splinters and smashes, the hood of my car getting scratched to pieces and I see his men rush out of the booths. Turning my attention back to the road.

The drive to Elena's pack is quick since the roads are pretty much empty, Eli alerts the women in Elena's pack to stay off the roads, and I am surprised they listen because when I pull onto the long driveway, they are nowhere to be seen.

"Eli, where are you?" I ask him via the mindlink.

"Helping Michelle grab the kid's car seats out of Elena's car."

"Good. Can you bring the boys to the packhouse?"

"Nanny duty?" Eli asks.

"Yep, bring Michelle if you want," I tell him, pulling up out the front. I spot Sondra sitting in her rocking chair, a smoke between her lips, rocking back and forth.

Climbing out of the car, I move toward the stairs.

"She's upstairs with Marco," she tells me.

"Is she conscious?"

"She was last I checked. That's why I am down here. She is angry I called you," she tells me, and I nod, opening the door and walking inside the house. The moment I open the wooden door and step inside, I am slammed with the scent of her heat, I almost choke on its potency, and my pupils dilate. Khan shoves forward, and it takes everything to shove him back and retake control.

I follow her scent, finding her in the bathroom attached to her room. Marco is kneeling beside the bathtub, drenched, and has one arm under her head. Elena is passed out, and Marco looks over his shoulder while I try to remind myself he is not a threat to her despite him holding my naked mate.

"Thank fucking god," Marco snaps.

"You should have called!" I tell him pushing him aside, he still holds his hand under her head, but now I can see her. Her skin is flush, her body heat so hot, the room's mirrors are foggy, and her scent is sinfully addictive, making me instantly uncomfortable.

"They took my phone, and I couldn't leave her. None of them wanted to call you, not even Sondra at first." I nod, unbuttoning my shirt, knowing my skin will ease some of her pain and lessen her heat until I get her home. Scooping my arms under her body in the water. I find the water is hot from her heat. The moment I grab her, her eyes fly open.

"Axton?" she murmurs weakly and she can barely hold her head up. Her skin is so hot she is making me sweat. Yet despite her not wanting me near her, she can't help but to lean into me, seeking out my skin and scent, maneuvering her. I place my hands under her ass and hoist her higher. Her legs wrap around my waist, and she sighs, yet I can feel she is fighting the urge to mark me. Her instincts tell her to, which makes me realize why she didn't want them to ring me. She knows she will mark me, she won't be able to help herself.

"You can go back to hating me tomorrow. For now, you fucking need me," I growl at her when I feel her cognitive mind reawaken and she tries to get out of my arms.

"Forgive me!" I whisper before sinking my teeth into her neck. She thrashes against me, fighting as Khan shoves his intention behind it, forcing her to submit to us. Yet she is fighting a losing battle, especially while she is in heat. Khan would also dominate her in this sense, and it's a natural instinct for the female to submit while in heat. Despite her being an alpha, she is still female. It doesn't take her long before she collapses against me falling unconscious. I pull my teeth from her neck, angry she would suffer for days because she is so damn stubborn!

Marco tosses a towel over her body when I turn around. "I'll drive you," Marco says, walking out of the bedroom. I follow him. We walk downstairs, and he snatches his keys off the kitchen counter and moves to open the front door.

"Wait, you're taking her?" Louise says, looking at me nervously.

"Well, I ain't listening to them go at it like rabbits!" Sondra snaps at her from her rocking chair.

"Sondra! Don't be crude. That's my daughter you're talking about!" Louise scolds her.

"Well, what did you think he was here for? A fucking tea party?" She retorts. Louise rubs her temples and shakes her head, and I follow Marco down the porch steps.

"Chuck a good one into her; it might put her in a better mood." I raise an eyebrow at Sondra while Louise scolds her for her dirty language.

"At least someone is getting laid around here," she huffs, and Marco chuckles, opening the back door to his car.

CHAPTER FIFTY-ONE

Sliding across the seat with Elena on my lap. I notice Eli and Michelle grabbing the boys and placing them in my car. Relief fills me knowing the boys are coming with us and I will have help with them; I can't leave the boys out here, or Elena will fret, and it will make her heat so much worse. Plus, I have no idea how long her heat will last. Marco decides to wait for them while I maneuver Elena's unconscious body to a more comfortable position in my lap. Once Eli and Michelle are following, we leave, heading down the long driveway.

The drive is quiet until we reach the halfway mark, and Elena remains unconscious from marking her again, all while Khan paces anxiously in my head. My skin ripples with the urge to mate her, yet her heat has dimmed a little from my bite and because I'm near. I just hope it doesn't flare back up in the car, or things may get a little awkward for Marco.

"Any more attacks?" Marco finally speaks, and I shake my head. I'm still a little annoyed he didn't tell me earlier she was in heat, but grateful he was there to help her, even if it meant he saw her naked.

"No, thankfully, none since Derrick has been gone," I answer. Everyone thinks he is behind it, but Marco and I believe differently.

"It's not Derrick, but whoever it is helped Derrick to escape. It's a setup. They're trying to cover their tracks," Marco states. "He's the perfect person to frame since he is on the run," he adds, and I agree.

"Well, we know it isn't Osiris. He also has petitioned the council to have an election. They want to throw me from my seat." I tell him.

Marco laughs and shakes his head. "They can try. They'll be dead if Osiris holds the seat." I sigh but nod. Checking Elena, she is breathing steadily, her nose buried in my neck, when Marco stops, showing his ID to the border patrols.

"Do I need to take care of this mess when I head back?" Marco asks me, looking at the ruined boom gates when I spot Soyer talking to some of Osiris' men. As Marco's car passes, Soyer gives him a nod, and he waves Eli through, who is driving my car behind us to keep going.

"No, Soyer will handle it. I am leaving my men on the borders of Elena's pack. I can't leave them unprotected. She'll kill me when her heat finishes if no one is out there." I tell Marco.

"I will be staying out there anyway; the women will be safe. Hopefully, you can convince Elena to move back to the city; I will work on Sondra. If not, I might take time off work to look after her at the ranch." Marco tells me with a heavy sigh.

"At least then I will be closer to help with this entire strigoi situation," Marco adds, and I nod my head.

"Unfortunately, I don't see that happening any time soon, Elena is angry, and she'll be angrier that I took her."

"I don't think so; Elena is smart. She knows it's the safest choice. She also isn't as angry as you think. She looked more hurt that you planned to destroy her land, not angry." Marco adds.

"I can only hope so because this traveling between and constant worry for them out there is driving me crazy." Pulling up at the house, I see Eli pull up behind us. Climbing out, I pull the towel covering Elena's naked body up higher and look at Eli.

"We will stay in the guest house out the back with the boys," Eli tells me.

"I'm not sharing a room with you!" Michelle snaps at him.

"Correct, because you're sharing a bed!" Eli retorts, and I shake my head at them.

"I will be glad to get rid of her for a few days. She and Sondra argue like cats and dogs!" Marco mutters to me.

"I heard that, Marco!" Michelle yells at him.

"I meant the other Michelle!" he calls back.

"Who?" she asks, her brow furrowing.

"You know the other one!" he shrugs. Turning, I peer over between them, and she seems deep in thought for a second. Her face then twists into a scowl. "There is no other Michelle!" she snarls.

"Whoops, my bad, must have got you confused with someone else." Marco laughs, and she flips him a rude finger. I chuckle and quickly say goodbye to Marco before heading inside the house through the garage while listening to Michelle and Eli argue as they go around the side of the house and to the studio out the back with the boys.

"Make sure those shutters remain down! If not, come inside; I can watch them and deal with Elena."

"Yeah, right. Once Elena wakes up, the only thing you'll be able to do is deal with her. They'll be fine, and yes, the shutters will be down!" Eli mind links back.

Walking up to my room, I lay Elena on the bed, wondering how long she would be knocked out. Sitting on the edge of the bed, I watch her for a second and pull the sheet up, covering her so I am not tempted to sink myself inside her while she is asleep.

My cock is painfully hard, her scent driving me to the brink of insanity, so I know she must be slowly coming back to consciousness. From where I am sitting next to her, I can feel her temperature rising, her scent becoming so potent I am struggling to think clearly.

Despite knowing I am the only one that can break her heat, nerves have set in; she is going to be furious. However, it explains why I've felt off for the past few days. She can't expect me to allow her to try to ride out her heat, hoping it breaks; it angers me that she tried. For days she suffered, and her anger for me outweighed her reason.

CHAPTER
FIFTY-TWO

Feeling the bed move, my head snaps in her direction, and I swallow as she stirs, her eyes blinking open. Now that I'm near, she can sense me so much stronger. Her ability to recognize anything other than me in the room with her is completely gone as primal instinct overrules her.

"In this state, she'll mark us," Khan reminds me, and you would think satisfaction would rush through me at his words, but only hesitation does instead. I didn't want her mark by default; I wanted her to give it to me because she felt I was worthy of her. Another thing she'll be angry about when she comes to her senses.

Then there is also the issue of her being extremely fertile, and since I am her mate, it is almost guaranteed that I will knock her up. Just the thought of that makes my stomach twist; I can imagine her hatred, especially with the boys not even a year old. This is not how I imagined her first heat would be. Now I am second-guessing even touching her but also knowing I have no choice.

I guess, I just imagined we would be on good terms by now. That she would want me, but knowing she doesn't is making this extremely difficult. Even as her lust-filled hazy eyes meet mine, doubt fills me. Am I taking advantage of her? That worries me most: would she wake up tomorrow and think I am just another Jake, another Alpha asshole taking something from her?

Elena purrs, her eyes turning glassy as her senses overwhelm her, and the moment her skin brushes mine, it is like fireworks have exploded on my skin as sparks rush everywhere. A feral growl tears out of me, making me lose focus. If it weren't for Khan in my head, reminding me to focus, I would have answered her calling. Khan is the only thing stopping me from mating her, and I focus on his voice as she crawls into my lap.

I lift my arms, allowing it but also not willing to touch her. Her mouth moves instantly to my skin as she sucks and licks my flesh. Her scent is intoxicating, and now she is awake; her heat is much more robust, and the desire to take her is much stronger, too. The intensity of it causes me pain as I refuse to give in to urges.

"She'll forgive us. We can't help it if she marks us." Khan reminds me.

"But can she forgive herself; I don't want her mark because she is driven by senses. I want it because she wants me to have it."

"Isn't it the same thing?" Khan asks, also fighting his desires, and he is the only thing stopping me from acting mine out right now.

"Yes-no, kinda..... She'll regret it; I know she will," I tell him.

"Then we don't let her," Khan says as if it is that simple, and I feel her claws slip down the sides of my ribs, my hands still in the air, as I try not to maul her. I hiss, feeling them slice down my skin and her claws sinking into my abs as she claws at my pants. I grit my teeth before grabbing her. A groan leaves me as I pull her closer, and she purrs, pressing closer as I wrap her legs around my waist and lean forward.

Reaching into the top drawer of the bedside table, her teeth slice through my bicep, then her face moves to my neck. I drop my chin, stopping her from sinking her teeth into me as instinct tells her to claim me.

Elena growls when I deny her, and my hand rummages, finding

the handcuffs I chucked in here and forgot about and a box of old condoms. My face twists at the thought of using them; I am hers, yet until she says so, she is not mine. I glare at the foil packet as I take one out, not wanting to use it but knowing I should.

It is the right thing to do, she may not be able to help her heat or her instincts, but I can at least not use it against her or take advantage of her vulnerability—How things have changed. Going back a few weeks ago, I would have used her heat to trap her, to get her to mark me. But seeing how good we get along when we are both trying to make the bond work, I want it to go back to that place where she doesn't hate me and wants to be around me.

Twisting, I press her against the mattress and shake off the carnal desire to fuck her until she screams. Instead, I handcuff her, pinning her wrists to the headboard. My hands shake terribly as I sit back on my heels between her legs, her body squirming as her heat rises and pain starts to cripple her at the loss of skin contact.

"Shh, Lena. I will make it stop. I'm trying here, okay? I just need to keep my head." I whisper to her. Those words are easier said than done when she locks her legs around me, yanking me to her. Her heat overwhelms me as I blink back the haze she is forcing me in.

I'm not sure how much of Elena is actually present during her heat, but I hope some part of her is here with me, so she knows I wish things were different, so she knows I don't want to hurt her, or take her while she is angry with me.

Yet the moment her voice pleads for me, I know some part of her is under the baser instinct, that some part isn't purely driven by Lexa's needs or their heat. "Please, make it stop, just make it stop, Axton," she growls, the sound turning to a purr, as her canines slip past her lips, her eyes turn black a charcoal. "Axton," she moans, her legs locking around my waist tighter.

"Be patient," I tell her. "I'm just…."

My eyes bleed black as I feel Khan's instincts seep into me, unable to hold out any longer, her heat becoming too tempting to fight against. My hands fumble with my pants before my claws slip out, shredding them to pieces, and the next second I am shoving her legs open. And not as gently as I wanted, as all restraint slips away along with any real cognitive thoughts, instead, I'm solely consumed by her heat.

"Axton, please," she whines, and my lips crash down on hers.

CHAPTER
FIFTY-THREE

Elena

His scent is the first thing I notice when I groggily wake; it perfumes the room, enticing senses I never knew existed. My body feels foreign and so hot. Burning and aching for him, I'm high on his scent as I breathe it in. My eyes flutter open as Lexa's instincts painfully become mine. Axton sits on the edge of the bed, his head in his hands, making me wonder why he is so far away, I need him closer. So much closer.

His presence alone has become an addiction, one I want to feed, making me crave him, luring me closer. It's like the world no longer exists, and we live on our own plane of existence together, and right now, all I can focus on is his intoxicating scent, luring me to him.

Moving my limbs, they don't feel like mine, purely driven by instinct, he startles. Some part of me wants to know why he looks so conflicted, yet my heat rising, and the blood in my veins boiling, pulsating makes any thoughts slip away easily. Every piece of me calls for me to go to him as I crawl into his lap.

The mate bond demands his touch, but he seems hesitant to give it because he puts his hands up. I bury my face in the crook of his neck. His scent is overwhelming; it's intoxicating.

His entire body trembles underneath me. Tomorrow, I will feel embarrassed about my actions, but right now, I couldn't care less as long as the pain that is becoming torturous eases.

Axton growls, pulling me closer, and my lips attack his neck when he leans forward; my hands claw at him, needing him closer, not that I understand how that is possible. My body feels strange, tingling, and I want to climb inside him, which makes no sense. He pulls my legs around his waist, and I moan as his hard chest presses against my heated flesh.

Yet instead of giving me what my body and the bond craves and needs, he twists and presses me against the mattress. The next second, he handcuffs me, pinning my wrists to the headboard; the metal clamping tightly around my wrists. I struggle against the restraints, needing to touch him, needing his skin. Yet he sits back on his heels between my legs. My body squirms as my heat rises and the pain intensifies. What is he doing?

"Shh, Lena. I will make it stop. I'm trying here, okay? I just need to keep my head." he whispers to me. Confusion wraps around me for a second at his hesitation. Isn't this what he has wanted, and now he is denying both of us? Why?

I lock my legs around his waist, yanking him to me. He growls, the sounds savage but sends a thrill through me. Yet still, he does nothing. It drives the bond insane, and the pain washes through me tenfold at his refusal.

"Please, make it stop, just make it stop, Axton," I growl, the sound turning to a purr as my canines slip out, the bond demanding me to mark him and make him mine. "Axton," I moan, legs locking around his waist tighter, refusing to let him escape me.

"Be patient," he tells me. "I'm just...." Axton groans and pulls back slightly, his entire body shaking.

His eyes bleed black. His hand's fumble with his pants before he shreds them to pieces, and he shoves my legs open, pressing his weight down on me. A moan escapes my lips at the relief his skin against mine offers.

"Axton, please," I whine when I feel his hesitation once more. The next second, his lips crash down on mine hard.

Every inch of my skin is covered in goosebumps. My breath hitches when I feel his tongue delve between my lips, tasting every inch. I feel like I am on some sort of high, which makes it hard to think straight. I can't concentrate. It's all too much with his harsh grip and brutal lips, molding around mine. Somehow, he only manages to turn me on more instead of offering me any sort of reprieve. I want nothing more than to feel his teeth sinking into my skin and let him devour me. Yet once again, he fights instinct and pulls away.

What the hell is he waiting for? Isn't this what he wants, to tie me to him so I can't escape him? I don't care what he does as long as he stops fighting the damn bond.

"Axton, please," I gasp, but a moment later, he takes my ability to speak away from me when he kisses me again.

My heart beats out of my chest. I want more. I need *so much* more. Yanking on the handcuffs, wanting to touch and pull him closer, he grips my wrist, stopping the action. My fight makes my wrists ache, so I allow him to explore my mouth with his tongue.

I flinch underneath him as I feel the cold air against my skin. How can I feel cold, and yet I feel hotter than I ever have before? He pulls away, sitting up, and I am blessed by seeing his muscular torso. I want to reach out and touch him, but the handcuffs prevent my movements. His pitch-black eyes watch me as he runs his hands down my sides to my hips. The sensation makes me shiver when he moves his hands to spread my legs, pushing them flat against the bed.

Leaning back down, he gently brushes his lips over mine briefly, then his lips travel down my jaw and neck, trailing down my body. His mouth latches onto one of my nipples while his hand squeezes the bottom of my breast before it moves to the other, and he flicks and plucks it. It doesn't take long before a needy whimper escapes past my lips.

"So beautiful," he murmurs, moving lower, but he doesn't give me a chance to really respond when I feel his hot breath sweep over my pussy; I lift my head looking down at him, needing him to touch me, anything to relieve the burning sensation that riddles through me. However, his focus is between my legs.

Dark, hungry eyes watching me squirm in anticipation. He wants to devour me, and I am done denying him; I'm done pretending I don't want him just as badly. With this man, everything just feels like it makes sense like this is how it was always so supposed to be. Right now, it seems crazy to deny him, deny myself.

CHAPTER
FIFTY-FOUR

I've longed for this moment for ages without knowing it or allowing myself to admit it. Now, though, that desire is undeniable and uncontrollable.

His dark gaze lifts to mine, and I gasp when his lips sweep across my core. Squirming in his grip, a moan leaves me, which earns a growl from him as his tongue runs between my folds. My head drops back on the pillow, eyes fluttering closed at the sensation.

He laps at my heated flesh, teasing my clit with slow strokes, earning a breathy moan from me, and I buck against his face. He growls, fingers digging into my thighs as he picks up speed, his tongue relentless leaving no part untouched.

"Yes," I moan out, my eyes rolling into the back of my head while his hands grab the back of my thighs, lifting them higher so he can slip his tongue inside me. "Ah," I whimper. He moves higher and starts to nibble and lick my sensitive clit harder and faster, making my walls clench.

All I can do in response is take it and buck my hips against his mouth— the bond craving more, greedy for it.

He sucks on my clit, massaging it with his tongue, and my hips rock against his face, the sensation pushing me over the edge, and I come undone.

I moan through my orgasm, my body locking up tensely and then quivering against his mouth. Axton's tongue laps greedily. He groans, his tongue slowing while I ride out the waves of it; the heat easing enough that I can finally think straight. Only it doesn't last long; having not been satisfied, and craving something more than his mouth can offer, it flares back up.

Axton, sensing this, sits up, moving back between my legs. He yanks at me a little, hooking his muscular arms around the backs of my knees and holding me up. With one hand, he guides himself closer until the tip of his cock is pressed against my soaking-wet heat.

His eyes dart to mine, and it's almost like he's waiting for me to tell him to get off me, waiting for my rejection.

He slips inside of me. My body is forced to get used to his large size stretching me. Having not had sex in so long, it feels foreign. As he pushes inside me, I feel every inch of him and my breath hitches.

"You okay?" he asks me, his voice husky. His lust-filled eyes looking hazy. So fucking sexy.

I nod my head. "Don't hold back," I moan, moving my hips. His eyes flicker at my words, and a deep growl resonates around me. My hands yank on the handcuffs, wanting to touch him, pull him closer and force him to fuck me.

"Axton," I moan as he continues watching me. "Please."

Almost as if my begging triggers him, his arms and shoulders ripple, and he leans down, his hands fist the sheets on the mattress, and he pulls out before slamming into me.

Soon, the pain and discomfort warp into something else as his pace picks up. Quicker and harsher, he pounds into me, each thrust making my breast bounce and my walls clench. I whimper when his tongue trails down my neck, lightly biting down on my delicate skin.

But still, he doesn't slow his pace; he continues thrusting into me, bringing me closer. My eyes open to see his jaw clenched, his skin glistening with sweat.

He pulls out and then roughly pushes back in. My body is burning from his size as he becomes more brutal. I am wet enough to make up for it, and the pain from his harsh thrusts only complements the pleasure.

I throw my head back, and my mouth falls open as he picks up the rhythm. Utterly at his mercy, he controls my body as he thrusts inside of me, softly yanking at my hips to meet him with each thrust, the sensation putting strain on my wrists. Axton thrusting deeper, harder, sending me blind with bliss.

"Fuck..." My breath hitches when his thrusts shoot through my body like electricity. I can feel him everywhere, making my entire body buzz. The sensations are overwhelming, and he is savage as he continues to fuck my body into the mattress. "Oh, god--" He chuckles—such a beautiful sound.

He moves one hand between my legs, pressing his thumb on my clit, caressing me in circular motions. I can barely take it anymore when my toes curl, and my entire body shakes. The moan that leaves my lips sounds like a shout. My body quivers as I reach the edge and fall blissfully over it, making everything so bright and so sensitive.

He leans back down over me, and his mouth and teeth maul my throat. His canines dig into my skin, only adding to the pleasure writhing through me. My canines slip out when he pulls back, squeezing his eyes shut as he focuses on the sensations that shoot through his body, and he stills inside me. My walls clamp down around him, and he groans, sinking his teeth into me before I can mark him. He pulls his teeth from my neck, and my eyes flutter as I fight to remain conscious.

"I love you, Elena," he whispers, kissing my lips softly. I want to reply. Tell him I love him too, tell him I want to mark him, but the moment is stolen when he marks me again, and coldness seeps through me as my heat abates before I am sucked into the abyss of nothingness.

The sun lighting up the back of my eyelids pulls me from sleep. Blinking, I sit up to shield my eyes. I am lying across Axton's chest, who is passed out. Pushing off his chest, I peer around, trying to remember how I got here. My mind feels foggy, my body feels sticky, and I am drenched in his scent. Fragmented memories rush to the surface, and I feel Lexa purring in contentment in my head, still sleeping off the effects of our....heat.

My heart races a little quicker with that knowledge and the way I mauled Axton. My eyes move to his neck, and I touch my own. Hissing at the dull ache of his bite, dried blood caked to my flesh.

CHAPTER
FIFTY-FIVE

Staring at my bloodied fingertips, I see the bruises around my wrists and my lips part when I notice the handcuffs hanging from the headboard.

"It was so we didn't mark him," Lexa says sleepily, coming forward.

"He doesn't want us to mark him?" I ask her, my stomach sinking at the thought.

"What, of course, he does. He was worried you would hate him if we did it while in heat."

"But that wouldn't have been his fault?" I tell her, and she sighs; while my eyes scan the room, the first thing I notice is the bag beside the bed. Curious because it reeked of his scent, I pick it up and find condoms making me quickly drop it, to notice the empty box beside it. I scrunch up my face, yet glad he thought to use them.

I try to remember last night, but the images are grainy, and some are downright embarrassing. Looking down at Axton, he looks peaceful with no lines marring his handsome face. He looks relaxed and content. My hand moves down his chest, and he tugs me closer with a groan. I stifle a giggle as he sluggishly tucks me closer, his hand fumbling above his head, reaching for the handcuffs.

Enjoying his sleepy reactions, thinking I'm still riddled with heat, I trail my fingertips down his side. "No, no more. It's broken," he whines, rolling into me like he can just crush me into the bed and go back to sleep. His heavy arm draped across my chest and shoulder as he chucks his leg across my waist.

His scent fills my nose, his neck a mere inch from my lips. Lifting my head, I suck on his skin, my lips trailing across his skin, making him shiver. He groans, his arm moving awkwardly for his hand to fall over my mouth.

"Khan, I tap out. You're up!" he whines, burying his face in the pillow next to my head. Chuckling, I lick his hand, and he turns his face toward me. Blinking hazily he presses his lips against my cheek muttering something about needing sleep.

Gripping his wrist, I pull it from my mouth, and he growls, clearly over fucking, making me laugh. "Climb aboard while I catch some sleep, help yourself," he mumbles. I try to push him off, but he doesn't budge instead, he starts snoring softly. With my one arm free, I try to push him off, kissing his shoulder, and he groans, his eyes opening to snatch the handcuffs.

"Greedy heat-ridden she-wolf, you're lucky I love you," he huffs.

"I love you too," I snicker as he sits up, half asleep; I pull him closer by wrapping my legs around his waist.

"Wait..." he growls, blinking rapidly and yawning. I raise an eyebrow at him as he yawns, unwrapping my legs from around him.

He grabs my wrist, clamping the handcuff on it, and catches me watching him. His brows furrow then he jolts. "Elena?"

"Axton." I chuckle, shaking my wrist at him.

"You're awake?" he says, cupping my face with his hand.

"And you're handcuffing me!" I tell him, and he blinks down at me for a second, then his eyes widen, his lips parting.

"It's not what you think, I...I'm not holding you here." he fumbles for words and for the key off of the bedside dresser.

"I'll undo it," he rambles.

"He's cute when he's scared of us." Lexa laughs.

"Scared of our reaction," I correct her. Axton, lets me go, leaning over and reaching for the key that sits right on the edge, his hand clutching the bedhead.

"I promise it's not what it looks like....I...." I clamp the other side of the handcuff on his wrist, and he freezes, peering down at me. His eyes move to his wrist, now attached to mine.

"What are you doing? I promise I have the key."

"I don't want the key. I'm just making sure you can't escape me." I tell him, moving quickly. I wrap my legs around him and twist. He makes an oomph noise as I reverse our positions, so I am now straddling his waist.

"Lena, I swear.... Ask Khan. I wa–" my lips cut his words off. He freezes beneath me, and my tongue traces the seam of his lips. He jerks away from me, giving me a concerned look.

He sighs, while I lean down recapturing his lips. Axton mumbles against my lips about me still being in heat. "I'm not in heat, Axton," I tell him, pulling back. He watches me for a few seconds.

"The boys?" he tilts his head to the side, observing me.

His free hand gripping my thigh, he runs his hand up my leg watching me. I shiver, but he clearly doesn't get the response my heat would give him because his brows furrow.

"With Eli and Michelle in the studio out back," he says cautiously.

"My pack?"

"My men are watching them, and Marco is with them." I nod my head, already knowing the answers I am asking. Axton and I, despite fighting, he has always come to my pack's aid when needed, so I knew even with me out of the picture, he wouldn't abandon them.

His lips part, and I can feel him tugging on the bond, feeling for my reactions, the heat that no longer exists. He goes to say something, but I cut him off.

"I'm not mad." I tell him.

"You're not mad?" he asks, and I shake my head.

"Maybe a little," I tell him. But I am completely the opposite of mad. I see the question in his eyes and feel him trying to lure the answer from the bond, but I block him out, and he sighs.

"Then why this,..." he glances at his wrist. "Just get it over with then; I am not accepting you rejecting me again, though—" I shake my head, my wrist is cuffed to him.

"This is so that you can't escape me. You forgot something," I tell him, lacing my fingers through his.

"I did?" he seems far too confused of a morning, much like me without my morning coffee, yet I never felt more clear-headed as I stared down at this gorgeous man, my mate. Mine.

"Yes," I smile down at him, feeling my canines lengthen slowly. "You forgot to let me mark you." I purr before ripping his head to the side and sinking my teeth into his neck. He grunts, his hand going to my hair, his finger tangling in it.

His blood floods my mouth, coating my tongue when I feel the bond explode, blasting right open as his emotions rush into me. I choke on the feelings rushing through me. Pulling my teeth from his neck, I run my tongue over his neck, sealing it before pressing my lips to his neck. He shudders, his hand fisting my hair.

"I love you," he whispers.

"I know....I love you too," I whisper, pulling back, and he lets me go. His hand moves to my face, and he cups my cheek.

"You know what you've done, don't you?" he worries.

"Yes, I made you mine as I am yours," I whisper, leaning down and kissing him. He lets out a shaky breath, kissing me back.

CHAPTER
FIFTY-SIX

Axton groans against my lips and tugs me closer so my body is flush against his. He rolls, shoving me on my back, and I wrap my legs around his waist when he pulls away. He looks down at me, and I move my hips against him, smiling deviously.

"Please, I think you rubbed the skin off it. It's basically raw meat at the moment," he whines, and I wiggle my hips beneath him again. He grunts, dropping his head on my shoulder.

"Fine. I'm starting to wonder if you only marked me so you can take advantage of me," Axton breathes out before chuckling.

I laugh. "That is only half the reason," I tell him.

"Hmm, what's the other half?" he asks.

"You are nice to look at too, and we make cute babies together," I shrug.

"Is that right?" he huffs, and I laugh. His breath fans against my neck, making me shiver when he collapses on top of me. The air in my lungs rushes out in a wheeze.

"Axton!" I rasp under his weight as I'm crushed into the bed; I try to shove him off.

"I am not just some fucktoy, Luna. I will not tolerate being spoken about in such a derogatory way," he snickers. I jam my fingers in his ribs, only to learn the man is not ticklish.

"Axton! Off!" I growl, and he laughs.

"Nope, pretty fucktoy is broken; I need new batteries. How about an IOU, though I'm pretty sure you do owe me a new cock since you broke mine." he chuckles, but he lifts his weight slightly off me. He peers down at me with a coy smile on his lips.

"Quite the predicament you have found yourself in, Luna," he purrs, nipping at my jaw.

"Yes, it appears I am being crushed by an alpha-hole, now off!" I taunt, and he purrs, running his nose across my cheek to my ear. He inhales my scent. Our scents are now mingled from me marking him, and the bond is complete. His lips travel down my neck when Lexa comes forward sluggishly.

"We need to get the boys and speak with the packs. Now we've marked him, we need to get them in one place, we won't be able to handle being away from him for long," Lexa yawns, and I sigh. As much as I want to laze about with my mate, I need to get up and check on our sons and my pack.

"The boys?" I ask him, and he groans.

"Ten minutes, please," he groans, rolling on his back and pulling me on top of him. His free hand trails up my spine. I close my eyes, enjoying the sound of his heart beating beneath my ear. This is how it should have been from the start. Yet our stubbornness and pride got in the way, as well as our anger and rivalry.

Lifting my head, I prop my chin on his chest, staring at the mark that now lies etched into his neck. "You're regretting it already?" he asks, but I shake my head, trailing my fingertips over it. Axton shudders beneath me, and his cock twitches against my thigh. Sparks rush over every inch of me where our skin is in contact.

"No, I was just thinking this is how it should have been," I tell him; that thought makes me a little sad. We've wasted so much time hating each other that we forgot we are supposed to love each other.

Exhausted so much energy on why we shouldn't be together,

forgetting we were destined to be. Axton nods his head slowly and bites down on his lip.

"No reason it can't be now," he finally whispers.

"You could always move back to the city, Elena. We could organize—"

"Yeah, I suppose it's time; I can't manage two packs on my own," I sigh, yet he is still rambling on, giving me every reason he can conjure as to why I should move back to the city, having not realized I just agreed.

"I'm even willing to let Sondra move into the–" he glances down at me, and I raise an eyebrow at him, a silly smile on my face.

"Wait, you said yes?" I nod again.

"Really?" he asks, his brows pinching.

"Well, that is a waste of my night; I had this entire speech ready. Me and Khan worked on it between fuck breaks," he muses.

"Well, in that case, I better hear it, then. Depending on what you say, I may need to change my mind," I chuckle.

He tilts his head to the side, watching me, his fingers skating down my face, and he tucks my hair behind my ear. Turning my face, I kiss his palm, and he smiles.

"Who would have thought I only had to fuck your brains out to make you move in with me?" he laughs. I roll my eyes at him when his arm snakes around my waist, hoisting me higher so he can kiss me. His lips are soft and warm against mine, gentle as he licks across the seam of my lips. Smiling, I kiss him back, my tongue tangling with his.

Suddenly I feel like I found my new favorite thing, kissing Axton. His fingers tangle in my hair as he deepens the kiss, tongue fighting with mine when he sucks my lip into his mouth, nibbling on it and teasing the swollen flesh. Eventually, he lets go, and I pull away and catch my breath.

"We should get the boys and head out to the pack; I need to tell the women to start packing." I groan, knowing how much of a task this will be.

"Wait, what... Now... as in right now?" Axton blurts.

"Is that a problem, Alpha?" I taunt, and he clamps his lips shut and makes a strange, strangled humming noise.

"Nope, not an issue. We can have it done. I thought you would say a week. What's a day?" he quips a little too fast.

I raise an eyebrow at him. "To pack Axton, not move. I'm good, but I'm not that good that I can move an entire pack in a day," I laugh. He sighs, looking relieved.

"Thank god, because I was thinking I was going to have a house full of women because I still need to clear out a few floors on the hotel." he chuckles. I peck his lips, moving to climb off him when I remember the handcuffs. Axton reaches over and retrieves the key, unlocking them. I rub my wrist.

Getting up, I wander into the bathroom to wash the sweat and remnants from last night off. A few moments pass and Axton enters the bathroom, sliding the shower door open and stepping in behind me. His hands instantly go to my hips, and he presses his lips to my shoulder when his phone starts ringing. He lets it ring out, only for it to immediately begin ringing again.

"Maybe you should get it?" I tell him, and he growls but slides the door open, stepping out. He wraps a towel around his waist, then moves into the bedroom, leaving the door open.

"Hey Marco," I hear Axton answer. Silence follows for a few moments, and I shut the shower off.

"Why, where are you?" Axton asks, and in his tone of voice, I shut the water off. Grabbing a towel and wrapping it around me, Axton is already moving around the room, snatching clothes and tossing them at me. My heart beats quicker when I feel the mind link opens up. My mother's tether tugging, and the next second, her voice is in my head.

"She's gone, Elena. She's gone. I can't find her!" she sobs hysterically.

"What's happened?" I ask, ripping my towel off and tugging on the clothes Axton tosses at me.

"We're on our way. What's the address?" Axton says, snatching a piece of paper. "We'll check the bakery, while you check the old rogue commune," I hear Axton tell Marco.

"Mom?" I order, and Axton hangs up the phone, turning to face me.

"Sondra, we all woke up and she was gone, her car was gone and she hasn't returned. Marco is out looking for her with the pack," my mother tells me, and my blood runs cold as I try to take in her words.

"We'll find her, Lena," Axton tells me, but I shake my head, snatching his keys off the dresser, and run for the door.

CHAPTER FIFTY-SEVEN

Axton

We left the boys with Eli and Michelle, knowing having to get them will only slow us down. Elena is a nervous wreck beside me, and all she has done is panic, conjuring up the worst-case scenario. What if the strigoi got Sondra? Or her father came back for revenge, or what if Osiris is behind it?

I have a feeling Sondra is missing because she chose to go missing; the strong old bat takes shit from nobody, so I doubt if someone came after her, she would go quietly.

"She may have run into town," I tell Elena, and she nods, staring off vacantly out the window. Her bottom lip quivers, and she presses her top teeth against it.

"Elena, we'll find her. Marco has gone to check the commune. We can check in town; she is probably at the bakery, eating all the cupcakes," I try to reassure her, and she turns her head to look at me.

"She's dying, Axton," she answers, and I swallow. Yeah, Marco had said something about taking care of her, but she looked okay the last time I saw her.

"We'll find her," I answer. We have to; I don't think Elena will cope with not knowing.

"Don't go to the bakery. Go to Mary's café," Elena whispers, and I glance at her. I nod my head, taking the next turn to head down the main street of the small, derelict town.

Pulling up along the curb, I don't see her car anywhere or any sign of her. Elena gets out to check the old café, letting herself in with a set of keys. She pauses at the door, and I stop on my way to the bakery to watch her. Her hands shake as she tries to get the key in the lock. Fear slivers through the bond, yet she is determined to find Sondra. Forgetting the bakery, I walk over to her and grab the key from her hand. She glances over her shoulder at me, and I brush my lips against her cheek and unlock the door.

"You don't have to go in there. I will check it out," I tell her. Elena, however, shakes her head.

Pushing the door open, Elena sucks in a deep breath. "How do you have a key," I ask her, and she sighs, glancing at me.

"Sondra bought this place for Mary, turns out Jake never bought it, so once her death certificate was in the place, it was handed back to Sondra, who in turn gave it to me."

"And you kept it?" I ask, a little shocked. She sighs, stepping inside further, and my stomach drops, feeling her anguish. "Have you been back here...you know, since?" I stop myself, only now realizing how much this place torments her.

"No, it's why Sondra gave it to me, she wanted me to burn it down, yet I couldn't bring myself to step inside it," she whispers while looking up at the ceiling of the apartment above.

The place is mostly empty, though the fridges are full of old fizzy drinks and outdated milk. Other than that, my men had cleaned the place pretty good.

Elena stops near the basement door that is ajar and glances at me. "Want me to check?" I ask, and she nods her head. Nodding once, I quickly rush down the stairs to the pitch-black basement, my vision adjusting as Khan steps forward. We peer around the place, and I walk to the back, calling out for Sondra but don't find her. However, I do find the cage that Mary and Alisha were both kept in. Turning around, I head back upstairs to find Elena, only she is no longer in the shop. I can feel she is close by, so I pull on the bond, using it to find her.

Climbing the stairs out to the back area, I see the apartment door open and rush up to find her. Stepping inside, it feels like déjà vu when I spot her. She holds the same look on her face. Back then, I thought she was petrified of me finding her shacked up with another man. Now, seeing the same expression, I recognize it for what it is. This place, her prison for so long. Something I used time and time again against her.

It is exactly the same as all those months ago, and I kind of regret not getting my men to clear it out. As I wander over to her, she is staring at the bed. I slip my arms around her waist, tugging her back against me.

"She's not here," Elena says, and I nod against her shoulder. Noticing the chains and cuffs on the bed, I swallow guiltily. Khan had tried to tell me, but I was angry; I only believed what I wanted to believe and chose her father's words over my mates.

Instead of helping her, I hurt her more. "Sondra once said that some things she wanted to take to her grave," Elena murmurs.

I turn my head on her shoulder. "This is one of mine," she whispers.

"Well, you know the saying, two can keep a secret if one is dead. Jake is dead, Elena," I tell her, but she shakes her head.

"No, he's not because he is seared into my memories. He got the easy way out. He took it to the grave, while I live with it," she murmurs.

"But you get to live, Elena. He hurt you, but—"

"He did more than hurt me, Axton. He broke me." she croaks. Her lips quiver and the bond feels as broken as the words sounded leaving her lips.

"Then I'll rebuild you, help put you back together again. It's my fault you were here anyway. You wouldn't have run, if I hadn't leaked that video."

"You were angry I rejected you," she tells me with a sigh.

"That's still no excuse for hurting someone I claim to love, I should have listened to Khan; I was just so focused on my plans to take down your father, too focused on my dreams I forgot you would have them too," I tell her. She nods her head but adds nothing, she doesn't need to.

I know she's forgiven me, I can feel it, I just hope she can forgive herself. Because right now, all I feel is her guilt. She feels guilty because she ran, but what option did she truly have? Guilt over Alisha, but how was she supposed to know her best friend was a vamp? Guilt for allowing it and not fighting back, all those things play on her mind, yet now sensing her thoughts so clearly. I realize she was doing the best she could with the hand she was dealt.

Unfortunately, that meant allowing some things to protect others, and now I see why she didn't try to run, the risk to Alisha and our sons outweighed the risk to herself. Her sanity, her body, and her heart were a sacrifice she could live with, losing them she couldn't. So she played along and... prayed I would come save her. Instead, I broke her all over again.

"Come on, we should find Sondra," she breathes out, turning and walking out of the apartment. I follow, closing the door behind me when cigarette smoke wafts to me, Elena looks back at me before rushing down the steps to the back of the café. Following her, she steps out the back of the store and I spot Sondra sitting in a green weathered plastic chair. She has a smoke between her lips. She is deathly pale, her skin clammy, and sweat glistens on her neck and forehead.

CHAPTER
FIFTY-EIGHT

"Sondra," Elena breathes, and Sondra looks up. She smiles, but it doesn't look right; it's forced, and I can tell she is in pain.

"I see you found me," she murmurs before coughing and choking on her cigarette. Elena instantly rushes over to her and rubs her back. Reaching for the glass of water on the table, I pass it to her when Elena snatches it and sniffs it. She scrunches her face up, passing it back to me. I sniff it, finding it is vodka, not water like it appears to be.

"Grab a glass of water from inside," Elena tells me. Sondra continues to cough but holds up her hand, it's shakes terribly, but she snatches the glass off me. Elena watches her worriedly and glances at me.

"Call an ambulance," Elena tells me.

"You'll do no such thing. Can't a woman die in peace?" Sondra snaps at her.

"I don't want you to die at all." Elena retorts.

"Well, it is not up to you; I want to die and die I shall. Not even the gods will stop me from croaking this time, the grim reaper is knocking, and he wants an accomplice; I have volunteered," she says, only to wheeze and start coughing again.

"I feel a hospital would be far more comfortable than this plastic chair. If you insist on dying, wouldn't you rather die in comfort?" Elena asks her. It's funny watching them, they have their own love language, and it comes out in short replies and sarcastic words thrown at each other.

Sondra sighs, her fingers white as she grips the table, and she leans back. Blood dribbles from between her lips, and she shakily wipes her mouth on the back of her hand.

"Why here, of all places?" Elena demands.

"You know why, Elena. Let's not play pretend. Besides, I didn't want to drop dead next to Marco. Only when I got here did I find this whole dying ordeal is taking a little longer than predicted, I kinda believed I would croak going over the bridge, but seems Floyd is trying to torture me more by dragging this shit out. You hear me, you old bastard, I am coming for you, not even death will save you from me!" she yells at the sky, shaking her fist. I raise my eyebrows at her.

"Oh stop looking at me like that! Now be a love and fetch me another glass of vodka, if I am going to hell, I am going drunk!" she huffs. Elena presses her lips in a line but nods for me to do as she asks, walking over to Sondra's car, I grab the bottle only to hear the chair scrape across the ground. Glancing back, I see Elena helping her to stand, but Sondra smacks her hands away, making Elena toss hers in the air.

"I'm coming, I'm coming, just hold your damn horses," Sondra mutters.

She stands upright, and wobbles on her feet. "I'm driving!" Sondra declares.

"Like hell you are, you may want to visit the grim-reaper but I sure as hell don't!" Elena scolds, snatching her keys before Sondra can off the table.

"Oi muscles, get here and help carry a legless old woman to the car," she snaps, clicking her fingers at me.

Chuckling, I walk over to her and scoop her up while Elena grabs the door.

"Now, now, stop that. Why so handsy!" she snaps at me.

"Exactly how am I supposed to grab you if I can't touch you?" I ask her. She seems to think for a second.

"He has a point," Sondra babbles to Elena. I set her in the seat of her car, but when I go to close her door, she clicks her tongue.

"Weren't you getting me a vodka?" she asks and I glance at Elena over the roof of the car. She sighs but nods and I quickly grab the bottle and her glass.

"Life's too short to wait for you to pour me a glass, just give it here, I'll show you how real women drink!" she tsk's. She swigs from the bottle and nestles back in her seat, pulling a cigarette from her packet. Elena climbs in the driver's seat and starts Sondra's car. On the drive home, I ring Marco and the relief in his voice is evident.

He tells me he will meet us back at the packhouse, yet the longer we drive, the more Elena keeps glancing in the mirror at Sondra. Peering over my shoulder, Sondra is leaning to one side, head slumped forward, bloody drool seeping from her lips and her unlit smoke has fallen into her lap.

Sondra mumbles to herself in her half drunk stupor and I turn back to the front. However, just before we arrive, the bumpy dirt road must wake her because she speaks.

"I always hated this place," she speaks, and Elena's eyes dart to her in the mirror. We say nothing, instead listening to her ramble.

"It was never home, not to me. It was a prison."

"So where was home, Sondra?" I ask, peering over to look at her. She laughs and shakes her head.

"Not here, wasn't there either. The closest to home I ever got was my shitty apartment next to Marco. Every other place was a prison, just a little shinier than the last." she murmurs, looking out at the fields. Elena stops the car halfway up the driveway. She swivels in her seat, looking back at Sondra, and I can tell she is barely holding it together.

"So, where do you wanna go?" Elena asks her and Sondra smiles sadly.

"Home, but it doesn't exist any more, not for me." Sondra says.

"We made this place a home. The women here love you like family," Elena tells her, and Sondra nods.

"Home is where your heart belongs, a piece of mine is here, but it's not my home. Those women are a pack, family. But home to me isn't a place. It's a someone. Someone I could never have."

"Marco?" Elena asks her, and she sniffles and nods. Elena looks at me, and I nod, letting her know Marco is on his way.

Elena keeps driving until Sondra tells her to stop. Women have gathered outside the packhouse. We sit in the car for a second when Sondra points to the old willow tree on the hill.

"That looks like a nice place to croak, I can see the shit hole for what is up there. What do you say muscles think you can carry me up that hill?" she asks me.

"Depends if I can touch you?" I ask her.

She slaps my arm. "How would you carry me, if you can't touch me?" she scoffs, and I open my door and climb out of the car.

CHAPTER
FIFTY-NINE

Moving to the rear of the car, the women crowd around, and I hear Elena trying to regather herself. Trying to slip a facade she has worn for too long back on. Clearing her throat, she moves to take one of the blankets her mother rushes out with.

Opening the rear door, Sondra grabs her vodka bottle, and I pick her up moving to the front of the car. Only when I do, Elena's entire pack is on their knees, baring their necks to Sondra. Sondra smiles and then shivers, Elena moves to wrap the blanket around her, and I start climbing the hill.

However, when we reach the top, Sondra speaks. "I was wrong about you," she tells me, making me glance down at her.

"Now I know you're dying, you just admitted you're wrong about something," I tell her and she chuckles softly. I sit on the ground and I prop Sondra between my legs so she can lean against me. Elena sitting beside me.

"You're nothing like your father, I used to think you would be just like him, having grown up in his image, but now I see you were just another of his victims." Sondra tells me, and I swallow.

"I'm sorry, I couldn't save her; I couldn't save any of them. If only

I had the courage to do what I did to Floyd back then, we may be having a different conversation. Maybe none at all." She muses.

"You couldn't have predicted the outcome of being with your mate, Sondra," Elena whispers.

"You're right, but I could have stopped it before he took more lives. I had plenty of opportunities. I just didn't take them. Same as your fathers, I could have ended them, but I didn't. Instead I convinced myself I would be the same as them if I did. Instead, I was the same because I sat back and did nothing." she sighs. Elena shakes her head but Sondra reaches out and grips her hand.

"But you two are different. You're both who you are in spite of your father's. Defeated them, conquered the trauma instead of passing it down to the next generation."

Elena laughs. "That is yet to be seen," she chuckles.

"No, I've seen it," Sondra tells her, and Elena looks at her.

"You left despite loving him because he was toxic. You didn't use your boys as an excuse to stay. You used them as your excuse to leave. So I know you will do the right thing by them if you're willing to break your own heart for them." Sondra tells her.

Sondra looks over her shoulder at me. "I mean no offense by that. I'm not just referencing you, but her father. She could have gone back and asked for forgiveness, but she didn't."

"Yes, you did, but it's okay," I chuckle.

"Yeah, I did. But it's the same for you, son. You overrode your ego and are trying to make up for your mistakes. That is more than your father ever cared to do. No, he would just beat her down until there was nothing left but a compliant shell of a woman. Therefore you are not the same, Elena is not beneath you, she is your equal. That is people's biggest mistake in life, heart, and ego. Sometimes, they follow their heart and stay not realizing they're giving them the power to keep breaking it. In turn they raise their children broken. Other's can't see past their ego to know their flaws so they can't work on fixing them. Neither of you are those people, neither of you are your fathers,"

"My childhood was good, Sondra," Elena tells her. "It was only when I grew older did dad turn into that." Elena sighs.

"But not for your mother, do you think she would hold the same answers, dear? She put all her time and energy into you kids hoping you didn't make the same mistakes, hoping he would be the man he said he was. It was only until he didn't keep his end of the deal that she realized she was lying to herself. Just like me with Floyd," Sondra tells her. She lifts the bottle to her lips.

"Gosh, who would have thought you were so depressing drunk, give me that." Elena tells her, taking the bottle and swigging from it, Elena chokes coughing and spluttering.

"Geez what is that, jet fuel?"

"Almost, I once fired my tractor up with this shit," Sondra tells her, taking the bottle back.

"You two promise me you won't ever sacrifice life for love," Sondra says. Elena's brows furrow and so do mine.

"It sounds funny now, but that is what I did. I sacrificed life for love that wasn't really love, just some twisted version of what I perceived as love. You two will be different, because both of you want the best for each other."

"It wasn't until I was old that I suddenly found myself comfortable in my own misery. It took me killing Floyd to realize I hated the person I also loved—years of living a step behind him, becoming and morphing into his shadow while mine faded away. So caught up in everything to do with him that I forgot what I wanted. Forgot who I am and who I truly loved." Sondra sighs.

"Instead, I became what he wanted me to be, just like your mothers did for your fathers. They sacrificed themselves until nothing was left, and now yours is trying to rebuild her life, just as I had to. And yours, Axton, is dead because it took me too long to realize I could have stopped it."

Elena drops her chin on her knees, watching the sunset. Sondra lifts her hand, brushing it down her hair before her hand falls limply to my leg and she clears her throat.

"I'm not saying this to hurt you, either of you, I'm trying to explain. I'm not saying your mother was wrong, Elena, she did what she thought was right at the time, just as I did, but it was because I was blinded by the mate bond, as she was. You become comfortably familiar in it. You spend so long with someone you eventually lose yourself within them. They slowly break the pieces off that you thought you could live without. Just like me, your mother lost herself, and it took her leaving to find herself again."

"We aren't the same," I tell Sondra and she nods.

"Resentment and sacrifice are the two things that anchor us, pull us down and slowly drown us. Resentment that he didn't see how much he was breaking me. Sacrifice that I allowed him to do it, sacrificing my own happiness allowing him to decide when I received it because my ego got in the way to notice my own toxic traits. I convinced myself that love was holding me here, but it wasn't, it was fear of losing everything that I sacrificed for, in the end what I thought I was gaining was nothing, instead I lost everything."

Hearing a car I glance over my shoulder to see headlights as Marco races to the packhouse. "You two are different, I know because I have seen it, you work well together, but fight for each other even when fighting against each other. Floyd never fought for me, it was always one sided." I tug the blankets higher, noticing the goosebumps lacing her skin.

"Floyd would have let me burn in the flames if it meant saving his own skin," she looks overhear shoulder at me and inclines her head. "But he'd walk through them and burn with you while trying to save you, rather than leave you behind." Sondra tells her.

"Like Marco?" I ask her and she nods.

"He tried to save me so many times, unfortunately I was too stubborn to realize. I thought he was on his brother's side, not realizing the only reason he stuck around was because I was with his brother." she sighs, sipping from her drink before coughing, blood spills from her lips. And Elena rubs her back.

CHAPTER SIXTY

Elena

Hearing a car door, Axton glances over his shoulder and so do I, only to see Marco climb out of his car, looking rather disheveled. "Marco will be here soon, he's on his way." I tell Sondra, but she shakes her head.

"He doesn't need to watch me die, the woman he fell in love with died when she married Floyd. He needs to hang on to her, not this withered, broken body that has suffered too much and lived longer than it deserved." Sondra murmurs between sucking in deep breaths. If only she knew how wrong she was, she deserved so much more than the hand she was dealt. Everyone makes mistakes, learning from them is redemption, and she learned from her the same as I learned from mine.

"How about you let me decide which version of you I love because last I checked there wasn't a version I didn't," Marco says, suddenly appearing next to me. Sondra looks up at him and so do I. He nods for me to move, and I take that as my cue to get up, allowing him to take my place, and he takes Sondra from Axton, setting her between his legs.

"You shouldn't be here, I don't want you to see me like this," she snaps at him.

"Shush. Fine, I am not here for you, I am here for me, to see a stubborn old brat off." he tells her while wrapping his arms around her tiny frail body. Sondra sighs, leaning back against him.

Getting up, I move toward Axton, and we both move to leave to give them some privacy.

"Where are you going?" Sondra asks and I look at Marco who pats the ground beside him.

"Can't leave me here with this leech, what if he drains me dry?" Sondra snips at me and I chuckle.

"Your blood is so old it's like powdered milk running through those veins, I wouldn't want to catch wrinkles," Marco tells her as I sit between Axton's legs.

Sondra laughs and Marco kisses her temple before propping his chin on top of her head. We sit in silence for what feels like forever, listening to her breathe, each breath she takes, there is a longer pause between, that leaves me holding mine.

I can see my pack sitting and standing along the porch waiting, watching in silence.

"It should have been us," Sondra rasps.

"It should have been," Marco replies, turning his head slightly and resting his cheek on the back of her head while rocking her back and forth. Tears stream down his face as he closes his eyes, his lips quivering as he rocks her.

"In another life," he tells her and she tries to speak but it comes out in a wheeze, blood spewing from her lips. Her death draws on and I feel like walking off. Yet she asked me to stay so I remain. Each second that passes I wish her next breath is her last, just so I don't have to listen, just so she isn't suffering anymore.

"It's time to go old girl, what are you hanging around for, it better not be for me?" Marco asks her, his voice shaky as he gets the words out. Her hand twitches and she grabs him, her body convulsing as she tries to suck in a breath. Each wheeze grows louder than the last, her panic screaming back at me when she opens her watery eyes. Marco breaks down, and nods his head.

"I'm here, I'm here," he tells her and I look away, unable to watch her suffer. I press my face into Axton's chest, and he grips my hair, his hands covering both my ears just in time before I witness Marco break her neck. But I still hear the faint crack, closing my eyes, I suck in a deep breath as silence falls and Axton moves his hands, and kisses the top of my head.

Besides my own breathing and the sound of Axton's heart against my ear, I hear nothing for ten beats. Then I hear Marco wail, the sound so heartbreaking I never want to hear the sound again. It screamed how much he loved her, how much it hurt to lose her. It screamed his torment, a few seconds later the howls of my pack ring through the air as they screamed theirs.

Screamed for a woman that didn't realize she saved all of us, instead, she believed she failed us, but she never did, no she taught us who we are. I was never the Alpha of this pack, Sondra was, she created it and handed it down to me. Sondra was the true Alpha of 'Elysian Fortuna Moonlight Pack' She had created our piece of paradise, and Fortuna is a second chance, and she gave that to all of us. Only now do I realize we were also hers, a second chance at finding herself.

CHAPTER
SIXTY-ONE

The next week passes in a daze, one I wish stayed forgotten. Marco hasn't spoken, just sat in her room for the entire time, only leaving for her funeral. Axton and I have tried to get him to leave, knowing he needs blood but nothing we do seems to work. Yet as each day passes he slips further into psychosis, induced by his insatiable hunger. After the second day when we realized he hadn't fed since four days before Sondra's death, Axton having counted the blood bags in the basement, he forbid me going into the room by myself.

Which is hard because one thing I know is Sondra wouldn't want us moping, life goes on, and things need to be taken care of. So, for the past two days, I have done nothing but organize housing and work details for our move to the city. Axton today is dealing with never ending strigoi attacks, his absence from the city really amped up the attacks, so much so Osiris having taken over for a mere week, called him begging him to come back to help since the city has been in a panic state since the first one, on the night of Sondra's death.

We couldn't seem to catch a break and even the boys are teething so it's been a never-ending clusterfluck. Having finished packing up the kitchen I walk to the closet to start that task next. Most of the pack was already in the city, the trucks having picked up the women's belongings yesterday, so there is only the main packhouse left to move. My mother and Luke are moving into the penthouse apartment Axton owns. So today we are planning to pack what's left of the pack house for the truck arriving tomorrow.

Reaching the top shelf, Axton's arms wrap around me from behind as I pull down the box from the top cupboard in the huge linen closet. "I need to head into the city," he whispers, dropping his head onto my shoulder.

"How long? I can meet you at the packhouse tonight, mom and I should be done here by this afternoon hopefully," I tell him and he nods and then sighs.

"Has he come out?" Axton asks me, and I shake my head peering down the hall toward Sondra's room. None of us have touched her room. Most of Sondra's belongings we have put in storage for Marco to go through when he's ready, despite him claiming he wants nothing.

Axton exhales, kissing my cheek then wandering down the hall toward her room. "I put the boys in their bouncers downstairs. Luke is watching them while your mother brings some boxes up from the basement," he tells me as I follow him. Axton stops at the door and knocks, but like usual Marco doesn't answer so he pushes the door open. Marco is still sitting in her rocking chair, staring at her bed, his fingers steepled under his chin, with a dark expression on his face.

"Marco?" Axton calls out while stepping into the room. Axton moves cautiously, stepping in front of him.

"Get up, Marco." Marco says nothing, but leans back in the chair, watching Axton.

"I could have changed her," he mumbles. His voice was rather raspy after so long of barely speaking.

"Sondra didn't want that," Axton reminds him.

Marco rocks back and forth in her chair and nods. "No, she didn't. Maybe if I convinced her when she was younger she may have taken the offer, but I was too late. We were always too late. Fighting against time, looking for the perfect opportunity which never came and when it did, she was too old to take it. She believed she was a burden to me." Marco says, looking over at me.

"Always too late. I was too late to stop Floyd from marking her, too late to stop their wedding, too late at telling her I love her. Always so focused on work, waiting for an opportunity that never came. I missed my opportunity to save her. Instead, I willingly gave her up to him thinking that is what she wanted when all she wanted was for me to save her from him." Marco whispers, Marco rubs a hand down his face, looking rather tired, it makes me wonder if he has slept at all, or if he has just been lost in his own head.

"And now that is the burden I carry, the burden of time. Time I thought I never had and will never get again."

"So why are you wasting more of it by sitting here?" Axton asks him.

"Time is irrelevant without her now. I was always fighting to get back to her, and now I have no reason to keep fighting; I already lost any time I perceived as valuable," he chuckles.

"I wasted it, and because I did, it killed her." Marco states.

"I don't know, but your crazy is starting to show and if Sondra was here, she would be beating it back into its box. So instead of wasting more of this never-ending time you have, why don't you come do something productive with me, like save the pack that Sondra worked so hard to build from being eaten by a strigoi?" Axton suggests.

Marco pauses and seems to think for a second. Yet Axton is right, so long in here and he is starting to show sides of him he usually kept hidden. He wasn't even trying to hide his fangs, usually he did, mostly he tried to keep what he is hidden. However, now he dropped the mask and doesn't seem to care.

"I can't go into the city. I am not even sure I can leave this room right now, Axton. Your scent is enticing enough. If I step out there, I may just kill somebody. Sondra would be furious if I killed somebody, especially one of her own." Marco tells him, only as he speaks the words do I realize why he is in here. Lost in his own thoughts, he ignored instinct for far too long, leaving him trapped and making him ravenous. The only safety was in this room, away from temptation.

"Are you trying to make me look bad? Damn, Marco, I swear you just like the damn taste of me. Blood bags not doing enough for you these days, you have a freezer full downstairs?" Axton snaps at him while unbuttoning his jacket. I stare at him, wondering what he is doing before looking at Marco. Axton shrugs off his jacket, tossing it on Sondra's bed, and shakes his head.

"I just fucking ironed this shirt too," Axton huffs, unbuttoning his white button down shirt. He hands it to me and I hesitantly step into the room, only for Marco to move with speed I miss. Axton's threatening growl sends shivers down my spine when Marco moves with a blood crazed gleam in his eyes. Axton cutting off his path toward me as if he expected it. Marco shakes his head, staggering back and blinking rapidly.

"Mark my mate and I mark your chest with a stake," Axton growls, while Marco shakes his head, his body twitching and he swallows.

"Elena, leave the room. Shut the door behind you, please." Axton says calmly, holding his shirt out to me. I glance at Marco then Axton who stands chest to chest with Marco. My hands shake as I take his shirt, rushing from the room as he asked. My heart thumps erratically in my chest when I peer back in.

"Close the door, Lena. I'll be out in a minute," Axton tells me. Lexa urges me to listen, but I worry for my mate. Reluctantly, I shut the door. The moment I close the door I hear a savage growl, and struggling. I hold my breath, and Lexa presses to the surface in case Marco comes out.

Pain flickers through the bond fleetingly, as I hear stuff being smashed around and my hand twitches for the door handle. I can hear fighting, hear that Axton shifted when I hear a loud thump which makes my heart jolt in my chest. When silence falls, I grip the handle, only to hear Axton's voice.

"Did you have to take a chunk out of me? I'm not a fucking steak, you damn cannibal," he scolds. Exhaling in relief, I open the door to find Marco pressed to the floor, Axton straddling him naked, having shifted back. He has a huge bite mark on his arm, ribs and even his shoulder blade. Blood cascades over his chest and back and I near faint at the sight of him. Axton looks like he had a blood-bath, puncture wounds in his neck yet not in the correct place to mark him. Marco, however, is also in the same state, Khan having torn him to pieces. The room is nearly completely upturned, and stuffing from the mattress covers the floor like snow.

"Your balls are touching my fucking leg!" Marco snarls.

"Your teeth were in my damn neck, so I guess we're even!" Axton retorts. I clear my throat and both of them look at me.

Axton looks down at Marco pinned on the floor and Marco wipes his mouth with his thumb, before sucking the blood off it.

"Wow, well this is awkward, just one man's balls on another man's leg, a few love bites, nothing sordid, just a drive-thru snack, nothing to see here," Marco quips. Axton growls at him, shoving him off his feet.

"Clearly, he likes to be the top! I don't know how I feel about that," Marco says, dusting himself as he sits up.

"Those were my good pants," Axton snarls, standing up.

"And that was my good hand, you damn savage! You know you're poisonous to me, right?" Marco snarls, holding his hand up to show Axton. I look at his hand to see where Khan had bitten him, his hand black and looking infected.

"Fuck!" Axton curses.

"I'm fine. I'm too old for such a pissy bite to affect me," Marco tells him. Axton snarls, reaching for his hand.

Marco jerks it back. "We don't need to hold hands afterward. Your mate is right there, have you no manners," Marco snaps at him and I raise an eyebrow at him while Axton rolls his.

"I can see why you and Sondra got on so well, the same snarky sarcastic sense of humor," Axton snaps as he bends down, snatching his jacket and holding it up. Claw marks shredded through it. He groans. "Hers was far better," Marco replies, and even now, with his normal facade back in place, I can still see the mention of her name causes him pain. Just now, not in a blood craze, he has better control of his emotions to mask it.

"You can borrow one of mine. I have few in the car," Marco says, back to his normal self.

Marco moves to the dresser, the only thing really left intact. He picks up a photo from it.

"Next life my love, next life we'll get it right," he mumbles only just loud enough for me to catch. Axton watches him worriedly, then grabs a sheet, wrapping it around his waist. A few minutes pass and Marco seems to be slipping back into the same depressive mood.

"Marco?' Axton calls, drawing him back to us. Marco jumps and sets the photo back down. He clears his throat and straightens his shoulders.

"We have work to do." Marco speaks, walking out of the room and past me without so much as a glance back. Axton wanders out slowly and sighs.

"Reckon, he'll be alright?" I ask him, and he shrugs.

"No idea, but at least he is out of this room." Axton tells me. He presses his lips to mine briefly. "I will see you tonight." he sighs. "Now to go try to squeeze into one of his damn suits, or I am going to the meeting in this old sheet," he chuckles, and I hold his shirt out to him. He takes it, pecking my cheek.

"I love you!" he calls over his shoulder.

"Love you too," I chuckle, watching him leave. When he does, I turn back to close Sondra's door. Sucking in a deep breath, I pull it closed and get back to work.

CHAPTER
SIXTY-TWO

A xton
  Later that night.

Unlocking the penthouse apartment, I show Louise around. Luke races up the hall, but I can tell she is nervous about being back in the city.

"You know you and Luke can stay at home with me and Elena until you're comfortable?" I remind her. She peers around, forcing a smile onto her face.

"Don't be silly, besides you and Elena need some time to yourselves, and some privacy." Louise tells me.

Sighing, I start twisting the key off the key ring when I hear Luke sing out. "Can I have this room?" he calls to his mother and I glance down the hall, he is in Elena's old room. I haven't been here since the day after she left me the second time. Unable to stay here, her scent was on everything, though I had sent a cleaner to tidy the place.

"No, I changed my mind, I want this one!" Luke sings out a second later, wandering into my old room.

"Pick whichever one you want, just not the main one, that's your mother's," I tell him and he huffs.

"But this one hasn't got a bathroom." he whines, wandering back to Elena's old room. I chuckle and so does Louise as I pass her the keys she'll need. I also write down the security code.

"Fridge and pantry are stocked. I sent Eli out earlier, and—" I wander down the hall to show her the linen cupboard knowing they'll need fresh sheets and towels; the others are probably a little stale and dusty.

"Towels, linen. Phone is on, and packhouse number is beside it. Also the receptionist downstairs has all the pack numbers and you have the mindlink!" I tell her. She smiles and wanders to Elena's old room and I see Luke sitting on the end of the bed opening an envelope.

"What have you got?" Louise asks him and I am about to wander down the hall when I hear her scold Luke.

"You don't open other people's mail."

"It's not other people's mail, look it's Elena's handwriting," Luke says and I stop. I glance back at the door.

"Exactly Elena's handwriting, meaning it is not yours!" she tsk's and I hear her sigh. Turning back to the room, Louise comes back out with the envelope, holding it out to me.

"It is addressed to you," she says. I take it, turning it over and indeed it is Elena's handwriting.

"That must have been the letter she said she left that we never found," Khan tells me. I nod, putting it in my jacket pocket.

"Aren't you going to read it?" Khan asks.

"Not sure I want to here with Louise, I doubt it has anything good in it," I tell him and he growls, knowing I am right.

"Elena said she'll swing by in the morning to grab you with the boys on the way out of the city, the truck arrives at the packhouse after noon," I tell Louise only for her to growl. She spins around, pointing a finger through the door at Luke.

"No jumping on the bed!" she scolds. I chuckle, shaking my head and wandering off when she sings out.

"Thank you," she says and I stop at the front door. I give her nod, before gripping the handle and walking out, excited to get home to my boys and my mate.

When I reach the bottom, I check security and make sure patrols are run around the building before climbing in my car. Shrugging my jacket off, I toss it on the passenger seat but grab the envelope out. Turning it over, I read the front, recognizing her handwriting easily. The front of the envelope reads.

For the mate I love to hate.....Axton

Opening the envelope, I suck in a breath wondering what she wanted to say back then, yet I also wonder why the cleaning lady never mentioned finding it. Pulling it out, Khan presses forward also wanting to read, well invade my thoughts with his running commentary while I read it.

> Axton,
>
> You have probably figured out I am gone by now. So I wanted to explain. But first things first, I am not coming back, so don't look for me, though I will find a way to contact you to let you know the boys arrived safe. I have picked out the names already, and one might surprise you. I wish it didn't have to be this way, but I don't see this working out when you only see me as property. Though I was willing to try, only this time you weren't.
>
> I never ran off to be with Jake... someone I thought was a friend, turned out to be a monster that will forever haunt me. But not as much as you will. You haunt me for a different reason though. Jake I never wanted. What he did I never asked for or wished for. I never loved Jake. What he did haunts me, his

touch repulsed me, and sometimes I can still feel his hands, feel his fingers wrapping around my throat. Feel his breath on my neck. The fear of him haunts me.

But you? I loved you, even though you were hurting me too. And you haunt me for a very different reason.

You have no idea how much I prayed to the moon goddess that you would find us. That my father would. Anyone. But mostly you. I carry your sons, so I knew they'd be safest with you, I thought I would be. I once perceived hope as a fantasy, a conjured-up idea that you would come save us. Believed in it wholly, believed you would come for us and you did.

The relief of seeing you walk through that door was so immense. Finally I could breathe... Only instead you stole my breath. You rejected me. I just wanted to touch you, know the nightmare I found myself in was over, know our boys were safe, that I was going home. I didn't even care about where home was as long as it was going back with you.

Only instead of being my freedom, you just became my next captor. I went from one cage to another, only this time I actually loved my tormentor.

I'm sorry I ran the first time, and I see what a mistake it was, but can you honestly say you wouldn't have done the same? Stomped down and destroyed by one Alpha, yet I was expected to run into the arms of another? Another Alpha who decided it was okay to destroy me as long as he got his end game.

To me, you were just as bad as he was, you wanted to enslave a mate, my father wanted to enslave a daughter, then Jake wanted to enslave a blood bag, a toy, something for him to torment and play with. He played with my body, ruined it. But you played with something far more valuable, my heart.

Only you didn't just play with it. You broke it. Showed me how replaceable I am, showed me what it would be like to be loved by you, which is not the happily ever after I dreamt about.

Always pick the lesser of two evils. So I picked you to place all my hope in, but it turns out you were worse than them all. You were worse because when you found me; I thought I would be given the opportunity to be your mate, equal because mates are supposed to be, only you showed me we're not.

Instead, I just became your breeder, a means for an heir. I thought I could forgive you, and even after everything I truly tried. Yet now stuck in my golden cage, the mirage that was once hope has now dissipated.

I'm done being a prisoner, I'm done being in someone's shadow, but most of all, I am done being disappointed. Everyone expects something of me while I am told not to expect anything in return. I wanted a mate. Even now, I am waiting for you to come home, waiting for you to change your mind, because despite hating you, I still want you, still love you. It may be the bond, it may not be, but you hurt me, as I hurt you, but I won't let you hurt our sons.

I refuse to live like this, I can't. I also won't let you take them from me.

You wanted a child. I guess you got what you wanted, 2 of them in fact, too bad you can't have them without their mother.

I will not apologize for running this time. This time I am not running because I am scared of being with you, this time I wanted you. You just didn't want me. So this time I am running for our sons and a future I know I don't have with you. I hope you find what you're looking for Axton, I just hope it's not me.

Because if there is anything I know about hope. It's that it's always better conjured up than finding it in reality because once you find it, you realize how easily it is crushed.

Bye Axton.

P.S. I'll be stealing your car and raiding your safe.

PPS. Tell Khan I'm sorry, and I love him, but you? I hope you choke on my metaphorical ghost dick!

Also the laxatives were totally Lexa's idea, she decided to double your dosage, though it was mine to throw out all the toilet paper. Happy shitting!

Love, Elena x

My stomach sinks reading her letter and I fold it back up. Khan is quiet and my guilt nags at me. I knew I was hurting her, it was my intention back then, but not anymore. I fucked up, we both did.

"And now we make it up to her," Khan tells me.

"You mean I have to make it up to her, she said she loved you, she told me to suck her dick!" I tell him.

"Well, then you suck her ghost dick!" Khan orders, and I chuckle.

"Though I must admit the toilet paper was a shitty move," Khan agrees with me as I start the car to drive home.

"You reckon? I had to wipe my ass on a pair of socks!" I tell him and he laughs.

CHAPTER
SIXTY-THREE

There's something about doing laundry that always made me feel at ease. Perhaps it's because it is something I often did with my mother when I was a child. Or perhaps it's because it is a way to show Axton how much I want to be here with him. Folding the boys' basket first, I put them away, using that time to also check on them. Both Kyan and Bane are sleeping peacefully in their beds, their cheeks rosy from teething.

Humming quietly to myself, I return to the laundry and put away one of my dresses, then move along to Axton's shirts I ironed earlier, hanging them up before moving to the clothes left in the basket. Soon only his ties rested at the bottom of the laundry basket, and I bend over to pick up a few of them, ready to put them away.

What I didn't expect was a large pair of hands firmly grabbing me from behind, grasping tightly at my hips. I yelp in surprise from the fright before I somewhat relax when I realize it is Axton, sparks rushing over my skin where his hands lie. He presses into my back and leaves a rough kiss on my exposed neck, causing me to shiver as his lips brush my mark.

"Axton." I chuckle, catching my breath. I drop my chin, feeling his warm tongue run over my neck, his stubble tickling. He pulls away, letting out a growl as he embraces me. I chuckle, trying to get my heartbeat back to normal as I crane my neck to look at him. "I didn't see you there. You could have sung out."

"Lost in thought?" his voice low and husky as he moves his hands upwards, grasping at my breasts through the fabric of my shirt—a t-shirt I've stolen from him. I let out a whine noise not wanting the distraction, but knowing I'll give in any way, unable to resist the bond, and also not wanting to. I tense up at his sudden, delicate touch. The mate bond's ability to awaken arousal is something I'm unsure I will ever get used to.

"Ax," I mewl while his touch awakens a longing inside of me, heat and sparks of arousal running through my veins. Axton, breathing heavily into my neck, makes me tremble in excitement when he soon starts to pepper kisses instead, making me cringe at his ticklish stubble.

"Stop! I have to put these away first," I whine at him when he bumps the ironing board, knocking over the piles I just folded and stacked on top. I growl at him, but he growls back.

"How about you leave it for tomorrow?" he offers. I hold back a laugh. When he says leave it tomorrow, he means he'll just hastily shove everything away. Not that there's much to put away. I did most of it already. "I can think of a few other things to do." he whispers, nipping at my mark.

"Though I must admit, I do like seeing you in my shirt, doing the laundry. So domesticated and *mine*." He laughs and I pull away, raising an eyebrow at him. Seeing Axton this riled up makes it hard to think straight, the bond being flooded with his desires only amplifying mine. My whole body heats.

Axton presses his crotch against my ass from behind, and I can feel the already huge bulge in his pants pressing into me. "What's got into him?" Lexa wonders, with a laugh.

I press myself back against him, and he groans.

"I think you have the right idea in mind," I tease back, as his hand slips beneath my shirt, fingers grazing my pussy. Ironing Elena, you're supposed to be ironing! Just this action alone makes the ache between my legs throb harder.

"Anything specific in mind?"

I didn't think I had a high sex drive, yet when home I can barely keep my hands off him. Turns out my nonexistent sex drive was because I hadn't met him yet. As long as I could get my hands on him, I didn't care what we did. I already know I will succumb completely, Axton being my undoing, and he knows it with his teasing touches and the dirty messages he was sending all day.

Now.

Tomorrow.

Forevermore.

He is mine, and I am happily his.

He chuckles, wrapping his arms around my shoulders before rummaging in his pocket. Glancing over my shoulder, I see he has a piece of paper.

I instantly recognize my messy handwriting and try to reach for it. My heart beats erratically, knowing the hateful things I said. We were finally getting along and the idea that a stupid letter ruining it nearly sends me into a panic attack.

"Don't read that!" I snap, but he holds me tighter, pressing his forehead against mine.

"I already did. I'm not upset," he whispers. "You're right, about all of it," he tells me. I exhale, trying to turn in his arms to take it from him when he clicks his tongue.

"I want you to undress for me, and then hand me one of my ties. So I can tie you up." I jerk away from him, only for him to hold me tighter.

"You want to tie me up?" I question. His eyes flicker, and he smiles seductively. "Scared, Elena?" he asks, gripping my hips and tugging me against his crotch.

"No..." I narrow my eyes at him, untrusting of his intentions, yet the bond tells me he is in a playful mood. He just wants me, but I know he has no kinks, so why the sudden desire to tie me up?

"Why?" I question, and he grabs me and then purrs, burying his face in my neck.

"You know why," he growls, nipping at my chin.

Just hearing the words causes my legs to tremble as my arousal spikes. The thought of being at his complete mercy and rendered to be nothing more than a toy always made me feel on the edge, terrified. Yet now with Axton, it excited me. Only Axton could turn my fears into desire. Axton won't hurt me. But I think that stupid counselor I had come out for the women three days ago got in his head. He's been weird since. She wasn't even there to see me, yet I somehow got hooked into it by Axton. How she went from a grief counseling to trauma one is beyond me. Lexa and I believe Axton set us up, he is the one that recommended her after all.

"Axton..."

"You've been handcuffed, you were fine," he growls, giving another push against me that made my knees almost give out. "I was in heat!" I tell him before losing that train of thought when I feel his hand cup my pussy and a moan escapes my lips.

"Please...I have," I needed to finish the folding, but his fingers distract me.

Axton lets out a seductive chuckle as he stops grinding into me. "Begging are we?" Axton asks.

"No!"

"Fuck if you won't, I will," Lexa pants in my head, wanting a piece of him.

It looks like he has already begun his teasing games. From this alone, I know I would become a needy, begging mess. All I currently want is to have my clothes ripped off of me so I can throw him on the bed. But why has he brought the letter out? And when did he find it? Once again, I lose that train of thought.

Axton's tongue runs over my neck, causing me to shiver as he teases my mark and sucks on it.

"In your letter." he purrs, lips trailing along my neck. He sucks on my mark and his arm barely slips around my waist before I crash to the floor.

"Lena?" he purrs.

"Hmm, the..." Axton chuckles.

"Yes, the letter." he hums.

"What about it?" I breathe, my hand reaching back to tug him closer. Desire courses through me. His hands on my body sending sparks everywhere.

"Do you remember what you said?" he asks. I shake my head, not caring in the slightest what that stupid letter said.

"Tell Khan I love him and you, you can suck my metaphorical ghost dick!" Axton growls, and I freeze. His tongue trails along the back of my neck to behind my ear, he flicks it before sucking and nibbling on it.

"I don't know about sucking your cock, but I will be eating this pussy." he purrs, his hand squeezing between my legs. A groan leaves me and my pussy throbs as his hand squeezes harder, fingers pressing against my opening.

CHAPTER
SIXTY-FOUR

He then lets go of me, takes the tie that had been in my hand, and backs away. As our eyes clash, I see his eyes filled with burning lust and desire. I quickly pull off the t-shirt I've been wearing and because it belongs to Axton, it is two times my size that it reached just above my knees. Every second without Axton's touch is torturous, and I want more, need more.

My choice to undress had been the right one, because I see the excited grin appear on Axton's face as he steps closer to me, carefully running his hands over my naked skin. His hands are firm and warm, and he leans in to place a kiss on my collarbone before he pulls away once more.

"Okay, fine. But burn that?" I tell him, pointing to the letter still clutched in his hand.

"On the bed first!" he commands, and I raise a brow.

"You want it or not?" he asks and I roll my eyes but obey his command and crawl onto the bed. Folding my arms across my chest I rest my back against the soft sheets as I wait.

Axton sets the letter down and I go to reach for it when he crawls up after me with the tie in hand. He shoves me back. "Hands above your head,"

I do as he asks and feel the thrill running through every inch of my body, my heart frantically beating in my chest as he grips my hands, firmly tying my wrists together with the tie. He pulls at them to make sure the knot is strong enough and not loose enough for me to get out of unless I use my claws.

It is arousing to feel the fabric slightly dig into my skin like this, leaving me completely restrained.

As he lets go of me, I hear him let out a soft laugh as he once more runs his hands over my body then he leans forward and kisses me. He wanders lower and lower until one of his hands reaches between my legs, coating his fingers in my juices as he rubs them back and forth.

I tip my head backward, enjoying his teasing, staring at the ceiling with half-open eyes as pleasure courses through me, just a simple touch already riling me up to this extent, has my body aching with a frantic need to be touched.

"Now back to your letter," Axton teases as he pushes two fingers inside of me, making me gasp at the sudden sensation of fullness. Axton thrusts right away, moving quickly as he thrusts upwards with skillful, hooked fingers.

"Are you listening?" yet my thoughts are focused on his fingers.

Pleasure rippling through me with every single thrust makes me writhe under his touch. Only he stops. "What?" I growl, annoyed.

"Just getting your attention." he teases, eyes flashing.

He continues to move his fingers in and out of me, causing the slow buildup of pleasure to make me go insane as I feel my walls tighten around him. He is so good at this, using just the right pace as my breathing speeds up and becomes quick and shallow.

"Axton... ah.... Axton..."

"Are you listening?" he teases.

"Yes, yes! I swear if you stop I will--"

"Steal the damn toilet paper and put laxatives in my drink?" he asks.

"Wow, you just killed it with that sort of dirty talk!" I growl, then pout. Axton chuckles and I'm tempted to kick him in his handsome face when his fingers move inside me again.

My mind becomes quickly clouded, lust and desire consuming me completely as I try to buck my hips upwards to match the rhythm of his fingers, craving more.

"Hm, so wet for me." he purrs, slipping his fingers out slowly.

"Ax," I beg, spreading my legs even further as he continues to shove his fingers inside me.

As the word escapes my lips, I feel him pull them out of me. I groan at the sudden loss of friction, desperately needing more of it. But the complaints are short-lived.

Axton brushes his fingers up over my core, and I shudder a gasp of relief rushing out of me as I roll my hips to meet his hand. He pushes two fingers into me, his eyes watching me when he bends down to suck on my clit, and I hum with pleasure. Fuck, I could never get tired of him.

My breath is raspy in my throat, and my arousal is maddening. Axton adds a third finger making me writhe, and the ties around my wrist draw tighter as I slide against the sheets. He increases his pace, swirling wetly around my clit while his fingers thrust against my walls.

He angles his fingers up and sucks harder, and it is enough to tip me over the edge. My body stiffens, walls clamping around his fingers, and I cry out, riding out my orgasm.

Axton grunts as he pulls his fingers out of me, he then wipes his fingers on the bed sheets. My entire body is trembling and I'm out of breath, as I tug against the restraints.

I watch him unbuckle his pants and pull them down just enough to expose his cock.

He gives me a seductive grin and groans as he positions himself over me, rubbing his cock against my folds slowly, all to tease.

"You want my cock?" he purrs and I wiggle, if I wasn't tied right now he would be sorry for teasing me.

With that, Axton finally pushes inside.

Slowly, so slowly that I'm about to go *insane* as I feel myself stretch around his thick length. "Fuck, Lena," Axton groans, sheathing himself inside me.

It almost sounds like a prayer, making me tighten up even more around him. He moves one of his hands upwards, grasping at my already tied wrists while he rests his other one on the mattress right next to my body to properly steady himself.

"Oh!" I gasp, when he pulls out thrusting back in, shoving me further up the bed with the force.

The pace is quick, his thrusts rough as he slams into me. I moan loudly as I feel myself tightening around him, my whole body trembling as the heat builds.

"Fuck, I love your pussy..." Axton moans from above, pulling out almost completely before he pushes back inside just as roughly, making me scream. All I want to do is to wrap my arms around him and pull him to me. But I can't, with my arms restrained.

"More," I breathe out, losing myself to his blissfully painful thrusts, Axton slams into me, harder.

Truthfully, I don't know what I'm begging for.

All I know is that I want more of it as I slowly feel myself dissolve under his touch. We move in sync, with me rocking my hips upward to the motion of his thrusts, making him delve into me even deeper.

It is so primal and intoxicating, it makes me unable to control myself as I needed more. It feels like I'm on the edge of my heat yet I know that is far off. He pants loudly, and I feel his rapid hot breath against me as he leans in closer, capturing my lips. "Please, Ax," I mumble against his lips

"I know," Axton growls.

He let go of the mattress with his hands and moves it to rest between us. He grazes his fingertips against me, never stopping his thrusting for a single moment. I whimper in anticipation. His thumb roughly presses down on my swollen clit as he starts circling the area—I lose it completely.

After just a few more seconds, I hit the edge and completely fell over.

"Axton..."

My screams echo through the bedroom as I hit my peak, feeling the ripples of pure fire run through me in rough, quick waves. My pussy squeezes around him while he keeps thrusting. Axton laughs, his lips slamming down mine, to muffle my cries. "Shh, the boys are sleeping next door," he chuckles. I don't get to answer as his hand falls over my mouth, the other hand gripping the headboard as he slams into me, harder, his thrusts brutal as he chases his own release.

He follows me over the edge half a minute later, moaning my name as I fall still beneath him when he curses, moving to rip himself out of me.

I lock my legs around his waist.

"Elena, unless you want more...fuck." he curses again and I feel his cock twitch inside me, Axton has been very clear about wanting more kids, angry with himself for missing the boys' birth, so I am not worried.

"It's fine," I breathe.

Now with the arousal out of our system, we look at each other trying to steady our breathing. My arms feel like jelly, and Axton brushes the backs of his fingers against my cheek.

"I love you," he whispers.

"I love you too," I breathe out. He pulls out of me and then unties my wrists.

"I wasn't too rough, was I?" he worries but I shake my head.

"I love it rough when it comes to you," I tell him as I sit up next to him, pressing my lips to his.

Axton pulls me on top of him, his arms slipping around my waist while his other hand trails up and down my spine and I yawn.

"No, sleeping. You promised to help me go over the pack files," he tells me. I yawn again, unable to stay awake and he chuckles.

"Looks like I'm going over them myself." he quips, pressing his lips to my forehead, and he sighs.

CHAPTER
SIXTY-FIVE

The shuffling of papers wakes me from my slumber, the room dim, the only light coming from the lamp on Axton's side of the bed. Rolling over, Axton has a stack of papers on the bed and scattered across his lap.

"What are you doing?' I yawn while stretching.

"Pack documents, also looking over treaty agreements," he tells me, yet his brows furrow in confusion.

"What is it?" I ask him.

"Elder Stiles from the Crident Pack." He mumbles to himself and I sit up.

"The missing Elder?" I ask and he nods, showing me the paper. I take it, glancing down at it.

"He signed a treaty agreement with my father's pack?" Axton nods.

"Yes, expanding borders, appears your father was in debt to the council. That isn't what I find strange though, or surprising, it's that he signed his pack over to Osiris." I glance at Axton, and he holds up another document.

"But they were estranged?" I tell him.

"Exactly, it also shows here that Elder Stiles dropped the claim for your father's land right here," Axton points out.

"So?" I ask, trying to figure out what he is trying to say. My father was the head council member. It is not uncommon for the council to sweep things under the rug to prevent it getting out.

"The date, he'd been reported missing three days earlier,"

"So it couldn't have been Stiles," I gasp.

"Exactly, but someone that had access to his portal."

"Osiris," I tell him and he scratches the back of his neck.

"But why would Osiris cut a deal with my father?" Axton shrugs.

"That's what I want to know," he says, grabbing another document from a box on the floor which I notice is his personal documents, the rest I can tell are from the council. I help him go through all the pack archives before Axton grabs the box, rummaging through it. Picking up the council documents, I find a USB fall out of one of the packages.

"What's this?" I ask him and he shrugs.

"Where did it fall out of?" he asks.

"No, idea it was sitting on the bed under all...this" I glance at the mess we made.

Axton takes it, looking at it then shrugs. "Wait here, I will grab my laptop." He tells me wandering off. I start packing up the files we went through already and move his box to the floor when I notice the document on top.

Nightfall pack ownership papers, Axton's pack. Only it isn't just about his pack records on its own, Marco's signature on the bottom ruling the death by challenge, yet when I pick up the envelope under it; Axton suddenly snatches it from my hand with a growl having come back into the room.

I watch him for a second. "What are you hiding, Councilman Axton?"

"Nothing, stay out of it. We aren't investigating me but everyone else." he snarls.

I press my lips in a line, offended that he still doesn't trust me enough to tell me even now I have marked him. He drops it back in the box, then moves to sit on the bed with his laptop.

He plugs the USB in and I watch the screen to see it is a news clip. "Ah, just Alpha Cane's story that was on the news," Axton tells me about to pull it out.

I move stopping him, having not seen the news clip. Axton sighs passing it over and the news anchor explains there was a car crash not far from the city. It then shows photos of the wreckage which is nothing more than burned remains, and crumpled metal. It then goes on to question the pack's future and who will take over the pack before Alpha Cane's picture comes up on the screen. Only the picture seems off to me when I realize why. He's in a hospital gown.

"Was Alpha Cane in the wreckage?" I ask Axton and he shakes his head, glancing at the screen.

"That's an old photo, the man is messed up. He spent a few years in an insane asylum, after his father declared he wasn't in position for the title," Axton explains.

"And that sent him crazy?" I question.

"No, he was never crazy. Rumor was Alpha Cane was going to out his father's underground dealings, so to shut him up, his father had him admitted." Axton tells me.

"Then how did he get out?"

"Marco helped. When I moved here and realized this is the city his family came to, I questioned his whereabouts. It seemed off, so I had Marco look into it. Marco got him out and Cane left to become a mechanic or something, he never returned to the city until his father and brother passed." Axton tells me. I nod feeling terrible for Alpha Cane.

"So back to Elder Stiles and Osiris?" I ask him.

"And Thomas," Axton murmurs and I look at him.

"How I didn't notice before is beyond me."

"Notice what?"

"This... he witnessed Elder Stiles agreement with your father, but

Stiles was already missing. None of this makes sense." he whispers the last part.

"Do you know what your father's debt was for?" he questions. I shake my head.

"Maybe ask my mother?" I tell him and he nods. "I will grab the pack files tomorrow once we get back from moving the last of the stuff out." I tell him. He sighs, and places the documents on the bedside table, packing up the papers when he picks up his box. I look away busying myself with a stack in front of me when he sighs. Suddenly the yellow envelope drops next to me. I look at Axton.

"Go on, you'll only snoop later," he growls, walking the box back to the walk-in closet where he has a safe.

"I wasn't going to snoop!" I tell him.

"No, but you're angry I won't tell you." he calls out as I pick it up. I sit it back on the bedside table now feeling like I've forced him to give it to me. Since when did relationships get so crazy?

"When we could suddenly feel him!" Lexa deadpans and I roll my eyes just as he comes out.

He growls, snatching the document. "I gave it to you!"

"But not because you wanted to." I remind him. He clicks his tongue and shakes his head when I feel embarrassment leak through the bond. He falls onto the bed opening it, grabbing some pictures out and dropping them in my lap. Picking them up he speaks.

"I shouldn't be Alpha," he tells me.

"The title would have been handed down to you anyway,"

"But they're right, the rumors, I never challenged him. I'd be in prison if Macro hadn't covered it up," I turn the photos over to find they're crime scene photos.

Only when I come to one of his father's body to I realize what he means. "You shot him?" I ask. No wonder there was so much speculation regarding his death.

"While he was asleep." Axton admits and nods to the next photo which is vastly different. Instead of it being in the room the body had been moved and looked like it was put through a shredder to imitate a challenge.

"Why would you keep this?" I ask, holding up the one of his father, in his bed, blood covering his face from the bullet to the head.

"I didn't, Marco wasn't initially at the scene first. That is one of the real crime scene photos that Marco had taken off one of the officers,"

"Which officer?" I ask. Axton shrugs, "Marco took care of him, too," I chew my lip and nod. Now it makes so much sense why he didn't want me to know. This information could ruin him and destroy his pack.

"Unfortunately, that photo somehow survived. Marco got it back for me before it was leaked."

"Someone got hold of the pictures?"

"No, Marco believes it was sent via text before Marco got there,"

"Sent to who?"

"Your father, he went to leak it to the news outlet here. Everything has to be run by the major investors of the station. Marco is one of them,"

"Wait, Sondra's?" Axton nods his head.

"Yeah, I didn't know Sondra existed or that she owned it or about Floyd being my mother's father, not for sure anyway. But I knew Marco handled a lot of this city's socials and news stations, being this is one of the city's he maintains through the supernatural council. So when your father came in with the photo, he thought Marco would be happy to let it out, not realizing my mother was Marco's niece, and I was like family to him. All your father knew was that Marco hated my father, he just didn't know why. He also didn't realize he was leaking a picture to the very man who helped cover it up."

"Yeah, I could imagine his shock when he learned of Floyd being Marco's brother and Sondra being the biggest stakeholder in the city since most of that is covered up by the supernatural governments.

That explains though, how a human woman could have so much control." I tell him.

"Control you now have since everything of Sondra's is now yours," Axton tells me, and I sigh. Just hearing that sounds daunting and leaves a target on my back.

"So, this is why you were after my father and why you leaked the sex tape?" I ask him. Axton exhales.

"Not the only reason, but part of it, yes. I needed him off the council because he was using that initially to blackmail me. When I refused, he went to take it to the local news station, Marco found it and compelled him to find out if there were any other copies, there weren't thankfully, but your father was not happy. However, we don't understand how your father got his hands on that picture or why it was sent to him, as far as we could tell, he had no links to the dead officer," Axton states.

I chew my lip. That is an issue.

CHAPTER
SIXTY-SIX

All night, it played on my mind. Even when I woke up, I suffered from the lingering effects of the dreams this knowledge caused. I had dreamt so many possible scenarios, my dreams plagued with nightmares of each one. I needed to figure out how everything links because I am positive there is a connection in some way.

Axton believes it doesn't link with what is happening now, but I think it somehow does. Some incessant nagging voice in my head that for once wasn't Lexa telling me we were missing something. Something vital. Just seems like too much of a coincidence that all Alphas are linked to Stiles, who's missing. And those same Alphas are out to stop Axton? And now me...

Axton passes me a travel cup full of steaming hot coffee. He had meetings today and is debating whether to cancel them. My mother and I still have a fair bit of packing up to do, having not finished everything yet. We still had to drag out the last of Sondra's stuff from her room that survived Marco from the other day; we would toss everything in storage to be sorted later.

"Are you sure you'll be fine?" Axton asks me for the hundredth time. It's almost like he believes I can't survive without him holding my hand.

"Yes, it won't take long. We'll follow the truck back," I tell him.

"If I finish early, I will come out and help," he says, leaning inside the car and pecking my cheek while I start the car. I place my cup in the cup holder while he pulls his jacket on. I watch him climb in his car before reversing and heading to the borderline to pick up my mother and Luke.

This morning its particularly chilly; the rains coming, and a storm was brewing silently; I could feel it, that strange, bizarre instinct to take cover settling over me, and the faint scent of moisture in the air, the dampening smell lingering in the breeze.

I chuckle, watching Luke climb over the front seats to squeeze between the car seats, his shoulders rubbing the seats. He doesn't seem to mind as he coos at his nephews while clicking in his seatbelt. My mother climbs in with a laundry basket of cleaning products.

"We are supposed to be emptying the place, not filling it with more junk," I tell her as she shuts the door.

"I want to leave the place clean," she tells me.

"Axton organized cleaners to go out there Thursday," I remind her.

"I know, but I don't want the cleaners to think we live like pigs," she snaps, and I raise my eyebrows at her and chuckle. Mom was one of those people you take on holidays, and she brought a bag of cleaning products to clean the hotel room before we left. She used to be the same back home. The house would be spotless before the cleaner came, and the poor girl would scratch her head, wondering what to do. I used to tell her to make it look like she was busy, or she would usually spend time re-stacking the attic or basement to kill time.

When we reach the house, Luke helps me drag the bouncers and playpen inside to set the boys up while we get to work. Checking each room is empty while my mother frantically cleans every inch of the house. Heaven forbid the cleaners actually had to clean.

Dragging the last box from the basement, I find my mother using the broom to sweep the cobwebs from the banisters. I set the box by the front door before stopping to drink some of my now lukewarm coffee. "Did Dad ever say anything about Elder Stiles to you?" Mom stops what she is doing and glances at me, her brows furrowing in confusion.

"Not really until your father found out I owned the pack. Stiles came to me and said he believed the pack was safest in my hands; I was trying to find something to use against your father anyway," she tells me with a shrug.

"So you didn't know Stiles was going to report dad?" she looks at me. Clearly, this is news to her too.

"What?"

"Yeah, Stiles and Dad were arguing. That is why Stiles wanted to give you the pack."

"No—" Mom's brows furrow, and I can tell she is genuinely confused.

"No, I told Stiles I wanted a divorce. He said your father wouldn't let me leave and that I needed leverage, so he overrode the system so I could send off the change of titles. I never put it in my name; I sent it off for it to be placed in your name. Your father didn't know until after I left, he only knew about the divorce. Stiles signed the paperwork for it." she tells me.

"Stiles signed those papers?" Mom nods her head.

"Yeah, said soon your father would come under fire, that he was glad because he was worried about what would happen to the pack, so he offered to help me forge the documents, kept them sealed from the other council members, or tried to, but somehow he found out. So I rejected him, and well, all hell broke loose," she sighs, glancing toward the living room to look at Luke. She smiles sadly, and I can see talking about my father is upsetting her, so I drop the subject, instead returning back to the tasks while wondering who told my father about the forged divorce papers.

Hearing one of the boys cry out, Luke sings out to tell me I've run out of diapers in the bag. I groan, and mom chuckles, scrubbing the stove top; who would have thought three measly stairs on the porch could make your legs burn so badly? I've trudged up them that much this morning. I'm surprised I haven't run tracks into them. Walking back out to the car, my phone rings, and I pull it from my back pocket. Axton.

"Yes?" I answer while propping the phone on one ear and shoulder as I start rummaging for the diapers I swore were left in the back pocket of the seats.

"I'm heading out to you now; only Soyer, Osiris, and Marco showed up. We finished early," Axton tells me, and I smile, digging under the seat.

"Great, I will see you soon," I tell him before hissing when I jam my thumb under something beneath the seat. I suck on it.

"What's wrong?"

"Looking for spare diapers," I tell him.

I rummage through the car, looking for the spares I always keep.

"I put them in the trunk," Axton tells me, and I groan before shutting the door, popping the trunk, and finding where Axton placed them.

"I should be around twenty minutes. Do you want me to bring anything?"

"Coffee," I chuckle.

He laughs. "Okay, love you, see you soon," he tells me before hanging up. Shaking my head, I move back toward the house when I hear glass break. I jog up the steps assuming mom dropped something.

"Everything alright," I sing out, closing the front door when my nose picks up a strange scent, my brows furrow, wondering where I've smelt it before. Shaking it off to the amount of cleaning chemicals mom has used. I move past the kitchen to notice mom is no longer there.

"Elena?" Luke croaks through the mind-link just as I round the corner into the living room. My mother has her hands out in some placating gesture, tears trekking down her cheeks. Luke clutches Kyan, who is wailing loudly in his arms, while my mother shields them with her body. My heart nearly stops when I see my father holding Bane.

CHAPTER
SIXTY-SEVEN

"Derrick, Please, give me our grandson," Mom sobs, holding her hands out for him, her steps slow as she approaches him. Luke has a gash down the side of his face, and I can tell he has met my father's claws.

"No, you're coming with me," he tells her. I have never seen my father look so...so...feral. He looked like a rogue, every part of it; he was dirty and shaking, insane. That is what happens to rogues when they've been on their own for too long, but my father hasn't been missing long for it to have this effect.

"Just let me take him. You're scaring him, please," Mom pleads, while my heart races as I figure out what to do.

"Luke, I need you to take Kyan out to the car and call Axton," I mind-link him, and he looks over his shoulder at me. The moment he does, my father's eyes dart to me, and he clutches Bane tighter.

"I'm taking her. She is my mate! You have taken everything from me, but you won't take her!" he says, rushing up the steps as he snarls at me, and I hold my hands up in surrender. Nodding my head.

"No one's taking her, but you need to give me my son, Dad," I tell him. Mom nods her head.

"Please, Derrick, I'll come. Just hand him over, please," she begs and sobs.

"Luke, go!" I snap at him when I see he is paralyzed by his fear. He jumps and races from the room and runs outside.

"You don't want to hurt him? He's just a baby," Mom pleads from the bottom of the steps. Only then do I notice the slash marks down the side of dad's ribs when he twists slightly. My eyes dart to my mother's fingers, which are coated in blood before they dart back to my father holding my son like he is a football and not a baby.

"Stand down, Lexa!" I snap at her, knowing we risk hurting our son if she shifts right now. The hairs on my arms rise as she presses against my skin, making it ripple.

"Dad..." I call out to him, stepping closer and Bane screams when dad moves too quickly, his eyes calculating my every move as I try to move closer.

"Come any closer, and I will drop him," Dad threatens, moving his arm over the banister. My heart nearly stops, and my breath hitches.

My mother shrieks, racing to the side to catch him, but Dad just holds him out in the air.

"I'll give him back, but she leaves with me," Dad says, eyes trained on me.

"Luke...Luke. We can give him to Luke. Then we can leave," she tells him, and Dad's eyes dart to her.

"I just want you back. I want everything back." Dad breaks down, huge hiccuping sobs wracking his body as he drops onto the step clutching Bane to his chest.

My entire body is trembling, and Lexa is filling in Axton while my mother climbs the stairs, and I can see the violent shaking of her hands as she reaches out for him. The moment she does, he latches onto her, and she has to grab the banister to stop him from crushing my son. I shriek in panic when I hear my mother murmuring. Consoling my father, trying to calm him down.

I hold my breath the entire time until she gets Dad to stand, and I find Bane is still in his arms. He sniffles and smiles. I can't hear what my mother is saying over the pounding of my heart in my ears. Yet whatever she says seems to work as he comes down the stairs.

I back up with my hands in the air and walk backward toward the front door, which is where my mother seems to be leading him when he breaks down again, only this time, she convinces him to give her my son. The moment I see him in her hands, I suck in a breath, finally able to breathe when I get the scent of gas in the air, making me confused.

"Love, I have to give him to El, so she can change him. He needs his mother."

My mother talks to him like she is talking to a child that she is trying to calm down when he clutches onto her, drops to his knees and hugs her. Hesitantly, she holds Bane out to me, and I shakily step forward before snatching him from her.

"Axton is on his way. I will be back...." I tell her through the mindlink, and she smiles sadly, tilting her head while my father rambles. She gives me a brief nod turning her gaze back to my father and sucking in a shaky breath, her bottom lip quivering as tears trek down her face.

She runs her fingers through his hair, trying to calm him, and I back up, turning for the door when the waves in the air catch my gaze, the same potent stench reaching my nose, making me turn my gaze to the stove where my mother was cleaning to see the knobs turned on.

It is gas.

My father roars, becoming angry, and I know I need to get my son out first, so I can come back for her. I race to the door and open it, the door slamming shut behind me, then I run to the car where Luke stands outside, peering in through the huge bay windows that line the porch where I can see my mother trying to calm him back down.

"Luke, get in the car and lock the doors," I tell him, but his grief-stricken face is on our mother when I hear a car racing up the driveway. Turning my head, I see the dust and know it's Axton. We just need to bide our time.

"He came out of nowhere. I...I went to get the bottle and returned, and he had him. He came out of nowhere," Luke sobs. I try to console him, but I have to get inside to help mom.

"Luke, I need you to listen to me," I tell him, shaking him gently. "Axton is on his way, but you need to watch the boys until he gets here," I tell him when I hear the mind link open.

"He will never stop, Elena," my mother says, and I pivot looking at the house, my eyes going wide when I see her pull the long stove lighter from her pants pocket.

"Take care of your brother for me," she tells me.

"No!" I gasp, stumbling toward the house, hearing the mindlink open further.

"Be good for your sister, Luke. I love you both," she tells us, and Luke screams, also catching onto what she means. He cries a blood-curdling scream while I race toward the house, and I can see her standing in the living room, seeing my father clutching onto her when she looks at me.

"Love you, sweetie," she says, clicking the lighter when I am a few feet from the porch steps. The spark turns to flame before the air inside the house ignites instantly, making it so bright my eyes burn when the house explodes. The shock wave throws me backward, knocking the air out of my lungs as I hit the dirt. The sound of the car windows bursting in the distance rings out loudly, along with Luke's broken scream.

I barely get to my hands and knees when I see him rushing toward the raging inferno. I scream for him, racing to stop him when Axton snatches him, catching him around the middle. I didn't even hear him pull up, but the frantic look on his face told me he had witnessed everything. Luke wails and thrashes in his grip, and I clutch my ears, unable to listen to him scream for her.

"She's gone, buddy. You can't save them." I just hear Axton tell him while my heart breaks for them. She sacrificed everything for us, and now she sacrificed her life.

CHAPTER
SIXTY-EIGHT

Axton

I watch in a panic as the house explodes and instinctively snatch Luke just before he reaches the threshold of the smoke-filled porch. The explosion was deafening, enveloping the packhouse in flames and smoke so thick that it makes breathing next to impossible.

Everything happens too fast for anyone to really comprehend and it was the last thing I was expecting when Luke mind-linked me to tell me they were in trouble and Derrick had shown up.

However, amidst all the chaos of screams and burning debris, adrenaline surged through as I pulled up, and I only just got to Luke in time when I raced forward to snatch him up. He had been standing so near to the entrance of the house before it burst forth with destruction. Tossing us back once again when the gas cylinders alongside the packhouse exploded a second time.

Grasping him tightly, his entire body trembles, and tears pour down his face as he stares in anguish at his now-destroyed home. Turning my head, I look for my mate. Elena stares motionlessly. Her blank expression makes my heart sink as she stares at the house, and

I can feel her mind racing to take it all in - she seems unable to connect the sight in front of her to reality.

Our sons screaming in the background makes me glance at the cars to see the front windows have burst, but lucky, the angle of the car prevented the back ones from erupting.

It feels surreal.

Luke continues to scream, and I choke back a whimper at what he just witnessed, unsure how to comfort him while trying to figure out where everything went so wrong. My arms remain tightly wrapped around him to protect him from the sharp debris and the heat from flames cascading around us.

Despite being held securely against my body, Luke wails for his mother and father, who I know have perished in their burning home.

Glancing at Elena, she stares expressionless from where she sits on the grass nearby, stunned into silence as she is confronted with the ruins that were once her home; all that is left behind are pieces of smoldering wood and a cloud of ash that seems to go on forever. Her emotions through the bond are tumultuous, grief, anger but also this strange sense of numbness like she can't comprehend what's happened as she keeps flicking between emotions. Lost.

"We can't stay here," Khan murmurs in my head as he comes forward, his despair also potent. His worry for our sons and mate, and his desire to protect them, is far stronger, keeping him level-headed when, just like me, he wants to break something and hurt someone for the anger of what just happened. We were too late, a few minutes earlier, and we may have been able to prevent this. If only I had canceled my appointments today, we would have been here.

Covered in soot and scraps from the blast, I stand, hauling Luke with me as I get up, and I cast one last glance at the burning wreckage, with Luke still sobbing softly in my arms.

I move toward Elena and offer her my hand. She stares at me, blinking back tears, a look on her face so heartbreaking it twists knots in my stomach. Her face is blotchy, her lips quivering, and she has a cut on her cheek.

"We need to go, Love," I whisper to her and reluctantly, she places her hand in mine. When she stands, her gaze is distant and empty. We make our way to her car. The windows in the front are blown out, and the boys scream inside, which seems to set her in motion as she rushes to pull them out, hugging them close.

The fear I felt from her when Luke mind-linked me, was so potent I nearly swerved off the road. It was stomach-turning.

We finally get the boys' car seats out and put them in my car.

In the distance, I can hear the sirens blaring loudly on their way to us. Mindlinking Eli, I tell him to get Marco so they can handle it because my mind is on one task and one task alone, and that is to get them away from here. Silently we begin our journey home. Along the way, I try to piece together what had happened and why our lives were suddenly upside down.

We drive in silence, just the sound of the car engine humming low and soft. I can feel a seismic shift within us as we make our way home. I feel helpless against this tragedy that has befallen us. As hard as I try, there is no way to undo this damage. But I can focus on the present and make sure they are safe from further harm.

When we finally arrive home, I hug them tightly, my arms trembling with relief as I lead Elena inside with the boys tucked in her arms.

"Luke?" she panics, whirling around, and I lift my hand, showing I have him. She exhales with relief while glancing down at Luke. He looks lost.

"It's okay, buddy," she whispers softly to him. Elena looks up at me, and I know that her strength will eventually get us through this. We are family, united together in love, and nothing can break that bond. As long as we have each other, we can survive anything.

She will get through this.

"They're gone," Luke murmurs. I watch as Elena swallows down her grief, her eyes turning glassy and her lips quivering.

She takes a deep breath before gathering her courage and nodding resolutely.

"Yes, they are gone," she whispers back, her voice thick with emotion. "But we still have each other."

"But what will happen to me? Where will I go without mom?" Luke asks, and I blink down at him.

"With us, Luke," I murmur. "You'll always have a home with us," I tell him, and he nods sadly.

I wrap my arm around Elena and pull her close. We will weather this storm together, no matter what comes our way. The pain we feel now will eventually pass, but the love that binds us will last forever.

We can survive anything as long as we have each other, and so can Luke with us by his side.

"I'll settle the boys. I need to change them. Can you?" Her eyes move to Luke.

"I'll remain with him," I tell her, and she nods, yet I can tell she was trying to remain strong for him, even when her heart was breaking.

I pull Luke close, and he buries his head in my chest. I hug him tightly while Elena turns away to take care of the boys.

CHAPTER
SIXTY-NINE

I've barely caught any sleep. Worry for Elena keeps me awake at night, knowing she is not coping with the loss of her mother. All week she has done nothing but work, leaving before I wake and coming home only to crawl into bed. I miss her terribly, and so do the boys, but I know all too well what this sort of loss feels like, so I let her go. Although Khan wants me to step in, he doesn't like how much she is working. It has almost become an addiction to her. I just hope after today; things can go back to normal. Today is their funeral, and when I feel her move and roll out of bed, I reach for her before sighing when my hands only manage to grab air.

"We have to be at the funeral home by ten. Service is at 10:30," Elena reminds me like she is reminding me to grab milk on the way home. Sighing, I climb out of bed.

I help her pack the few items she needs for today and take a deep breath. We drive in silence to the funeral home; none of us are ready for this, yet it is something that must be done, and because Sondra's funeral was supposed to be the day after the explosion, we have decided to join them. So today, we lay two to rest, though one I don't know how to feel about. Derrick had done so many wrongs, yet he was still her father and Luke's. I could feel Elena wanted to hate him, wanted to be angry, but no matter the things he had done, she still loved him.

Reaching over, I try to grab her hand, but she is quick to move it away. "Elena?" I murmur, pulling into the car park.

"I know what you're doing and don't. Tears won't bring them back," she says, staring vacantly out the window.

"There is nothing wrong with being emotional, Elena. You don't need to be strong for everyone." I tell her looking in the mirror, I peer at Luke, his headphones in as he stares vacantly out the window. Kyan is banging his rattle against the side of his car seat trying to get his attention.

"Strong is all I got left right now, Axton. My pack has had their entire lives turned upside down, and they don't need another crying pack member. They need an Alpha," Elena snaps before shoving the door open and climbing out of the car.

Elena moves to the trunk to pull out the stroller, and I move to help her before getting the boys out. Michelle pulls up beside us and instantly jumps out to help, and takes the stroller.

However, Luke doesn't climb out of the car, and Elena looks around for him to find him sitting between the two car seats staring out the window. Elena leans in and waves him forward, and he climbs over the seats, falling into the passenger seat, but still, he refuses to climb out. Elena looks at me, and I step forward, trying to coax him out of the car. When he still refuses to get out, Elena crouches beside him, fixing his tie and buttoning up his suit jacket.

"We can't stay out here with you, Luke. I have to go in."

"I will just wait in the car," Luke says, and Elena glances at me over her shoulder. I shrug, not understanding why he doesn't want to go in, and she sighs heavily, turning back to face him.

"Don't you want to say goodbye? If you don't want to go in, I won't force you, but I think you'll regret it if you don't," she tells him.

"It's not that I don't want to say goodbye. It's that everyone will have nice things to say about Mom, but what about Dad? I don't want to listen to them speak badly about him. He wasn't perfect, but he was still ours," Luke says, breaking down. Watching Elena, her lip quivers, and she nods, rubbing his back in understanding.

"Nobody will speak badly about him, I promise," Elena assures. Luke looks up at her, his eyes are puffy with the surrounding rings from crying.

"I won't let them, okay," she tells him.

"You promise?" Luke asks her, and she nods, leaning forward and pressing her lips to his head. When she stands, she offers him her hand, and Luke reluctantly takes it, allowing her to pull him to his feet. Locking the car, I place my hand on Elena's back as we walk inside. The atmosphere is somber, yet there is a sense of peace in the room. We are welcomed by familiar faces of the funeral service people, and I can tell Elena is trying to take comfort in that as they discuss the service, and she tells them no one is to speak for her father.

I swallow, watching as the woman in charge of the service appears confused before understanding crosses their faces, and their eyes go to Luke. Opening the mind-link, I open it to our pack while blocking out Luke's link, warning them if they haven't got anything nice to say to keep their mouths shut regarding Derrick. It wasn't uncommon for packs to list a person's crimes when they depart. In fact, for those that betray their pack, a service is rarely held, and if it is, it's not the sort of service one would expect. No, it's usually not held in their honor but in their victims, giving them a chance to speak about the pain they caused them to set them free of the past of hurt.

Knowing this, I used to wonder sometimes if my funeral one day would match my father's, or if people would be sad to see me go. I have no doubt now that'll make up for my failures because no failure is bigger for me than not being there for Elena when she truly needed me, and if my mate can forgive me, I can live with everything else bad I've done because her opinion of me is the only one I care for.

While we wait for everyone to arrive, I watch Elena as she stands alone next to the casket, her eyes dark with her grief as she stares at her parents' coffins. My heart aches for her, and I wish I could ease her pain. I wish I could shield her from all of this, but I cannot. I can only stand helplessly by her side, offering silent support.

Luke makes his way over to her, and I notice her eyes flick down toward him, tears threatening to spill, but I know she won't let them. She is strong-headed and will not let her emotions show, even though she is in immense pain. She is trying to stay composed for her mother, also for Luke, and is showing the courage it takes to do so.

CHAPTER
SEVENTY

Even when her brother breaks down and sobs, Elena remains standing tall and dignified. Her hand grasps his shoulder as she tugs him closer. She turns, leading him to his seat. Elena's face is expressionless. Her face is a mask of stoicism as she keeps her emotions in check. Despite the tears threatening to spill, her jaw is set in determination, and her gaze is distant, as if she is looking far away from the present moment.

I know what she is doing. She is placing her own emotions on the back burner in order to remain present for her family and pack. She remains composed and gives her brother the support he needs at this time while neglecting that she needs it herself.

It is almost impossible to believe that it has already been a week since the explosion. As I look around the room that is filling with our packs and friends, the sadness of who everyone has lost begins to sink in a little deeper. Even though they're gone, their memory lives on in all our hearts—a reminder of what Louise had done for her children. Even in death, she still managed to bless us with her love, leaving behind her daughter and my sons, whom I will cherish forever.

I take a deep breath and try my best to compose myself as more family and friends arrive. Everyone is quiet in reflection as they embrace Elena, offering their condolences.

Just like the past week, she slips effortlessly into a facade of being okay, when I know she is anything but. I notice how her hands shake, and how she tries her best to steady them when someone speaks, telling those present to switch their phones off and take a seat or stand where they're out of the way in aisles.

The service begins, and I can feel my heart break as I watch Elena struggle with her emotions. There is no doubt that this loss has changed our lives forever.

I step forward and wrap my arms around her in a tight embrace, feeling the tremors of emotion that ripple through her body as the last of our guests enter.

The service is a solemn reminder of how fragile life can be, and how quickly it can all change. With tear-filled eyes, we say goodbye to an amazing women who will remain in our hearts forever. Louise sacrificed her life to save her kids and grandkids. And lastly, Derrick, who caused a mix of emotions amongst everyone by the looks on their faces, yet no one stood up and gave a speech for him when the woman waits with the microphone in her hand, looking expectantly at the crowd.

When I see Elena's head turn to look for someone with a friendly face for Derrick, I watch her swallow and glance at Luke. No one rises to give a eulogy for Derrick, and I know Elena didn't have one planned, so I am surprised when once again Elena rises. Murmurs break out as they wait for her anger or heartache, but Elena is a pillar of strength as she takes the podium and speaks for the one man no one dared to.

"I know most of you expect me to get up here and condemn my father for his actions, condemn him for being a terrible Alpha. But I can't do that and I won't. Despite his flaws, he was still my dad. So I won't speak of his mistakes because we've all made those. We just haven't carried them to our graves yet; we still have time to redeem ourselves for our failures. He wasn't given that. So, I will not speak of the man, but I will speak for my father,"

Luke lifts his head beside me, staring at his sister, waiting to hear what she has to say. Leaning over a little I squeeze his shoulder.

"Growing up, he was a good father, at least to Luke and me, for the most part. Growing up as the alpha's daughter came with great responsibility, but it also came with great pride. The love and care he showed us can never be taken away or erased.

So today, I will honor my father and his legacy. He may have been a sinner in the eyes of some, but in mine. He'll always be the man I grew up believing was bigger than life, someone to look up to and who loved his kids and his pack.

He was the one who taught me how to hunt and how to survive without modern conveniences. My father made sure I understood our pack laws, our rituals, and traditions before I could walk. He taught me leadership skills from a young age.

He taught me how to ride a bike, how to drive, fight and hunt, and he made me into an Alpha despite never giving me the title. I had to fight for it. That's what he taught me. He brought me up in his image, and although his character has not, as of recently, been painted in a good light, he'll always be an Alpha, that is a title no one can take from him, yet the least important title he held. His greatest title will be that he was once a great father and that I will always be daddy's little girl. And Luke will always be daddy's little Alpha."

I look at Luke, who has tears in his eyes, and know that he is thinking about all their memories together with their father. I know she did it for Luke, but I also know she believed the words she spoke.

As the service ends, I squeeze Elena's shoulder and offer her a small smile; she nods once and after the coffins are walked out; I take Elena's hand as we walk out of the funeral home with Luke when I spot Michelle with the stroller; the boys tucked inside.

"Did you get it?" Elena asks Michelle and my brows furrow.

"Elena, we should–" Elena dismisses her with a wave of her hand, and Michelle reluctantly looks beneath the stroller, pulling out some folders. I peer over Elena's shoulder as she takes them, flipping them open.

"What's this?" I ask.

"Pack lists. I need to organize housing. There still isn't enough room at your apartment building." I almost groan. Can't she take a day off?

"Elena, I'm sure that can wait," I tell her, but she shakes her head and walks off. I sigh, looking at Michelle, who watches her nervously.

I follow her as she reaches the car, opening the trunk and back doors to put the boys in. I grip her shoulder.

"Are you okay?" I whisper, looking into her eyes, yet her jaw clenches, and she swallows, pulling her gaze from mine.

"I'm here for you if you need anything," I whisper softly as Elena slowly turns to face me. She nods, her eyes void of all emotion, but despite everything, she manages a small smile that I know is fake.

"I'm fine," is all she says, but I know she's not. Despite Khan's protests, I don't press the matter. Instead, I help her get the boys in the car.

"You need to do something!" Khan snarls angrily at me, and I am beginning to think he is right. She keeps going like this. She'll burn out.

CHAPTER
SEVENTY-ONE

Axton
    Elena hid in my office the moment we got home and has been in there for three hours now with the door closed. I can hear her on the phone organizing housing for her pack members.

Looking for an excuse to go in there, I make her a coffee. Popping my head into the living room, Luke is watching TV with the boys. He glances at me before turning his attention back to the TV.

"I wouldn't. She'll bite your head off," he warns, knowing his sister too well. Walking into MY office, she is on the phone, staring out the window as she talks to someone on the phone. Elena glances at me, and I hold up the mug, and she points to my desk as if I don't know where it is.

Setting it down, I sit in my chair across from her. She's so focused on the conversation that she doesn't even blink when I focus all my attention on her.

"Just find them. There has to be a record somewhere," Elena says into the phone before hanging up. She turns to me, and I can see the exhaustion written all over her face.

"If you're here to lecture me more about working--"

I hold my hand up, stopping her. "Just checking on you," I admit, and she sighs, reaching for a box of paperwork I recognize to belong to her father. She and Luke went home the other day to rummage through her old house and came home with mountain loads of paperwork. Luke returned with a few of his old belongings, too.

"How is the housing situation going?" I ask her, watching as she digs through the box.

"Sorted now," she tells me, opening up a folder and flicking through the sleeves.

"So, who were you on the phone to then?" I question, and I can feel her annoyance at me distracting her.

"The Supernatural Council. I am looking for records on Osiris," she tells me, and my brows furrow in confusion.

"Why?" I ask, a little shocked. Elena sets the folder down, shrugging off her blazer and tossing it on the brown leather couch.

"Because after the other night, I've been doing some digging about my father's debt. So we know he was stealing money from the council, and he got into some gambling debts. Stiles found out and confronted him. Then he ends up dead, but where has Osiris been this entire time?" she asks me, and I shrug.

"Well, after going through my father's files, I found something interesting. Once a month, money was coming into a separate bank account that my father held. I linked that bank account to Osiris. I checked Thomas' old accounting files, which I could rummage up, and after my father sold the laundromat to Thomas. I noticed Thomas started receiving money monthly into the laundromat account, which was how I caught Thomas in the first place, through these deposits he couldn't explain, but before that, it was going into a secret account my father had, as soon as my father sold the laundromats to Thomas he started receiving the same monthly figures. My father and Thomas were working with Osiris."

My mouth opens in shock, and I can feel my heart beating out of my chest. "Do you think Osiris was the one who killed his father?" I ask her, and she chews her lip, a thoughtful expression slipping onto her face.

"Possibly, but I know he is linked to it somehow," she says, not looking sure herself.

"Would Elder Stiles report Osiris, though, since he is his son?" she asks.

"I know they had a falling out. That is all I know."

Elena sighs. "So what we know is my father was working with Thomas and Osiris. He stole money from the council to pay back a gambling debt which was from before he sold the laundromats to Thomas," she says thoughtfully.

"Without the extra money coming in from the laundromat, he couldn't afford to pay the debt, so he stole the money from the council," I tell her, and she nods.

"Still doesn't explain where Stiles is," I tell her.

"What if Stiles found out about Osiris being linked to the laundromats?" she questions.

"If I have had to guess, I'd say Osiris killed his father," Elena tells me, "which is why I requested all documents on every alpha in the city."

"Am I under suspicion?" I chuckle.

"No, of course not. I never requested your files, just Soyer's, Osiris', Thomas', and Cane's."

"Why, Cane's?" I ask curiously.

"I know he's a friend of yours, but something about the accident doesn't add up."

"Like what?"

"The fact he lied about where he was the day of the accident, but that isn't all. Did you know Cane was the product of an affair?" she asks me, and I blink at her.

"Excuse me?" Elena shrugs.

"There is a reason he was never made Alpha. It had nothing to do with not wanting to take the position."

"What do you mean?" I ask, leaning forward and bracing my arms on the desk.

"The day of the accident, his father picked him up from an insane asylum. Yet the reports say he was never in the car."

"So? Just means his father dropped him home before he headed back here, he did have a home in the town he lived in, and not surprisingly, I told you he spent time in one," I tell her.

"The address he had listed was for an old lady, his biological grandmother on his mother's side."

"Biological grandmother? Cane is adopted?" I ask, and Elena shakes her head.

"So, Alpha Lyle had an affair,"

"Yep!" Elena tells me, but that makes no sense to me.

"Then what, Alpha Lyle stole him from his bio mother?" I ask, trying to piece together what she is telling me.

"No, she died giving birth to him. Alpha Lyle's Luna." She tries to explain, but I cut her off, getting confused about the story.

"Luna Grace?" I question.

"Yes, Luna Grace made out Cane was her son to cover up the fact Alpha Lyle had cheated on her with a woman named Dana. That is why Pete, despite his record, was to be the next Alpha. Apparently, the entire pack petitioned against Pete taking over; it's why the title was never handed down to him." she explains.

"Yes, I heard rumors of that. It's why his pack is so small and was no longer council worthy or recognized for a seat in the council. Those that opposed Pete taking over, Lyle banished or killed, which dropped their numbers." I tell her. She nods, sliding a piece of paper over to me, and I find it is Cane's original birth certificate.

"See, Cane is an illegitimate child of Alpha Lyle; and a she-wolf named Dana. Pete is only his half-brother, and if you check his birth certificate, you'll see, Luna Grace is not listed as his mother."

"Well, that explains why his brother always hated him growing up," Khan tells me, and I have to agree.

Both Lyle and Pete were exceptionally cruel to Cane. Come to think of it, it makes sense that I never saw Luna Grace ever step in at the pits, she never threw in the towel for Cane, yet I had witnessed several times she did for Pete. And there were plenty of times Cane was nearly killed in those pits.

"But that isn't the most shocking part. There is no information about his bio mother, Dana, at all, and his grandmother died two months ago," she tells me, and I sigh—another dead end.

"Well, how about we figure it out once the supernatural council sends the paperwork? For now, come have a break," I tell her, praying she listens, and this doesn't turn into another argument. There is no point in combing over all these documents until we have those documents. So best just to wait, though I could probably get Marco to get them quicker. But I need Elena to have a break.

Unsurprisingly, she shakes her head and opens her mouth to speak, but I cut her off.

"Now, Elena!" I snap at her, sick of her burying herself in ridiculous amounts of work that can wait. The look she gives me is one of shock, and I don't want to pull rank over her, but she is leaving me with no choice.

"Excuse me?" she growls angrily.

"You're done for the day. Now up, you can come and spend time with the boys. You know your family!"

"No, I have to--"

"It wasn't a choice," I tell her. Elena's eyebrows raise, and she sits back in her chair, folding her arms across her chest. But I know if I don't get her to slow down or stop for a while, Khan will come forward, and as much as I don't want to order her, I will. She needs sleep!

Shaking my head, I pinch the bridge of my nose and exhale. "I don't want to order you, but Khan--"

"Don't put the blame on me, asshole," Khan grumbles as if he wasn't the one who threatened to make her submit yesterday if she didn't slow down. Then today, he told me to do something about her working so much.

"Khan, what? Will make me submit?" she snarls, and I grit my teeth.

"No, but I will. You need rest. So either you come willingly, or I order you to take the next week off. Eli and Michelle can handle pack business. It's why they're our Betas." I tell her, standing up when Elena goes to argue, and I curse at her stubbornness.

"1..." I count, and she snarls.

"You did not just count like I am a damn --"

"2... Elena. What's it going to be?" I tell her. She curses and shakes her head.

"Fine, commanding you it is then... 3," I tell her, moving toward her.

"Fuck! Fine, I am getting up." She snarls before I reach her as she jumps up from her seat. She storms out of my office, shoulder-barging me as she does.

I exhale, heading out after her and finding her rummaging through the linen cupboard for a towel. She glares at me when she spots me before stalking off up the stairs to take a shower.

Great...

CHAPTER
SEVENTY-TWO

Elena

Grabbing a towel from the linen cupboard, I almost groan when I notice Axton coming up the hallway after me. Quickly shutting the door, I rush toward the stairs, trying to escape him. The shower is calling my name, just as I climb a few steps, I hear the boys cry out. Glancing over my shoulder, Axton stops mid-stride. He presses his lips in a line, giving me a look that says our little tiff is not over.

His hovering lately is driving me insane. Everywhere I turn, he's there! Breathing down my neck like he thinks I am about to have a nervous breakdown. I'm not, I'm just focused. Walking down the hall toward our room, I hear the boys fall quiet. Why son, why? Just cry for five more minutes, so I can shower in peace....

I know Axton is just worried about me, but it's not helping. I feel suffocated and frustrated, like my every move is being scrutinized. Taking a deep breath and reminding myself that he's only trying to help.

Stepping into the bedroom, I am flooded with light. I squint, moving around the spacious bedroom to the windows to close the curtains.

"What do you expect? You've been in that dark-ass room most of the day," Lexa snaps at me.

"It wasn't dark."

"You had a lamp on, which indicated to me that it was dark." Lexa argues.

"I had the blinds open," I retort, quickly shutting the windows on the next set and then the curtains. Although I am relieved she is talking to me, she has been quiet the last few days, leaving me in peace without her incessant whining.

"You know I can hear your thoughts, right? Incessant whining, your bitch ass whines more than me," she huffs, and I snicker then curse when I stub my little toe on the corner of the huge plush king-sized bed taking up the center of the damn room. A loud gasping groan leaves my lips at the pain and my bent toenail as I hop on one foot, clutching my toe while trying to breathe through the pain.

"Serve you right, for thinking I'm annoying!" adds Lexa's annoying commentary while I hop on the other foot, a towel over my shoulder while clutching my toe.

"Oh, stop being a baby. You shift and break bones all the time," Lexa continues.

"That doesn't mean it doesn't hurt any less!" Lexa rolls her eyes at me. I suddenly want to kick the bed, but after what it did to my toe, I think it would win that one too so I think twice about punishing it. Regathering myself, I wiggle my toes and then head into the bathroom.

Moving to the double vanity, I set my towel aside and remove my earrings and necklace, placing them on the counter. I undress quickly, hanging my clothes on a hook on the wall near the bathtub that runs along the window. Once I'm done, I start the shower and step in, letting the scalding water cascade over my body.

His scent fills the steamy air and makes me groan as I hear the bathroom door creak open. See, I can't even shower in peace.

"Did you think you could escape me?" Axton chuckles. I turn around to face him. "I did once...." I remind him, not that I have any intention of escaping him again even if he has been extremely clingy lately.

As I turn around, his eyes run the entire length of me. He's leaning against the vanity, his eyes smoldering with intensity when they finally lift to mine with a devious smile on his lips. "As if you would ever escape me again," he growls, folding his arms across his chest.

"If I wanted to go, I'd go. You would never find me or catch me," I tell him, raising my eyebrows in challenge. He takes a step forward, his eyes flashing with amusement. "You're already caught," he purrs, and I can't help but shiver in response. "Oh, really?" I mock him with a playful smirk.

His eyes flash with amusement, and he pushes off the vanity. "Don't deny it," he says, his voice low and deep. I swallow hard, my heart racing. He reaches for the hem of his shirt, his eyes never leaving mine as he slowly peels it off. His muscular body is toned and sculpted, with firm and full pecs, defined abs, and strong arms that are covered in intricate tattoos. His biceps are also decorated with intricate designs, winding around his arms and ending at his wrists. I could admire this man all day and not get bored.

My cheeks flush as I take in his impressive physique. His broad shoulders, perfectly chiseled jawline, and toned chest send my pulse racing. He looks powerful, and every part of him screams Alpha.

"More like you'll be screaming Alpha," Lexa mutters as she drools over our mate like he is a piece of meat to be devoured.

My eyes follow his hands to his pants. In one quick motion, he unzips his jeans, letting them fall to the floor before stepping out of them. "I thought you were escaping?" he taunts as he grips the shower door handle.

I reach for it, but he rips it open, invading my shower. His eyes flicker as he steps in. Water cascades over his body, steam billowing and fogging the glass. He looks down at me, meeting my gaze, and I take a step back, my back pressing against the wall. He takes a step closer, and all I can do is watch, mesmerized, as he moves closer. "You won't ever escape me again," he purrs as he presses his hard chest against mine, his hand gripping my hip as he presses closer.

The mate bond goes berserk with need. While his hand trails over my hip and skates across my ribs when he suddenly cups my neck in his hand, his fingers grazing along his mark on my neck. I shiver, which makes him smile.

"Not with this," he murmurs.

He takes my hand in his and kisses my palm. "You're mine," he murmurs, and I can feel all of my resolve melting away. The steamy air wraps around us, and the electricity between makes my earlier anger fade to the back of my mind.

Yeah, I'm definitely caught, I think to myself when his lips crash down on mine. His hands are rough but gentle against my skin. His touch ignites a fire inside me, and my heart starts beating faster. All too soon, he pulls away, breaking the kiss.

CHAPTER
SEVENTY-THREE

"Well, you seem to be in a better mood now." He chuckles.

"I was until you stopped," I growl, wrapping my arms around his neck.

"I thought you wanted to escape me?" he laughs.

It is still irking me, but it is mostly forgotten. "You ordered me," I tell him, still a little annoyed.

"I don't want to order you, Lena. But you need to slow down, I don't want to be your Alpha. I want to be your mate, but I won't watch you run yourself into the ground with exhaustion either."

"Well, unfortunately, you'll always be able to pull rank over me now that you've marked me," I tell him. He frowns slightly and I let him go. Mates are supposedly equal yet everything in our nature says otherwise. It's a little disappointing that no matter what I'll always be at a disadvantage compared to him.

"That is what trust is for," Lexa tells me and I sigh, knowing she is right.

Axton and I shower quickly so we can organize dinner and bathe the kids. Hopping out of the shower, I put my pajamas on, and head down stairs with Axton right behind me.

"I'll start dinner if you want to grab the boys?" I tell him when we reach the bottom. We part ways and I head for the kitchen. I start rummaging through the pantry and then the fridge grabbing ingredients out when I hear my phone ring. Looking over at the microwave, I see Axton must have put it on the charger before he came upstairs to invade my shower. Wiping my hands on a tea towel, I pick it up and notice it is Marco.

I quickly answer it. "Hey, what's up?" I ask him, turning back to the frying pan where I was cooking my ground beef and onion for my spaghetti.

"I have the files you requested from the council," he tells me.

"Huh? I only just ordered them today?" I tell him.

"Well, one of the supernatural court's officer's delivered them personally because the council hasn't been able to get a hold of me."

"Right. So why are they looking for you?" Marco sighs.

"What is it?" I ask him when I hear someone in the background talking.

"Who are you with?" I ask him.

"Soyer, I needed him to let me into the council chambers here, I didn't have my keys. I was at the club across the road when the officer showed up to escort me back to the courts. I put your documents in your filing box for you." Marco explains.

"Okay—what aren't you telling me? Why are you being escorted?" I ask him just as Axton comes out, setting Kyan in his high chair, and Luke follows with Bane doing the same. Axton straps the boys in then comes over bumping me out of the way to take over.

"We are all under suspicion, I guess you and I will be next. But that is not all, the human governments might be getting involved with the entire strigoi situation," Axton glances at me overhearing him and he gives me a questioning look.

"Wait, you're under suspicion for being strigoi and me?" I ask him.

"No, no, that is a different matter."

"I'm not following," I tell him now, becoming confused.

"They want to interview me about your parents, with everything going on with your father they are wondering—"

"They think I killed my parents?" I ask gobsmacked they would think that.

"Yes, and they think I covered it up. I have to go but I'll fill you in when I—" I hear the jiggling of keys and a door shut when Marco speaks again. "Why is Cane here?"

"What?" I hear Soyer ask in the background.

"Probably parked here and went to the club. I'll find him so I can lock the gates. Go, I'll find him and ask him to move his car." I hear Soyer tell him.

"Right… Elena, your documents are in your filing box, I will let you know what is going when I know,"

"Fine, but stay in touch." I tell him. We hang up and I turn to look at Axton.

"Marco will handle it. Don't stress over it." I nod my head, taking over dinner again. Axton wanders off while I set the pasta in the boiling water, he soon returns with his laptop and sits at the table and opens it.

Luke is playing his video game while the boys munch on their toast in their highchairs while waiting for me to finish cooking. "What are you working on?" I ask Axton.

"Payrolls," he answers and I nod my head. Ten minutes later dinner is cooked and Axton pushes his laptop aside and gets up to help me set dinner out. Yet my mind is on those files, knowing they hold the answers I need so I barely remember dinner at all. Until Axton is clearing the table which makes me look up.

"Sorry," I mutter knowing I zoned out.

"Come on, help me get the boys bathed so we can have an early night," he tells me and I stand up. Luke is stacking the dishwasher and I move to grab Bane. His face covered in spaghetti sauce. I chuckle wiping his face with his bib before following Axton to the hall. Stopping, I peer back at Luke. "You ok?" I ask him and he looks over at me, dish in hand. He gives me a thumbs up and I nod watching as he turns back to his task.

The night seems to end in the same routine except now I am staring at the ceiling twiddling my thumbs bored.

"Why don't you pick a movie to watch or something?" Axton suggests and I look over at him. He has spent the last few hours checking his laptop every five damn minutes.

"What are you waiting on?" I ask him.

"The notification for the quarterly taxes?"

"It's nearly midnight. Check it in the morning," I tell him.

"Supernatural courts don't sleep. It's twenty four hours. And Marco put an urgent request on it." Axton says and I see him refresh his portal again. Shaking my head I lean over him to steal the remote when I hear his laptop make its notification jingle. Falling back against my pillow I start flicking through the many apps on the TV when he groans.

"What?"

"My laptop is about to die," he curses and I sigh.

"Can I email it to yours?" he asks.

"Can't it wait until morning?" I ask him, becoming annoyed that he told me I can't work but he's done nothing but work all damn night.

"I need to send it off, it's past due," I groan. Just as I got comfy. Getting up, and tossing the blanket back, Axton jumps to his feet.

"I'll grab it," he tells me. quickly leaving to head to his office to retrieve it. "Why do these apps have so many movies, how are you supposed to pick?" I ask Lexa, when nothing catches my attention. Axton returns and hands me my laptop. I unlock it.

"Password is your name."

"That's it?" Axton asks and I nod.

"That is the shittiest password, anyone could guess that."

"I have two factor authentication. Why, what is yours?" I ask him.

"Your date of birth."

"And you think my password is shitty, and I know you don't have two factor authentication," I tell him as he unlocks my computer. My phone bings and I approve it being unlocked while he takes a seat.

"Yeah, good point," Axton mumbles, sitting beside me. He finds whatever he sent to my email before tapping his chest and I raise an eyebrow at him. He pats his chest again.

"Elena, now," he growls and I roll my eyes and move closer only for him to jerk me so I am half laying on him.

"Fuck sake, I can't see the TV now!" I whine.

"Because I want to show you something." Axton purrs burying his face in my neck. He taps my laptop screen and I glance at it. My brows furrow, confused at what I am looking at because it has nothing to do with taxes or what he claimed he was doing. Instead it's the title for his pack.

"What?" I ask him peering up at him.

"I don't want to be your Alpha, Lena," Axton murmurs. "I want to be your mate,"

"You're Alpha," I remind him.

"Not on paper," he tells me and my head jerks back to the screen. My eyes widen when I see his name is gone and mine in its place as the Alpha. I blink at the screen. He gave me his pack....

"Axton, I don't want your pack. I have two,"

"Now three, I may be Alpha, but I will never be your Alpha, now we are equal," he whispers as I stare at the screen. "I'd rather be your Lupha." he chuckles and I look at him.

"Lupha?" I chuckle,

"You can tell Michelle, I said thanks for the honorary title, I thought she had a speech impediment until I kept hearing your pack call me it," he laughs and I smile.

Axton grabs the laptop, setting it aside before turning back to me. A devious smile on his lips as he leans down, pressing his lips to mine. "I love you, Alpha." He mumbles against my lips, and I chuckle.

"Love you too, Lupha."

"Is it weird that I don't actually hate it? I can get used to it," he chuckles.

CHAPTER
SEVENTY-FOUR

Elena

    Axton and I spent the night watching movies, or I did because he fell asleep about twenty minutes in. I have been listening to him snore quietly ever since. Flipping my pillow over, I try to get comfy. However, my mind is on what Marco had said earlier about us being suspected of for my parents' murder when, in fact, it was a murder-suicide. One done out of my mother's love for us, but I now wonder if it was also to put herself out of her own misery of living with a broken mate bond. I can't imagine that torture.

    My mind doesn't want to switch off, conjuring up every scenario from the past couple of days. How rapidly our lives have changed. I can't remember how we got here. How did our lives get to this point? It seems more like I am thinking of someone else's memories, not mine. Or maybe I am still in shock and grief that is making me feel like an outsider in my own life. I want to find a way to make sense of the chaos, but it feels like I am grasping at straws. I feel like I have been living in a parallel universe with no control over my life. I just want to go back to the way things were. The way things were when our lives weren't so broken. So once again, in the dead of night, sleep eludes me.

My mind keeps churning, working in overdrive, and my body refuses to rest. I can't shake the feeling of restlessness that keeps me awake, and I know I need to find something to occupy myself.

My thoughts fixate on the files Marco left for me at the council chambers. It is almost as if they hold the answers to all of our problems, and I need to find a way to access them. I won't be able to rest until I have those files. As I sit up in bed, my eyes adjust to the darkness, I know I have to go get them.

So, I slip out of bed, being extra mindful not to wake Axton, who always seems to have a way of sensing when I am up to something.

The only problem is they are sitting untouched in my filing box at the council chambers. With a sense of guilt, I get dressed as quietly as possible, not wanting to wake Axton. He stirs but rolls over, blissfully unaware of my escape. I tiptoe to the closet, and grab some clothes. I grab a pair of dark jeans, a black sweater, and a pair of black tennis shoes. Glancing over my shoulder toward the bed, I quickly dress and grab my keys from the bedside table before heading out the door.

Guilt washes over me as I sneak out of the house, but my need for answers outweighs everything else. The night air is cool and crisp as I step out of the house, the moon casting its pale light over the world around me. I gently pull the door closed and rush to my car. Putting the car in neutral, I let the car roll down the driveway and onto the street. With one last parting glance at the house, I start the car. He won't even realize I left, and it is like a ten-minute drive.

I move quietly through familiar streets. The city streets are eerily still and silent, the darkness only illuminated by the occasional streetlight. I can feel the tension in the air, and I feel a chill run down my spine as I drive. The streets are coated in a thick layer of fog and I can barely see the white lines on the road and the outlines of the surrounding buildings.

The quietness of the city is unnerving, making my senses on high alert as I near my destination.

"It's the curfew, remember? The entire city has a curfew now. You're freaking out for nothing," Lexa reminds me and I exhale, having forgotten all about the city being on lockdown during the night. A guilty feeling still nags at me, knowing I am sneaking around at this hour knowing I am violating my mate's rules for the city, but my curiosity got the best of me.

Pulling up at the council chambers, the gates are open. "Crap, Soyer must have forgotten to close them," I curse and Lexa grumbles in my head, but it saves me from unlocking them. Upon pulling into the parking lot, I find it deserted. No cars in sight. I turn the car off and reach into my purse, which I left in the car. I rummage through it, looking for my keys and pass card for the security doors inside. Finding them, I shove my door open and climb out.

The council chambers at night are hauntingly eerie. The only sound is the occasional wind gust through the deserted parking lot. The darkness of the night is only broken by pale moonlight. The fog seems to add to the sense of dread as I look up at the huge building cast in shadow by the skyscrapers surrounding it. As I approach the council chambers, the shadows in the windows seem to come alive. I know it is just my paranoia, and Lexa has a fun time making fun of me as I make my way to the huge doors.

I place my key in the panel and the sliding doors open. I rush inside to the alarms and flip open the box to turn the alarms off; however, when I look at the panel, I notice they already are off.

"Gee, I know Marco was in a rush, but damn, this is just plain careless," Lexa mutters to me.

Closing the alarm panel, I move to the next set of doors and unlock them with my card. I push through the turnstiles and head toward the filing room, turning lights on as I pass.

Once again, I use my card to open the door and flick the lights on. They flicker and buzz before turning on and illuminating the place. Rows of hardwired cabinets line this room. Each pack has its own row. Mine is at the back by the far window covered in steel bars. I wander toward the back, where my filing cabinet and postal box are.

I set my bag on the desk in the far corner near my filing cabinet. I slide my card through the swipe code, it turns green and opens the door for me to slide out and rummage through. I find the envelope sitting at the top and grab it out. Shutting it with my hip, the cabinet bings telling me it's locked, and I wander to the desk to check everything is here when suddenly the lights go out.

The room is plunged into darkness, and I stare at the ceiling and instantly reach for the lamp on the desk. It doesn't turn on. "Well, duh. The power is out!" Lexa tells me and I groan at my stupidity.

"Just grab it and let's go," Lexa tells me. My eyes adjust to the darkness and I move back to my purse, cramming the file into it. I pull the strap over my shoulder when I notice the parking lot lights are still on. "Aren't the city lights on a different grid?" Lexa asks. "Maybe," I offer when I notice two cars in the rear parking lot through the steel bars.

"Wait, aren't those Soyer's and Cane's cars?" Lexa asks as I peer out into the eerie, foggy parking lot. I lean closer peering out the window. "Maybe they walked to the club across the road and caught a taxi home," I mumble to myself. Shaking my head, I turn around, head down rummaging at the bottom of my bag for my keys. However, I walk into a wall. I stagger back, when a set of hands grip my arms. A growl tears out of me and I lift my gaze, finding Alpha Cane. I exhale a breath of relief.

"Geez, Cane." I slap his arm trying to catch my breath after the fright he just gave me. "You nearly gave me a heart attack." I laughed aloud. He stares at me, and I wonder if he is drunk.

"Did you come to collect your car? Is Soyer with you? Make sure you lock the gates on your way out," I remind him, about to step past him when he steps in my path. I look up at the man. He watches me with cold eyes that seem vastly different. It takes me a second to figure out why, the whites of his eyes are red. I squint at him. "Cane, are you alright?" I ask him. While Lexa presses anxiously against my skin, a shiver runs down my spine and dread pools in my stomach. His aura feels off. Different.

"I actually liked you," Cane tells me, speaking slowly.

"Pardon?" I ask, confused.

"But you just had to snoop, couldn't leave things be." He snarls. The next minute, I see his fist fly toward my face. Everything happens so fast that I didn't expect it. His fist connects with the side of my head so hard I see literal stars. With more force than that of any werewolf I've encountered.

Darkness swallows me seconds before I hit the ground, my ears ring loudly, and my head seems to have developed its own heartbeat as it throbs violently. Footsteps barely reach my ears, and I try to remember what is going on. Am I dreaming?

"It didn't have to be this way; I never asked for this. But you forced my hand!" Comes an angry voice when suddenly I feel, hear, and see nothing.

· CHAPTER ·
SEVENTY-FIVE

Axton

I jerk awake, my heart pounding in my chest and drenched in sweat. Peering up at the ceiling, I try to figure out what woke me. Was it just a nightmare? I can't remember the dream if it was. Something feels wrong. My body is on alert, my senses heightened, and overcome with a sense of fear and dread. I can feel the adrenaline pumping through my veins.

The room is dark and silent, broken only by my panting breaths.

"Elena..." I mumble, feeling her side of the bed. As I feel around for her body sleeping next to me, I find her side cold, as if she hadn't been there at all.

Fear creeps through my veins, and I sit up, looking toward the bathroom, but no lights are on either. I slowly sit up in bed, taking care not to make any sudden movements. Straining my ears, I listen for any sound that might indicate the cause of my unease. I can hear my heart beating in my chest and my breathing rhythm, but nothing else.

I reach for my lamp and switch it on. My eyes dart around the room. I jump out of bed, looking frantically around the room for any sign of her, while feeling for her through the bond. As I tug on the bond, Khan awakens.

"What is it?" Khan asks me. It takes a second for him to realize we can't feel Elena. It's almost like she is asleep, but we can usually feel her, sense her dreams, something. But we got nothing.

"Why can't I feel her or Lexa?" Khan panics.

"Maybe she is asleep in the boys' room?" I offer.

Stumbling blindly towards the boys' bedroom door, I poke my head in to find them both sleeping soundly. When I turn around, my eyes are drawn to the bedroom door. Seeing it open, I knew it was closed when we headed to bed. Fear courses through every fiber of my being, and I grab whatever clothes are closest and rush out of the room, heading toward Luke's room. Shoving his door open, he jerks awake and rubs his eyes.

"What?" he grumbles, while my eyes scan his room for any sign of her. My heart sinks when I realize that she's not there, and I look back at him in despair.

"Axton?" Luke mumbles, staring at me. Luke's face was filled with confusion, his eyes still heavy with sleep. He is wearing a pair of bright blue pajamas, and his hair was ruffled from the sudden awakening.

"It's probably nothing. Go back to sleep," I tell him before shutting his door.

Racing out of the house, I'm hit with cold air that feels like a slap in the face. I look for her in every direction, but nothing—no trace of her. As I step around the side of the house, the heavy air with dense fog made it difficult to see more than a few feet ahead. The fog dampening the sound of my breathing. Even the moon shines weakly through the haze, casting an eerie glow on the front yard. I stand still, listening carefully for any sound that may indicate where Elena is, when I notice her car is gone.

Panic builds within me; all I can think about is finding her. Pulling on our bond, I concentrate on reaching out to her. I search for any sign that will tell me where she went.

But even as my bond stretches, it reaches the end of its tether. Khan also feels for any sense of direction. He reaches farther than ever before, but there's still nothing to be found. She's gone, and deep down, I know I have to find her before it's too late...

As I open the mind-link, I feel for Eli. Forcing myself into his head. He groans, waking up.

"What is it, Alpha?" He groans, half asleep.

"Have you seen or heard from Elena?" I ask him, which has him suddenly wide awake.

"What, no... Why?"

"She's missing, and I can't feel her. Send Michelle to watch the boys and Luke. I need to find her. Something is wrong; I can feel it." I tell him, and I hear him opening the mind-link to our warriors to send out a search party while I race back inside.

Grabbing the house phone, I dial her number, but it goes straight to voicemail.

I try not to panic as I wait for Michelle to arrive, running through scenarios in my head of what could have happened and why she is gone. But no matter how much I think, nothing is coming to me, only white noise in my mind. Finally, Michelle comes bursting through the door. The moment she does, I snatch my keys and phone off the table and run for my car. I race down the steps, and only when I reach the final step do I suddenly feel her. My mind-link opens quickly, and I reach out to her.

"Elena?" I call out to her.

"Axton," she murmurs, her voice barely audible.

"Where are you, babe?" I ask, knowing something is wrong. The pain hits me like a tidal wave, my head throbbing to its beat; I can feel her disorientation and confusion as if it were my own.

"Elena, stay awake. Where are you?" I ask firmer. Khan presses beneath my skin. "She's east of us," Khan tells me.

"It's Cane..."

"What's Cane?" I ask her, trying to keep her awake, so I can feel which direction she is in.

"He's the strigoi..... He...." she mumbles through the link, and my brows pinch when I feel her fading again. I lose focus on the bond when pain courses through the front of my face and the side of my head.

"Listen to my voice, Elena," I command her. "Keep your eyes open and stay awake."

Knowing we didn't have any more time, I rush to the car, throw my door open and start it up. The engine roars to life under me as I push hard on the accelerator and take off. I reverse into the mailbox as I pull out of the driveway.

"Elena?!" I yell when I get one word before she cuts out completely. "... Chambers."

"Elena?"

I call out to her, trying to focus on the road and the mind-link.

"Elena?" The bond dies once again, and I lose her, but we have one direction.

"Chambers?" I mutter under my breath.

"Marco sent the papers she filed for to her filing box," Khan tells me.

"The council chambers," I gasp, forcing the mind-link open before telling my warriors to head to the council chambers. Pressing the button on my phone, I ring Marco telling him to get back here before I hear fighting, and I know he will kill anyone in his way to get back to us.

Hanging up, trusting he'll find a way to get back here, I ring the one person I don't want to, Osiris.

"This better be important to wake me at such an ungodly fucking hour!" he answers after a few rings.

"I need your help. He got Elena." I hear movement as I race through the streets, taking a corner far too sharp, and the car slides out, the back end smashing into a telephone pole.

"Who has her?" he asks.

"Cane... Cane is the strigoi!"

CHAPTER
SEVENTY-SIX

E lena

"Elena! Elena!" Axton's voice yells through the mind-link, waking me. I blink, my head pounds to its own beat. My vision even feels like it's pulsating, and my ears are ringing.

"Come on, baby. Stay with me," I try to focus on his voice. Try forcing myself to stay awake.

"I can feel you. We're on our way."

"Stay with me, babe," Axton tells me, and my head rolls on my shoulder when someone grips my hair, jerking my head back, and I come face to face with Alpha Cane. Alpha Cane is a strigoi. However, he looks vastly different. The whites of his eyes are blood-red, while his dilated pupils are pale yellow. His skin is pale, and his face is gaunt.

He looks nothing like the man that I've come to know. It's hard to wrap my head around the idea that they're the same person. This man resembles a monster you'd see in your nightmares, not in the waking world. His body is thin and wiry, but I know not to underestimate him because of his size. Strigoi are powerful and strong. His long fingernails are sharp against my cheeks, and his teeth are sharp and jagged. He moves with supernatural speed as he glances over his shoulder, sending a chill down my spine.

It takes a few moments for my memory of what happened to return.

"You with it, Elena?" Cane says, slapping my face. I groan, the slightest tap worsening the pounding in my head. "Is she alright?" I hear a groggy voice.

"I think so." Cane mumbles, then he lets me go. He steps back, and I dazedly look around to find I'm tied to a chair. It smells rancid down here, and it only takes me a few seconds to learn why. I'm in the tunnels under the city.

The tunnels were dark and damp, the smell of mildew and sewage filling the air. Along one wall were TV screens connected to surveillance cameras located throughout the city, allowing Cane to easily watch over the entire place. It is clear that Cane had set up a base of some sort in the tunnels, with a few chairs and tables scattered around. The flickering of the TV screens cast eerie shadows across the walls. Cane paces, clutching his hair like a madman, muttering to himself.

"What have I done? What have I done? Axton will lose his mind when he finds out."

"I didn't want it to be this way. I never asked for this!" he growls, spinning to look at me.

He points a long, slender finger at me. "You, this is your fault. You had to snoop. Why couldn't you let things be?" he growls when I hear another voice.

"Just let her go. We can still fix this. We can get you help...." come another voice, making me turn my head to see Soyer. He is also tied to a chair, and he is in a bad way. Blood covers him. He has huge slashes across his chest. Blood is matted in his hair. His face is twisted in pain, and his breathing is labored. Eyes wide and fearful, and he is clearly in shock. His clothing is torn, and his body is trembling, as if he is struggling to stay conscious.

"Shut up. Shut up. Shut up!" Cane shouts, pacing back and forth, talking to himself. I stare at Soyer, who looks half dead, his wounds too extensive as his wolf tries to heal him.

Hearing a groan, Soyer whimpers, and Cane stops his pacing. Turning quickly, it sends my eyes down at Soyer's feet, and my eyes widen when I notice his mate lying on the ground. She groans again, and he starts thrashing in his chair.

"No... Leave her, Cane. She won't tell. SHE WON'T TELL!" Soyer yells at him when he grabs her hair, ripping her onto her knees. She cries out, and Soyer tries to shift in his restraints, but he's too badly injured, his body stops.

"Use me... Use me!" Soyer screams at Cane. Cane turns his head, looking at Soyer, and smiles the most sadistic grin.

He then sinks his fangs into her neck, and I notice the multiple bite marks covering his mate's body and neck. She screams, and Soyer roars, thrashing so much in his seat it tips over. Tears stream down my face, and I feel the mind-link open up.

"Where are you?" Axton urges, and I peer around frantically. Trying to get my foggy mind to work.

"Um... I'm in the tunnel. You need to get here. Bring help! You need to find us."

"Which ones?" I try to think because I have no idea how long I was out, yet the smell tells me these tunnels are linked to the sewage system.

"The... I think it's the---" Suddenly, Cane is standing in front of me and grips my face, his nails piercing my cheeks, making me cry out.

"Who are you mind-linking?" he growls, blood covering his lips and dripping off his chin. My eyes dart to the side at Soyer's mate's crumpled body on the ground, lying motionless. Her body is covered in multiple bite marks. Several parts of her clothing are ripped, and her pants are missing completely. I hate to think about why her pants are missing.

Her blonde hair is now caked in blood, partly obscuring her face where it has fallen, which is pale, looking like she has lost a lot of blood. Blood is dripping from her neck, and her eyes are closed, so I know she has lost consciousness. Soyer tries to nudge her with his foot, which he manages to get free of his restraints when the chair fell.

"Burn in hell, you fucking monster." I scream at him. Alpha Cane snarls, all glamour removed. He is the stuff of nightmares as he smiles sadistically, his face covered in her blood when he speaks.

"Wrong answer!" he snarls, and the next second, all I see is darkness.

CHAPTER SEVENTY-SEVEN

Axton

Trying Alpha Thomas and Soyer again, but neither answered. Giving up, I growl, pulling into the council chamber's huge iron gates. "She's here; I can feel her," Khan tells me. I nod because I feel she is close also.

My stomach sinks as I pull into the parking lot next to her car. I stare at the huge council building. The night was foggy and dark, illuminated only by the faint yellow light of the moon peeking through the thick clouds. Lightning in the distance, just breaking through the fog, makes everything look white with each flash. The smell of rain in the air raises goosebumps. We will get a huge storm, that I am certain of. The feel of the surrounding air is charged, not like when I first left; it was chilly, and now the air is warmer and thicker.

In the distance, I can see pack members carrying flashlights, fanning out, and searching the area for Elena. The council building looms before me, a large, imposing structure made of dark stone walls. Its windows were high and barred. Climbing out of the car, I hear a loud engine. This makes me turn toward the gates in time to see the lights of cars entering the gates. One of them is Osiris' car pulling in. Of all my rivals, I didn't think he'd show up. He parks his car beside mine, and I watch as he steps out. He looks around, surveying the area, and then strides toward me.

"Sorry, I got here as fast as I could. I drove by Soyer's place to see if he was home. Neither his nor his wife's car were there." Osiris tells me, and I nod, looking up at the building.

"Come on," I tell him, knowing our men were waiting for one of us to let them in. Jogging to the front door, I unlock it and rush in to turn off the alarm, but it's already off. Osiris tries the lights, but they don't turn on. Osiris turns to one of his men. "Find the circuit breaker. Get these lights back on." Osiris orders as our men start rushing inside to search the building.

"And you're sure she is still here?" Osiris asks, and I nod.

"The bond, I can feel her, but she isn't conscious," I tell him as Eli rushes in, just in jeans, his chest bare, and his hair poking in every direction.

"Anything?" he asks, and I shake my head.

"Slater found Soyer's car around the back with Alpha Cane's. On the street, they found Luna Amy's car."

Osiris calls his men to the foyer, handing out orders and telling them which sections and floors to check.

"We'll check the filing rooms and this level," Osiris tells them as they break off into groups. My pack is out searching the surrounding buildings and outside.

We searched every room of the council chambers before moving down a corridor toward the archive room. It is the only room that has been checked on this floor. Yet, I am certain she is here. She feels close. Stepping into the dusty room, the power still isn't on, making it difficult to see.

The archive room is large and from floor to ceiling with towering shelves of musty books and old documents. This room is covered with dust, and the windows are shuttered and barred. The room almost appeared lost and forgotten in its condition. You can tell no one has been down here in a while, at least not since technology came in.

"You check that side; I'll take the back," I tell Osiris, and we split off.

As I make my way through the shelves, I take in the dusty old books and documents. Most of them are yellowed with age. Some are ancient manuscripts written in languages I couldn't even begin to identify. I pass by a shelf filled with artifacts from long-forgotten packs, and a few shelves of old maps and globes. As I walk down the narrow shelf corridor, I feel for the bond. "I didn't think you would show up," I say to Osiris, turning to look at him.

"Why wouldn't I?" Osiris asks me.

"Because it's me," I answer honestly.

"We may not see eye to eye, Axton, but that does not have anything to do with your ability to run this city. I know firsthand how challenging it is and admit it is a lot to take on."

"Is this your way of apologizing?" I ask.

"Nah, my reasons are more selfish than that," he tells me, and I stop.

"Huh?"

"My father is still missing, or have you forgotten?" he asks me when I turn to the next aisle, only to run into him.

"I haven't forgotten," I tell him.

"You just believe what everyone else believes, that I killed him," I shrug because that is what I believe. Osiris nods once and then peers around. "Did you?" I ask him, and he sighs heavily.

"My old man and I may not have gotten along, but he was a terrific father. I was just a terrible son, but we fixed all that. We sorted everything out," he shrugs. I side-eye him, not believing him.

"Besides, I thought you were the strigoi, so I guess we're even." Osiris tells me, and I stop.

"You seriously thought I was a strigoi?" I ask, a little shocked. I thought he was trying to turn the city against me, not that he actually believed the nonsense he spouted.

"Well, you're always hanging with that bloodsucker."

"Marco," I correct, and he nods.

"Yeah, and it made sense why this strigoi was never seen or caught. You could have easily covered it up. That is why I went after your seat on the council."

"Is that why you also went after Elena?"

"Nah, that was just to get under your skin. Not that I would have minded had she taken me up on the offer," I growl at him, and he puts his hands up in mock surrender and laughs.

"What, she's fucking hot," he shrugs, and Khan presses forward, not liking how he speaks of her. We reach the doors to the corridor when, finally, the lights flicker on.

"Finally!" Osiris says, tossing his hands up in the air.

"So why did you come back? Your father went missing the moment you showed up here. Kind of makes you look guilty," I admit.

CHAPTER
SEVENTY-EIGHT

"He called me back. He wanted me to give evidence against Derrick. Only when I got here, he was already missing."

"Because you reported him missing." I state.

"Look, I know it looks suspicious, but I didn't kill him," Osiris says, and I can hear underlying anger in his tone.

"Wait, what evidence did you have to give against Derrick?"

"My father wanted him off the council. He found out about his true identity, who he used to be. I told my father to let it be and that I'd handle it. He refused. Said he had evidence that Derrick and Thomas were dealing and trafficking women again with Alpha Lyle," I stop.

"Alpha Lyle? As in Cane's father?" Osiris nods. I hold up a finger, trying to piece this puzzle together.

"Now I know you're lying. Elena found the bank statements...."

"With my name on them, yeah." Osiris digs in his back pocket. He produces his phone, unlocks it, and presses a few things on the screen. He then turns the phone around to show me. Supernatural council ID. "I was undercover and have been for three years, but I don't work directly with the supernatural council; I work with the human government agencies. It's why I have been gone so long."

"So that is what you meant when you said I wasn't the only one with friends in the council," I exhale.

"Exactly,"

"Well, if you're in the supernatural council, why do you hate Marco so much?" I ask.

"Do you have any idea the links to the underworld he has? His brother was a crime boss, not just in the supernatural world but also in the human cities. He covered up for him. I investigated him in my first year. However, nothing would stick until my boss pulled me from the case and said I was stirring up trouble, but that is part of the reason I started looking into Derrick. Derrick worked for him, he used to be in the Winter Ridge pack before his father banished him for selling his pack members. Only when he left did his father realize how much money he was bringing the pack and that his son was getting them out of debt."

"Winter Ridge pack?"

"You know, the pack that was killed by their mates. After Derrick left, his father almost declared bankruptcy, so he started dealing drugs for Floyd. When that wasn't enough, he started selling the women, who in turn sold them off to—"

"My father," I finish for him. Wait, killed by their mates? Elena did mention briefly that Noleen recognized Derrick before she died.... I just thought she was one of the women sold. Well, clearly, she was.

"Wait, what happened to the women?" I ask.

"No idea. They were never caught. But I gather that they fled when they learned that the Alpha was planning to sell some children. From the evidence, I have seen those poor women were passed around the pack even by their mates, practically tortured. I guess one day they just snapped."

"Elena's pack," Khan tells me, and I nod to him.

"Our pack."

"I looked into you too when I found out that you moved to this city; I warned my father away from you. He said you weren't like your father, different. I didn't believe him. So I did some digging and found out Marco covered up that you killed your father. It wasn't until I moved here that I got the full story of what happened to your mother, so I don't blame you. He deserved it."

"Wait! You knew all this and still thought I was strigoi?" I ask incredulously.

"Just because I said I understood why you did it doesn't mean I liked you." he laughs.

"And why don't you like me again?" I ask.

"Because you were getting in the way of my investigation against Derrick. Both of you were constantly in the media, drawing more attention to the city I was currently investigating, so I stepped in."

"He was blackmailing me! I had no beef with him. He started it," I tell him, and Osiris looks away.

"Yeah, well, I didn't know the full story then."

My brows furrow, confused, before my eyes widen. "It was you.... You sent Derrick the photos?" I ask as the sudden revelation hits me. Osiris looks away.

"Aren't we looking for Elena?" he asks, and I know I am right.

"We can multitask." I growl at him.

"Yes, I found an old phone when investigating your father's link to Derrick and came across Marco's link to them. I then had someone make a copy of his swipe card and broke into his office. That is where I found the phone. I then sent the photos to Derrick, hoping it would get you kicked out of the city." Shaking my head, I can't believe this shit.

"Yet you've been all buddy-buddy with Thomas, Derrick, and Cane since you got here."

"Gotta keep up appearances, haven't you heard the term? Keep your friends close, your enemies closer," Osiris asks, and I glance at him.

"Be glad I wasn't trying to be your best friend, Axton. Because that would have meant you were my enemy," he tells me as he checks the bathrooms. I check the men's, finding them empty. Coming out, Osiris is stepping out of the women's.

"Empty," I tell him.

"Where to next? She isn't here. My men haven't found anyone upstairs either."

"No, she has to be close."

"What about the tunnels?" asks Osiris.

"Maybe she found a way down there." My stomach sinks as I remember they were sealed off years ago after a fire broke out in them back when I first moved here.

"Sealed off, if she can just stay awake long enough for me to feel her location," I tell him.

"Can always check anyway. Might as well be thorough." Osiris shrugs.

We all descended into the basement together and followed its winding corridors until we reached two massive gates blocking access to the tunnels beneath the council.

Having searched this floor, we regroup with our pack members in the main foyer.

Osiris quickly hops into action and takes over. I am thankful because I can barely think straight, and worry about my mate consumes my mind. He orders three of his men to check Alpha Canes packhouse for me, while sending the rest out to check neighboring businesses and houses.

I send half of mine to close off all city access points and lock the place down. As our packs take off as ordered, Osiris, Eli, and I turn back to our original mission and head toward the security personnel area to check out the basement.

As we turn to leave, we hear Alpha Thomas yell out to us from behind. "Any luck finding her?" he asks while jogging over quickly.

"Nothing yet," Osiris explains. "But Axton is certain she is here." He glances over at me with a knowing look.

"I came as soon as I heard your voicemail," Thomas tells us, and I can't help but feel a little confused since I hadn't sent any such message. Khan speaks up, then.

"Osiris probably left a voicemail for Thomas," Khan tells me.

CHAPTER
SEVENTY-NINE

Osiris and I descend into the basement together, Thomas and Eli go to check the old park amenities out the back of the council to check the tunnels there. Walking down the winding corridors until we reach two massive gates blocking access to the tunnels beneath the council. We could see the old and weathered stone walls, showing signs of wear and tear from years of use.

As we got closer to the gates, we could feel a chill in the air, the wind whistling loudly in the tunnels. Moving toward the back of the basement, we come across the old tunnel system, and it is, as expected, completely sealed off with bars. Osiris shines the flashlight into the dark tunnel, illuminating the ancient cobblestone walls and the thick layer of mold and mildew that has settled over everything.

Peering over his shoulder, I can just make out the old rusted pipes along the ceiling and the occasional rat scurrying around in the shadows.

"Nothing," Osiris says when I hear the faintest noise.

"We can check."

"Shh," I tell him, holding up a finger.

Bending down, I listen. Osiris instantly fell silent, but I thought I heard a banging sound like old copper pipes being banged on. When I don't hear it anymore, I rise to my feet.

We turn for the stairs when Osiris grabs my arm just as we hear it again. We both turn slowly, looking at the tunnel system. Moving toward the bars, I glance around the room, looking for something to break them. Peering into the tunnel, Osiris hands me a flashlight, and I shine it down the tunnel.

"Elena!" I shout. Silence for a few seconds when I hear Soyer's voice. It is faint, but I know I am not mistaken.

"She's down here," I look at Osiris, and his eyes widen. "Find something to break these bars," Osiris rushes off, but returns seconds later with nothing. Digging my phone from my pocket. I ring Thomas, knowing Eli had left to search the old tunnels under the amenities block of the park out back with Thomas. I could feel he was mind-linking with the patrols on the borders.

The phone rings a few times when Osiris grips one bar. "Grab the other. We might be able to open it enough to squeeze through," Osiris tells me. I place the phone on the loudspeaker, grabbing one bar while Osiris grips the other. We bend the bars, creating a gap when Thomas finally answers.

"Hello?" he grumbles, sounding half asleep.

"Thomas, where are you? Bring some men and flashlights, along with a crowbar, to break these bars off," Osiris tells him. I place my foot on the brickwork, using it as leverage to pry the bars further apart.

"I'm at home. You want me to do what? What time is it?" My blood runs cold, and it is like a bucket of ice is tossed over me. Osiris' head snaps up, and his eyes meet mine. I can see the question in his eyes. If Thomas is at home, who is upstairs with Eli?

"That's not Thomas," Osiris murmurs when we hear rancorous laughter.

"Well done, Alpha. You are correct." A sinister voice has us both turning to find Thomas standing by the stairs. Only he isn't alone,

Eli's limp body is over his shoulder. He cracks his neck, and in the distance, I can hear Thomas demanding to know what is going on.

Khan presses beneath my skin, and Thomas' body shudders and ripples. It is like a veil is lifted, and Cane suddenly takes his place. However, this man is not the Cane I spent countless hours in meetings with and grew up with.

This Cane is a strigoi. He walks closer, stalking us like a predator hunting its prey. My skin ripples with the need to shift, and the moment Cane lunges at me just as I lunge at him, giving Khan control. Khan tears into Cane's arm at the same time Osiris shifts to help.

CHAPTER
EIGHTY

Elena

I groan as I come to, my head pounding to its own beat, and my limbs ache and feel heavy. "Elena! Psst..." I hear someone calling out my name, and I lift my head, turning it in his direction. The moment I move my head, blood trickles down my face from where Alpha Cane hit me. I squint. Even the dull lights down here are hurting my eyes. Peering over, I realize it is Soyer. My vision clears enough for me to see him still strapped to a chair not far from me, with a worried expression on his face.

"Can you slip out of your restraints?" he asks urgently while glancing over his shoulder and then past me in the other direction the tunnel travels. He inclines his head at me, motioning towards the metal cuffs that bind me to the chair.

"See if you can get out of your cuffs. Try to shift. You're our only chance," he tells me, and my eyes dart to the floor where his mate lay.

"Is she..."

"She's not dead, not yet anyway. But if he feeds on her again..."

he doesn't finish, and I nod, letting out a shaky breath while trying to feel for Lexa when pain courses through my stomach, making me scream. I double over in the chair, my breath stolen by the searing pain that leaves me gasping for breath. Only it is not mine but Axton's, which instantly has my mind going to the boys.

With a surge of determination, I try to free myself from them, but they are too tight, while calling for Lexa to wake up. Just when I thought all hope was lost, one of the cuffs suddenly snaps when Lexa shoves forward abruptly, feeling our mate. My entire body jerks forward, and we nearly fall face forward off the chair, my hand slapping the ground is the only thing that stops us. Lexa forces my arms and wrists to break, allowing my other wrist to slip free of the cuff.

"Where is Axton?" she panics.

"I don't know!" I tell her through gritted teeth as I fall on my side. My legs are still strapped, twisted awkwardly, and my claws slip free, cutting through the rope that binds my legs to the chair.

"I've finally managed to get a hold of my pack. They've just got here. I finally opened the mind-link. They're working on blocking the tunnel exits with your pack."

Dazedly, I crawl toward Soyer. "Where did Cane go?" I ask, and he looks at a camera mounted on the wall of the tunnel we are in. Looking at the cameras, I can see the council chambers and the streets where pack members are searching for us.

"How long until your pack finds us?" I ask.

"Not sure, I know they just got here. I don't know what tunnel we're in," he tells me, then nods toward the screens covering the walls. Turning, I see cars racing into the council chambers while Axton's men race toward them.

Suddenly, there is a loud thud in the distance, followed by shouts and yelling from somewhere deeper within the tunnel. This makes me glance over my shoulder.

"Quick, use that crowbar over there," Soyer says, nodding toward a bench filled with tools and miscellaneous crap. Staggering, I get to my feet, trying to find something, when pain rips through my side, making me clutch the counter.

Opening the mindlink I feel for Axton, but can't hold it long due to my head pounding, making me unable to focus. Grabbing the crowbar, I try to bend the metal arm of the chair he is strapped to. Then I attempt to pry it under the cuff. It doesn't work. His hands are purple from how tight the handcuffs are that are cutting off his circulation.

"Just do it!" Soyer tells me. I blink at him, wondering what he means. "Now! We haven't got time. My mate is dying. Do it!" Soyer yells at me, and I hear the savage sounds of men fighting, growling, and banging coming from somewhere in the tunnel. Clenching my teeth, I turn back to Soyer and lift the crowbar before bringing it down on his wrist. He lets out a pained groan and tries to pull his hand out, but nothing.

"Again!" he demands, and I bring it down, breaking his hand and wrist more. The sound is sickening when suddenly the fighting stops, making me pause to look down the tunnel. I hear cursing, recognizing the voice as Cane's, and my eyes widen.

Soyer rocks back in his chair, and I turn back to face him and lift the crowbar. "No, go take my mate and get out of here," Soyer says, and I glance down at his mate on the ground.

"Go!" He hisses at me, but I know I won't be able to carry her fast enough. Hearing footsteps, I race back to my chair, setting it back in place. Leaning the crowbar against the back of the chair, I can hear Cane getting closer and quickly take my seat, pretending to be still knocked out.

Dropping my head forward, and resting my arms along the armrests while praying he doesn't notice the cuffs aren't attached. Seconds later, he enters this part of the tunnel. His footsteps seem loud when I hear a thud, and something hits my foot. I don't dare lift my head to see who it is until I hear Cane muttering to himself as he leaves. Lifting my head, I find it is Axton's body. I lurch out of my seat, tapping his face. He groans, and I clamp my hand over his mouth while glancing over my shoulder.

"Set me free before he returns," Soyer whispers, and I lift my head. I don't want to leave Axton, but we'd need two people to help get him up. Rushing over with the crowbar, I break his other hand, and Soyer grits his teeth.

CHAPTER
EIGHTY-ONE

I hear his bones cracking as he slips free and starts undoing the restraints on his legs when the sound of footsteps returning reaches me.

Soyer looks at me in panic, and I race back to my seat again. Osiris is dumped on the ground this time, and I hold my breath, watching Axton's face near my feet when Soyer talks.

"Water, please." Soyer chokes out. Cane mutters something and wanders off, and I hear rustling before lifting my head slightly when I feel a flicker of something through the bond. My eyes drift back to Axton to find him looking at me. His eyes are pitch black, and I know Khan is forward with him. "When I say to, you fucking run," he mindlinks, and I realize he is just pretending to be knocked out.

"Do you hear me?" My eyes widen as I peer down at him.

"I'm not leaving you," I reply.

"Yes, you are. You run and don't come back, promise me." I shake my head when I hear Cane.

"Wait...what have..." I hear Cane begin to say when Soyer tackles him, and they fall and hit the ground at the same time. Axton lurches to his feet when Soyer is thrown off. Soyer's body slams against the wall with startling force and speed before he hits the ground. Cane gets to his feet, and just before Axton reaches him, Cane spins with inhuman speed and kicks him. Axton's body flies past me down the tunnel, and Cane roars. Stomping past me, he heads for Axton, and I grab the crowbar leaning against the chair and come up behind him.

The crowbar slices through his flesh like butter, and the sound of metal-piercing flesh echoes through the air as I drive it into his back. The entirety of Cane's body goes rigid. Then slowly, he turns to face me. In the distance, I see Axton getting up, but my attention is fixed on Cane, whose eyes are locked on mine. The crowbar — now coated in blood — punctured straight through him, but he doesn't seem to care. With an almost feral snarl, he pulls the crowbar out of his body and flings it aside.

I back up, feeling the intensity of his gaze upon me like a physical weight. His eyes bore into mine, and his lips curl back into a snarl as he stalks toward me and goes to grab me when I am shoved out of the way from behind.

I land next to Soyer's mate and see Osiris is the one that shoved me, and Axton is once again attacking Alpha Cane. Axton and Cane both lunge at each other with a ferocity that rivals wild animals. Axton delivers a swift kick to Cane's chest, sending him flying back, and Cane retaliates when he gets up, blocking Axton's next blow before returning a punch that sends Axton to the ground. Cane then grabs the crowbar and swings it at Axton, but Osiris pushes Cane, making him miss his target. Everything happening with blurring speed in such tight confines makes everyone almost impossible to track.

Axton then lunges at Cane, tackling him to the ground and pummeling him with his fists. The two of them fight fiercely, with neither gaining the upper hand. The fight is brutal, with both men grunting and hissing as they exchange blows while Osiris is trying to get back to his feet, looking rather dazed.

The walls of the tunnel copping a beating in the tight space, when Axton is flung against another wall like a rag-doll. I can see why strigoi are so feared. They are unmatched rivals. Something not meant for this world. My scream is deafening when I see Axton crawling to get to his feet.

My scream rings out loudly, echoing off the walls, when I see Cane pick up the crowbar to deliver a lethal blow. However, Soyer suddenly blocks it with his shoulder, throwing his body over Axton's head. I hear a sickening crack that would have been Axton's head had Soyer not used his body to shield him.

Soyer screams in agony, and Axton shoves him away just as Cane brings the crowbar down. However, this time, Axton's hand grabs it mid-swing. Pain slivers up my arm through the bond, but Axton doesn't let go.

Instead, he swipes Cane's feet out from under him just as Osiris shakes himself off and gets to his feet. Looking around, I grab a screwdriver off the counter just as Cane backhands Osiris into a wall. The air leaves his lungs in a loud wheeze, and I run forward, stabbing the screwdriver into Cane's neck repeatedly just as Axton is pulled to his feet by his grip on the crowbar when Cane stands.

His face twists in fury as Cane grabs my hand that is holding the screwdriver when I stab him again, and he squeezes. I feel my hand break and scream, losing my grip on the screwdriver when Cane swings his arm down and back, catching me under the ribs. I go flying back and hit the wall, which knocks the air out of me. Groaning, I lift my head in time to see Axton headbutt him, making Cane let go of the crowbar.

Cane stumbles back toward me, and I barely move in time as he falls over Soyer's mate's body on the ground. Axton lands on top of him, and I scramble to my feet, wheezing to catch my breath.

Cane and Axton land heavily on the ground while I try to get to the crowbar when Axton lifts his head to look at me.

"Run!" he commands, his eyes blazing, and I feel his aura blast me when he suddenly shifts. Khan's size obscures half the place. Werewolves are not made to fight in such tight confines. The command freezes me on the spot, sweat beads on my neck, not wanting to leave my mate. When Khan starts mauling Cane, his teeth tear into his neck. The next second, Khan's furious voice booms in my head.

"Run!" he screams the command through the link, and unable to fight it, I take off running when I hear footsteps racing toward me.

My eyes widen when I see pack members barreling into the tunnels, having located us. I point the way I just came when I hear a feral snarl, and Marco shoves past Thomas, who has finally arrived to assist. "It's Cane," I rasp out, and Marco nods, shoving past me and disappearing from where I just came.

"Elena, get out of here!" Alpha Thomas yells at me. Yet as I continue to run, I find I can't catch my breath and stagger when I near the tunnel exit into the basement. I clutch the wall, and my vision blurs as I peer through the bars to see Eli's lifeless body heaped on the floor.

Gasping, the pain makes my lungs burn. Tilting my head in the direction I came from, Khan's command keeps trying to force me out of the tunnels. I stagger, using the wall to hold myself up as pain drags through my chest with each breath. My vision dulls and blurs.

My breathing comes in short pants, each breath agonizing as pain replaces the adrenaline, and I clutch my chest. Only when I do, I feel something protruding from it. Dazedly, I glance down and blink at what I'm seeing.

The screwdriver is embedded in my chest between my ribs, my hoodie completely drenched with my blood, making it stick to me like a second skin. My fingers wrap around the handle, intending to rip it out when I fall forward and collapse when I'm unable to catch my breath.

CHAPTER
EIGHTY-TWO

Axton

Adrenaline surges through my veins as we get knocked aside with a heavy punch. Elena makes a run for it as chaos erupts. Alpha Cane moves with lightning speed, delivering a sidekick that sends us flying toward the counter. I'm forced to dodge falling objects as my heart races in my chest, and we're forced to shift back.

Cane grabs the back of my neck before I even have a chance to get up, slamming my face into the concrete once, twice. However, I am ripped back the third time when Cane is hit. Lifting my gaze, I see Osiris with the crowbar. Breathless, he staggers, catching himself on the wall. The crowbar slips from his fingers, and I reach out to grab it and spin around to use it. Cane shakes his head, black blood streaming down the side of his face, and he growls, revealing his sharp jagged teeth.

Clambering to my feet, I see two of him, my vision doubles. His face twists, and he swings at me, his claws raking down my chest. I see the blow too late, only being able to step back. Blood spews from my chest when I trip over Osiris behind me, landing on my ass. My head bounces off the cement floor, and I stare dazedly at the concrete ceiling, the blue fluorescent light flickering when Cane steps over me.

Running can just be heard in the distance, shouting, and Cane looks in the direction the voices are coming from before sneering and glaring back down at me.

"Give up, Cane. There is no escape from this. The place is surrounded," I rasp out between pained breaths.

"You're right, there's not, but if there is no escape for me, then there is no escape for you either." Cane sneers, reaching for me when I hear slow clapping. Cane pauses, he lifts his head, and I turn my head to see Marco strolling into the tunnel like he is merely taking a walk in the park. Pack members rush up behind him when Marco raises his hand, forcing them to halt.

"Wait, this tunnel is barely ten feet wide. What do you think this is, a game of Tetris? Twister?" Marco snarls as my warriors stop behind him. Cane growls, rising to his feet, his claws slipping from his fingertips as he stares down his new opponent.

"Seriously! Look at the size of him and me. This isn't the human centipede. Nobody needs to be tasting nobody's ass today. So back it up a little and give me some room to work with–" Marco looks at Cane and makes a funny face. Cane steps over me with a growl escaping him as he moves to face Marco.

"Well... If it isn't Gloom and Doom himself. Don't you think it's overkill? Nobody likes Dracula these days," Marco comments with a smirk. "They prefer vamps that glitter and fart fairy dust." Cane did not appreciate the jab and growls back at him. Marco steps closer, seemingly unfazed, which makes me concerned because Cane has done nothing but rag-doll us down here. But then again, Marco is a vampire, and an old one at that.

"So serious question..... Do you sparkle in the sunlight or just go poof and burst into flames?" Marco asks, and Cane growls.

"I'm just asking because you look like you just crawled out of a crypt," Marco teases. I blink at him, wondering what he is doing...

Marco places his hands in the air in mock surrender, a cunning smile on his lips.

"Now, don't take this the wrong way. I'm sure you have no trouble with the ladies, but just a little advice. Most like their vamps with a touch less deathly pallor, but who knows, maybe it'll become the new trend. You could call it 'Undead Chic'," Marco shrugs.

What in the world is he doing?

It takes me a second to figure out why he is fucking around in such a dire situation when I see Osiris helping Soyer get his mate out of the way, who's been trampled; god knows how many times. Marco is merely playing distraction, biding them time.

Cane's eyes glow red with fury, and he growls menacingly. "You think you're funny, Marco? Let's see if your jokes provide enough entertainment while I rip your throat out," Cane spits.

A grin spread across Marco's face. "Ah, such eloquent words," Marco retorts. "Let's see if you can back them up." With that, Marco lunges at him, aiming a punch at Cane's face with striking speed, making him stagger back.

Marco and Cane trade powerful blows with astounding strength and agility. As I crawl toward Soyer and help him stand, it's an all-out war. My men rush in to grab his mate and Osiris. When Marco is kicked, his body flies past me and into the concrete wall, cracking it under the force. I gasp, waiting for him to fall, but Marco lands on his feet. He growls, his eyes blazing as he runs at Cane, both clashing violently, and Soyer and I just get out of the way. We turn back to witness a violent display.

Despite Cane's agility and strigoi reflexes, Marco is just as quick, but he knows how to use his speed and strength to his advantage and soon has his arm is locked around Cane's neck. Blood splatters across the tunnel as Marco tightens his grip and his legs lock around Cane's waist.

Marco gets one hand free and pulls down on Cane's jaw. The sickening tearing sound is grotesque when Marco sinks his claws through the bottom of Cane's mouth and then twists sharply, ripping his bottom jaw off. Cane screams and thrashes, bucking in his hold, while Marco grits his teeth, twisting Cane's head before ripping it off and spraying me and Soyer in blood. He then collapses on his back, breathing heavily, while my vision turns funny. The bond suddenly falls silent.

Marco rolls Cane's body off him and sits up, pointing at two pack members. "Burn it, barbecue. Just don't eat it," he says, rising and clutching his knees. He looks over at me.

"I thought the fucker had me for a second," Marco breathes when one of the warriors comes running toward us. Osiris stumbles over to me when some pack members take Soyer's wife, and he grabs Soyer's other arm.

"Still think I'm strigoi?" I chuckle before coughing. Blood sprays across my hand, and I wipe my mouth, shaking the searing pain the cough causes off. We are making our way back when I hear Marco's voice.

"What is it?" Marco demands, looking at one of Osiris' men, who is staring at the only unbroken screen on the wall. Marco gets up, and I can tell he just fed Soyer's mate some of his blood, his fingers dripping off it as he rises to his feet. We stop, and Marco taps the TV screen. "Where is this place?" he demands. My brows furrow, and Osiris tilts his head before I look at him.

"I'll check," he mumbles, and I continue half-dragging Soyer when I hear Osiris speak.

"Dad?" I stop, turning slightly, wondering if I heard right, when one of my pack members starts screaming out. "Alpha! Alpha!" I see it's Slater when he barges through—a bewildered look on his face.

"It's Elena..." His words sent my blood cold, and I let Soyer go, shoving him at Thomas, who catches him before chasing after Slater. A little further down the tunnel—My heart nearly stops when I spot her face down on the concrete. I quickly roll her over, tapping her face. I get no response when I notice the screwdriver stabbed in her chest.

"No, no, no!" I panic. Her face is pale as a ghost.

"Get help!" I scream, lifting her up gently, barely noticing the warm liquid that trickles through her shirt onto my hands.

I run with her in my arms, tears streaming down my face as I mentally beg for her to hold on. Suddenly, the bond weakens, and so do my legs as they give out from under me. Khan howls in my head as I clutch her, tears trekking down my face as I feel her slipping away from me, the bond fracturing, splintering like shards of glass cutting through my soul, fading away with her.

"Where is he? Where did he run off with her?" I hear Marco's voice boom in the tunnel. My mind blanks when suddenly she is ripped out of my arms. Marco yanks the screwdriver out, and I lunge at him.

"What are you doing?" I yell at him, pressing my hands down on her wound, trying to stem the bleeding, when I notice she has stopped breathing, her heart beating so faint, pausing and sputtering between beats.

"Choose... either she lives or dies," Marco tells me, and I stare at him, confused.

"Choose, Axton!" Marco yells at me, snapping me out of my head.

"Save her," I beg.

"I can't promise what she'll come back as. My blood could heal her or change her," he tells me. She would hate me if she comes back a vampire, but I can live with her hating me if it means she lives.

"I just got my family back. I am not about to lose them all over again," I tell him. Marco nods, biting his wrist and holding it over her mouth when suddenly her heart stops.

"Fuck! No, you need to ingest, Elena! You can't stop now!" Marco screams at her.

CHAPTER
EIGHTY-THREE

Axton

"How is she?" Marco asks, jolting me from my thoughts as I stare at Elena in the hospital bed. A breathing tube is down her throat, her skin is deathly pale. Marco's blood barely kept her alive long enough to get her to the hospital. Doctors have been trying to figure out why she hasn't woken up and isn't healing entirely. Leaning back in the stiff blue chair, I peer up at Marco and shake my head.

"No change, it's been hours, and she still can't breathe on her own. Her lung has healed, no punctures, and the bleeding around her heart stopped. They said she'd be dead if you hadn't given her your blood. The screwdriver was the only thing stopping her from bleeding out before we got to her," I tell him.

"Lab results haven't returned yet?" Marco asks, and I sigh, shaking my head.

"No, they said a couple of hours." Marco taps my shoulder and nods toward the door. "Come on then. There's no point sitting here. Besides, we are about to raid Cane's pack. Maybe you can get Soyer to join us?" he hasn't left Amy since they got here either.

"I'm not leaving her."

"She won't be alone," Michelle says, making me lean back to peer around Marco. She has the boys in a stroller. Eli battered and bruised beside her, but he is otherwise okay. Luke steps into the room, his eyes widening when he sees his sister before rushing toward her. Jumping to my feet, I grab him before he reaches her, locking my arms around his shoulders.

"She's okay. She's alive," I whisper, kissing his temple. He nods his head slowly, his eyes locked on his sister.

"I can't lose her, too," Luke whispers.

"I know, and you won't. She'll be fine once they figure out what's keeping her in this state," I promise him, though I just hope I don't have to break that promise.

"I need you to watch over her for me until I return. I have to help Marco." Luke stares up at me.

"You're not leaving me?" I shake my head.

"Never, I'll be back," I tell him, and he sighs but nods, so I quickly let him go. Giving the boys a quick kiss, I leave with Marco, stopping in the room next door. Amy is also unconscious, but Marco said she is in transition. She died on the way to the hospital, luckily, she had Marco's blood in her system. Stepping inside the room, Soyer lifts his head from the bed at her side.

Amy's hands are cuffed to the frame; apparently, when she wakes, she could turn rabid or suicidal. Evidently, the transition from werewolf to vampire is different from human to vampire. With instinct telling them they were an abomination, I couldn't imagine being one thing before becoming another, one you were raised believing is your mortal enemy.

"Get up, stop moping. She'll be fine. You two are depressing me!" Marco tells Soyer.

"What if she wakes?" Soyer questions.

"Then we will head back, but for now, both of you need to leave this hospital. Supernatural law says raids need to be approved by three council members and overseen. Unfortunately, Osiris can't sign himself, Cane is dead, Elena is knocked out, and Thomas is all that is left."

"Can't he override it? He works for the government!" Soyer asks.

"Human government, and currently, I'm suspended for attacking a court officer."

Soyer reluctantly gets up, and I know he only does it because he is driven by the need to pay back Osiris. Osiris was an enemy who turned out actually to be an ally. He didn't need to help, and I honestly thought he wouldn't. But he showed up anyway without hesitation.

We all leave the hospital, climbing into Marco's car. The trip is silent, all of us consumed with our thoughts and worries until we arrive at the front of the Cane's pack borders. Osiris is waiting, leaning against his car, a cigarette between his lips. He tosses it when we pull up beside him.

Climbing out, he throws his hands up. "Fuckers won't let my men pass. Despite feeling that the pack link is broken. They said I needed a warrant!" Osiris snarls.

"Which is why we're here," I tell him just as Thomas pulls up. He quickly jumps out of the car, warily eyeing Osiris, making me wonder what happened between them.

"Sign the fucking documents, and I will tell the council you are innocent!" Thomas glanced at us, then at Marco, like he expected to be arrested at any given second.

"He threatened my mate. What did you expect me to do? Derrick dumped the debt on my hands when he dropped that laundromat on me!"

"Sign the papers. My father is in there!" Osiris roars at him.

"Are you sure? Your pack said they felt the pack link crumble that day?" Soyer questions.

"I know, I felt it too, but it's him, I know it's him, I know what my father looks like."

Soyer nods, moving toward his car, and Osiris pulls the paper from his pocket. Soyer quickly signs it, and so do I and Thomas.

When done, Osiris stomps over to the main guard, slamming the paper against his chest.

As we crossed the pack borders, it was clear the pack was in disarray. The houses were boarded up, the lawns unkempt, and the people seemed fearful. There is an uneasy silence as we drive to the packhouse, and the tension is palpable. The windows on the passing houses are boarded up, and the doors. People are wary of anyone they don't recognize. The pack has been through a lot, and they are clearly still dealing with the aftermath, making me wonder how Cane kept all this from us.

When we pulled up to the packhouse, it was clear the house had seen better days. The windows were boarded up, and the door was locked. We had to break the door down to get in, and the stench of the place hit us immediately. Inside, we found people locked in cages, and dead bodies piled up in the corner, the stench of death and decay was overpowering. "No wonder his pack is so terrified," Marco comments.

We quickly make our way to the basement, where we find a tunnel that has been dug out, leading to the city tunnels. It is clear that Cane used the tunnels to smuggle people in and out of the pack. There are more cages down here and more dead bodies, the place has an eerie feeling to it.

We unlock the cages, and I can hear someone has called for ambulances when I hear Osiris. "Dad!" he screams, racing past me to a cage in the far corner. He clutches the mesh before peering over at us.

"Get me something now!" he yells. Marco rushes over, and so do I. Peering into the cage, I find Stiles. The elder stares blankly at his son for a second before he gasps, clutching his son's fingers through the mesh.

CHAPTER EIGHTY-FOUR

"You returned?" Elder Stiles croaks out. Elder Stiles is gaunt and skinny, his skin pale and dirty. He looks weak and frail, and his eyes are filled with sadness and despair. He wears tattered dirty clothes, and his hair is disheveled. It is clear that he has been through a lot of suffering. "Of course I did," Osiris said, reaching out to touch his arm. "I'm here, dad."

Elder Stiles looks up at me with tears in his eyes. "I thought I'd never see you again," he murmurs, his voice full of emotion. "I should have listened. I should have let you handle it." I could see the sadness written on his face and the relief in Osiris' eyes. Marco gets the cage unlocked, and Osiris rips it open. He drags his father out, hugging him tightly. "We need a medic down here!" Osiris shouts.

Elder Stiles held on to his son, his face covered in tears, murmuring his apologies. Marco had already called for a medic, and soon we were surrounded by medical personnel helping those in cages and tending to Elder Stiles. We follow them back to the hospital. Thomas also jumps in with us, telling his Beta to take his car.

Climbing into the passenger seat, Marco starts the car when

Thomas speaks. "What a mess. I still can't wrap my head around that Cane was the strigoi all along and that not one of us noticed," he grumbles. I am still trying to wrap my head around it, too. "It's hard to believe that someone we trusted could be so deceitful," Marco says, shaking his head in disbelief.

"And that is precisely why it is so shocking. You considered him a friend. No one wants to believe their friend is a monster. No one wants to live with the 'what if's', what if we could have done something sooner? What would have changed if we had?" Thomas nods in agreement, while I wonder if his words also refer to Sondra.

"No one would have seen this coming," Soyer adds. He's right. We all thought Cane was some neglected son, an alcoholic. It turns out he was just a great actor.

"I don't believe he meant to be bad," Soyer states, and I look over at him. He shrugs. "He turned crazy. I hate him for what he did to ---" he breathes. "For what he did to Amy," he choked.

"But I know he didn't intend this. He told me himself."

"Told you what?" I ask, and Marco also glances at him in the mirror.

"About the accident, he was in the car with his father and Peter. They died on impact. He was trapped with their dead bodies for three days. His legs were pinned beneath the dash. He said he was dying and needed blood. He fed off their dead bodies for three days."

"Yes, living blood heals us quickly, but drinking from someone dead turns us strigoi," Marco explains.

"Cane said he didn't know until he couldn't control it anymore."

"There's still no excuse," I tell him.

"No, you're right. It's no excuse, but it kind of helps to know he didn't want to be a monster. I remember him as a child. The kid was scared of his own shadow." Soyer laughs.

"Then he became the thing that haunted them..." he trails off.

"I overheard that Stiles caught him in the act, trying to get blood from the blood bank. He then ordered Stiles to turn rogue and abandon his pack. It severed the pack link, making everyone think he was dead," Marco tells me, and I nod, having overheard the same thing.

"I still don't get why Cane came back in the first place," I mutter, but it is Thomas who answers that one.

"Alpha Lyle was dying, and so was Peter. Peter had liver cancer and was given three months to live. Lyle, a year, not that he cared for much after he lost his mate."

"Luna Grace?"

"Yeah, you don't remember?" he asks, and Soyer nudges him, and I shake my head.

"He wasn't here then."

"Oh, right, she killed herself when Lyle killed her sister. Told Lyle, she hopes he feels as dead inside as she does," Thomas shrugs. My eyebrows raise, having not expected that answer.

Pulling up at the hospital, we climb out and head to the third floor. The hospital was bustling with activity, people coming in and out of the revolving doors, the sound of beeping machines, and shuffling feet echoing around us. The smell of disinfectant hangs heavily in the air, and the sterile white walls make the fluorescent lights burn brighter. As we make our way up to the wards, the smell of antiseptic grows stronger. The walls look even brighter and more sterile when alarm bells go off, and nurses rush toward Soyer's mate's room.

"Amy?" Soyer gasps, racing toward her room. We all chase him, and I stop at the door when I see Soyer trying to calm his mate down, who has escaped her handcuffs. Amy was frantic. Her face is streaked with tears as she shakes her head, her eyes pleading with Soyer. "I can't do this. I won't become a monster like him," she sobs, her body trembling as she clutches the nurse, whose eyes are wide and petrified.

Marco enters, but Soyer holds his hand up, giving him a pleading look. Amy is in hysterics, her body shaking uncontrollably and tears spilling down her face. She holds a nurse hostage. Her grip tightens around the scalpel pointed at the nurse's throat. Her eyes are wild with fear, desperation, and anger, pleading with Soyer.

"You can't make me!" Amy screams at him. The nurse trembles, her eyes wide with fear, and her breathing is erratic. When Marco steps further into the room, Amy spins, watching him, but Soyer speaks.

"Amy, baby, let the nurse go. You don't want to hurt her," Soyer pleads, and Marco moves, but Soyer puts himself between his mate and him.

"Please, she fucking scared!" Soyer begs Marco. Marco backs off, and Soyer's hand reaches out for Amy, the tremble in his hands obvious when I see motion out of the corner of my eye. Turning my head, I see Luke peering out wide-eyed, and I point back to the room, telling him to go back inside. Luke does as I ask when I hear Soyer pleading with his mate.

"Amy, I can help you. Please let the nurse go. I know you don't want to hurt her." Soyer says, his hand reaching for the nurse.

"Why would you even want to touch me after what you saw that monster do? After what he did?" Amy screams at him.

"You're still mine; nothing anyone does will ever change that. I'm here, and I'm not going anywhere." Amy shakes her head.

"You deserve someone better. Someone untainted. I won't ruin your life!" Amy screams at him. She shoves the nurse away. The nurse screams, and Soyer moves, snatching the scalpel blade before she plunges it into her neck.

"You are my life!" he screams, clutching her neck. He presses his forehead against her. "You dare to take your life, but you take mine first. I won't live without you!" He tells her, his blood streaking down his arm, spilling onto the floor.

"No life is worth living without you. You're the only thing worth living for," he tells her, and she breaks down, shaking her head. Soyer pries the scalpel from her hand, tossing it aside and clutching her to him. He holds her tightly, rocking her back and forth as she cries into his shoulder. He whispers comforting words, and seeing he doesn't need help, we back away when he grunts. He takes a step back, his hand clutching her hair.

"That's my girl," he says, and I realize she's feeding off him. He clutches her hair, and Marco moves in case he must intervene. Soyer shakes his head, letting us know he can handle her, and we pull the door shut.

Moving toward Elena's room, Michelle peers out the door. "Is she okay?"

"She'll be fine," I tell her, stepping past her to check on my mate. Luke has fallen asleep in a chair. Eli is passed out on the couch, both my boys lying on his chest.

"Any change?" I ask Michelle.

"No, but the doctor just went off to get her lab results," Michelle tells me as I sweep Elena's hair from her beautiful face. Moments later, the doctor comes in with a clipboard in hand, wearing a white lab coat.

"Anything?" I ask, and he nods slowly.

"It appears Marco's blood healed her lung and the graze on her heart." He tells us, and I nod, knowing that. "When you started CPR, you kept her heart pumping for long enough, but now we're faced with another problem."

"Elena's body is in shock. Her body is trying to reject his blood."

"So, what does that mean?" I ask.

"It's perfectly normal, Alpha. Her body recognizes something foreign is in her system, so it has shut down to protect itself. We've seen it before. Its natural bodily instinct is to stop his blood from reaching the placenta and altering DNA." I blink at him.

"Placenta?" I ask, thinking I misheard, and Michelle's hands cup her mouth in shock.

"Yes, Alpha. Luna is pregnant." I shake my head.

"No, we have baby boys?" the doctor's brows furrowed.

"Well, yes. But that doesn't mean she can't fall pregnant. In fact, she is actually more fertile after a successful pregnancy," Doc explains. Marco clamps a hand on my shoulder, and I am grateful because I don't know if I want to faint in shock or jump with joy.

"We'll schedule an ultrasound in a few days. For now, we want to keep an eye on her levels." Doc explains before walking out.

CHAPTER
EIGHTY-FIVE

E lena
         13 weeks Later.

"No, I don't want to go in there," I tell Axton as I stare up at the hospital. How could I be pregnant? What the heck am I going to do with three babies?

"Lena..." Axton groans frustrated. I have missed the last two appointments, some part of my brain conjuring up that as long as I don't have the ultrasound as proof, I can pretend I'm not pregnant. I'm too busy with the boys and Luke. Then there is work. Axton sighs and gets out of the car, I watch him walk around to my side, but before he opens up the door, I shove the lock down.

"Elena..." I ignore him, turning to the front and staring out the windshield.

"No, I am not going. Let's just go home," I tell him, folding my arms across my chest. He digs in his pocket, unlocking the doors, and I push the lock down again.

"You are being a brat!"

"And you are being a jerk! I don't wanna get fat and push a watermelon out of my coochie. You go drink a gallon of water and have someone squeeze your bladder if you want a baby so bad." I tell him, and Axton facepalms himself.

"Please get out of the car!" he groans, unlocking the car again. He yanks on the door handle, but I press the lock just in time.

"One….." he counts, and I raise an eyebrow, knowing he ain't going to do shit.

"Two… Don't make me bring Khan forward!" he snaps at me.

"Three!... That's it. You're in for it now." he growls, and I roll my eyes. His entire body shudders when he suddenly taps on the window again, and I look out to see his eyes pitch black, and Khan has come forward.

"Elena?" he breathes.

"Nope, you don't scare me. What are you gonna do? Huh… Fight me?" I ask. I've been in a salty mood since Axton removed all the coffee from the house, replacing it with decaf. That just defeats the purpose of drinking coffee!

"Why don't you want to go in? This is our third appointment, and you have missed the other two," he demands. I ignore him, refusing to go. We can try the fourth appointment, I think to myself. Allow me a little longer in denial.

"Axton will buy you coffee…." my eyes narrow to slits as I peer out at him. Lies!

He pauses to think for a second. Lexa wanders forward. Axton is convinced that Khan "deals with my tantrums" more like he bribes me.

"I wonder what he'll offer up this time?" Lexa asks, and I snicker. Khan was a teddy bear.

"I'll get you ice cream…."

"Oh, and skittles, but only the red ones," Lexa shoves forward and tells him.

"And gummy bears,"

"Fine, but unlock the car," Khan tells her, and I fight against her.

"I'd rather go without!" I snap at her.

"You are getting your ass out of this damn car. Aren't you even the tiniest bit curious?" Lexa asks me.

"We can smuggle a small jar of coffee, but if you get caught with it. You deal with Axton!" Khan tells me, and I smile to myself.

I release a deep breath before unlocking the door. Khan grips it, ensuring I don't slam it shut. Standing up, I feel Axton return through the bond. "Finally." he breathes.

"You better not be lying, Khan," I tell him.

"Never, we'll stop on the way home."

"Stop where?" Axton asks.

"To get my coffee!" I tell Axton.

"You lying brat, I did not say that." I hear Khan speak, outraged that I snitched on him.

"Ha, now I know you're lying." Axton huffs.

"I promised her gummy bears," Khan states, and I scoff.

"Don't forget my red skittles!" Lexa growls at him.

"Red skittles?" Axton shakes his head, leading me into the hospital to the ultrasound floor.

As I walk, I think about the gifts Khan promised me and smile to myself. Maybe this won't be so bad after all.

Axton leads me into the ultrasound room, where an older lady is already there waiting for us. Her eyes sparkle when she sees Axton walking in with me, and a knowing look passes over her face.

"Finally, you made it, Luna," she says, and I purse my lips before lying on the bed.

The ultrasound technician rubs some warm goo on my stomach before pressing the wand to it. Axton holds my hand tight as we wait for the image of our baby to appear on the screen. However, the longer she takes, the more anxious I become, especially when she turns the screen away and tells us she'll be right back. I glance at the Axton, who also looks just as worried as I feel.

She returns with a doctor who also goes over me, using the device to scan me, making a lot of grumbling noises, and I am on the verge of losing my damn mind and demanding answers.

Finally, I hear those three words that mean everything: "It's twin girls." We both let out a collective sigh of relief when he finally speaks.

"Wait! Did you say twins?" I ask, sitting upright, and the doc turns the screen.

"Yep," he points them out while I stare at the screen bewildered. Four babies under two?

"Alpha has got good swimmers, it appears," Doc chuckles.

"Damn right I do, take one load get one free," he states. "Two for four!" he says victorious. I shake my head at him.

"Need to bottle that shit up and sell it," Axton chuckles, and I shoot him a glare.

"Not that I would, can't give away my super sperm," he says.

The technician lady then takes over and points out all the babies' features—the arms, legs, heads, and tiny hearts beating away. I am both equal parts anxious and excited. While Axton is just excited. Yeah, because he isn't one, that's gotta push them out!

"That is so many diapers," I whisper as I take my seat in the car.

"We'll figure it out, there will be a team of us," Axton says while I nod my head.

The drive home is quiet and peaceful as we both think about our future with our two sets of twins. I had completely forgotten about Khan's promise until Axton pulls over at the general store. He looks at me expectantly. A second later, Khan shoves forward, blocking out Axton.

"You snitch!" He snarls at me and I chuckle.

"Well, I think it is only fair since I am now eating for two babies; I can get two jars of coffee," I tell him.

"Not a chance." He says, shoving his door open. I open mine, following him into the store, and I see his skin rippling as Axton fights to come forward. How bizarre it must feel to have your wolf block you out.

"Go on, hurry," Khan tells me, and I know he is struggling to keep

Axton out. We do our shopping, and I climb in the car with my goodies.

Putting my seatbelt on, I stuff a handful of gummy bears in my mouth, munching away while trying to hide my two jars of coffee under the bag of diapers.

Axton steals one of my gummy bears and starts the car. When we reach home, Axton reaches over to grab my bag from me. However, I don't let go. He raises an eyebrow at me, then his brows furrow.

"What's wrong?" I shake my head. Axton goes to take my bag again, but I jerk it from his grip and jump out of the car. He's not stealing my jars of coffee.

EPILOGUE

Elena

Six months later.

Life has become a chaotic whirlwind of laughter, tears, diapers, and midnight feedings. Sondra and Louise, our twin girls, are the newest additions to our growing family. Our once-quiet house is now filled with cooing, crying, and bickering between Kyan and Bane, who are now on the move and have turned into little terrors.

As I look around the house, getting ready to leave to go to the supernatural council, I can't help but feel a sense of pride and gratitude. Our family has grown so much in such a short time, and we're learning to adapt and love each other more with each passing day.

Axton has been incredible, taking his role as Alpha and father very seriously, which is a relief given the tumultuous world which our sons were born into. He's been present for every sleepless night, diaper change, and mealtime, juggling his duties as an Alpha and father effortlessly.

Our pack has also been an invaluable help, stepping in whenever Axton and I needed some time for ourselves or when we had to attend to our pack duties. The pack members have become like extended family, always willing to lend a hand and support us in any way possible. Surprisingly, all three packs have just about merged as one and get on well after everything that happened. For the first time, we all feel a sense of home within the city.

Kyan and Bane are adapting well to their new roles as big brothers. They adore their little sisters and can often be found playing with them or making them laugh. However, we have to watch them like hawks too, now that they're on the move. They're constantly getting into everything. It's heartwarming to see the bond forming between our children and to know that they will grow up surrounded by love and support.

Our days are now filled with laughter, love, and the occasional tantrum. We've learned to embrace the chaos and cherish every moment with our children. The sleepless nights and endless diaper changes are worth it when we see the smiles on our children's faces and feel the warmth of their love.

"Michelle and Eli are here." Axton sings out to me. They've come to watch the boys. Today we hope to put everything behind us finally, praying that the courts rule in our favor.

Giving the kids a quick kiss, I explain everything to Michelle, who rolls her eyes at me. "Go, I know how to make a damn bottle," she chuckles, waving me off. With one last glance at the kids, I reluctantly leave, following Axton out to the car.

It is the first time Axton and I have been away from our kids since the twins were born. Despite the importance of the council hearing, I can't help but feel a sense of urgency to return home. So, sitting in the supernatural council chambers, I find myself anxious to get back.

I know we're here to witness a historic moment in the werewolf communities. One that could potentially change the lives of many she-wolves. The women from my pack are awaiting the verdict for their exoneration after being accused of killing their abusive mates. If they aren't exonerated today, Axton will have to announce a punishment to the council, seeing as most packs handle pack business and crimes themselves, yet they still have to show proof of such crimes being punished.

Over the last couple of months, Axton has fought tirelessly to change the oppressive laws that prevent she-wolves from leaving their mates, even in the most dire of circumstances. The current laws have resulted in countless she-wolves suffering in silence, unable to escape their mates' torment.

As the council members file in, the room falls silent. All eyes are on them, and I sit up a little straighter. Axton and I exchange a hopeful glance, knowing that the outcome of this verdict could be a turning point for our kind.

The head council member clears his throat and begins to speak. "After careful consideration and thorough review of the evidence presented, we have unanimously decided. The accused pack members are hereby exonerated of all charges relating to the deaths of their mates." Marco then rises, reading out the names of every one of the women in the pack. It's not until the last name is read that I finally suck in a shaky breath. They are finally free, free to live without fear, free to live without having to glance over their shoulders wondering if the council is watching them.

The room erupts in gasps and murmurs. Still, the head council member continues. "Additionally, we recognize that the existing laws have long been a barrier for she-wolves seeking to escape abusive relationships. As a council, we have decided to remove these laws, effectively granting she-wolves the right to leave their mates in situations where their safety and well-being are compromised."

A wave of relief washes over us, and I can't help the smile that splits onto my face. This is a huge step towards a fairer society for all werewolves. "Furthermore, the supernatural court announces that the women of the Elysium Fortuna pack are hereby exonerated of their crimes."

As we leave, Marco catches up with us. He was part of the deciding panel. "Thank you," I tell him, and he shakes his head.

"No, they never should have been charged in the first place. It's about time some laws are redefined and looked into. Hopefully, this is just the start of change," he tells us.

"Are you--" Marco looks at Axton, who nods. Marco smiles while I watch their quiet exchange. "I'll catch you later, Elena," Marco tells us before heading inside the council courts again.

As we travel home, I notice that Axton seems anxious as we are nearing the city. Axton is tapping his fingers against the steering wheel, and his gaze is constantly shifting from the road to me. His face is lit up with anticipation, and his posture is tense, as if he can't wait to get home. He's clearly excited about getting home, but there's also a hint of nervousness that he's trying to conceal.

"Are you okay?" I ask him.

"Yes, I'm excited to get home." My eyes narrow slightly while I wonder what is wrong with him.

"What?" he asks with a playful smile.

"You've been bouncing in your seat the entire way home," he shrugs.

"I wanna get home to the kids," he tells me, and I sigh. Yes, the kids have been on my mind all day too, and I can't wait to finally be home, so I can take these darn heels off.

However, upon arriving home, I noticed cars lining the street.

"Axton, what's going on?" I ask, and he smiles mysteriously. When he pulls up in the driveway, Axton leads me out to the backyard. Here, we find all of our packs celebrating the announcement that the laws have been changed, and the women have been exonerated.

The atmosphere of the party was one of joy and relief. Everyone is celebrating the announcement and knowing that their lives would be changed for the better. The backyard was a flurry of activity: people laughing and talking. A bounce house was set up for the kids, and now I understand Axton's excitement to get home.

"When did you organize this?" I ask, glancing at Axton.

"I mind linked Eli to let him know the good news," Axton tells me while I glance around. The grass was freshly mowed, and the trees were in bloom. Tables were set up around the yard perimeter, dotted with plates of delicious food and drinks. Music played in the background. Upon entering, we are surrounded by pack members, and we become separated from each other.

Yet as the night goes on, I know I have to get the boys to bed. The girls are safely tucked in their stroller, which Axton has been pushing around with him possessively, so he can use them as an excuse to escape as he pleases.

Looking around, I spot Michelle grabbing them off the bounce house with Eli and Luke. I am about to go over and help when Axton calls for everyone's attention from the back porch. Stopping, I turn to look at him, and then he waves for me to come to him. I point to the boys, and he rolls his eyes, rushing down the steps to retrieve me. He covers my eyes.

"What are you doing?" I chuckle.

"Keeping the one promise no one else did," Axton whispers, leading me up the stairs. My brows pinch, wondering what he means as I stumble up the steps, only for Axton to keep a strong grip on me.

When he turns me around to face everyone, he removes his hands. I gasp, seeing Axton on his knees before me, along with all three packs. Axton bears his neck and pledges to me, naming me the Alpha of their pack. "I, Axton Levin, Alpha of the Nightfall pack, hereby step down as Alpha and name Elena Bardot as the new Alpha of our new pack, Elysium Fortuna pack. I pledge to serve her and the pack according to her directions and help her lead our pack to a bright and prosperous future. I swear to always honor, protect, and obey her and to love and honor her as our Alpha." The packs pledge their loyalty to me as their newly appointed Alpha, declaring me the Alpha of the Elysium Fortuna pack after Axton.

Overwhelmed with emotion, tears welled in my eyes. Axton rises and gently wipes them away. "I told you I don't want to be your Alpha. Only your mate," he whispers.

"You didn't have to give up our pack," I murmur.

"For you, I'd give up the world," he tells me before leaning down and kissing me briefly. Axton wraps his arms around me, and I see Michelle moving toward us, Bane over her shoulder, and Kyan tucked under her arm like a football. I chuckle, watching her wrangle the boys when Luke comes racing up the steps toward us. "Alpha," he smirks and I mess his hair.

"So what's next?" I chuckle when Kyan escapes Michelle's grip, making her chase after him.

"You marry me," Axton whispers. I gasp, peering at him over my shoulder. Axton smiles, his eyes twinkling with joy as he gazes at me. "I will be honored to be Lupha of the Elysium Fortuna Pack, but only if you become Mrs. Elena Louise Levin. Will you marry me?" Luke then holds up a small velvet box, passing it to Axton, and he pops it open. He presses his lips to the side of my neck.

"So, Alpha, what's it going to be?" he murmurs. A smile splits onto my face as I hold my hand up for him. "Yes..." I breathe.

About the Author

Join my Facebook group to connect with me
   https://www.facebook.com/jessicahall91

Enjoy all of my series
   https://www.amazon.com/Jessica-Hall/e/B09TSM8RZ7

   FB: Jessica Hall Author Page
   Website: jessicahallauthor.com
   Insta: Jessica.hall.author
   Goodreads: Jessica_Hall

Also by Jessica Hall

Authors I Recommend

Jane Knight

Want books with an immersive story that sucks you in until you're left wanting more? Queen of spice, Jane Knight has got you covered with her mix of paranormal and contemporary romance stories. She's a master of heat, but not all of her characters are nice. They're dark and controlling and not afraid to take their mates over their knees for a good spanking that will leave you just as shaken as the leading ladies. Or if you'd prefer the daddy-do type, she writes those too just so they can tell you that you are a good girl before growling in you ear. Her writing is dark and erotic. Her reverse-harems will leave you craving more and the kinks will have you wondering if you'll call the safe word or keep going for that happily every after.]

Follow her on facebook.com/janeknightwrites

Check out her books on https://www.amazon.com/stores/Jane-Knight/author/B08B1M8WD8

Moonlight Muse

Looking for a storyline that will have you on the edge of your seat? The spice levels are high with a plot that will keep you flipping to the next page and ready for more. You won't be disappointed with Moonlight Muse.

Her women as sassy and her men are possessive alpha-holes with high tensions and tons of steam. She'll draw you into her taboo tales, breaking your heart before giving you the happily ever after.

Follow her on facebook.com/author.moonlight.muse

Check out her books on https://www.amazon.com/stores/Moonlight-Muse/author/B0B1CKZFHQ

Printed in Great Britain
by Amazon

51393575R00219